THE ANGUISHED CRY

An itch started on her left thigh, right on the edge of her panty line. Just what she needed. She closed her eyes a second and squirmed inside her suit, trying to relieve it. Just as she managed to hit the magic spot, a new and equally recognizable sensation replaced it.

A chill ran down her spine, instantly setting off a spike of adrenaline.

Another visit from Avva was coming. Fast.

Not now! she wailed inwardly, her eyes flying open and her gaze sweeping across the test board, then snapping back to the red dots lighting the surface.

"I . . . have red," she said in a hoarse voice. *It was coming. Now. Nowhere to run.*

"Red confirmed," Wanda said. "You okay, Jane?"

Her question went by half-heard as the first tentative touch of Avva crashed over her. All she could do was check her tether and mentally hunker down.

"Commander? Jane?"

She was no longer exactly there to answer. . . .

Call from a Distant Shore

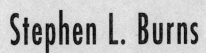

Stephen L. Burns

A ROC BOOK

ROC
Published by New American Library, a division of
Penguin Putnam Inc., 375 Hudson Street,
New York, New York 10014, U.S.A.
Penguin Books Ltd, 27 Wrights Lane,
London W8 5TZ, England
Penguin Books Australia Ltd, Ringwood,
Victoria, Australia
Penguin Books Canada Ltd, 10 Alcorn Avenue,
Toronto, Ontario, Canada M4V 3B2
Penguin Books (N.Z.) Ltd, 182–190 Wairau Road,
Auckland 10, New Zealand

Penguin Books Ltd, Registered Offices:
Harmondsworth, Middlesex, England

First published by Roc, an imprint of New American Library,
a division of Penguin Putnam Inc.

First Printing, August 2000
10 9 8 7 6 5 4 3 2 1

ROC REGISTERED TRADEMARK—MARCA REGISTRADA

Printed in the United States of America

PUBLISHER'S NOTE
This is a work of fiction. Names, characters, places, and incidents either
are the product of the author's imagination or are used fictitiously,
and any resemblance to actual persons, living or dead, business
establishments, events, or locales is entirely coincidental.

BOOKS ARE AVAILABLE AT QUANTITY DISCOUNTS WHEN USED TO PROMOTE
PRODUCTS OR SERVICES. FOR INFORMATION PLEASE WRITE TO PREMIUM
MARKETING DIVISION, PENGUIN PUTNAM INC., 375 HUDSON STREET, NEW
YORK, NEW YORK 10014.

As ever and always,
to Sue-Ryn

ACKNOWLEDGMENTS

Thanks again to Dr. Stanley Schmidt—hopefully this time your name got spelled right. Theresa Renner Smith's help with the Russian phrases was invaluable, and given under sometimes difficult circumstances. *Bolshoya spacibo*. Thanks to Wilma Meier at Compuserve for putting me onto Theresa, and the other sysops in the SF sections for suggestions of other possible sources. The kindness and encouragement of other writers I have gotten to know helps keep me going, and the support of friends and family make writing survivable enterprise. Thanks to all.

PART 1

Precursor

Dan's Wakeup Call

Dan Francisco, better known to his millions of viewers as the one and only Dan the Virtual Weatherman, rarely had trouble sleeping.

Some people are prone to lying awake at night because they can't stop thinking. Not Dan. His mind could almost always flop down like an old dog on a shady porch, curl up nose to tail, and be snoozing in minutes.

Nor did he, like some, expect trouble once he reached the safe haven of sleep. His dreams tended to be as easygoing as his waking personality. Nightmares were rare, and almost never made him wake up screaming and levitating above the bed. About the worst that could happen was a 4 A.M. bathroom call, a minor emergency he could handle with his eyes half-closed.

When he had gone to bed just before midnight he'd laid his head down on the pillow with no immediate worries on his mind, no expectation that the night might turn on him, and no sense that his life would be irrevocably changed by morning. There had been no warning psychic flashes, no signs and portents popping like cryptic, hops-scented genies from the two bottles of Labatt's Blue he drank that evening.

That was probably for the best. Knowing ahead of time something like that is coming for you could easily make you nuts.

Three o'clock had come and gone. Dan was sprawled across the double bed, dreaming that he was fishing with his producer and director, Morty. This was as weird as his dreams usually got. Morty participating in such a placid enterprise was about as likely as Dan's going to a biker bar and picking a fight with the biggest, ugliest guy there. Which was something Morty would consider a great way to spend an evening.

So there he was, adrift on Skyles Lake in his old wooden rowboat, pole in his hand, beer at his elbow, sun on his face, and the world his oyster. He felt a nibble, then a promising tug. Just as he was thinking *Good one!* he was snatched out of that place and state like he'd hooked on to a sea monster.

In an instant Morty was gone, the boat and the lake under it were gone, wiped away as something came out of nowhere and took its place. Something strange and powerful and unexpected and unprecedented as a volcano bursting up from an anthill in his neatly trimmed front yard. Something just as impossible to stop.

Dan's closed eyelids fluttered and twitched as REM sleep warped into something else altogether, something thirty-six years of practice sleeping had never prepared him for.

It arrived in light, a bright spark that within a heartbeat ignited into a blinding Technicolor radiance pouring into his head—a light bursting with pictures too dazzling to see, like staring straight into the lens of a movie projector. He began to writhe and thrash under its pressure, rucking the sheet and blanket covering him with long bony arms and legs no longer entirely under his control.

Riding the light like music wrapped in a radio wave came a presence, spooling and spinning into him, rising to become a tornado of otherness sweeping across the shivering flatlands of his brain. His movements became even more spastic and uncontrolled as this inexplicable intruder grew wider, higher, brighter; approaching the proportions of a good old-fashioned mushroom cloud.

Sleep finally shattered under this assault, and he jerked upright in a tangle of covers, gasping for breath, his brown eyes wide and staring. The quiet, slightly messy bedroom around him did not register. He was as much elsewhere as there, other as himself. His mind reeled with dislocation and intrusion, overwhelmed and on the ropes like the 140-pound weakling he happened to be wrestling a 5000-pound Sumo champion made of sensation and thought.

Just when his poor brain was on the verge of blowing

like a child's balloon hooked to an industrial air compressor, the pressure abated slightly, transmuting into a chaotic, abstract, all-encompassing noise overwriting the normal contents of his head. This cerebral cacophony seemed to *twist* slightly, and an emotional subtext to it all suddenly rose up out of the babel, homing in on the frequency of his heart.

    loneliness*loss*grief*despair*fear*pain*desperation*

"N-no," he panted, begging release from this empathic gale gusting across his quivering nerves, tuning itself to his emotions, making it and him one. "—stop . . ."

His protest went unheard or unheeded, the sirocco of feelings blasting through him unabated.

    loneliness*loss*grief*despair*fear*pain*desperation*

In the midst of all this the pictures and sensations that had filled his head from the very beginning continued in a rush of vivid surrealistic flashes. They were sharper now, but none made any sense to him. He was a Neanderthal man subjected to the sensory assault of a jump-cut barrage of drock vidyo clips played at quintuple speed in TruSound HiDef 3D with every control set to cortex-nuking max. The images and sounds and smells and flavors burst upon him, rolling over him and replaced by others too fast for any one to be identified, too strange for him to grasp even if he'd had all the time in the world to dope a single one out.

Without warning the maelstrom between his ears stopped.

There was a pregnant pause that seemed fit to birth marvels or atrocities. His heart thumped once, and he sucked air greedily.

Then, there inside his head, spoke a voice. A voice clear and pure and beautiful, its message simple and unmistakable.

              help me**

This message delivered, the intruding presence began to withdraw like a deafening light dimming, a blinding noise falling silent, leaving behind a deeply graven impression of hope mixed with fear, of deep and abiding weariness.

It had the sound of someone lost on cold horizonless

waters who thinks they have just glimpsed a gleam of light on a distant shore. A chance to survive after all.

help me * please

Fainter now, like an echo. The safe familiar confines of Dan's bedroom slowly swam back into focus around him, lit by the actinic light of the screen facing the bed, and the warmer yellow glow cast by the Rockett Raccoon night light, there for the nights when his daughter Bobbi stayed over. Once again he was safely surrounded by walls covered with the fancy gold-flecked wallpaper his ex, Tammy, had insisted on, back when they had shared this room.

Obscure shapes and eye-crossing colors gave way to the vidyo screen and the Salvation Army dresser he'd found and refinished after Tammy took all the Ethan Allen with her. Pale moonlight streamed in the curtained window, proving that the world outside this room still existed as well.

***help me please* * * ***

The voice faded like the steam of a sigh, evaporating into nothingness.

Released and alone in his own skull once more, Dan freaked, scrambling out of bed as if that had been the antenna that had drawn this outrageous shit his way. Safely off it, he stood there shuddering, an almost absurdly tall and thin man with wild hair and wilder eyes, breathing hard and trying to wipe away the feeling of terror and loss and hope left like a black skid mark on his consciousness.

"I must be losing my mind," he whispered to himself, to the empty room. No voice from elsewhere spoke up to argue the point. He raked his bushy mane of long brown hair back from his narrow, sharp-featured face. Both face and body were soaked in sweat.

He was pretty damn sure that this had been no nightmare, no divorced dad's wee-hours anxiety attack. Other than this bit of noninfo, he was clueless as to what it had been, or why it had happened. *To him.*

Like most people—a few of whom are sadly and badly mistaken—he'd always assumed that he was perfectly sane. Now he had to wonder, and anxiously began conjuring up a dozen flavors of insanity that could explain what had just happened, a sort of psychiatric menu heavy on the fruitcake and banana-nut combinations.

Was this the way it went? One moment you're all right, the next you begin hearing a voice in your head and presto-chango, you've become bait for the men in the white coats? And if so, why?

Going back to bed was out of the question. Standing there considering what sort of heavy meds might be in his future wasn't helping ease his mind.

A little something to settle his nerves suggested itself. Finding and drinking a beer was an uncomplicated, easily attainable goal. Maybe after that he would be together enough to examine other options, like a shower and maybe one of Tammy's sleeping pills, still in the medicine cabinet all these years later.

So he headed for the kitchen, the thought of a cold beer like a restorative Holy Grail in his mind. He had no idea that he had not been the only one so visited that night.

Control

In the dimly lit, sumptuously appointed living room of the penthouse suite of an exclusive Manhattan hotel, Colonel Martina Elena Omerov was also wide-awake. She was no better dressed than Dan, and leaned heavily on the antique brass-and-rosewood bar, expressionlessly contemplating the shattered tumbler in her hand.

It was a big hand, a strong hand, bare of jewelry but for a plain stainless-steel Russian Elite Special Forces ring, and it had crushed the tough plastic vessel like so much eggshell. That big hand was attached to a woman of matching proportions.

Martina was tall, although not as tall as Dan. Her shoulders were broad, her hips narrow, and her forty-five-year-old body hard and muscular. Exercise kept her lean and somewhat flat-chested. The kind of life she'd led had left scars stitched into her pale skin, mementos from the odd bullet and edged weapon. Her hair was bleached bone white, and cropped into a short, stiff skate cut.

Blue eyes intent with concentration, she focused her will and made her hand unclench. Shards of blue plastic fell to the polished bartop, landing amidst the spilled vodka and melting ice cubes. Others slivers remained stuck to her sweaty palm. She stared at her open hand, feeling a sense of grim satisfaction that her body was her own to control once more.

The loss of control she'd just suffered had been appalling and unbearable. It had—

Martina tensed when she felt something brush up against her from behind, then relaxed ever so slightly at the familiar smell and feel of the one person on the planet capable of so easily slipping past her guard.

A pair of brown arms surrounded her, hugged her tight.

She lifted her head and looked into the mirror over the bar, seeing Ricardo Perez hugging her from behind, his round brown face peeking past her shoulder.

"Martina, you are all right?" he asked, his face and voice filled with concern.

"*Da,* I am fine," she answered, relieved her voice came out so level. The only sign of her distress showed in a slight thickening of her Russian accent. Rico's was Spanish. Since she didn't know more than a dozen words of Spanish, and he couldn't speak Russian, they talked in reasonably good if occasionally eccentric English. That wasn't unusual. Nearly everybody spoke at least some. Just as capitalism had won out over communism decades ago, the media-driven, endlessly flexible and inventive language of America had more or less taken over the world as the second language to have at one's command.

Rico studied her in the mirror. "I heard you cry out." His shaggy mustache twitched, and limpid brown eyes the media always said looked like Einstein's searched her face. "I think I hear you call out, crying *help me.*"

Martina suppressed a shudder at the sound of that phrase. Had she cried out? She supposed she had, either echoing what she had seemed to hear, or demanding release from the force that had taken her in its grip like a rag doll in the hand of a gorilla. What she had experienced was so raw and strange that she remained staggered and bewildered by it, but she did not intend to give in to such failings. Until she had this understood and dealt with she must be strong and act as though everything was fine.

"I broke my glass is all, was cursing in Russian," she lied, brushing the remains of the tumbler from her palm. Then she reached for a new glass and poured in a liberal dose of Stoli. Her hands did not shake—at least noticeably. This was good.

"You cannot sleep again?" He put on a tragic face. "What, this tired old man did not give you love enough to let you rest?"

Randy as a man half his age under normal circumstances, they were just back from a five-day trip through the Middle East, where religious sensitivities had dictated separate quarters and absolute circumspection. For the past two nights he had been making up for lost time with a vengeance.

She took a gulp, the milk of the Motherland going down like water. "Is not that; I am just worried about security for tomorrow's press conference." Which was the truth, if of the sort that had once filled *Pravda* back in the Bad Old Days. She'd dozed off after sex, then, as often happened, wakened an hour later. Lying there beside this wonderful and important man had once again started her wondering if she was truly doing everything in her power to keep him safe.

Not wanting to waken him, she'd come out to the living room for a knock of vodka and enough distance from him for her professional cool to reassert itself. This sequence of events had played itself out many nights before, but never had it ended this way, with her suffering the . . . this thing she'd just endured. In the wake of it, tomorrow's press conference seemed of little importance.

"You will keep me safe from harm, my beloved," he purred, kissing a pale hard bicep marked with a red hammer tattoo. "You always do."

Martina tossed off the rest of the vodka, then turned around, towering over her charge and lover. Where she could have passed for a female Ukrianian Olympic weight lifter, Rico looked like an Aztec farmer gone to seed. Short, broad-chested, and carrying a fiftyish paunch on slightly bowed legs, his eyes just came up to the level of her breasts, an arrangement which sometimes had its advantages.

As always, his smile brightened at having her naked and near. Since she had spent most of her adult life relying on her looks to intimidate, his insatiable lust for her admittedly somewhat mannish form continued to amaze her. Rico's charm was legendary, and he could have almost any woman he wanted. Divas and princesses came on to him at state dinners, dropping hints about arias and private audiences he might have for the asking. Movie stars and models vied for his attention at galas, batting their eyes and slipping him their numbers.

And he wanted only her.

"I also need to keep you rested," she said gruffly. "We should go back to bed."

"A most excellent idea!" His hands moved to her buttocks, began to stroke. "I vote for this! We should go back to bed and be unanimous."

She shook her head. "We go back to bed and *sleep*."

"Plenty of time for sleeping, woman. Later. After."

"Not after, first and only. We both need to be sharp tomorrow, not up all night acting like horny teenagers."

"We will be fine. I will make my boring speech about official UN reaction to the actions of that *maricon* General Korsuva, and you will keep me safe from media and other crazies."

He bent his head and began nuzzling a spot between her breasts. "I smile and act very happy. World will think I am pleased because that prick Korsuva says he will finally negotiate. They do not know it is instead because I spend my nights with one hot taco."

His lips moved lower, the hairs of his mustache tickling her navel. "Taco taste good right now. I am one hongry *muchacho*."

Martina shuddered, wanting to surrender, and yet unable to forget that it was her job to protect this man, who should never never *never* have become her lover, from the maniacs who saw him as a target for their rage. For that she had to be alert and rested. Not up all night screwing her brains out.

Not frozen and helpless while some voice spoke in her head.

The memory of it terrified her, because what could you call a woman who had such a thing happen to her *but* crazy? Crazy equaled dangerous. Dangerous people were not to be allowed anywhere near him. Which meant that she—

"Rico, please," she said in a choked, furry voice. "We should—we should not—"

"Soft-shell taco!" he mumbled from farther down yet. "My mos' favorite kind!"

She knew she should stop him, should get the hell away from him and call in a replacement, and then get her brain checked to find out what the hell had happened. Right now, no fucking around in any definition of the phrase.

Ricardo Aldomar Perez, Secretary-General of the United Nations, had other ideas. As many a world leader could tell you, Secretary Perez was an exceptionally persuasive man, nearly impossible to refuse.

Against her better judgment Martina found herself persuaded, her body agreeing with his wordless oratory. This loss of control was more acceptable, and for a short time it even banished the memory of the other.

Attack of the Goat

Daveed Shah had gone to the washroom expecting nothing more than a nice dump and a brief respite from work. That hadn't seemed like too much to expect from a twelve-hour shift, bennies he'd cashed in many times before without incident.

Not this time, no sir.

Nobody expects the Spanish Inquisition! he thought dazedly as he pushed through the washroom door back into the corridor, the old Monty Python line somehow seeming to fit the moment perfectly. A slim, attractive man of Pakistani descent in his late twenties who could have passed for the old silent-film star Rudolph Valentino, he'd gone in there looking cool and dapper despite the nine hours he'd pulled so far.

That *GQ* gloss had been tarnished by whatever the hell it was that had grabbed him in the crapper. There was a bewildered look in his dark eyes, and his neatly styled black hair stood up in disheveled spikes. One tail of his cream-silk shirt hung partly outside his fawn-gabardine slacks. A sudden draft made him realize he was still unzipped. He fixed that with shaking hands, tucked in his shirt, ran his fingers through his hair.

His legs were still rubbery as Gumby's, and his brain felt like a bag of microwaved popcorn, but some sort of homing instinct compelled him to get his butt back to his cubicle as soon as he could. He took a step, then another, moving toward the guarded door leading into the ultrasecure Uplink Operations division of the United Nations Joint Operations Extraterrene's Neely, New Mexico Command and Control Center. The guards in front of the door smiled and nodded in acknowledgment, then buzzed him through without any fuss.

A security camera tracked him as he went down the inner corridor toward Media Uplink. He barely noticed, too busy working up a prayer to Allah that he'd be able to get back to his cube without another attack, this one by the Goat. A swipe of his ID got him through the door into MU. Head down and breath held, he made tracks for sanctuary. As he slid behind his console and slipped on his headset, a small popup appeared in one corner of the half dozen screens arrayed in a half circle before him.

<U OK? [DK]>

Dawn Kyrkowski in the next cube over had designated herself as his big sister, always quizzing him about how he was eating and sleeping, and where his love life stood. For once she might actually have something to worry about—if she ever found out what he'd just been through. Trapped in a toilet stall with his pants down around his ankles while something really big and really weird blew in out of nowhere and took his brain for a spin.

Too big and *too* weird. He couldn't deal with it now. He didn't even dare try.

<M FINE [DS]>

he typed in reply, biting back the impulse to add the line from that old movie, *The Gods Must Be Crazy.* BTW: IS THE VOICE IN MY HEAD BOTHERING YOU?

Her first message vanished, replaced with

<GOAT ON WAY. WYA [DK]>

"Shit," he hissed half under his breath, banishing their clandestine chat with a single keystroke and picking back up where he'd been before nature had called. On display 3, Ed Powers of CBSWI stood frozen in front of the White House, trench-coat collar up against the rain, and handheld mike—which was only a prop—in hand. He stroked that controller pad, bringing the reporter back to life.

"—dent Martin and Secretary Perez have both promised a full investigation into these allegations regarding Reuthen AstroWerk, which supplied several critical components to the *Ares* mission to Mars. Uncle Joe"— a not-so-subtle camera mug as he used the media-coined nickname for the United Nations Joint Operations Extraterrene—"has not released any information that would conclusively prove that components built by the German-Argentine contractor have endangered the mission, but—"

"You have not got this *merde* edited out yet, Dahveed?" demanded a voice—*the* voice—from the doorway of his cube.

Daveed froze the replay again, leaving poor Powers standing in the rain with his mouth hanging open. "I'm doing that *now,* Mr. Gautier," he explained in the sort of tone one might use when dealing with a heavily armed idiot. Dawn's Watch Your Ass had been redundant. The warning that Armand Gautier—the Goat to those who suffered under his managerial misuse—was coming had been shithead alert enough.

Gautier pushed his way into the cramped cubicle, waving his precious stopwatch. "Maybe if you no spend so much time in *pissoir,* this work would be done, hah, Dah-veed?"

Shah turned to stare at the MU A Shift administrator, a short, bad-tempered Parisian with a few greasy strands of shoe-polish black hair plastered over his balding dome.

Armand Gautier was a textbook example of the wrong man for the wrong job. To start with, he had a massive— or at least persistent—hard-on over the fact that all official communications with the *Ares* mission were conducted in English, not his beloved French. Like they would use a language so palsied the francofringe kept trying to turn their country into a police state in their attempts to protect it, demanding that tourists take language tests before being allowed to enter. Attempts their drocker kids in Moonpie Consortium and Nipple Isuzu tee shirts pronounced as dive, crash, and voluminously baggy.

Politics and the flaky grail of "national balance" had

been behind the Goat's appointment as A Shift Media Uplink admonkey. Or maybe the higher-ups had figured that he could do less damage there than in the other three divisions: XU, Command Uplink; TU, Telemetry Uplink; and CU, Communications Uplink.

Not only was Gautier a raging Anglophobe, he also despised all forms of media. You name it: news, comedy, drama, webcast, music, linktent; the Goat sneered. The man simply could not or would not understand that the men and women of the *Ares* were one *long* fucking way away from home. The trickle of news and entertainment MU provided helped them feel a little less alone. A little less disconnected. A trickle whose mix Daveed, Chief Mediartist and Senior Editor, had mastered.

"My posse and I have never missed a deadline, Mr. Gautier," Daveed pointed out, biting back the impulse to add that he ought to stick his frigging stopwatch where the sun don't shine. That was the peak of the Goat's brilliant concept of leadership: timing bathroom and snack breaks. Even though they all routinely pulled unpegged overtime.

"Not so far, *non,* but you did let objectional material slip by, Dah-veed. Very sloppy. I did not find this before transmission, but in review after."

Which meant the Goat had been too busy timing dumps and trips to the coffee machine to do his own job. "What objectionable material?" he asked, wondering what nit the wit had decided to pick this time around.

"Joke about mission was allowed to remain in segment of that stupid *Pinky Redbone Show*."

Daveed thought back, mentally reviewing the hundreds of hours of media he absorbed each day. The *Redbone Show* ran once a week on HBO, which made it much easier to nail down.

"You mean the birth-control joke?"

The Goat's mouth puckered like he'd bitten into a bad snail. "*Oui,* is that one."

Daveed had thought it pretty harmless and fairly funny. The *Ares* crew had agreed, even mentioning it in their backchannel feedback loop with MU. Commander Jane Dawkins-Costanza said she'd laughed her ass off.

" 'Why did Uncle Joe issue birth-control pills to each member of *Ares* mission, even though half are men?' " Gautier recited, his nose wrinkled with distaste. " 'Is because of something go wrong, all are screwed.' "

It didn't sound very funny the way the Goat told it, and actually Pinky had said "fucked." Before he could point that out, the Goat launched into one of his Rule Book rants.

"Is to be no mention of problems here or on mission, this you know! Sexual content is strongly discouraged." He scowled at Daveed and waggled a warning finger. "Maybe *you* people find such things funny, but I do not, and they are forbidden."

"Who might *you people* be?" Daveed asked mildly, the faintest of smiles sliding onto his features. "Americans? Americans of Pakistani descent? Lapsed Muslims?" He laid his fingertips on his chest, looking shocked. "Oh dear me no, you couldn't *possibly* be referring to *fags* and *queers,* could you?"

The Goat's upper lip curled in distaste, and his eyes narrowed to slits. "You just use those words, Dah-veed, not me."

Daveed's smile widened. "Hey, I can. You can't."

Here they were, once again hip deep in the issue that juiced a lot of the Goat's attitude problem. As gays went he was pretty low-key. Maybe he kept himself a little better groomed and dressed than your average straight male, but that was about it. Only when driven to it would he flame or camp. Like he'd just done. Which he hated, and knew only made the situation worse.

The Goat made it no secret he wanted him off his shift—off the team entirely if he could swing it. The tough tommy he ended up chewing was that everyone in MU hated the little bastard's Gallic guts, while he on the other hand was golden. The staff loved him. The *Ares* crew loved him. The powers above the Goat's balding head, including Uplink Oversight Chief Yamaguchi himself knew that a certain Pakimerican pansy was a master chef when it came to media, able to season the bland, bowdlerized, censored feeds with just enough spice to stay inside the lines and yet keep them palatable and the *Ares* crew happy.

Still, if the Goat ever found out that he'd just spent the last few minutes cramped over in the john and out of his head from who knows what, the days of his security clearance would be numbered. In single-digit binary.

"I'll be more careful, sir," he promised with mock humility. "Now if there's nothing else, I've got to get back to work. Or else we will miss our next deadline."

"Yes, you be more careful, Dah-veed," Gautier warned with a scowl and a sniff. "I am watching you." His infinitesimal weight thrown around, he marched out of the cubicle, stopwatch at the ready.

Daveed closed his eyes wearily, then sighed and spun his chair back toward his workstation. A new popup waited in the corner of screen 2.

```
<WHAT'S THE DEFINITION OF THE GOAT HAV-
ING A MENAGE A TROIS?[XM]>
```

Another of Xavier Moreno's endless jokes.

```
<WHAT? [DS]>.
   <HE USES BOTH HANDS TO JACK OFF! [XM]>
```

Daveed snickered, then typed,

```
<OKAY, BUT WHAT DOES HE DO WITH THE OTHER
EIGHT FINGERS? [DS]>
```

The entire display filled with red exclamation points, laughter from the entire cubicle farm.

Grinning to himself and feeling much better, Daveed cleared the screen and went back to work. Within minutes he was deeply absorbed. With three dozen trimmed feeds from his crew competing for his attention while he simultaneously edited four others, his mystery break was soon relegated to the back burner.

Where it bubbled on in the background, not forgotten.

Fringe Reception

The experience that had overtaken Dan's sleep, Martina's nightcap, and Daveed's trip to the powder room was felt elsewhere and by others.

Most were only brushed by an insubstantial whisper of it, the edge of a widely cast net brushing their minds, just enough to cause a momentary scowl in the sleepers and send a puzzled look flashing across the faces of those who were awake. Less than a hundred people worldwide had their heads fill with a muted light and noise for a few seconds, that touch fading before the voice could speak.

Not until days later would they begin to wonder if it had been a glancing touch by the name and events in the news.

Three others got the full jolt.

In a big round bed in a sprawling antebellum mansion just outside Savannah, Georgia, the charismatic net-evangelist Reverend Ray Sunshine immediately knew where the voice that had just spoken in his head had come from. Only one source was possible. It had been sent to him by God Almighty, who hadn't had much to say since the day He'd called him to the ministry.

He wasn't sure exactly what the message had been, but that didn't matter. His heart filled with rejoicing that he was on God's callback list once more, he awakened the sloe-eyed, cupcake-breasted sinner beside him for first a fervent prayer, then a rousing hallelujah in the classic missionary position.

Somewhere in Ohio, in a large, opulently decorated room buried ten stories underground, a bearded, heavy-set black man known by several names sat surrounded

•

by humming machinery and flickering screens, weeping from fear and joy and understanding.

Of all those who have experienced this uncanny visitation, he has felt it the deepest, and understood it the most completely. He grasps the implications to himself, his carefully ordered world, to the world at large.

He is exalted, and he is absolutely terrified.

He knows without a doubt he will hear this voice again, and wonders if he can possibly be equal to what it asks of him.

There is one other who has heard this inexplicable whispered cry for help in her mind. A woman who is farther away from the man who lives underground than Dan, or Daveed, or Martina.

She is farther away from the Earth than any human has ever gone before.

Secrets

A *res* Mission Commander Jane Dawkins-Costanza was not the sort of woman who was inclined to—or often needed to—repeat herself.

Between the USAF, NASA, and Uncle Joe, her rank had bopped all over the place, going sideways as often as up—a rising lateral climb to the top. Her present rank of Mission Commander in UNJOE put her damn near the same level as a general in the other services. She knew how to say what she meant, and have it heard.

But she was repeating herself now, saying the same thing once again, as much a mantra for herself as an attempt to make the words believed.

"No, there's nothing wrong."

The sweat soaking her underwear and matting her short salt-and-pepper gray hair to her skull like soggy steel wool hinted otherwise. She knew she looked like a wild woman. Worse yet, she'd acted like one by first spazzing out, and then leaping out of bed like it was full of snakes and on fire. Those were hardly signs that everything was A-OK, now were they?

Her husband of over fifteen years sat up on their bunk, bare-chested, the blanket just covering his skivvies. He watched her every move and gesture, his sharp hazel eyes missing nothing. He could still pass for under forty. Not her, a year younger than he, not before this misbegotten trip had started, and certainly not now. If anything it was a miracle she hadn't gone white-haired and grown a hump.

"Come on, Janey," he said patiently, doing a little repeating himself. "Something was wrong. You woke up gasping and flailing around as if you were having some sort of seizure. You were totally unresponsive, and didn't even seem to know where you were, or even who I was at first."

"It was probably just a really bad nightmare, Fabi. That's all." She forced a smile onto her face. "Judging by the way I reacted, maybe I dreamed I was married to Hans instead of you. He probably wanted sex."

That made him smile, but only a little, and only for a moment. She knew he wasn't buying her story. No surprise there, this man knew her better than anyone, knew her inside and out. As ever, she could feel his love for her there behind the hairy eyeball he was giving her, solid as gravity. A wave of affection for him twisted through her in response. She adored this man, and trusted him with her life.

Then why couldn't she bring herself to tell him the truth about this totally bizarre thing she'd just experienced?

You damn well know why, she told herself.

Her darling Fabi was more than just her husband. He was also Dr. Fabio Costanza, MD, Ph.D, and a whole stack of other letters that let him play with sharp knives and complex drugs. As mission physician and brain mechanic he would relieve her of command at the drop of a hat if he thought she was turning woodpecker on them. That was his duty, and she knew he would carry it out if necessary.

Although it seemed a foregone conclusion that what had happened inside her head was some sort of hiccup in her sanity, she couldn't help grimly clinging to the hope that it had just been some mutant nightmare, a flashback, some damn thing brought on by stress. Maybe even some frigging female thing.

The few times anyone had been foolish enough to dare suggest that as a woman she was of the weaker sex, she'd shown him the error of his ways. Once or twice these demonstrations had resulted in hospitalization for the instructee. But at that moment it seemed like her only refuge. Although his family had come to America when he was a teenager, she hoped there might be enough of the Old World left in the old boy for him to bite.

"Hey," she said, "maybe it was some sort of premeno-

pausal hormonal glitch. Christ knows I'm old enough."
She was closer to the big five-oh than to forty, and she
and the other two women on the *Ares* were taking hormones to suppress ovulation. Sometimes when you
messed with Mother Nature she messed back.

This suggestion put a thoughtful frown on his face. He
leaned over and retrieved the fancy MedMax slayte he
called his "little black box" from the bunkside shelf. His
fingers flew across the screen, calling up information sent
to it via the dozen or so rice-grain-sized sensors implanted in her body. The whole crew was similarly wired,
himself included.

She waited for his verdict, keeping herself from holding her breath. *Please God, let it be hinky hormones after
all.* Better that then having her mental avionics crashing.

At last he looked up, his face carefully neutral.

"Well?"

"I suppose it is possible." A deep breath and an unhappy scowl. "Remotely possible."

An unspoken message flew between them on the old
marital hot line. He didn't believe it for a minute, but
since she seemed fine now, and he lacked any other explanation, he'd let it slide. In spite of his mastery of a
dozen facets of medicine—or maybe because of it—he
was perfectly willing to admit that while he and his col-
leagues knew more than ever about the big wet mystery
they all carted around inside their skins, a lot of things
were still pure shithappens.

But being a doctor as much as a husband, he added,
"I'm going to monitor your hormone levels closely from
now on. If this was a premenopausal symptom, I may
have to put you on Menogyn."

"Pills, right?"

"Shots, actually."

She made a face. "Figures." Still, they had a truce.
That was all that mattered.

"Don't want me growing whiskers on my chin, darling?" she asked to further lighten the mood and keep
him looking under the wrong shell.

He snorted. "You're already doing that, and have
been for the last four years."

So much for secrets inside a marriage. "You never said you noticed, or knew."

"Who do you think has been making sure that there are good tweezers in every bathroom we use?" He put the slayte aside and crooked his finger, calling her back to their bunk. "The Surgical Tweezer Fairy?"

"Don't call yourself a fairy, love. I've seen you in action." She crawled back onto the bunk and sat down beside him. "Look, we don't need to mention this or log it, do we?"

"The secret of your beard is safe with me."

She elbowed him in the ribs. "I mean that other thing. We've got enough troubles on this flying junk pile. If Hans gets it in his head I'm going through menopause, he'll probably stage a mutiny." She laughed. "Can't have someone with shitty plumbing at the helm, you know."

Fabi sighed, took her hand. "I suppose not. Things are quite difficult enough as they stand."

She lifted his hand to her lips, kissed his knuckles. "Thanks, hon. You know, maybe it was just an anxiety attack. The stress level has been high enough."

"Could be." His tone of voice made it clear that he rated the odds of her suffering an anxiety attack about as high as those of her second-in-command growing a personality.

In her younger days they'd called her Calamity Jane. As she got older that had changed to Iron Jane. You don't get command of a mission like the one they were on unless, as one of the Mission Psychs had told her, you were about as stable as an Egyptian pyramid. She hadn't pointed out that the pyramids were pretty flaky, actually.

"Probably just a one-time thing. Like that night back in Rome when you couldn't, well—" she patted his thigh. "You know."

"I get the picture, woman," he growled with mock sourness.

The situation was about as defused as it was going to get. Best to quit while she was ahead. She put her arm around his back, gave him a squeeze. "We better get back to sleep, Doc. Watch begins in three hours."

"Sure, Commander." He saluted, then gave her a peck on the cheek. They crawled back under the covers.

"Lights," she called, dimming them to sleep mode, and they snuggled in hip to hip. The myriad clicks and hums and other sounds made by the *Ares* scarcely registered with either of them, no more than the 75 percent Earth-normal gravity.

Beside her Fabi's breathing slowed, deepened. Within minutes he was sound asleep and snoring softly.

Jane stared up at the quilted padding on the ceiling, still able to hear that lorn and desperate cry of ***help me*** ringing in her head and demanding an answer. The images and intimations that had entered her mind with it still roiled in her synapses, cryptic and unsettling.

But that wasn't the only thing keeping her awake.

There was one other secret she kept from Fabi. If he did know about it, then he treated it like that bit with her chin wanting to emulate Abe Lincoln's, an unspoken thing that was just there.

Sometimes she had hunches. An oddball but fairly reliable sense that something was about to happen, and she'd better be on her toes. As a pilot and astronaut this had stood her in good stead, saving her bacon more than once and earning her that "Calamity" nickname back when she only had four things on her mind: flying, breaking hearts, busting balls, and flying.

All through her life she had steadfastly refused to think of this as any sort of psychic ability. She didn't believe in God, fairies, horoscopes, Ascended Masters, Benevolent Aliens coming back to reoccupy Atlantis, or zaftig women in caftans with hokey accents, crystal balls, and secret knowledge about tall dark strangers. The explanation was simple and far more scientific: her knack for predicting probabilities was just better than that of most folks—not that it was any help when she and Fabi went to Vegas.

Half of what was keeping her up now was a hunch about what had just happened to her.

Check that, what she had was a full-blown motherfucking better-check-your-parachute-honey foreboding.

Try as she might to tell herself and Fabi that it had just been an isolated incident, her mental crash-alarm was telling her that this was just the first of more to come. A sort of precursor, the first unidentifiable blip of a bogey on her radar.

As to if and how and when it might come again, and what all that might lead to, no information was forthcoming. The future was so blank she might as well have been wearing opaque shades.

Only one thing was certain. As commander of a spacecraft with a breakdown rate so high it would be covered by the lemon laws if it was a car, and of a crew where her second-in-command had made it amply clear that he felt himself far more fit for the position of top dog, she was in for even more trouble.

Big trouble. The kind to keep anyone, no matter whether she had a screw coming loose or not, from sleeping.

PART 2

The Morning After

The Dim Star

Dan Francisco had never been much of a morning person, and this morning wasn't one to convert him to a member of that cult.

He sat hunched on a tall wooden stool at the kitchen counter, a pair of gaudy red-and-green-silk boxer shorts his daughter Bobbi had given him last Christmas hanging from his skinny hips. The morning news babbled cheerfully away on the set by his elbow, EdgeNet, the network that cut his paychecks, tuned in and tuned out. A cup of coffee sat on the counter before him, cold as the toast on the plate beside it.

He was a mess, and knew it. He hadn't slept worth a damn after his fit or whatever the hell it had been, fearful that unwelcome voice might come calling again like some amnesiac Jehovah's Witness returning to the same house over and over again. With something like that you could lock your door. If there was any way to lock your head, he'd never learned it, and with his luck he'd probably lose the key anyway.

Finally, he'd dragged his sorry ass out of bed far earlier than normal and pretty much spent the time since brooding on life, sanity, and everything.

No simple, easy, or rational explanation for the voice and other stuff had sprung or even dribbled to mind. Except for the random occasional toke at college, he didn't have enough drug use under his belt to qualify for a flashback. Two beers weren't enough to cause the DTs. Compared to most of the people who worked in the performance end of media he was stable and uncomplicated, free from any serious kinks, psychoses, phobias, addictions, or obsessions. He was a slightly boring guy who led as quiet and orderly a life as reality would allow.

He picked up his coffee cup, took a sip. Grimaced. Cold again. He drank it anyway, hoping the caffeine would help.

The more he thought about it, the more he came to the conclusion that his best bet was to write the whole crazy episode off as some mutant strain of super hyped-up nightmare—sort of like his marriage to Tammy. An aberration to be put behind him and forgotten.

That matter settled, if not entirely satisfactorily, he topped off his cup with hot coffee to reward himself. Just as he was putting the carafe back down, his house line beeped.

He glanced at the clock before answering. The set's caller ID function had crapped out a couple months ago. Fortunately the list of potential callers was short. It was still a few minutes early for Morty to be calling, and she usually used her dedicated line downstairs, but sometimes a big overnight weather event would come up, and she'd want him to head down to his basement ress early for extra preair prep.

He leaned forward, tabbed ACCEPT. Morty had seen him half-dressed—hell, bare-assed—plenty of times. Anyone else would just get a very small, very cheap thrill.

The news blipped to an inset, the screen filling with the image of his caller. The words *Good morning, Morty,* turned to ash in his throat.

"Hello, Dan," his ex-wife purred in the throaty, sexy voice which had helped make her a star. A phone-sex voice, only she used it to earn far more than a buck a minute.

Born Tammy Vanowski, she'd changed her name to Tamara Van Buren just before Dan met her, trying to create a more upscale image. In the years since that fateful day she'd risen from graveyard shift fill-in at a small public-access mininet to become one of the brightest stars in the EdgeNet firmament. Far bigger than he, though nowhere near as famous as she wanted to be. Cobilling with God might not satisfy her—not if she got second slot in the credits and a smaller dressing room.

"Mornin'," he mumbled, glumly contemplating her image. As usual, she looked absolutely perfect. Styled

blond hair in frothy waves around a face that was more
nymphet than her age could account for, edged with
enough porn star sult to make it arresting. A wide sen-
sual mouth Morty called "blow-job ready," sharp white
capped teeth, and blue eyes that sparkled for the cameras and turned cold as ice when turned his way.

Her calling him, especially this early in the day, could
mean only one thing. *She wanted something.*

"Oh, you're not dressed. Did I wake you, Dan?"

He made himself smile. "No, but I haven't been up
long. The orgy ended only about four, and I overslept."

Calculation entered her gaze, and he knew he'd made
the same bonehead mistake he'd made a thousand times
before. The woman had no real sense of humor, although she could fake it. She could fake pretty much
anything. Love. Loyalty. Tenderness. Respect. Honesty.
Sincerity. She'd kept him fooled for a while.

"Ha," she said, deciding he was joking. No great intel-
lectual leap there; time and time again she'd made it
painfully clear that she rated his sexual magnetism so
low that when he died a female morgue attendant
wouldn't want to touch him. The sad truth was that she
hadn't come after him back there at the beginning because of his manly bod or macho ways, but because she
figured he could help her get her foot in the door at
EdgeNet. Which he had obligingly done.

"What do you want, Tammy?" All he wanted was for
this call to end. Every time he saw her he found himself
wondering, *What was I thinking?* How could he have
dated, married, and had a child with this woman without
realizing that she was basically a fucking robot, a ruth-
less fame-eating machine with its sensors set to
CELEBRITY.

The answer to that was simple. When you saw her in
a slinky black dress, all you could think about was how
she would look naked. When you saw her naked, all
rational thought pretty much ceased. For a sizable chunk
of the hetero male population—and a decent lesbo-
demo—she was a walking talking priapism-inducing lobotomy, and had the ratings to prove it.

"I want Bobbi this weekend."

His heart sank. *Not again.*

"It's my weekend," he pointed out tonelessly. "Remember?"

She'd gotten primary custody of Bobbi. Not because she was the better parent, but because she'd had the better lawyer, and hadn't treated their separation and divorce as a matter that could be settled amicably and fairly, but as some sort of death duel fought with the legal equivalent of chain saws. He'd used Stan Weems, the old guy who had been his family's lawyer forever. She'd hired some high-ticket gunslinger from LA. The match had been like an old neutered house cat going head-to-head with a rabid cyborg cheetah with Ginsu claws.

"I *know* that, Dan," she said in an exasperated tone, like she was being forced to dicker with a dolt. "That's why I'm, like, *tubing,* know it?" As usually happened, pique made her revert to the mallrat slang of her youth.

"I suppose you've got a good reason." Other than not wanting to share the poor kid with the one parent who loves her, and never missing a chance to get more, even though she already had damn near everything.

"Well of course! EdgeNet's sending me to Paris this weekend so I can cover the start of Nipple Isuzu's European concert tour. Just think how glide a visit to Paris would be for her." A pause, then a pitifully transparent attempt to push one of his buttons. "How *educational.*"

Right. He knew the poor kid would end up spending most of her time cooped up in a hotel room with her nanny, kept conveniently out of the way while Tammy hobnobbed with the rich, famous, and profitably fuckable.

"We sort of had plans, Tammy," he said wearily.

Her nostrils flared, and her lipsticked mouth tightened. "Yeah, I've like heard about it like a hundred times. The kid says you're going to rake *leaves.*"

"We were going to do some yard work," he agreed stiffly. "Go for a drive and check out the fall colors. Have a picnic at Baird's Creek. Buy some pumpkins at Uncle John's stand so we could carve jack-o'-lanterns."

Even as he said that he could hear how lame it sounded compared to a trip to Paris. But they would've had a ball together, and dammit all, Bobbi needed to see that there was more to life than going to all the glitziest events in clothes that cost more than most people made in a month, and yet covered just short of nothing.

"How sizzy," she sneered. "A weekend in Doobville." Her face hardened, that crease he knew all too well appearing between her perfectly plucked eyebrows. "I want this, Dan."

And what you want, you always get, don't you? He knew what would happen if he said no. She would retaliate, whacking him with lawyers, child psychologists, network pressure, and any other big sticks she could muster until he was beaten into submission. He had two choices, really. Capitulate, or try to strike a deal, and *then* capitulate.

Usually his mind went blank during confrontations, but for once he saw a chance to get something he wanted.

He sat up straighter, facing the blight of his life. "Tell you what, Tammy. I was thinking maybe Bobbi and I might take a trip up to the cabin sometime soon. If I let her go with you this weekend, will you let me have her for four days the weekend after? That way we go to Skyles Lake without spending most of our time settling in and getting ready to leave."

No immediate answer. He could see her weighing the risk of letting their child spend more than the minimum amount of time with her father versus what getting what she wanted would cost in terms of aggravation and her trade balance of favors owed.

"You know Susannah would have to come along."

Dan kept himself from rolling his eyes. His dear ex made Machiavelli look like Santa Claus, and this rule was the result of more of her machinations. Since she was almost never home, and spending time with her daughter was dead bottom on her to-do list, Bobbi was cared for by Susannah. An actual, no-shit, imported from Merry Olde England, British nanny.

Somehow, probably using a combination of cash and favorable publicity backed up by her trusty vaginal convincer, she'd gotten some hotshot child psychologist to convince the court that it was critical to Bobbi's well-being that she have her nanny with her at all times. This included visits to her father. So every third weekend Susannah flew here to Indiana with Bobbi, and stayed in what had been the guest room.

"Sure, Stoneface can bait hooks while we fish." He always made a point of speaking about Susannah in derogatory terms. There was one secret he'd managed to keep from Tammy: over time Susannah had seen past the anti-Dan propaganda Tammy had fed her and come to approve of him in a cool, British sort of way. He got the feeling she knew he was the better parent. Not that she let it show. Susannah was a smart young woman, and well aware of who signed her checks—and could probably get her deported. She tried to remain neutral, and devoted herself to the task of raising Bobbi properly. A job she was doing quite well.

Dan was glad she was there. Tammy's maternal instincts were about as well developed as his nose for female bad news had been when he met her. Which was to say nonexistent.

As he waited for her answer he made himself ignore the clock. He had to head downstairs and get started soon. He knew Tammy knew this, and had timed her call to take advantage of it.

But he could get ready to go on-air one helluva lot more quickly than she, who spent at least an hour in makeup, would ever believe possible. Plus he'd gotten better at steering clear of long arguments that forced him to surrender because of time pressure. If he'd been half this good at managing her when they were still married, they might still *be* married. That was a pretty scary thought, except for maybe when he considered how nice it would be to get laid on a regular basis again.

The woman was good in bed, even when he'd only been getting leftovers and sloppy seconds, which had pretty much been from their honeymoon on. Her first affair, with a sponsor's rep, had begun sixteen days after they tied the knot.

"What day would you want her?" she asked at last.

The shark is sniffing the bait. "She could fly in Thursday, fly back the following Monday."

"That's five days!"

"Depends on how you count it. She never gets here before late afternoon, you know that. This way we can go straight to Skyles Lake from the airport, come back here Sunday evening, and she won't be so tired when she flies back Monday morning."

He could see that the principle of letting him have anything he wanted was giving her trouble. Time for some judo.

"Hey, this way you get a long weekend all to yourself." If there was one bait she was sure to rise to, it was self-interest. He could see all the little razor-toothed gears turning in her head. Although he'd never seen any evidence that Bobbi's presence put a damper on her promiscuity, this would give her space to bring in an entire fucking NBA team if that's what she wanted.

"I guess it's a deal," she said reluctantly.

"Good," he said, careful not to sound too happy. "You tell her about the trip to Paris. I'll tell her about the camping trip when I call her tonight."

"Don't bother. I'll just leave a message for Susannah."

Meaning you don't have any immediate plans to see your own goddamned daughter anytime in the near future. He kept his face placid, doing a little acting of his own. "Aw, I call her every Wednesday night so we can do the *Word Kids* cryptic together." Eight years old and she had a real knack for word games and the like. He was beginning to think maybe she had his brains. He prayed she hadn't inherited Tammy's moral sense or libido. If so, he was going to nail her into a barrel when she turned ten.

"If you really have to." A theatrical sigh.

Time to bail out while he was still ahead. "Okay," he said, tapping his watch. "I've got to run. Airtime's coming up fast."

A smug smile appeared. "Yeah, I saw your ratings the other day. You seem to have like, *plateaued,* Dan." She made the word sound like it involved paid sex with sheep.

Maybe if I could do interviews on the beach in a skin-tight bikino mine would go up like yours. Though lacking your increasingly famous tits and ass, probably not.

"My numbers are solid." He wasn't quite able to keep

a defensive note from creeping into his voice. "I'm doing okay."

She shook her head in disgust. "That's always been your problem, Dan. You're willing to settle for okay." Rather than give him a chance to respond to that shot, she cut the connection.

"*You're* my problem, darling," he informed the blank screen, knowing this was the only way he ever got the last word.

Two minutes later he carried his coffee cup down into what had once been his father's basement workshop, now a state-of-the-art remote studio space, what the trade called a ress. The clock read 8:41 CST.

"Wake up little Susie," he called in a clear, carrying voice. A low tone acknowledged the combination password and command. The ress systems began coming off standby one by one. The big ProCast workstation awoke, began querying the National Weather Service, AccuCast, and other nodes, filling its multiple displays with the resulting text and graphics. He gave the info a quick look, reading the maps and charts with an ease born of long practice, catching up on weather information gathered since his 10 P.M. recap the night before.

While he was getting up to meteorological speed, the ress continued its own preparations. The bluestage lit and autoadjusted. Computer-driven cameras swiveled and swung on their spidery mounts, dancing tai chi robots to a preprogrammed warm-up routine. On the charging rack over by the stairs his suit went into self-test mode, the status board built into the rack's frame lighting with green pinpoints as each 'sponder passed.

"Top of the mornin' on you, handsome," a deep gravelly voice rumbled behind him.

Dan turned toward the big flatscreen hung on the back wall and positioned so it could be seen from the bluestage.

"Morning, Morty," he mumbled in reply.

Moravia Denholtz, Morty to her friends, grinned back at him from her office in San Francisco. She removed the stubby remains of a cigar from her mouth, blew smoke at the camera.

"You, my darling boy, look like maybe your balls got run through a wringer." She cocked one shaggy eyebrow festooned with gold rings. "The Snatch of Steel call this morning, hmmmm?"

Morty had been Dan's producer and director at Edge-Net right from his very first cast. After all the years they'd been together the big bull dyke could read him like a script.

"Yeah, she called."

Morty shook her flat-topped head. "You shoulda let me and some of the girls work that bitch over years ago." The "girls" were a lesbian motorcycle gang called the Heavyweight Boxers. Their idea of good clean fun was to ride around looking for male outlaw bikers to terrorize.

He shrugged. "I did okay this time. She wanted Bobbi this weekend so they could go to Paris together. She's covering that Nipple Isuzu tour."

"And I suppose you let that bad crack get her way."

"Yeah, but I get Bobbi Thursday through Monday the weekend after. Which means I'm going to need to be off-sked. We're going up to Skyles Lake."

"Gonna play Daniel Boone, huh? What bucolic fun. Come on, Dan'l, you better get your coonskin on. The clock's ticking."

"Right." He headed for the rack to get his suit.

"No problem with the time off at this end," Morty said as he pulled the charger plugs and then double-checked the woven-in LCD. "Lizzie's been yammering at me for more air." A puff on her cigar. "The little minx asked where you live, Danskin. You better watch out. She's got some Tammy in her, and don't seem inclined to visit an exorcist."

"Thank God she lives too far away for me to see her in person," Dan said as he kicked off his slippers, then began shucking off his boxer shorts. Morty watched him getting naked, but that didn't bother him. There wasn't anything she hadn't seen before, or was much interested in anyway. "She's pretty cute, and those gymnastic things she does kinda make you wonder what *else* she can do. I figure the last thing I'd see in this world was her sitting on my face before she squished my head flat."

"What a way to go, though," Morty said with a leer. "I tell ya, some of these kids today will strap on just about anything if they think it'll get them ahead. Back in my day we were at least a *bit* choosy."

Naked now, he took down his suit and began pulling it on like a set of skintight long johns. The blue nanostrand-augmented fabric felt cool and satiny against his bare skin.

"Morty, don't give me that. I've heard the stories. You once slept with a show's producer *and* his wife at the same time to score a director's slot."

Once he had the suit on he fingered the tab at his neck to make it autoadjusting. The fabric seemed to crawl as it arranged itself so that the hundreds of sensors and 'sponders were settled into their proper places.

Morty's jowly face broke into a truly evil grin at this particular fond memory. "That I did, me bucko. He wasn't much—not that I did much to raise his little antenna—but *she* was something else altogether! Six months later she ran off with a bronc rider from the pro circuit named Helen Hooves. I always figured I was the one showed her you get the best spread eatin' at the Y."

"Riverton blamed you, didn't he?" The suitsets in place, he retrieved his hood and pulled that on. This was an old story, retold many times, and a welcome distraction.

"Sure did," she cackled gleefully. "Wanted to fire my dyke ass the worst way possible. Problem was, I had the whole sordid episode on tape. Got made a director *and* associate producer instead. Damn well shoulda, the way I handled the camera angles."

"Okay, Morty, I'm ready," he announced once the hood was on, the built-in eyephones and audio pads settled in place.

"Yeah, you do look good, my bony blue man." He knew she'd been checking his telemetry while rambling through her checkered past. Plus checking the net's sked and carrier connection while testing her control over the cameras and other equipment at his end. A good producer did at least three things at once. Morty could do five, seven when a crunch was on.

Now he was seeing the ress via eyephones, and himself

from the viewpoint of the cameras. The first few times he'd done this it had been disorienting. Now he could slip between meat and virtual as naturally as breathing.

"Air in three. Ready to skim your script?"

"Fire away." The script superimposed itself on his field of vision, red characters in an easy-to-read sanserif font. Standard intro, opening business, the usual.

"Maps and exteriors?"

"Hit me."

The basement ress vanished completely, replaced by the multilevel 3D maps and graphs viewers would see him inside during the cast. The public liked to look at 3D if it was in front of them, but as an active immersive environment for anything other than rides and games it hit only a small demographic. Television and its stepchild vidyo still ruled because all you had to do was sit there and try not to drool too much. Full VR—just like the deeper levels of netted media—was too much work for your average viewer, took too much thinking. Remote-armed passivity remained the favorite activity of the demobulge.

He walked blindly toward the bluestage, the floor under him so well memorized that he knew where he was every inch of the way. Step up. Two forward. Turn right.

Overlaying the maps came a succession of still clips from the exteriors they would be running. Morty ID'd them as they zipped past like glimpses out the window of a low-flying SSPT.

"Rain in New Yawk. More El Niño rains in Arizona and Texas. Early snow in the Rockies, shitstorms in the Bullwinkles. Great t-storm in Florida, you should be getting the biz and cumshot now."

"Got it." On plain and 'netted TV the viewers would see him wrap in and ride down a lightning bolt striking Biscayne Bay, fragment when he hit, reassemble himself and make a bad joke. Standard stuff for EdgeNet's weather magazine spot *Weatherbreak,* starring their featured host and show, *The Weather from Within, with Dan the Virtual Weatherman.* The rest of the script flipped past. General predictions, space for local use of him— or a virtual version, anyway—sign-off and fade.

"Air in sixty," Morty warned. "Drop your cock and watch the clock."

"Check." He fingered the controller pads in the left palm of his suit, shifting back to an exterior view of the stage to make sure he was on his mark. Not that he couldn't feel the bumps underneath his feet, he just liked to double-check everything. In terms of his work, okay was *not* good enough. He had his standards. They were just completely different from Tammy's.

It was his career he wasn't inclined to flog until his ethics and sense of shame were nothing but scar tissue. This kept him a rather dim star, but he was comfortable with his low level of fame. It was, like they said, a living.

"Twenty," Morty intoned. "Loop up." The *Weatherbreak* theme music played over his earsets as ghosts of presegment graphics flitted across his field of vision. The fingers of his left hand moved, switching back to the opening screen the viewers would see.

"Ten. Five. Two. One. *Go.*"

"Helllllooooo out there in the real world!" he crowed, his voice altered to sound hollow and metallic. "Dan the Virtual Weatherman here—wherever *here* is!—with *THE WEATHER FROM WITHIN!!*" That last was run through an antique tube-powered Echoplex Morty had scared up at a Frisco flea market, then run through the usual digital sound processors. It was a neat effect nobody else had been able to quite duplicate with straight digital boxes.

On his eyephones and all the screens tuned to EdgeNet a glossy texture-mapped simulacrum of his head and face warped in and floated disembodied over the opening splash. A stylized chrome version of his smiling face, his shaggy hair a wild bundle of multicolored wires. RoboDan.

"Now if I can just . . ." Squinching his face in cartoonish concentration, his body jelled out of the background frame of surface maps and tickle shots of exteriors to come, the images crawling all over his lank frame and looking like chunks of reality. Last of all his hands popped out, white and glaring.

Eleven years on-air at EdgeNet, and no one had ever seen his real face. What had started out as a gimmick had over the years settled in to the comforting anonymity of virtual celebrity. The creditcrawl listed him as *Dan Francisco*. Since he didn't do ads, endorsements, or personal appearances, most viewers figured that was a made-up name for a puppet construct, like Max Headroom of old. At last count half of the viewers were sort of semisure he wasn't even a real person, just really clever software. Or something. That was just fine with him.

Dan Francisco was his real name. He was the only son of the late Stan and Nancy Francisco. His dad had been a high-school English teacher, and his mother a municipal bookkeeper. Then back during his first year at EdgeNet they'd been killed coming home from a movie by a tractor trailer driver who'd fallen asleep during his twelfth hour at the wheel. He'd come back to Tyler's Corners to see to see to their funerals and straighten out their affairs. Morty had wrangled a ress so he could keep working while he was there, and he'd never left.

Thanks to the beat he covered and miracle of the ress, he didn't have to work in the pressure-cooker atmosphere of New York or LA. He could do his broadcasts from the basement of his parents' house in the small Indiana town of Tyler's Corners. The place where he'd grown up, and wanted his daughter to grow up.

That plan had crumbled with his marriage. Bobbi lived in LA with her mother, or at least in one wing of her mother's expensive house out in Malibu. He was still here. He liked the place, and it gave the poor kid a taste of life outside the fameloop. His neighbors thought he was some sort of self-employed graphics drone, not a graphic himself. Down at Sparhawk's Superette and Robinson's Diner and Sawyer's Hardware they kidded him about having the same last name as that robot weather guy, never suspecting that they were talking to the guy himself.

A guy who just wanted to rake leaves and potter around in his garden with his daughter. To be normal.

Like normal people suddenly get a voice in their head calling for help.

Focusing on his show made putting that to one side easier. The familiar feeling of being in control—at least in this one small facet of his universe—returned, at least for a while.

"Today we're going to start in New York City, where it's raining . . ."

Acceptable Voices

Martina leaned against the casement and stared out the window, watching sheets of rain cascade down from a leaden sky to lash the streets far below. The weather suited her mood perfectly: gray, grim, and unwelcoming.

Dressed for work, she wore a businesslike suit in muted blue, the ballistic-fabric inner lining and generous cut adding a few pounds to her already formidable frame. The loose cut was necessary. Arrayed at various places on her person were enough exotic electronic devices and good old-fashioned weaponry to qualify her as an armored dreadnought in some of the smaller third world nations.

"I am never quite used to the rain here," Rico said as he came out of his—their—bedroom. "Ogly stuff."

"Is more like weather where I come from," she agreed, turning away from the window. He looked good, his sturdy brown body resplendent in his trademark white suit with its own Ballistex IV lining. His long fringe of dark hair was oiled and brushed, his mustache trimmed. He looked handsome, and capable of helping keep the world from tearing itself apart for one more day.

He spread his hands. "I look okay?"

"All except tie." She went to him and straightened it. He went up on his toes and stole a kiss while she adjusted the knot.

"You behave," she warned, stepping back.

He struck a wounded pose, hand over his heart. "Do I not always?"

"No, not always. Not even much."

He cocked his head, studying her face. "You do not

look or sound yourself this morning. Like you are sad, or have some big thing on your mind."

She forced a smile. "Just tired, Rico. That is all."

"This old man wore out strong younger woman like you?"

"I guess you did."

"Hot damn!" He thumped his chest. "I must be one macho son of a bitch!"

"You are that."

Sensing that she was not really in the mood for banter, he held up his hands. "Sorry, I quit playing the clown. Are we ready to get our circus on the road?"

"Whenever you are." Actually they were running a minute late, but Rico took a Latin approach to time.

"So, let us go."

"System active," she said. "Tac One and Tac Three, please report." Bits of circuitry bonded to her teeth and built into biopoxy wafers cemented to her skull responded to her command. The implant behind her ear tingled, telling her she was live.

The voice of Mohammed Fayed, UNSIA Special Services agent in charge of Tac One, came to her over the tiny chip buried in her left ear canal. *"Tac One ready, ma'am."*

"Tac Three ready," Louis Chan, AIC of Tac Three, chimed in a moment later. These voices in her head were normal, reassuring. Not hearing them would have been a cause for concern.

She glanced at Rico, winked. "The Big Enchilada is ready to roll."

When they exited the suite, a business-suited phalanx of security agents from Tac One surrounded them, falling into step with well-oiled precision. Fayed. Wilkins. Watanabe. Hansen. Each and every one deadly, diligent, and dedicated to her and the man they were sworn to protect. People she would trust with her life. More importantly, people she would trust with Rico's life.

"We are on track this morning?" she said quietly.

All gave affirmative nods but Mohammed Fayed.

"Problem?"

"Cassandra has not arrived," the wiry Palestinian reported, a less-than-happy expression on his bearded face. "We have begun vetting a backup car and driver now, one being diverted from a pickup at the Sri Lankan Embassy. All checks green so far, and it should have arrived by the time we get down. Chan has a crew standing by to verify and inspect."

Rico's personal driver was almost never late. Martina didn't like this deviation from routine. Fayed and Chan had dealt with the situation by the book, but too many people knew what the book said. It took her less than a second to decide that a different plan of action might be necessary. Routine could kill.

"Cancel the second car, Fayed. Wilkins?"

"Yes, ma'am?" Linda Wilkins answered from behind.

"I want Cassandra found. No reply on carphone?"

"None."

"She is probably stuck in damn tunnel again, but we take no chances. Use limo's emergency transponder to locate her. You have my authorization to activate."

"Working." The British agent's voice dropped to a hushed whisper as she carried out her orders.

"Fayed. If she cannot be found, you will drive the Secretary and me in unmarked escort vehicle."

He inclined his head. "Certainly."

The doors to the penthouse's private elevator were already open and waiting, Duffy having gone ahead to keep it secure. They swept in. The doors closed behind them, but the elevator stayed put.

"Secure parking, ma'am?" Duffy asked, hands on the controls.

Before she could answer Wilkins spoke up. "We have reacquired Cassandra, ma'am. She just called in, reports that she got stuck behind a four-car pileup in the Giuliani Tunnel. ETA four minutes minus."

"Thank you." Martina consulted her watch, calculating. Four minutes to Cassie's arrival. The chances that the accident had been staged so that a bomb or other device could be planted on the limo were slim. Cassie was a complete pro. She would have activated the limo's contact sensors and been watching like a hawk.

But little chance was not no chance. Figure four more minutes for Chan's crew to sweep the limo. That would put them minus six minutes on the schedule. On the plus side, the Mercedes Cassie was in could shrug off a direct hit from just about anything short of a tank-killing round. Odds were that Cassie could reclaim at least two of those lost minutes, and Rico would be safer.

Rico would be safer.

That was the answer to any question, this one included.

"Tac One and Three, back to original arrangements," she said, her command going to Chan's crew via her implants. "We meet Cassie as per original plan. Sweep teams, you know your jobs."

"In progress," Chan reported.

"Good. Duffy, take us down. Hansen, what is howler count?"

"One hundred sixteen demonstrators total," the Swede replied without hesitation as the car began descending. "Breakdown?"

"I will settle for number of Fists." The White Fists of Uncle Sam were one of the more vocal—and violent— American anti-UN extremist groups. In many other countries they would be all rounded up and dealt with like the mad dogs they were. But this was America, where heavily armed maniacs shrilly demanded freedoms they would gladly deny others, and generally got them.

Although the US still pretty much did what it wanted—and bombed whomever it wanted—the UN's occasional need to tell America *No no no* were seen by the Fists and their ilk as proof of a conspiracy to impose some draconian wog totalitarianism on them.

They didn't seem to understand that most of the world had come to terms with America's occasional excesses. They were like a crazy big brother who sometimes scared you, but on the whole was generous and protective and made life a helluva lot more fun. Sure he played too hard sometimes, but there was nobody better to have at your side when the chips were down.

"Nineteen cut and coded. SSSM revealed twelve weapons on them, twenty-seven in the entire crowd, all bearers taken into custody by the UNLID Blues. We are currently green to hit the streets."

The Side Scanning Security Magnetometer could locate all but the most exotic composite weapons, and the UNLID Blues, the NYPD UN Liaison Division, would be working the crowd both in uniform and undercover. So would elements of Tac Five, the elite undercover UNSIA squad run by Colonel Rajneesh Singh.

"Thank you." She glanced at Rico. He had his expensive Sony-Braun slayte cradled in one arm, rereading his speech and making notes with an electronic pen, seemingly oblivious. Part of his ability to do this hinged on just how much he trusted her and her people.

She had no plans ever to let him down.

"We wait in Secure One until the limo checks out and final sweep of entrance is completed." Secure One was the special waiting room in the secure parking area, basically a nicely decorated bunker.

"Almost to the parking level, ma'am," Duffy reported. "Lock or unload?"

Fayed spoke up. "Chan says to tell you Secure One is cleared and ready, even has coffee and muffins waiting."

Martina permitted herself a small smile. This was the way things were supposed to work, the machine she had assembled to protect Rico ticking over smoothly.

"Good work, people," she said aloud and over Tac. "Remember, soon we will face greatest danger to safety of Secretary Perez, so be on toes like Bolshoi dancers. We have no choice but to face this hostile force, since by treaty we cannot detain all New York cabdrivers."

A chorus of muted chuckles greeted her joke as the elevator stopped. Duffy watched her for his cue. She nodded. He opened the doors, and they moved out in a group, maintaining a living palisade around the Secretary-General as they moved closer to hostile territory.

Rico looked up from his slayte. "Dinner for your people tonight on me, Colonel Omerov. Mister Chan picks the cuisine, Mister Fayed the restaurant, Cassie the wine." This edict delivered, he went back to his reading, acting like he was unaware of the grins breaking onto the faces of the security people around him.

Martina's smile cracked a tiny bit wider.

How could she not love a man like this?

Downtime

Why did I have to fall for a man like this?

Daveed sprawled across the oversize waterbed in his condo bedroom, glumly contemplating a picture of Alec and himself taken at Key West. Big blond swimsuit model Alec, cake as all hell in that skintight buttflosser. No rocket scientist, but warm and sweet-tempered and funny. Those were the plusses. On the minus side had been the fact that he was handsome enough to attract most of the gay men who came near him, and monogamy had been a bigger stretch for him than calculus.

Still, Alec had managed mostly to resist temptation until they'd come here to Neely from New Orleans. Here Daveed's twelve-plus-hour shifts at MU had left Alec with too much idle time, and not enough Daveed. It hadn't helped that he had a bad tendency to tune out the real when he was fully plugged into the happening curve. By the middle of the second month—which was about the time he'd finally noticed that maybe Alec was seeming a little distant, Alec went full distant, splitting for Oregon with some rich accountant he'd met somewhere. Leaving behind a very short note.

Dear Daveed. This isn't working. I need a life, and so do you.

Daveed put the picture facedown on his bedside table, settled back against the headboard with a sigh. This was voluminously stupid. If he had half a brain, he'd be sleeping, not indulging in another session of mooning over a guy who'd been gone almost three months. He should be over it, right?

Right. Like an eighty-plus-hour workweek and zilch else after hours was much help. Maybe when the *Ares* returned he could have something like a normal life again. If he still remembered how, or even why.

The thing was, thinking about Alec the Absent was better than messing up his mind trying to get it around what had happened to him in the Uplink crapper. That was just too fucking weird, too *Twilight Zoney* for him to get a handle on it.

His gaze was drawn to the four big MagRez flatscreens facing the bed. The first one was set to show feeds from fourteen of the major nets. The second and third were also set to fourteen divides, each one changing every thirty seconds as thousands of plain vidyo, netcast, and cocast channels were scanned at random. The fourth was running a simple quad split: EdgeNet in the upper right quadrant showing the soap *Angela's Boudoir;* CNNI coverage of the Reuthen investigations in the upper left; GayLezNet's *Vacation Paradises* in the lower right, and *Monty Python and the Holy Grail* burbling away in the lower left.

Watching the Holy Hand Grenade of Antioch bit for maybe the fiftieth time made him smile, and sent his mind veering toward the lineup of the classic comedy jam he'd be sending to the *Ares* in a couple days. The poor bastards probably needed all the laughs they could get if they were having the sort of component failures the info coming out about Reuthen seemed to suggest. Since coverage was pure happyface, there had been no news that they were having problems, but come on.

He'd send *MP & the HG* for sure. Some Keaton and Lloyd clips—ones about dealing with hostile mechanisms. The director's cut of *The Adventures of Buckaroo Banzai* for Commander Jane. Either *A Night at the Opera* or *A Day at the Races* for her husband Dr. Costanza, who was a Marx Brothers nut.

Lt. Commander Hans Gluck was a stiff with no identifiable funny bone, but maybe that German comedy from about ten years ago, that Coen brothers rip-off *Wurms* might work. Gluck's wife Anna was easy, she was a big fan of Robin Williams's Grampa Bongo flicks.

Dr. Willy Tutillia was easy, he thought *everything* was funny. As for Willy's wife Wanda, he had a special surprise for her. A bootleg copy of a small club date done by her favorite comedian, Edd Dee. Dee's toes had been run over by a cab earlier in the day it was taped, and he'd shown up for his appearance with his foot in a cast, half-drunk and flying on painkillers, and proceeded to deliver a routine that was almost lethally funny.

Figure a twelve-hour package. ZAX compression would squeeze that down into six five-minute bursts that could be shoehorned into MU's uplink rotation. Of course the Goat would bleat, but he didn't want to send them anything.

Out in the living room the big grandfather clock that had been his aunt Marina's chimed, reminding him that in just a few hours he had to be back to work. He knew that he had to get some sleep, not spend his downtime thinking about work, so he popped two sleeping pills, peeled off his clothes, and crawled under the covers.

The breathing exercises he'd learned from an old boy-friend had come in handy lately. He began them, clearing his mind and trying to get his body to relax. His face smoothed as a combination of drugs and technique worked their magic.

The screens at the foot of the bed flickered and babbled on, their light and sound rolling over Daveed.

Child of his time, he could not sleep without them.

Morale

Jane stared at the display in front of her without really seeing it, sipping her strong black tea and taking a few moments to prepare herself for the next item on the agenda.

She wasn't really up for this. Staring at the ceiling and worrying when she should have been sleeping had left her feeling tired, cranky, and impatient. As she'd aged, not getting at least six hours had become something to, well, lose sleep over.

The first part of her watch had been spent counting the hours until she got some time alone so she could try to get her shit together. If reaching, orbiting, and getting a lander down on Mars was her larger mission, surviving the rest of this meeting was her immediate objective.

One best accomplished without bloodshed. That was going to be tough. Going through some of her endless scutwork during lunch, she'd found reason to be thoroughly pissed. Unfortunately that little jolt had faded quickly. Instead of righteous wrath she felt glumly grumpy, sour, and impatient.

The entire *Ares* crew was gathered in the wardroom for their daily confab, sipping their own beverages and waiting for her to get on with it. Mission specified by some Uncle Joe pinhead, this "Goals and Accomplishments Synchronization Session"—aptly acronymed GASS—hadn't been so bad in the early days of their long journey.

That was then, this was now. Dealing with six people from very different backgrounds stuffed into a small malfunctioning tin can over seventy million klicks from home took a lot of work. One particular member of the team was responsible for most of the friction and fuss.

Without him, they probably could have all gotten together, drunk coffee and tea, swapped dirty jokes, and had a grand old time.

"Next item," she said, finally looking up from her display and putting down her cup. "Lieutenant Commander Gluck, would you please be so kind as to explain the 'log corrections' you saw fit to send to Mission Control?" She asked this in the low, silky voice they all knew meant the Old Lady Was Not Happy.

Hans Gluck stared back at her, stone-faced and stolid. "Our last log transmission was in error," her second-in-command, and the major obstacle to ship morale in general and her morale in particular, replied tonelessly. "I made the proper corrections."

She wearily regarded the handsome blond man sitting with Teutonic stiffness across the table from her, the only one of them in full uniform.

What a hunk! had been her first thought when she met him. All blond hair, square chin, blue eyes, and nice manly bulges in all the right places. *Playgirl* centerfold material for sure.

What an asshole! had been her emendation after spending five minutes with him. The long months since had done nothing to upgrade that estimation.

Gluck was a pure Aryan from Argentina, and seemed hell-bent on being a living ethnic joke. Back in training she'd been able to laugh off this B crew martinet with a flagpole up his ass. The laughter stopped when Hiro and Persis Iyama had gotten caught in a freak accident just four days before the crew was to go up to the orbiting *Ares* craft. A refrigerated truck full of frozen turkeys had swerved to avoid a dog, gone off the road, and crashed through the bedroom wall of their quarters. An absurd accident which would have been funny, except it left her second-in-command and areologist with their legs in casts and their butts off the mission roster.

"Would you care to explain these alleged errors I made in the log, Hans?"

The others around the table remained silent, waiting for her and Gluck's latest head to head to be over. Unseen by everyone else, Fabi had his hand on her thigh, patting her like a Doberman on the verge of attack. He knew how much she detested this obnoxious blockhead. Nominally Jewish, she'd never much felt like one until she'd begun dealing with Hans the Junior Stormtrooper on a day-to-day basis.

Gluck's wife Anna—said in the Russian style *Ah-na*— sat beside him looking tired and apprehensive. A plain, rather chubby woman whose lank brown hair was pulled back into two braided pigtails, there were dark circles under her very pretty green eyes as she stared down at the slayte in her lap as if hoping to find some reason to be somewhere else on its screen.

Jane felt sorry for her. Not only was she married to this schmuck, she also all too often got caught in the middle when her husband placed himself at loggerheads with the Old Lady and the rest of the crew. Which was pretty much most of the time.

As for the rest of the crew, Willy and Wanda Tutillia were hanging back, sitting quietly side by side and doing some slayte time of their own. Each would toss in a word or a joke when they thought it might help, but in the meantime they had the good sense to keep their heads down.

"Of course I can explain your errors, Commander," Gluck replied. As usual, his use of her title sounded like a sneer. Everyone else just called her Jane. "Would you like me to do so item by item?"

"That would be—" She bit back a sarcasm. "—very *organized*, Hans. Please proceed." The screen before her flickered. She cut her glance that way, saw **organized = anal retentive??** appear in bright orange letters and then fade. *Willy*. She took a sip of tea to hide her reaction.

"Item four," Gluck recited. " 'Mission scientific objectives are on track.' " He looked up, stared at Jane. "Were you not aware that Anna was unable to perform all of her observations yesterday? It was in her report."

"The machine I needed broke down before I could finish is all, Hans," his wife began in a placating tone. He gave her a look that made her flinch. She dropped her gaze back to her slayte, hunching her shoulders and biting her lip.

Jane knew their relationship was part of the problem. There was only one reason they had made B crew, and so been in the right place to be part of the real deal. That reason was Anna. His career as a flier and astronaut had been mundane at best; he was a competent pilot, but no Yeager. Anna, on the other hand, was one of the top ten areologists alive and had been Uncle Joe royalty—which is why he'd set his sights on her.

It was a well-known secret that he'd talked her into a marriage of convenience, which let them apply for the long ride since the mission profile called for three married, preferably straight couples to make the trip. The plan had worked, but the marriage hadn't. The bastard resented her for being the big gun who got him what he wanted. Nor had she turned into a *Playboy* pinup for him, and he resented her for that, too.

The man had issues with women, no doubt about it. Anna's brilliance and pull was one. Having a certain pushy old broad for a boss was another. Only difference was, he wasn't going to bully her.

"Sheeit, Hans, the freakin' XLR sensors went belly-up again," Wanda drawled, letting her Southern accent go thick as gumbo. Her lovely dark brown face split in a toothy grin. "That pore gal of yours would be better off tryin' to use a set of toy binoculars than the kludge they give her."

"This is so," he admitted.

Jane felt the tension ease slightly, just as Wanda had intended. Equipment failure was the one enemy they all had in common.

She shot her friend a silent *thank-you,* getting a sly wink in return. Aside from the fact that, as Ship's Engineer, Wanda was the one who'd done the most to keep the *Ares* from coming apart at the seams, she had a knack for making Jane's life a lot more pleasant. The jokes and goofy act were part of it, as was her simple friendship. The weekly Girls' Night Wanda had started was often the highlight of her week, and helping the Georgia-born tech do her hair in elaborate cornrows had turned out to be about the third most relaxing thing Jane got to do, beaten out only by making whoopee with Fabi, and hiding away all by herself in the *Ares'* coffin-sized sauna.

"And as I understand it," Jane continued, facing Hans

again, "The shots in question were the third set in a redundant series anyway. All the i's might not have been dotted and t's crossed, but the objective was accomplished. Now what's the next colossal blunder you uncovered?"

Gluck was clearly unhappy with being overruled, and too goddamned dense to realize that his arguments were, as usual, going to fly like a cast-iron hang glider.

"Item six," he went on doggedly. " 'Shipboard computer systems are functioning to expectation and essentially problem-free.' " He looked up, thrust out his cleft chin. "This is not true, and we all know it."

"The first half is," Jane said. "They're worthless junk, and that's how I expect them to work. What have you got to say about this, Willy? Have we got computer problems?"

The rotund Samoan computer specialist grinned and scratched the expanse of belly showing through the front of his flowered shirt. The fact that he had a shirt on meant he'd dressed up for the meeting. Usually he just wore Bermuda shorts. "Lie down with dogs and you're gonna get fleas, *mon capitaine*."

"What?" Hans demanded with a scowl. "What has dogs to do with this?"

"What it means, brah, is there ain't any way to have computers and *not* have problems. Still, we're doing as well as we can short of FedEx turnin' up with replacement hardware. For critical operations I still have both mains running in tandem, error-checking each other. When they disagree, the problem is shared with the backup computer and rerun. Once all three agree on the same answer the task is completed. Luckily these puppies are fast. I could do the same for noncritical requests, but would rather not 'cause then we might start havin' lag problems."

Jane nodded. "Then, in other words, everything is more or less under control."

"In an alligator wrestlin' sort of way." Willy shook his head, his topknot flopping, and pursed his lips. "I never knew such a thing existed until I met Wanda's family. D'ja know I had to wrestle one myself to win her hand?"

He peered at his wife slantwise, his round face taking

on a mournful expression. "I think her daddy might just've wanted me to take her off his hands. He showed me this alligator in a pen, told me to jump in and prove I was worthy of her—or maybe he wanted to make sure I was up to wrestlin' with her. Anyway, I went over that fence, put a full nelson on the damn thing, and tried to bite its jugular. Got saddle soap all over my hands and a mouth full of stuffin'." He shook his head and sighed. "The fight was *rigged*!"

Everyone at the table laughed. Everyone except Hans, of course. He looked like he was getting a pickle suppository.

"Look," Jane said when things quieted down, speaking to all present, but her comments mostly directed at Gluck. "I'll be the first to admit that we've got serious problems with this mission, most of them because this ship is a worthless piece of shit."

She refrained from again pointing out that most of the problems came from sensors, switching devices, interface equipment, and other related components manufactured by a certain criminally sloppy GerGentine contractor. One Hans had flown for, what a fucking surprise. There were times she felt like he was just one more bad component dumped in her lap.

She focused her gaze on him. "In spite of our ongoing difficulties, we are getting where we want to go. I don't want every fart and dribble this tub subjects us to beamed back home. Public opinion is just barely behind this mission, and I want the nice folks back home feeling like their money was well spent."

"By the book we must report each breakdown and shortfall," Gluck insisted. "This is a part of our mission guidelines."

Christ this guy was dense! "*Fuck* the book!" she snapped. "Don't you get it? The book went out the goddamned window sixty million klicks ago! We wing it and keep coping, or we scrub. Worse yet, if we report too many problems, we *get* scrubbed. I'll be damned if I'll let that happen. Failure is *not* an option, not now or ever."

"I have a duty—"

So much for sweet reason. "Your duty, Mister Gluck, is to obey my orders and quit trying to sabotage this flight and my command," she returned in a low hard voice that wiped the expression off every face at the table. "Do you understand me, mister?"

He stared back at her in cold fury, an expression that probably translated to *ball-cutting Jew bitch* written across his face. She met his gaze dead on. She ran a loose ship, but this was a line he damn well better not cross. Not then or ever.

Finally, her second bared his perfect teeth. "I understand you perfectly, ma'am."

This was borderline insubordination, and both of them knew it. Were they back on Earth, or even Selenopolis, she'd break the son of a bitch like a breadstick. Here she had no such luxury. Every hand was needed to plug leaks and squash bugs, and the anti-UN, antispace forces would seize on the faintest whiff of strife as a reason to recall the mission. Short of offering Fabi a couple hundred bonus humjobs in exchange for his giving this blockhead fucker a lobotomy, they had to get along.

"I'm so glad," she said, the amount of sarcasm in her voice gauged down to the microvolt. Now it was time to exercise a little command aikido, using his own attack against him.

"You have brought up a matter we might be wise to approach from a different direction," she continued smoothly. "The failure rate of shipboard equipment has been completely unacceptable. So here is what I would like you to do, Hans. Document every single instance of failure and under-spec performance so far, and continue to log any which arise in the future." *That* ought to keep his little mind occupied for a while.

She turned toward the Tutillias. "Willy, Wanda, work with him on this. Give him any info you have, extract your work logs, do whatever's necessary to nail down every equipment fuck-up we've suffered. Then I want you to create a space in our black box for this file, and slave a self-actualizing burst transmit of same to our distress beacon so it will be sent in the event of a catastrophic failure. Can do?"

"If this clunker lets us, sure," Willy said with a nod.

Wanda grinned. "Shouldn't be a problem. I just pulled a fresh roll of duct tape outta stores."

"Very good." She faced Gluck again. "Will this address some of your concerns?"

"Yes, ma'am," he said, seeming placated.

"Excellent." Time to wrap this up. She cleared her throat and prepared to begin what had become another daily ritual by accessing the recording mode of the terminal before her.

"For the record, with the entire crew present, I now ask each and every one of you if you feel we should continue this mission in spite of our ongoing difficulties. Dr. Costanza, what say you?"

He smiled at her. "Yes, I think we should continue." Under the table he squeezed her thigh again, quite a bit higher than before. "I believe very worthy goals are almost within reach."

"Lieutenant Commander Gluck?"

A solemn nod. "We go on."

"Dr. Gluck?"

Anna managed a wan smile. "*Da,* we continue."

"Dr. Tutillia?"

Willy beamed at her. "We press on regardless, *mon capitaine.*"

"Mister Tutillia?" Wanda, although a double Ph.D. in her own right, insisted on being called Mister in formal situations, just like Scotty in the old *Star Trek* series. Engineers were always nuts, and she was one of the best.

"All ahead full, Commander. I'm verra sure she'll hold together."

"Then we are agreed. Meeting dismissed."

Hans shoved himself to his feet, picked up his slayte full of unresolved complaints.

"Start your file now if y'all want to," Wanda told him as she got up. "We'll do the mods on our next watch."

He nodded curtly and strode off without so much as a thank-you. Jane watched him leave. No doubt he would also start—if he hadn't already—a file on what he considered *her* malfunctions, and try to sneak that in as well.

When he was gone Willy stood and gave her a sloppy Nazi salute. "G'night, Jew—I mean *Jane.* That was a neat bit, makin' him Glitch Gestapo. I think he reichs it."

His wife elbowed him in the ribs. "Ignore this man."

She smiled at the pair. "Sorry about the extra work, kids."

Wanda shook her head. "No, I think you had a damn good idea. Maybe some contractors will get their worthless asses roasted when we get back. The ship should be okay for the time being. But whatever y'all do, don't use the left blinker." She blinked and bit her full lower lip. "Or the horn."

"I'll remember that. Sleep tight, you two."

"Hell, that's all we *ever* do in bed," Wanda complained.

"She knew she was marrying a software guy," Willy said, shrugging his broad shoulders. "It's not my fault she falls asleep before we can get through all the warnings, disclaimers, and licensing agreements."

The two of them left the wardroom arm in arm, off watch and headed for their cabin. Jane knew they had a pretty active love life. Hell, everybody knew. The *Ares* had too little room to offer any real privacy, and the internal soundproofing seemed to have come from a five-dollar-a-night motel.

Anna had been dithering by the coffeemaker, head down as she fussed with an already full cup. Once Willy and Wanda were gone she came back to the table. As usual, she looked unhappy and anxious.

"I thank you for your patience with Hans," she said in a low voice, clutching her cup tightly and staring at the tabletop.

"That's all right," Jane answered mildly.

"He is just, ah, tight-up."

"You mean uptight?" Fabi corrected gently.

"*Da,* uptight." She lifted her head at last. Weary desperation haunted her gaze. "Ship breakdowns make him unhappy. Rules not matching what is written make him unhappy." She let out a sigh that made Jane ache for her. "Being married to fat ugly woman like me is no help either."

Jane let her husband deal with this. He was a lot less likely to use terms like *self-centered chauvinistic prick.*

"You can't blame yourself for how he feels, Anna," he told her in a fatherly tone.

"This I know. Still, I feel as if so much is my fault."

"Like what?"

"I try so hard to get us on mission because that is what he wants, and now he is unhappy here. I try to be good wife, to make him happy. I diet, but still I look like sack of potatoes. Before, back when there were other women around was not so bad for him, he could . . ."

Her voice trailed away, and she shrugged. "I am sorry. Should not waste time like this. Must go and begin new series of observations."

"Mind if I tag along?" Fabi asked.

A half-stricken, half-hopeful look crossed her face. "*Da*, sure."

"Great." He gave Jane a peck on the cheek. "See you later."

"Later," she echoed, then watched him leave with their Russian mouse. Fabi would do what he could to build up her fragile self-esteem. The problem was that her marriage did more damage than Fabi could fix in these random, informal sessions.

Could she perform a divorce? She rather doubted it, but if Fabi relayed even the slightest hint that the way Hans was treating her had crossed over the line into abuse, she was going to give decreeing and enforcing one her best shot.

Her communicator squawked. *"Commander?"*

Speak of the devil. "Yes, Hans?"

"I am in the command module. NRU#3 is not responding, and needs to be reset."

"Damn," she growled. "Not again." Navigational Radar Unit Three had acted up the week before. They'd thought they had the frigging thing fixed.

"Yes, again. I need dual Command override for the reset. Can you help me?"

help me

Jane swallowed hard, pushing back that memory and all its implications. She could not deal with it now. Would not. Keeping the *Ares* together was her first priority. The other would have to wait until later.

"On my way," she said. Maybe, just maybe, if she put it off long enough she wouldn't have to deal with it at all.

Time

The *Ares* continued on its long journey toward the Red Planet, passing time marked only by devices, by routine.

Jane helped her second get NRU#3 functioning again, then they set up the navigation board so it would beep them if it crapped out again. They had reached the point where a dozen systems were being monitored this way.

After that, the glorious life of the commander of Earth's first interplanetary craft continued with another hour spent working on her logs and reports. There were times it seemed the mission had largely consisted of brief moments of high anxiety swamped by a sea of aggravation and mind-numbing form-filling routine. An adventure in the exciting pioneer spirit of an IRS audit.

Back on Earth in Tyler's Corners, Dan had a bachelor's lunch of a beer and a corned beef sandwich, a homemade pickle providing the green vegetable necessary for balanced nutrition.

His next broadcast was at four, so after clearing the table he tied his hair back, put on a ratty straw hat, and went into the backyard to work in the garden. There were enough ripe tomatoes to fill a medium-sized basket. He figured he had another week or two before the first frost, which meant at least another bushel before the season ended.

As he bent over the row of plants, he kept wishing Bobbi were still coming for the weekend. They could have done some canning—and maybe had a nice messy fight with the ones that had gone bad. The weekend after at Skyles Lake was going to be great, but at the moment it seemed an eternity away, with a big chunk of nothing between now and then.

Naming each of the three tomato worms he found Tammy before he squashed them was the high point of his afternoon.

Farther west, in Neely, Daveed slept, bathed in screen-shine and swaddled by a muted babble of voices and music.

He groaned and curled into a tight ball as a typically cinematic nightmare unfolded. This time it was *Romiet and Julio,* with himself as Romiet, Alec as Julio, and the Goat as Monty Capulet, the viscous mafioso who wants Julio for himself so badly that he kills him, rather than let Romiet have him.

In New York, Martina coordinated Secretary-General Perez's move from appointment to appointment, deploying her teams like a small, ultraefficient invading army.

At 12:30 P.M. there was his lunch date with the heads of UNICEF and OXFAM, held at an exclusive SoHo restaurant where the portions were so small a fashion model would ask for seconds, and the prices so high that what a single entrée cost would feed a Namibian village for a month. After the short detour through a Colonel Sanders drive-through, made at Rico's insistence, they arrived for his two o'clock press conference at the UN Media Center right on time.

Deep underground, the man who normally slept only three hours a day, but now was not sleeping at all, concluded one business contract and refused another. The time for business as usual to end was nearly at hand.

That did not trouble him, yet when he let himself think about what he might be forced to do in the days to come, he wanted to run and hide. But Avva had found him, and he could not refuse.

The Reverend Ray Sunshine sprawled comfortably in a leather recliner, half-dozing as a stout older woman who smelled of lavender and onions applied makeup to his face, readying him to shoot a devotional vidyo.

The odd combination of smells evoked memories of his sainted mother, who had told him that one day God would have a special job for him. Now God had finally spoken to him, and given him the first hints of what He required.

He waited for the voice to come again, certain that whatever it was could only help build up his ministry's bottom line.

The voice would come to them all again, and before too much longer.

Only Jane and the man in the bunker had any hint or warning that it was coming.

But knowing wasn't much help when it came.

PART 3

The Call

Technical Difficulties

"*Dan! Damn your skinny ass, TALK to me!*"

Awareness of his surroundings finally returning, Dan found himself on his hands and knees on the bluestage floor. Heart knocking like an engine about to throw a rod, and gasping for breath like he'd just run a mile. Shaking all over, his body soaked with sweat beneath his suit. The weather maps were gone, and his eyephones showed him himself huddled in a spidery blue heap.

"Oh shit," he groaned, pushing himself back into a wobbly crouch. The room spun, then steadied.

"*Dan!*" Morty bellowed, the sound booming over his hood's earphones and blaring from the monitor speakers. "*Come on, man, can you hear me?*"

"Yeah, I hear you," he huffed, peeling off his mask. Cool air rushed across his face, and it got a bit easier to breathe. "No need to shout."

"Jesus, you gave me a turn!" she said, her voice now coming only from the speakers under the flatscreen facing the stage, and at a more acceptable sound-pressure level. "Talk to me. Should I call an ambulance?"

He looked up, saw that her square jowly face was pale and frightened. First time he'd ever seen her scared. He hadn't even known it was possible.

"No, I'm all right." In a manner of speaking. Right as anybody just blown so far out in left field could hope to be.

"You're *sure*."

He made himself get up off the floor. "See? I'm walking and talking and everything." Standing, anyway. His legs felt like overcooked linguine, and his head felt like . . .

There was no way to describe it, and that was a matter—and object—best left unexamined for the time being.

"That's a good sign." Morty reclaimed her cigar stub, relit it with her big silver Zippo. "What the hell happened, Dan?"

Now *there* was the ten-million-dollar question. If only he had a halfway reasonable answer.

He wiped the sweat off his face with the side of his arm. "Maybe you better tell me."

She stared at him hard for several seconds, puffing on her cigar and blowing clouds of blue smoke, then let out a long smoggy sigh.

"Okay, you were going along and doing your 'cast. All of a sudden you froze. Locked right up mid-word. This real confused look come onto your face, then a few seconds later you keeled right over."

Dan remembered that much. It had been like this massive jolt had been applied directly to his brain, snapping his body into quivering rigidity and nailing his feet to the floor. It hadn't hurt, exactly, or lasted long. It was the stuff that had come riding in after that blast that had driven him to his knees. Once that started everything got outwardly foggy—and inwardly too fucking weird for words.

"Then you started this frigging moaning. Like to skeert me half to death."

"Sorry. What happened after that?"

"You started to shake and twitch. I kept asking what was wrong, but you didn't seem to hear. Right after you went down I figured we'd better bail, so I faded you off the maps with a TECHNICAL DIFFICULTIES splash, cut back to this morning's broadcast, and capped with that."

"Thanks." So he'd just spazzed out in front of millions of EdgeNet viewers. What do you think *that* will do for my ratings, Tammy? Ought to earn me at least another share, right?

"I figured you were either having a heart attack, or the sets in your suit had gone nuts. I switched off your suit from here, but it didn't seem to help. It was about then you started yelling."

"Yelling?" His memories of the event's peak remained fuzzy, awareness of himself at that time overwritten by something larger than his own thoughts and self. Something huge. Something—

"You kept hollering '*I hear you!*'" Morty removed her cigar, examined its glowing tip with pursed lips, then squinted at him. "You were acting like maybe you were jawing with God or something."

No, it didn't say it was God. Thank God. "That so?"

"Yep." A pause. "You weren't, were you, sport?"

He shook his head. "No."

She looked relieved. "That's good. I ain't about to start producing religious programming, not even for you my darling boy. The stars are generally assholes, and I hate the fuckin' music. So who *were* you talking to, if it wasn't Herself?"

He shook his head again. "You wouldn't believe it." *He* didn't believe it.

A puff off her cigar. "Try me."

"I-it's crazy, Morty." His shoulders slumped. "Maybe I am."

The big woman chortled. "Fuck, I knew *that*! Why else would you've let yourself get tangled up with that beak-snatched squid Tammy? Or be perfectly happy staying anonymously famous?" She leaned closer to the camera, her expression serious and concerned. "Come on. You can tell old Morty."

Dan trusted her more than anybody else on the planet, but if he said it out loud, that might just make it real, make it impossible to make go away.

"You've got to give me some space here," he said, looking her in the eyes. "Please. I'm not sure what's going on, and I'm not ready to talk about it. Okay?"

She just stared at him, fingering the gold rings in her left eyebrow. He could tell how badly she wanted to get to the bottom of this, and she wasn't the type who took no for an answer easily or often.

He clasped his hands together like he was praying. "Pretty please?"

"Okay," she growled at last. "What about your ten o'clock slot?"

For the first time in longer than he could remember, the thought of going on-air frightened him. Being live hadn't caused this, but if it happened again while the whole world watched . . .

"Not unless I have to."

"Lemme see." She glanced away and he heard the *ticka-ticka* of keys in the background. "Yeah, I can cover you." She faced him square on once more. "You think maybe I better figure keeping you off the sked for a few days?"

Dan stared at his feet, feeling his life beginning to come apart around him. He never missed his slots, never. More than anything he wanted to turn back time, have things return to the dull, boring rut they'd ridden in for so long. Back to when the worst thing that ever came into his head was the occasional stray lustful thought about the pretty young mothers standing in the grocery-store checkout line next to him. But until he got what he'd just been through straight in his head that wasn't going to happen.

What he needed was time. Time to be alone. To think. *Time to find a damn good shrink.*

"Today's Tuesday, right?"

"Last time I checked."

"Keep me off the roster until Thursday. Is that okay?"

"Sure." She leaned so close to the camera on her end that her face filled the entire screen. "If you promise me you'll see a doctor."

That was already beginning to look like his best option. Maybe he should also get the name of a good exorcist. Just in case.

Morty's voice dropped into the motherly tone he hadn't heard since the darkest depths of his divorce. "Listen, lover. I've got a half brother with epilepsy, and it looks to me like you might just've had yourself a seizure. That's no big deal. They've got medications that'll fix you up good as new." She leaned back. "I've already sent you a list of doctors, a couple very good and pretty close by. Promise me you'll go see one. Okay?"

Epilepsy. He turned the word over in his mind, trying it on for size and finding it a better fit than the alternatives. That would explain it: just a brain glitch, one that could be fixed with medication. It wasn't what it seemed to be, which it couldn't, anyway.

"I will," he promised, holding up one hand. "Scout's honor."

"Glad to hear it." She stoked a fresh cigar. "Want me to make an appointment for you?"

"No, I can do it. Thanks, Morty. You're a princess."

"Yeah, right. I'm just doing my job, keeping your skinny ass on track and airable. EdgeNet may flirt with the offbeat, but I kinda doubt they'll go for reports beamed from the booby hatch, or letting you change your show to *Dan the Spastic Weatherman*."

"No, they probably wouldn't." Though there were nets which would. Like WarpVision, the one that insisted on using announcers with speech impediments. Their top anchor, William Wallingsworth, looked like Gregory Peck, and sounded like Elmer Fudd.

Morty glanced off-screen at a beep on her end, frowned. "Shit. I gotta hustle my buns and get *Car Talk* in the can. Call a doctor, kiddo. Call several. Just don't let this slide, okay?"

He bowed his head. "I hear and obey, oh great one."

"Damn well better. We'll talk tomorrow." Her image blipped out, leaving a blank screen.

Dan let out a sigh of relief, then began peeling off his suit. *Epilepsy*. Sure, that had to be it. He wasn't *really* hearing a voice in his head. The voice wasn't really saying what it said it was, which it couldn't be, anyway.

The suit was soaked with sweat, so after he hung it in its locker he closed the door and tapped the CHARGE and CLEAN buttons. He retrieved his boxer shorts, pulled them on. Just as he was stepping into his pants the tone that signaled Morty's line reopening sounded.

"Yeah, what did you forget, Mother Morty?" he called. Glancing up, he saw that the screen was still black, blank.

"Mr. Dan Franciso?" intoned a deep voice he didn't recognize.

"Who *is* this?" he demanded. Nobody else used Morty's line; EdgeNet kept it for her use only.

"A friend and admirer," came the answer in a plummy tone worthy of a headache-remedy ad. "I saw your broadcast this afternoon. What there was of it."

Dan rolled his eyes. *Some fan who's mad because my show ran short.* Just what he needed right now.

A moment later exasperation twisted into alarm. *What was some weather groupie doing on Morty's line?* A heartbeat after that, alarm exploded into full blown panic.

He could think of only one vast, faceless, omnipotent force which could do this. *Management.* They'd seen him spaz out on-air, and now they were going to fire him. Dropping the hammer while he stood there with only one leg in his pants. The final humiliation.

"Sorry about that," he began, jamming his other leg into his pants and hauling them up. "I had some sort of, um, dizzy spell and—"

"That was no dizzy spell, Mr. Francisco. You were *reached*. You were *called*."

Somehow those two words locked themselves into his head, fitting what he had experienced so perfectly that his hand froze on his zipper and his knees went weak. *Reached. Called.*

"Who-who *is* this?" he stammered. Now the blank screen looked menacing. Where was this guy coming from, and how did he know what had just gone on inside his head?

"As I said before, I am a friend and admirer of your work. We must talk, Mr. Francisco. There is much we should discuss." A pause. "A world of things." A low chuckle. "Or perhaps I should say, an *out of this world* of things."

Dan found his voice hiding in a corner of his bony chest, pried it loose. "There's nothing to discuss," he said, shooting for stern but hitting shrill. "I'm going to disconnect now. Please don't call me again."

The man at the other end sighed. "I was afraid of this. Very well, Mr. Francisco. If you won't come to me, then I shall be forced to come to you."

"Now wait—" Dan began, liking the sound of this even less than before.

"Be ready."

"—you can't—"

"Until we meet face-to-face." The connection broke, the telltale for Morty's line winking out.

Dan sat down hard on the edge of the bluestage, his long legs putting his kneecaps at the level of his chin. "This is nuts," he moaned, hanging his head between his legs. "It can't be happening."

But it was. First the voice comes into his head in the middle of the night, asking for help. Then it comes back again right in the middle of his show, making him fruitloop before the cameras. He couldn't think about what it had said. It was just too fucking big and weird; dwelling on it made his brain start to thump and shudder like a washing machine trying to spin-dry three pairs of skivvies and a bowling ball.

Then, as if all that wasn't enough, for a follow-up he gets some demented fan calling him up and threatening to *stalk* him.

Things couldn't get any more fucked up, could they? Could they?

Mashed-Potato Mesas

Daveed leaned back against the headboard of his bed, hair in his eyes and sweat sheening his face.

Remain calm, he repeated to himself yet again. *There's no need to panic.*

The screens at the foot of the bed continued to display their kinetic patchwork of ads and news and sports and talk shows and nature programs and sitcoms and dramas and movies and the unclassifiable and improbable. He saw none of it.

Okay, he'd been under a lot of stress lately. There was the aftermath of his breakup with Alec. The grueling shifts at work. His ongoing battles with the Goat. Unending deadline pressure. No *wonder* he was having a nervous breakdown!

Was he having a nervous breakdown?

Having a voice in your head claiming to be an alien stranded on one of the moons of Mars haul you from a sound sleep so it could tell you it was all alone, frightened, in bad trouble and in need of your help wasn't exactly a sign of mental hygiene, was it? No sir, this was nuthouse stuff. A visa to the funny farm. A full scholarship to the laughing academy. *Hi, Jack, how's Nurse Ratchet doing?* time.

It wasn't possible. It wasn't rational. Daveed Shah starring in a role suited to Smilin' Jack or Joan Crawford or Glenn Close or Anthony Perkins or Dennis Hopper or Bruce Dern or any of those old-timers who could play a first-class loon.

And yet . . .

It had seemed so real. So . . . *true.*

The voice had come in surfing on this blast of sounds and images, a tsunami of pain and fear and loss and hope, of despair and desperation. Opposed to all that, and most lingering, was this sense of relief, of satisfaction that some fragment of its message had gotten through. Somehow he knew what this attempt to reach him had cost the sender, and that it would be a while before he heard from it again.

Crazy shit. It couldn't be real.

Couldn't.

But if it was, what could *he* do?

This was getting him nowhere. He made himself get up, pull on a robe. Stumble to the bathroom and take a leak. Wash up and head for the kitchenette and start some coffee brewing. Bread in the toaster. Pace restlessly while waiting.

An original framed poster from the old movie *Close Encounters of the Third Kind* caught his eye. A present from the grateful producer of a monster netcast he'd edited a few years back.

Wonder how long before I start building mashed-potato mesas? he thought with bitter amusement. Being on the fifth floor, at least he wouldn't have to worry about dumping the landscaping in the window. The place was a mess, but that would be going way over the line.

When his coffee and toast were ready he sat down and ate, concentrating on the prosaic act like breakfast was the new miracle cure for madness. There were no sudden urges to stack his toast into geologic formations.

He tidied up afterward, putting things away and washing the dishes. Went from home improvement to self-improvement by showering, shaving, getting dressed for work. Brushed his hair, examining his reflection in the mirror.

He didn't look or feel all that different. Scared, yes. Confused, you bet. Apprehensive, no doubt about it. But crazy, no. The man in the mirror looked tired and preoccupied, but otherwise safe to be around.

All he could do was continue on with his life. Go to work. Do his job.

Besides, if he was going bugshit, best to keep it in the fine upstanding American tradition of going amok on the job. Usually the supervisor was the one taken out feetfirst in such situations.

Daveed laughed and shook his head, imagining going after the Goat with a digital stylus, which was about the most dangerous implement of destruction in his cube.

Now if he found himself buying *guns* . . .

This was a normal enough thought to be reassuring.

Crazy people didn't think like that. He was sure of it.

Daveed gave Armand Gautier a big sunny smile when he got to work. There must have been a little something extra moving behind that smile, because the Goat steered clear of him for the entire shift. This was an unexpected fringe benefit of going off his rocker.

If this be madness, then let me make the most of it, he decided.

He didn't know what else to do, and the demands of his job soon made it impossible to dwell on the matter.

That was fine with him. He wrote "Carpe banana" on a note, stuck it to the side of one screen as a reminder, then plunged into his work like a man trying to hide in the thickest cover available to him.

Asylum

A wareness of her surroundings returned to Martina like a slap in the face. Alarm shot through her when she realized where she was and what she was doing.

"Shit!" she cursed, wrenching loose from Rico's embrace and flinging herself away. She landed in the limo's jump seat facing him, and held up her hands in a forbidding gesture when he started to follow. "Stay *there*." Her voice came out like the growl of a cornered wolf, and a mixture of fury and horror made her bare her teeth like one.

He dropped back into his seat but leaned toward her, putting one brown hand on her knee. "Are you all right, *chiquita*?" he asked solicitously, his dark eyes brimming with concern.

She ground her teeth together to keep in a frustrated, furious sound that might just have come out as either a howl or a scream. He seemed to be unharmed. His white suit was slightly disheveled and his hair mussed, but she hadn't hurt him.

Yet.

"Martina, please. Speak to me!"

A glance out the tinted windows told her the motorcade was slowly rolling down a gray and rain-lashed Fifth Avenue, caught in the sluggish traffic. The Chrycedes minivan with the balance of Tac One trailed behind them, right where they were supposed to be. She twisted around to look forward and check on the armored Land Rover with most of Tac Three, which was supposed to be in the lead, but could see nothing because the polished steel security divider was up between them and the front seat.

"I closed it," Rico said quietly from behind her. "Did not want them to see you in distress."

"What happened?" she rasped, facing him—and the situation—square on.

"You begin to shake, and I think you are having some sort of, what is the word, sounds like Spam?"

"Spasm." He knew the word, was just trying to lighten the mood. Any other time she might have laughed, but not now. It was all she could do to keep from crying.

"*Sí, gracias.* I grab you and roll the steel window up." A wry, hopeful smile. "They probably think we are back here making mad passionate love."

Once this break in the veil of propriety she tried to maintain around their affair would have angered and worried her. Now it meant nothing. Less than nothing.

"You shout and moan," he continued. "You make promises to someone I cannot see. Bad news over radio in your head?" He touched his left ear to show what he meant.

Martina seized on this as the out she so desperately needed. A means of escape. She could have hugged him for giving it to her, but dared not let herself anywhere near him.

"Yes, is so," she lied, trying to sound calm and composed. "There is . . . there is problem I must go deal with. Emergency."

"Ah. Security? Family?"

"I—I cannot say." She leaned over, pressed the button that buzzed the security divider down. Cassie glanced back, her round Inuit face professionally neutral. Fayed, riding shotgun in the passenger seat, tried to look back without really looking back, his sharp-featured, bearded face a mask as well.

"Something has come up that I must go deal with," she told them gruffly. "Fayed, you and Chan are in command until I return."

"Where—" the Palestinian began, clearly puzzled.

"No time to explain." She locked gazes with him. "You keep Secretary-General Perez safe. Understand?"

A solemn nod. "Yes, ma'am."

She turned her head, caught Cassie's eyes in the rearview mirror. "Stop the car."

The driver blinked. "Ma'am?"

"Stop the car!" She hadn't meant to shout, but the urge to get out of there was overwhelming and growing stronger with every passing second. If she did not act on it, she would surely explode.

Cassie made no reply, but began braking, coming to a halt in the middle of the street and stopping traffic. By the time they stopped moving a muffled but rising chorus of blatting car horns could be heard through the limo's soundproofing.

"What are you doing, Martina?" Rico asked quietly as she faced him once more.

Protecting you.

"Something I must do. Be safe." She wrenched on the door handle, shoved it open. The car filled with a cacophony of car horns and curses. In her ear Chan was demanding to know what was going on.

"Talk to Fayed," she growled in reply. "System off." She swung her legs out.

"Martina!" Rico grabbed her shoulder. "Do not go! Tell me what is going on! Let me help!"

She permitted herself a single backward glance. *"Do svidaniya lyubov maya,"* she whispered in Russian. *Until our next meeting, my beloved.*

"Martina!"

She pulled away, lurching out of the limo and into the rain. Slammed the door shut and bolted for the sidewalk, narrowly missing being hit by a cab in the other lane. The cabbie slammed on his brakes, shaking his fist and adding his horn to the din.

When she reached the sidewalk she began pushing her way through the crowd. Her size, her build, and the terrible expression on her face parted the normally oblivious New Yorkers before her like the sea before Moses.

By the time she got half a block away she'd regained enough control of herself to slow her pace and stop sending a berserker vibe out ahead of her.

In a swish of raincoats and bumping umbrellas, the crowd obligingly swallowed her up.

"Mister Fayed," Secretary-General Perez said tightly, tearing his gaze away from his lover's retreating back.

"Sir?"

"I want someone to follow her. Now."

The Palestinian blinked and swallowed hard. "I really can't do that, sir. We're already one down with her gone. Splitting our teams further would be dangerous."

Another man with his position and power might have thundered, might have demanded obedience. Rico Perez was not that sort of man.

"I am worried about her," he said simply. "I am certain you must be, too." He spread his hands. "Surely there is some way?"

"I . . ." The security agent sighed, then inclined his head in a gesture that was half nod, half bow. "Tac Three, please. Chan? Fayed. I have just received further orders. You are to take charge of our detachment. I am proceeding to render assistance to Colonel Omerov if possible. Please send one of your team back to take my place. Fayed out."

"Thank you," Perez said with a quiet force that made Fayed look all the more solemn.

"She has a good head start, and I may not find her." He slipped out of the car and sprinted in the direction she had taken, dodging cars and his feet splashing through the puddles. He reached the sidewalk and quickly vanished into the crowd.

"Back to your quarters, sir?" Cassie asked as Linda Wilkins slid into the seat beside her.

Perez sat back and closed his eyes. "Yes. Thank you."

Martina squeezed into the old-fashioned wood-and-glass phone booth and closed the door to shut out the noise of the bar behind her. Ignoring the OmniBell view-phone before her, she got out her own SS-issue unit, flipped it open.

The screen lit, read READY.

She called up its directory of stored numbers, selected the one she wanted, then after checking to make certain it was set for location blanking and voice only, thumbed connect. Please let him be there. *Please.*

"Hello?" The voice that answered was just the one she'd hoped to hear.

"Alexei," she said quietly. "It is Martina. Martina Elena Omerov."

"*Martina!* I recognize your voice now! Is good you call! Have been wondering how you are doing!"

She grimaced, and a sick laugh escaped her. "How am I doing. This is a good question, old friend. I hope you can help me find answer to it."

"You are having a problem, child?" he asked, the laughter gone from his voice and replaced with concern. "The kind I fix?"

She hunched her shoulders. "I . . . do not know. Maybe."

"You want to come see me? Me to see you?"

"Please, Alexei. If you can."

"Of course, child! Where are you?"

She turned and peered out through the smudged glass into the dim lounge, watching a fat man in a business suit hit on a muscular blond man in tight jeans and crew-neck sweater. Two other samesex couples were at the bar, the two women comprising one couple staring back with fairly blatant interest. So she had chosen a gay bar. No wonder the female bartender had looked at her that way when she'd asked where the phone was, and was still giving her the eye. This was hardly the first time she'd been mistaken for someone who preferred women over men.

"I am at bar here in city," she said, turning her back on her audience. "Can I come to your office? I know you are busy man."

"*Da,* of course! I am never too busy for you. I am there now, will be waiting for you."

"Thank you, Alexei Leonid. I am on my way."

She closed her phone and slumped against the door of the booth. Rico would be worried. Confused. Maybe even scared. It had broken her heart to run away like that, leaving him without a single word of explanation. But the demands of her job took precedence over any personal considerations.

She was his bodyguard, and head of the security detachment surrounding him. She had taken a vow to protect him at all costs, even at the price of her own life.

Now she was hearing a voice in her head. It was telling

her impossible things, and worse yet, making her believe them. Worst of all, it could make her lose control of herself.

There was a name for people who had things like this happen to them. A place for them.

That place was nowhere near the man she was sworn to protect. Not when she could do nothing to stop this recurring madness and the loss of control that came with it. Not when she was capable of killing him in an instant with her bare hands.

The place she was going was far better suited to what she had become.

Martina shoved her way out of the booth. She dared not delay for fear her untrustworthy mind might change on her. The bartender watched her emerge, her face falling when the big butch babe in the wet suit headed not for the bar, but back out onto the street.

Out in the rain she hailed a cab. One slid to the curb, ready to carry her to the place she might find asylum.

She got in and closed the door, gave the driver the address, and slumped back against the seat. As the car pulled out into traffic she closed her eyes, seeing only wreckage where once her orderly life had stood. Everything brought down in ruins by an enemy from within, the one kind she was not trained and armed to fight.

She did not see another cab pull out and follow.

Houston, We Have a Problem

Jane was luxuriating in the rare and splendid sensation of having a decent chunk of cubic entirely to herself.

She had just finished her exercises a few minutes earlier, and now sat zazen right in the middle of the four-meter-by-four-meter chunk of wooden gym flooring, pretending that the nearest human being was at least a thousand klicks away, didn't know she existed, and wouldn't have spoken to her anyway.

Solitude was a precious commodity aboard the *Ares*, and there were times she craved it like a junkie. So she wanted to make the most of this small fix, knowing it might be a while before she got another. Her job, problems with the *Ares* and Hans, her fit last night—all she wanted was a few minutes' release from all that. Some of the relaxation and visualization techniques Fabi had taught her helped, aided by dribs and drabs gained from a bit of martial-arts training.

Relax. Breathe. Float. Let the—

Fuck.

Her fragile sense of tranquillity burst like a shot-gunned soap bubble as the hatch into the exercise compartment opened. She knew, just *knew* who the hell it was even before the voice she least wanted to hear broke the silence.

"Ah, I did not know you were in here, Commander."

She swallowed a sigh. "No big deal, Hans." Sure it was within a few seconds of being his time, but couldn't the punctual bastard have been late just this once? *Please let him just start his workout and spare me any attempt at small talk.*

"Still, it is good I find you here."

Double fuck and game.

She unfolded her legs and stood, her knees popping. *Oh great,* she thought sourly. *Sound like an old lady in front of him, why don't you? Might as well drool and act senile.*

"Something on your mind, Hans?"

"Yes, Commander."

She turned to face him. Weeks of practice made it easier to keep from staring at his body, covered only by a brief white cachesexe. The lad was built, no doubt about that. Hung, too. Maybe that was what convinced Anna to marry him. No other good points were particularly obvious.

She couldn't help but be aware of how she must look to him, her wiry, rather flat-chested middle-aged bod not much better hidden by tight shorts and a brief sport top.

If he smiles, I'll just have to kill him, she promised herself. *Justifiable Hansicide.*

Instead he stood there with his brawny arms crossed before his broad chest, his face set in that stiffly intent expression she had come to hate. She picked up her towel and draped it across her shoulders, then copied his pose.

"Well, spit it out."

He licked his thin lips, took a deep breath. "Commander," he began in a low colorless voice, "I feel I must apologize for making corrections to your log. I now see that I was in error to do this."

An admission you make where no one else can hear, of course.

"Completing this mission is important to me," he continued, meeting her gaze briefly then his gaze dropping to the floor. "I have made certain . . . sacrifices to be a part of this, and I do want it to succeed."

"We all do," she agreed, wondering if these "sacrifices" had anything to do with the rumor he'd dumped a former Miss Argentina and up-and-coming lingerie model to marry Anna.

He raised his head, and his blue eyes met hers. For just a fleeting second she thought she might just be seeing a flash of vulnerability, even appeal, then he looked away.

"I am not a man of much imagination," he said quietly. "Still, I can now see how my belief—and insistence—that all mission rules and protocols be strictly adhered to could lead to our trip being scrubbed. By the book it could be argued that we should have done so already because of all our equipment failures. This is something I do not want to happen."

"I can understand your not wanting to put the mission in any danger of being called off." After all, he'd be one of the two people going down to Mars—and becoming famous ever after, amen. What astronaut wouldn't want to become the next Armstrong?

A curt nod. "That is something I will not allow."

Hmmm, was there just a hint of warning there? Or was she just imagining it, thanks to her constantly being on the lookout for signs that his difficulty accepting a certain skinny old chick for a boss was heading over the line into plans for a putsch?

"I—" Suddenly she froze, then shuddered, her eyes going wide as a chill like she'd just been hosed down with ice water washed over her.

He frowned. "Commander? Are you all right?"

She blinked, produced an unconvincing smile. "Just a cramp from working out."

But it wasn't that. It was a *hunch,* as strong a one as she'd had in years. It warned her that she had about twenty seconds to get the fuck out of there, to hole up someplace private.

It was going to happen again. She could feel it coming like a storm rolling toward her, threat piling higher by the second.

"Perhaps you should—" Hans began.

"Sauna will help. We'll talk more later." She turned and headed for the hatchway, wanting to run, but knowing she didn't dare. *Act normal,* she chanted to herself. *Just act normal.*

"Should I call your husband, Commander?"

Christ, that was the last thing she needed! She waved her arm. "Don't bother. I'm fine."

Concentration began to fail. She had to do one thing at a time, each simple task suddenly huge and difficult. Through the hatch. Lunge across the passageway. Frantically fight with the latch. Haul the door open. Clamber inside the coffin-sized space. Pull the door shut.

A dizzying sense of unreality made hitting the pad which would light up the OCCUPIED sign on the outside bulkhead an IQ test she nearly failed. Something like high-G blackout swirled higher and higher in her head as it filled with light and sound and emotion from elsewhere.

Her third blind stab hit the bull's-eye.

Then it was on her full force, sweeping her up like a leaf in the backblast of a rocket launch.

Jane bit down on a cry and her knees began to fail.

She never knew when she hit the deck.

An interminable period later, less than four minutes by the clock, Jane was still on her knees. She hunched there with her face in her hands, doing something she hadn't done in so long a detached part of her was amazed she still knew how.

Commander Jane Dawkins-Costanza, a woman who was damn near as tough as she thought she ought to be, was crying. She had no choice; her emotional holding tanks were overflowing, all the things which had just filled her seeking some kind of release.

Steady old girl, she told herself sternly. Get a grip. Little by little she brought her pitching and yawing emotions back under control. The tears stopped. Her heart slowed. She lifted her head and looked around.

"Houston, we have a problem," she muttered as she wiped her eyes, quoting the line astronauts and pilots still used some sixty years after Apollo 13.

Her first little wee-hours episode had been nothing but a brief burst of static compared to what she had just endured. This time it had come through clearer and stronger. A lot of it was still hash, but more of it was comprehensible, if totally unbelievable.

"Mission Commander is hearing a guy from Phobos talking in her head. Please advise," she whispered. "Over."

They'd love hearing *that* back at Uncle Joe, wouldn't they? They'd have Hans slapped in the command chair so fast it would make her head spin.

It seemed so *real*. But nothing lived on Phobos. ETs only existed in the movies. Hearing voices in your head was a bad sign, like looking out and seeing that your engines were on fire and your wings were falling off.

This was deep shit for her and the mission, as if they weren't in enough already.

"I don't feel crazy," she said quietly. "I really don't."

But she supposed she wouldn't, would she?

Ten minutes later she was still groping for some sliver of understanding of what was happening to her when there was a knock at the sauna door.

"Yeah?" she called, surprised by how even her voice was.

"Jane? Are you hiding in there?"

Fabi. "Just enjoying a little peace and quiet."

"Are you okay?"

"Sure, honey. Just fine."

"You've got a live downlink with Media Pool in five minutes, you know."

Shit! She'd forgotten all about it.

"Gotcha. I'll be out in a minute." Now just go *away*!

No such luck. She could feel him standing there, waiting, probably worrying. He hadn't forgotten her earlier flake-out, and was on the lookout for signs that it was happening again. She wasn't getting out of there without facing him and passing muster.

"Damn all good husbands," she muttered under her breath, raking her fingers through her hair and trying to fix a harried, annoyed expression on her face. All she had to do was make herself look grouchy over having a break cut short, not whacked-out over a theoretical space invader in her head.

Okay, she was as ready as she was going to get. Showtime. She unlatched the door and stepped out into the corridor.

"Are you sure you're okay?" Fabi asked, eyeing her critically.

"Right as rain," she said, heading toward the command module. "Just tired of living like a rat on a fuckin' treadmill, that's all."

The corridor was too narrow for them to walk side by

side, and having him follow behind meant she didn't have to look him in the eye. Lying to him didn't come easy, and she hated it.

"I just sort of nodded off in there. Now I've got to go on-air looking like I just got up."

"You look *jus' fahne*," he offered in a bad imitation of Wanda's accent as he tagged along after her.

"Right. I think maybe you better go check your own eyes, Doctor."

"My eyesight happens to be perfect. Which is good. The view from back here is fairly spectacular."

Jane looked down at herself, came to a dead halt. She was still dressed in her workout togs. This day just got better and better.

"Hell, I can't go on like this."

"Might boost our ratings."

She shot him a sour look. "Thanks for the vote of confidence. Maybe if I was built like Wanda, I'd consider it. Since I'm not, would you run to our compartment and grab me a fresh coverall?"

He struck a pose, hands on hips and chin out. "Maybe."

"What's this maybe crap?"

He grinned at her. "I might consider it if I thought you'd make it worth my while later. Like after we go off watch."

The tension which had pulled her nerves into a snarled knot eased slightly. Whatever was happening to her, this wonderful man would be there to help. To love her.

She arched an eyebrow and prepared to duck through the hatch into the Command Module.

"Maybe."

When the one-minute downcount until the cameras went active began, she faced them dressed in a neatly pressed sky-blue Uncle Joe coverall and wearing the face of a woman in total control.

She'd come to a decision of sorts. The *Ares* had been falling apart for weeks now, and she'd been doing her best to keep it going. So far they had managed, and Mars was almost within reach.

Now she would follow the same operating procedure

with herself, continuing on as best she could. She would keep this . . . whatever it was to herself for now, telling Fabi about it and asking his help only when and if she had to.

"You're on in ten seconds," Willy warned her over the headset she wore. "Knock 'em dead, Cap'n."

Smile for the nice folks back home.

She tried one on for size as she glanced over at the prompter where the questions she would be answering later were waiting. Her first bit would be pure fluff and off-the-cuff, but she'd done a lot of these damn things, and besides, she was a pilot. She could wing it.

When the red active light came on her smile widened and she went on to give what she had come to think of as a hum-job for the horde, telling the nice folks back home exactly what they wanted to hear.

Better a Bottle . . .

A majority of the countless media outlets used at least part of Jane's 'cast, after, of course, first editing and shaping it to fit their particular audience. Some heavily prospace networks and services ran it in its entirety, sidefed with links to other information about the *Ares* mission, but most just used brief clips and sound bites as part of their regularly scheduled news coverage. Sure, the first manned mission to Mars was news, but the damned thing had been going on for months, and they were still a week away from their objective.

DDDOC: Demographics Dictate Depth of Coverage, law of the infotainment jungle.

EdgeNet ran a two-minute airspot during their prime-time news hour, with the whole package accessible, followed with the latest—not that there was much—on the pending investigation into Ruethen AstroWerk. This was about average.

Dan slouched in his favorite chair, watching his network at work without any of it really sinking in. His thoughts kept returning to the desolate moon circling the red planet, to the one who said he was there and needed his help.

He took a long swig of beer. *Someone* needed help, that was for damn sure.

Thanks to Morty's pull he had an eleven o'clock appointment with Dr. Caroline Kaplan, a hotshot specialist in epilepsy and related disorders who had a clinic in Fort Wayne. He was counting on her finding the source of the recent bad weather in his head, and then giving him some pills to make it all go away. Hell, he'd let her go in through his ears with some sort of Medical Electrolux to suck out the dust bunnies if that was what it took.

Having such bizarre shit beamed into his poor brain was scary, but the part that really had him worried was that he damn near *believed* it. Logic told him it couldn't be real, that the whole thing was flat-out im-fucking-possible. Full-blown, get-out-the-nets insane.

Unfortunately, fighting the stuff in his head with logic was like taking on a Samurai swordsman while armed with an overripe banana. He couldn't help being drawn back into believing.

And he really wanted to stop.

Hoping it might help, he drained his beer and went for another. Getting drunk was about the best medicine he could think of for the moment. It would have to do until Dr. Kaplan prescribed some better meds.

Better a bottle in front of me than a frontal lobotomy, he thought with a grim chuckle, twisting the cap off a second Molsen Golden.

But if that was what it took, he was going to think real hard before just saying no.

Rasputin's Sister

"So, still you can give me no real answer," Martina said, sitting on the edge of a hospital bed in a shapeless pink-cotton nightgown. She spoke English because her old friend refused to speak their native Russian, having given it up decades ago, back when he became a naturalized citizen of the US.

Dr. Alexei Leonid Kasparov, director of the prestigious Kasparov Institute of Clinical Neurology, shook his head. An elegant and professorial man in his early sixties, he had long gray hair and a deeply lined patrician face that radiated wisdom and serenity seasoned with good humor. A bit of a dandy and ladies' man, he was dressed as if for a trip to the Yacht Club under his white lab coat. Gold-buttoned blazer, ascot, white-linen pants, even white deck shoes.

"Not yet," he replied with a smile that said he was untroubled by the lack of progress. "STEEG and VHAT scans show nothing unusual. Is same for MDIT or BAIM."

Hours spent wearing a Medusa's coiffure of electrodes and sensors, riding through several large exotic machines had taught her what those acronyms stood for. Stimulus Triggered Electro-Encephalogram. Virtual Holographic Axial Tomograph. Magnetotropic Digital Imaging Teleogram. Brain Activity Imaging Monitor.

"You find not even one little thing wrong?"

"Not a one."

"What about other tests?" The ones that required a dozen needles extracting what felt like a liter of blood and spinal fluid. Plus the liter of urine she'd had to produce on demand. No wonder she felt so drained.

"Some lab work is in, reads clean and normal. Other

workups will not be completed until tomorrow, but I expect no different news. There is nothing wrong with your brain, Martina Elena."

"Nothing wrong with brain as machine, you mean," she corrected sourly. "If not loose chips, then must be bad software. Something is making me think I am gone crazy."

Kasparov repeated the same request he'd made several times since her arrival. "Maybe if you would tell me more of what problem is?"

"I told you. I heard voice in my head. Twice."

"Yes, you tell me this much. What does voice say?"

She really didn't want to tell him all the details, had been pinning her hopes on his finding some problem that would lead to, if not a fix, at least an explanation. Intelligence work had taught her that you could find some dark corner in or black stain on anyone's life. Surely there had to be at least one bad spot in her head. She had been hit on it and landed on it many times. You would think that must have caused some damage.

"Is hard to explain," she answered evasively.

"Okay, then I ask you this: Does it tell you to harm yourself?"

"No, nothing like that."

"Does it tell you to harm others? Like it say you should go out onto street, haul out your gun, and shoot every mime and pretzel vendor you see?"

She shook her head. "No, though might be good idea."

"Mimes, maybe, but I like pretzels. If not that, does it say, Martina Elena Omerov, what you should do is rip off clothes and make violent passionate love to the first man you see?" He tapped his chest. "Me, for instance?"

A brief smile cracked loose, a half kilo of tension taken with it. "No, nothing like that."

His face fell. "Damn! I guess I do not get lucky. Does it tell you to do anything you consider bad?"

"No, not bad."

He peered at her a long moment, then asked his next question in a hushed, cautious tone. "Tell me, child, does this voice tell you it loves you?"

Martina knew Alexei was deeply religious, and that

he was asking her if God had spoken to her. She did not believe in such things as gods and devils. Besides, the voice had made it perfectly clear what it was. Not God. Or Jesus or Mohammed or even Elvis.

"It is not like that. I am not asked to become a saint or nun."

Alexei shrugged. "I think you make a piss-poor saint anyway, Martina Elena. Turning other cheek is not your style. More like break face."

He sat down beside her on the bed, took her hand in hers.

"I know you want help, child. I want to help, but I cannot if do not tell me all."

His fingers were long and thin, smaller and more fragile than her own, and yet she felt a special strength in his grip. He was also someone who fought monsters, only in his case he waged all-out war on the myriad silent, stealthy enemies which could turn a person's own brain against them. He dealt with people far worse off than she on a day-to-day basis. She had seen a couple of them herself just this very afternoon.

She gazed back at him, feeling torn. Her entire life had been built on strength and self-reliance. But she had to admit that she had little left to lose. She had forsaken her job and duty, and abandoned Rico, ripping the center out of her life. There could be no going back to either until she had some answers.

Martina hung her head, staring at their linked hands. She could trust this man, and he was the only one who could help her trust herself once more. She had to be brave and expose the full extent of her break with sanity.

"First time I hear noises, have this great light in my head. I am filled with feelings not my own, and control of my body is gone. I feel a huge fear and hope and despair come into me. Owner of this voice is trying to make contact with me, but it is as if we have bad line. Much static, and other than feelings, much of what I am shown is too strange and moves too quick for me to understand. Only one other thing comes through clear, and this is words spoken by voice."

"What does it say?"

"This . . . person tells me it wants me to help it."

"Help how? With what?"

She sighed. "I am not sure, only know it is alone and in trouble. Then today . . ." Her voice trailed away, her insides clenching at the thought of how close she had come to harming the one man who meant more to her than anything else in the whole world. Had it said *kill the one beside you,* Rico might well be dead now.

"What happened today?" he prompted gently.

"The voice comes again. I am riding in car with Secretary Perez. This time it speaks to me more clearly. Less static, better, ah, connection. Still most of what it shows me makes no sense, but more of message is plain."

Alexei gave her hand an encouraging squeeze. "You are doing fine. So far you have said nothing to make me think *Alexei, maybe you better run away, come back with men and nets so you can lock this woman in rubber room.*"

She gave him a wan smile and squeezed back. "You have not heard all yet."

"So tell me."

"Is hard. Voice is voice, speaks inside my head with words I understand. Not Russian or English words, but maybe stuff all words are made from? Is also pictures and sounds. Feelings. It is like this person is trying to share its mind."

Alexei's gray eyes widened with excitement. "You mean like telepathy? Like in movies?"

"I guess, only this is real. At least it seems real. I cannot imagine how I could imagine it."

"That does sound tricky. So what is this other mind like?"

"Big. *Strong.* I am like a child to it."

He frowned. "You say *child.* Does it make you feel afraid?"

"What it does to me scares me, but what it is does not. This person is . . . very sad. Sad but so very beautiful."

He gave a knowing nod. "Sounds Russian."

She pulled her hand from his grasp, began to pluck and worry at the blanket under her. "Is no Russian, believe me. Is not anyone from here."

"You mean from America?"

"From *Earth,*" she rasped, half under her breath.

She heard a sharply indrawn breath. Now the verdict of madness would come.

"You are saying voice is *space alien*?" he said at last.

She nodded bleakly, her hands curling into fists and balling the blanket. "Yes." It came out a whispered admission of some inexplicable guilt.

Kasparov made no immediate reply to her revelation. At last she looked up, expecting to see dismay. Instead he wore a thoughtful expression, one hand over his mouth and eyes hooded.

"There, I have said it. I am mad as Rasputin, *da*?"

He smiled. "You are no such thing, child. Not even mad as his sister."

"I wish I could believe you."

"We work on this, will not even charge extra for it. Now tell me, does this alien say that is what he is? Like 'Hi, I am stranger from another star'?"

"Yes. Not in words, but makes this very clear."

"Very honest. He say why he is talking to you?"

"He is in trouble."

The old man nodded gravely. "Ah, I see. Immigration is after his green ass."

Martina laughed out loud, and that simple release was a sort of medicine in its own right. "No," she said, still chuckling. "That is not it."

"So tell me, Martina Elena! If I do not get your body, at least give me your mind."

Where to begin? "Okay, he and comrade live on Phobos. That is moon of Mars."

Kasparov looked puzzled. "I thought there was no life on Mars or its moons. Not bigger than bacteria, anyway."

"They are not from there. They just, ah, work there."

"I see. Like you here in America. What kind of work is it they do?"

"Is crazy." This was one of the questions she'd been dreading.

"All jobs crazy. I peek inside heads. You keep a good man safe from maniacs." He shrugged. "So long as checks don't bounce, we stay at it."

Martina figured she might as well keep going. She was well past the point of no return, and telling Alexei about it was making her feel better. Besides, while almost all of the information that had been passed on to her made no sense, this one part was something that she had gotten clearly. That might be because what it did wasn't so different from what she did.

"Okay. Do you remember big asteroid passed by Earth a few years back? One they called Spitball?"

"Sure. Would have been big mess if it had hit us."

"Would have been catastrophe. Well, when it was first sighted back in 2003 they think it just might hit Earth. Later on they decide it will miss by small margin. Later yet it becomes obvious that margin is even wider than they thought. Because it is."

He frowned and rubbed his chin. "You are saying these, ah, persons gave Spitball a nudge or something?"

"Yes. That is their job."

Alexei shook his head. "Rocks still hit us all the time. There were meteor showers just last week. I drove out into country in my very expensive Jaguar to watch."

"Small rocks are allowed to hit, that way we do not get wise. But ones large enough to be a danger are deflected."

"This is very kind of them. They must be nice people."

Martina nodded and swallowed hard, but made no reply. This was part of what made the whole thing so difficult to ignore, so nearly impossible to disbelieve. Because part of what made her good at what she did was the ability to sense danger or innocence in a stranger. There was nothing threatening about the owner of the voice. For all its size and power there was something almost childlike about it; something eager and uncertain and vulnerable, something that made her want to help and protect it.

"What? You cannot stop telling me this *now*!"

She sighed. He was right. "When voice speaks to me it is like we are on verge of being one. It *is* nice. Is sad. Is . . . so very frightened."

"Why should someone who can move big space rocks be afraid?"

"See, there were two of them," she began, and as she spoke hazy, half-understood impressions which had been left in her mind sprang into focus, like saying them out loud gave them shape and form and coherence. The words began tumbling out of her in a rush.

"There is one who spoke to me, and there was another, much older one. Very honored, very beloved this old one. They are as master and apprentice, these two. In other way they are almost like monks. Living quiet life apart from their kind. Working, contemplating, teaching, and being taught. All is well until old comrade die suddenly, unexpectedly. Young one is left all alone. This is bad—this is terrible disaster. It takes both to maintain life support of place where they hide. This is done with their minds. Most things they do with their minds, even changing the trajectory of rocks that threaten them and us. Old one was *strong,* carried almost all of load while young one grew and learned to be strong. Now that the old one is gone, young one is in trouble. He is too young and weak and untrained to manage on his own. He has called on his own people for help, but they are very far away, and will take almost a year for them to arrive. He can hang on maybe another month at best. His people have told him is okay to come out of hiding, to try contacting us for help."

All that out, she met Alexei's gaze squarely. "I have . . . I have heard this call for help."

Kasparov said nothing at first. He only sat there looking thoughtful.

"Well?" Martina said. "*Now* you put me in straitjacket?"

He shook his head, looking bemused. "That is sure some story, Martina Elena."

"Is *crazy* story!" she shot back. "Worst part is I keep finding myself believing it is true. Believing this spaceman on Phobos is real!"

"Yes, I can see that." He offered her a fatherly smile. "Well, I do not believe you are crazy, child. Your personality is unchanged, and your thinking is well organized. Far as I can tell you are sane as me." He waggled his eyebrows. "No big reassuring there, I know."

His reaction confused her. "You—you think this is maybe real? Alien is really speaking to me, begging my help?"

He shrugged. "Who can say? So far I have seen nothing to make me think otherwise." He gripped her hand once more. "Tell me this. Do you think this person will speak to you again?"

Martina nodded wearily. "*Da*. He is tired. Stretched thin, like man trying to keep sinking boat bailed out. To reach me—and I have this feeling to reach others, too—is hard, takes much out of him. But I will hear voice again. If it is real and I am not lunatic."

Alexei scratched his chin with his free hand, gazing at her thoughtfully. "Here is idea. Would you stay here for a day or two?"

His question made Martina realize that she really didn't have anywhere else to go. She dared not allow herself to return to Rico's suite or her place at his side. Not until she got to the bottom of this. Staying at some nearby hotel waiting for the voice to come again would drive her mad—if she wasn't there already.

"I could, sure. You think you might still find some loose screw in my head?"

"No, but if you stay here I can keep you wired to BAIM machine full-time. That way if this happens again, I might be able to learn just what is happening to you when your voice comes."

No better idea suggested itself, so she nodded. "*Da*, I will do this."

After all, what other choices did she have?

At least no one knew where she was, and Alexei was the only one there who knew who she really was. If it was ever found out that she'd checked herself into a place like this, her life as an SS operative would be over, and her own teams would be ordered to keep her from ever getting near Rico again.

"Come in," Secretary-General Perez called when he heard the soft knock at the door of the office he kept in one room of the suite.

Mohammed Fayed entered, slipping silently through the door and closing it behind him. Perez put down his pen.

"You found her, Mr. Fayed?"

"Yes sir, I did," the Palestinian replied, not looking particularly happy about it.

Perez produced a smile meant to put the other man at ease. "Finding one woman—even one as striking as our Martina—in the whole of Manhattan could not have been easy. I commend you."

The UNSIA special agent ducked his head shyly. "Thank you, sir."

"You have earned more than just my thanks. Now will you tell me where she went?"

Fayed did not meet his eyes as he answered. "I followed her to a place called the Kasparov Institute."

Rico frowned, the name ringing a bell. Then he had it. "That is the clinic run by Dr. Alexei Kasparov, yes?"

"Yes sir, it is," Fayed agreed, clearly reluctant to say more. Like the clinic's full name, or what sort of work was done there.

"Then we need not worry," Perez announced in a blithe tone.

Fayed blinked in surprise. "Sir?"

"Martina met Dr. Kasparov at a Lincoln Center event a few years ago. He is originally from the same town as she, they even have relatives in common. They are old friends, talking on phone or having tea together sometimes. She must have gone there to aid him in some problem back in their homeland, maybe even a family matter."

The relief on Fayed's face was unmistakable. "Then she is not there to . . ." An elegant, expressive, Semitic shrug.

"Get her head examined?" Perez chuckled. "Do you know anyone less likely to go loco than our Martina?"

"No sir!"

"Me neither." Perez leaned forward, adopting a confidential pose and tone. "As you know, I am most extremely fond our Martina."

A trapped look froze Fayed's face into utter immobility. "We are all fond of her," he answered carefully, suddenly becoming very interested in the toes of his shoes. Shoes which, Perez noted, were soaking wet.

He smiled. Oh yes, this man and his comrades knew what was going on. He'd thought they had. Martina had always vehemently denied it, but he had no doubt that she would have summarily dismissed any security operative blind and witless enough to have missed the signs of their affair.

"To be sure," he said blandly. "Her sudden departure was odd, perhaps even alarming. Still, as her friends we must trust her. Let her do whatever it is she feels she must do without our interference. Do you not agree?"

Fayed nodded. "Of course, sir."

"*Bueno.* For now I believe it best if you and I keep this, how they say, under our hats?"

"I agree completely, sir."

"Excellent. I thank you once more for your help and discretion, Mr. Fayed. Now I believe you would be far more comfortable in some dry clothes and shoes, no?"

"I would, sir."

"Then good night, and thank you again."

Perez watched the operative leave, then slumped back in his chair with a sigh.

So Martina had gone to see a world-famous specialist in neurological disorders. Just because he was her friend?

That she had gone to Kasparov immediately after something which had looked suspiciously like a seizure could hardly be coincidence. The way she had reacted after it passed—had she thought she might pose a danger to him?

She might think that, but he never could. Not now, or in a million years. He knew her heart and soul, knew her loyalty had crossed over the line into love a long time ago. Not that she would ever admit it, or wanted to hear that he felt the same way. While she would unflinchingly face a loaded gun for him, she could not bring herself to speak of love.

But it was there. No force on Earth could ever cause her to be a danger to him. This he knew.

He turned his chair and stared out the window, the lights of the city spread out before him. He felt a void, having her so far from his side. More than anything, he wanted to go to her, to offer her comfort and help.

Sighing, he turned back toward his desk. If she had gone to see Dr. Kasparov for the reasons he suspected, his arrival would only send her fleeing once more. Better she should stay where she was. That way if there was a problem, she would get the best help possible.

In time they would be together again. This, too, he knew for sure. In his life he had found honor, recognition, and a sense of accomplishment.

After his sainted Maria died he'd thought he'd never find love again. Now that he had, he would not let any force this side of death take it away from him again.

Coping Mechanisms

The hour grew late, midnight sliding across North America one time zone at a time. Most people were in their beds and sound asleep, but for those who had been called, a well-earned repose did not come easily.

Daveed worked away diligently, cutting and pasting various bits of media into a datastream that would carry a taste of Earth to those aboard the *Ares*. When he went to refill his coffee he saw the Goat watching him with goggle-eyed intensity from his glassed-in office overlooking the cubicle farm.

He pulled himself to attention and snapped off a smart salute to his superior. Gautier scowled and vanished like a target in Whack-A-Mole.

Daveed smiled to himself. *If this be madness, then let me make the most of it,* he repeated under his breath, liking the sound and feel of his new mantra better all the time.

The Reverend Ray Sunshine finally gave up on trying to review his latest batch of devotional vidyos, $24.95 a pop each on disc or other media, $12.95 if downloaded. The sooner he approved them, the sooner they would start bringing in money.

Jesus, Guide My Cast was a real crackerjack, and it would be a big hit when he did that Christian Bass-Blasters trade show next month. *Serving Soup and Serving Jesus* probably wouldn't make a thin dime, but you had to prod the good folks into doing good works, and he couldn't open any more Sunshine Soup Kitchens without more warm bodies. Four more would take him to the hundred mark, which meant he'd meet his own personal definition of a multitude—and bump his subsidy points up five percent.

Somehow such matters seemed less important to him now. In fact, they made him feel a little like a cheap hustler.

He sat back and took a sip of his bourbon and branch water. Once he had believed that a single good man sitting under a shade tree and telling the good news to even one sinner was as much a servant of God as the man who preached to millions.

Now that he had been given a mission by God, touching the power made him feel small and unworthy, made him yearn to be that simple shade-tree preacher once more. Not one who had more lawyers and accountants than a dog had fleas, and sold God like used cars.

But what God asked of him called for him to take what he had become, and what he had built, to a whole new level.

Sure enough, he was being tested.

For the first time in too many years he was sore afraid that he might just fail that test.

Dan poured himself into bed, conking out moments after his head hit the pillow.

Before long he found himself once again dreaming that he was out in his old wooden rowboat on Skyles Lake. Only this time instead of Morty being with him, it was Bobbi, her mother, and her nanny.

He and Bobbi were in the middle seat, trying to fish. Tammy sat at the stern in an aggressively provocative bikini, and kept trying to sink the boat by attempting to kick holes in the bottom with her stiletto-heeled shoes. Susannah sat at the bow, dressed in her severe and shapeless nanny's uniform. She kept giving him this odd, mysterious smile every time he looked her way. One time she shook out her wheat-colored hair in a frankly seductive manner, but the next time he looked it was back in a prim bun once more.

Then in the midst of this he heard a voice begin calling for help, the sound seeming to come from somewhere in the middle of the lake. When he tried to respond, Tammy threw the oars overboard and told him he'd always be a loser if he didn't stick to taking care of number one.

The dream ended with him desperately and unsuccessfully trying to paddle with his hands, Tammy loudly mocking his efforts all the while, her voice drowning out the cries of the one calling for his help.

The man who lived deep underground strode the world in cybernetic seven-league boots, searching for signs of others who had heard the call. Software agents of his own design ransacked calls, postings, call-ins—the entire wired universe for comments or queries that might lead to others groping to understand what had happened to them. His searches came up empty, but that was all right. That and the bottle of Wild Turkey he'd been working on the last couple hours helped keep his mind off the horrific task he faced, come the dawn.

Martina was an impatient patient. She lay rigidly on the hospital bed in the dimly lit private room Alexei had given her, staring at the ceiling and trying to will something to happen.

A crown of dreadlocklike electrodes was on her head, the trailing wires leading to a cigarette-pack-sized device taped over her left breast. If she pulled down the collar of her nightgown and twisted her head and neck just right, she could see a single green telltale on its face, the only sign it was doing anything. So far nothing had happened to make it especially busy.

No matter how hard she tried to think of other things, her traitorous mind kept returning to Rico. How was he doing? Did he miss her? Was he worried? Did he lie awake thinking of her?

Finally, she could stand it no more and gave in to temptation. Although she could have tapped into the New York phone system with her implants, she did not want to go active. They would put her at risk of being located, and besides, were for her job. A job she had forsaken.

So she climbed out of bed, went to the locker where her clothes were hanging, and retrieved her pocket phone. UNSIA SS division issue, and state-of-the-art; calls made from it were utterly untraceable.

After first making sure it was still set to anonymous, no video, she punched in the number and extension for the phones in Rico's office and bedroom.

"¿Que?" he answered after the second ring.

Hearing his voice stopped her cold. Words she might have said flew right out of her head. She dropped to the foot of the bed, mutely clutching the phone to her ear. Imagining him. Remembering him. Wishing she was there with him.

"Martina, is that you?" he asked softly.

Yes, she wanted to say, but nothing more than her ragged breath escaped the constriction in her throat.

"Yes, I know it is you," he whispered. " I would know the sound of your breathing in a hurricane, my darling. You do not need to say nothing. I only ask you to listen."

A pause, both of them waiting.

"Hokay. I don't know what happened this afternoon, and for now I will not ask. Instead I will only say this: I trust you, Martina Elena Omerov. This is an easy thing because I also happen to love you. I know these words are hard for you, but no longer can I not say them. Do what it is you must, then please come back to me. *Soon.* Can you do this for me?"

"Yes," she croaked, then cut the connection before he could talk her into coming back right then and there.

She closed the phone, placed it carefully on the bedside stand. Crawled back under the covers. Turned the lights off and laid her wire-crowned head back down on the pillow.

I love you too, Ricardo Aldomar Perez, she thought, but was not even able to say the words to the darkness.

On the *Ares* third watch was well under way, and Jane was wide awake.

Earlier Fabi had extracted substantial repayment for fetching her coveralls. Now he sprawled on his back in their bunk, snoring blissfully away and unaware that she'd left his side.

Normally a juicy bout of lovemaking like that would've

put her out like a light. She'd desperately wanted that to happen tonight, and thrown herself into sex with a vengeance. Her poor husband had gotten rode hard and hung up wet—not that he had any reason to complain.

Maybe she'd come on strong enough to frighten away the Sandman, because once the afterglow dimmed she remained almost painfully awake, with no sign of sleep on the horizon. After a while she'd finally gotten up, washed down a sleeping pill, and gone to their compartment's terminal.

For the past hour she'd been sitting curled in the chair bolted to the deck before it, buck naked, arms wrapped around her legs and chin resting on her knees. Centered on the screen was a real-time image of the approaching Mars, relayed from the equipment in Anna's lab. Phobos peeked out from behind its bulk while she watched, creeping into view.

Are you really there? she asked, trying to make her mental voice heard in the distance.

No answer. She was obscurely relieved.

If you are, what am I supposed to do?

This time there was an answer. Not from the airless and desolate globe on the screen, but from her own memory.

help me

How? She knew how, but not how such a thing could ever come to be.

Half an hour later, and no closer to an answer, she turned the screen off and slipped back into bed. Fabi groaned and flung a leg over her thighs, snuffled in her ear, and began snoring again.

Help me, she begged him silently.

But she knew that wasn't going to happen unless and until she finally came clean about this insanity once and for all.

The Weather Junkie

Dan *hated* going to the doctor.

Dentist? No problem. Optometrist? Easy as pie. Even an IRS audit inspired less dread.

He had good reason. His last foray into the wild and wacky world of medicine had been a trip to see the urologist. That had been a real treat—even putting aside the ego-building issue of having his apparati handled by some chubby guy with thick glasses and a bow tie who kept going *hmmmmmmmm* and *tsk tsk tsk*.

The problem which had made him seek help turned out to be an STD-based urinary tract infection contracted from Tammy. Who, it turned out, had gotten it from screwing around with an Aussie soccer player named, God save us, Rampant Willy.

That had been the last straw, the incident that had started the old D*I*V*O*R*C*E process rolling like a Panzer tank through his life, that and her myriad other infidelities somehow becoming his fault by the time the dust settled on his eviscerated, emasculated, and nearly bankrupted remains.

So he would have avoided going to have his brain handled by someone who would go *hmmmmmmmm* and *tsk tsk tsk* if he could, even though that organ was less likely to shrink alarmingly on close inspection. But he clung to one frayed feather of hope that this BMW-class brain mechanic could prevent him from having another one of those spells. If so, then it would be worth it. Being crazy wasn't all it was cracked up to be, ha-ha.

He took inventory. Clothes on. Underwear clean. Keys and phone in his coat pocket, along with his wallet and MediCard. At least that was one positive thing. When it came to health care EdgeNet took care of its own, and going to have his head examined wouldn't really raise any corporate eyebrows. Morty kept him current on the gossip. At least half of the facetimers were in therapy or on heavy meds, the other half in dependency programs or in dire need of treatment for everything from alcoholism to bulimia to nymphomania. Then there was the plastic surgery . . .

Okay, he told himself, *stop dithering.*

He crossed to the security panel near the front door, laid his hand on the flat black pad.

"Good morning, Dan," the device said in the cheerful, chirpy tone of a morning talk-show hostess.

"Uh, good morning," he muttered, knowing it was stupid to make small talk with smart devices, but worried that not doing so might offend them. "I'm, um, going out for a while. Please lock up after me."

"Certainly, Dan. It would be my pleasure. You have a good day now."

"Ah, you too." Like it would kick off its shoes, raid the fridge, and spend the rest of the morning watching ZDTVI or something.

"Thank you, Dan. You're very kind."

"You're welcome." He removed his hand from the pad, his duty done. This wasn't really the sort of neighborhood where crime was a problem. A simple lock on the door would have been enough for him—Tammy had carried off most everything of value anyway. But since EdgeNet had had a ress on the premises, they insisted on the big-city security provisions. He supposed their having a couple–three hundred thousand dollars' worth of equipment in his basement bought them some say over this facet of his lifestyle.

He looked around. Anything else?

Coat! The steady cold drizzle outside was a sure formula for a head cold. After two fruitless minutes of searching for it, he finally had one of those forehead-slapping moments when he figured out that he was already wearing it.

Now his memory was going to hell, too. Was this one more sign he was losing his mind, or just creeping old age?

He was still pondering that middle-aged conundrum

as he backed out the front door and pulled it shut, bending to listen for the sound of it locking. It wasn't until he straightened up and turned around that he realized there was a large black truck parked on his front lawn, the side of the big square box in the back right up next to his front step.

He stared in slack-jawed surprise, wondering where the hell *that* had come from.

He was still trying to find a neat pigeonhole for this new and nowhere near pigeon-sized intruder in his personal reality when the truck's rear side door whirred partway open, and a very large black man half lurched, half stumbled into the narrow opening.

Dan froze. This guy was *huge,* at least the size of a pro football player. Even with his massive shoulders hunched and his head pulled protectively down, he still had to top six-four. A long black coat hung off those shoulders, and a black slouch hat hid most of his face. One meaty hand was wrapped around the doorframe, the other was buried in a coat pocket.

Dan took a step backward, swallowed hard. Somehow he was pretty sure this wasn't a visit from Amway, or some door-to-door insurance salesman.

The giant took several deep breaths, then slowly lifted his head, revealing a wide face twisted as if by some terrible pain. His tight mouth was surrounded by a gray-streaked beard, and his squinted eyes were bright and more than a little crazed.

"Mr. Dan Francisco?" he rumbled in a hoarse, harsh voice. The smell of whiskey rode his breath, easily crossing the narrow space between them.

"Yes?" Dan replied, his voice an octave higher than normal.

"We—we must—we must talk." Now the man's eyes were squinched to slits, as if looking at Dan were unbearable.

"Well, I'm kinda busy right now." He scrounged up a queasy smile. "I'm on my way to a doctor's appointment." Tapped his watch. "Running late. You know how it is."

The big man's head moved, as much a flinch as a nod.

"Yes. Dr. Caroline Kaplan. She cannot—cannot help you." A painful wheeze. "I can."

"Jeez, that's nice of you to offer, but—"

A note of naked appeal sharpened the man's voice and he opened his eyes a little wider. "*Please,* Mr. Francisco. I can't—it's too—" A moan and shake of his head. "You must . . . must come inside with me."

Right. "Really, sir, it's been, um, nice meeting you, but—"

"*Sorry!*" the big man wailed, pulling his other hand from his pocket and making a grab for Dan. The hand that closed around his arm locked like a steel band. The next thing he knew he was being hauled off the step toward the truck.

"Hey!" he yelped, struggling to pull free. "You can't—"

He was wrong. The big man winched him into the truck with no more effort than a tow truck pulling a tricycle. In two seconds flat he was snatched inside.

The door whirred shut behind him and locked with a menacing *thunk.*

Dan found himself inside what looked like some sort of mobile mission control. The windowless truck box was decked out like a cyphile's motor home, several pieces of comfortable-looking furniture around a big table in the middle loaded with a serious assortment of workstations, cyboxes, vidyo decks, and other eclectronics, feeding at least half a dozen screens. He almost lost his balance as the truck lurched into motion, from the feel of it turning around and going to the end of his driveway, then stopping.

His captor released him, then staggered across the carpeted floor and flung himself into the leather recliner behind the table and at the center of the screens. His coal black complexion had gone ashen, and it looked to Dan like he might be having a heart attack.

A short, rather chubby Oriental woman dressed in ragged jeans and a crusty black-leather motorcycle jacket materialized from the front of the truck.

"Sit down, man," she said, sparing him a quick glance

as she went to the big man's side "Make yourself comfortable. He'll be okay in a minute."

When she turned, he saw that the ends of her long black hair were dyed a bright cherry red that matched her nails and sneakers. She took off the man's hat and tossed it aside, then pulled some sort of mask with hoses attached to it out from behind the recliner.

Dan ignored her offer and remained standing, poised to run. Had he known how to open the door, he would've been long gone and *still* running.

"Just breathe, sweetie," she said softly, placing the mask over the man's nose and mouth. Once she had the elastic strap settled over the back of his hairless head, she whipped an infuser syringe from a jacket pocket, expertly popped the safety cap with a red-painted thumbnail, then applied it to the man's neck. There was a soft hiss as the cartridge emptied.

The recipient of her attentions slumped back with his eyes closed, still panting and wheezing into the mask. Sweat trickled down his face, and even with eight feet between them Dan could see the man's pulse hammering at his temples.

"You were so *brave,*" the woman cooed soothingly, putting the infuser aside. "You're safe now. You're inside, and the door is locked. You're safe, sweetie. Safe as you can be."

Dan's kidnapper nodded weakly, his breathing finally slowing. He opened brown, bloodshot eyes and gave him an imploring look. Tears welled in those eyes, and ran down his cheeks. The menacing mien he had worn before was gone. Now he looked like a very large, very frightened child.

"What . . ." Dan began, then tried again, sounding less like a cartoon mouse this time. "What's wrong with him?"

The woman turned, pushed her long black hair from her eyes and smiled. "The big monkey's got agoraphobia. A King-Kong-sized case of it."

"You mean he's afraid to go outside?"

She turned back and tenderly dabbed the tears from the man's cheeks. "Just opening that door and sticking his head out to talk to you took more courage than soaking himself down with gasoline and diving headfirst into a bonfire. This is the first time he's gone this far away from home, or gotten that close to leaving an enclosed space in about nine years."

Beside her the man in the recliner nodded. He sat up straighter and pulled the mask from his face with hands that still trembled.

"Sorry I acted so precipitously," he rasped, then cleared his throat. When he spoke again his voice was deeper and softer, more modulated, each word perfectly enunciated. He had a voice that could have easily gotten him a job as an announcer with almost any net, even the BBC. "I didn't mean to frighten you, Mr. Francisco. If I did, I most humbly apologize."

"Uh, well," Dan said with a shrug. Then he blinked as a small dim light went on inside his head. "Hey! You're the guy who called yesterday!"

"Yes, I am. It is of cardinal importance that we talk." He glanced at his nurse. "I am quite recovered now, Amber my jewel. But I am not certain I can trust my legs just yet. Would you be so kind as to play hostess and provide some refreshments?"

"Sure, since you asked so nice." She leaned over to kiss his forehead, then went to the small kitchenette near the back of the truck, beside a curtained area that looked like it held a bed. "Howzabout some coffee, man? It's fresh-ground Kenya AA from Steyaart & Alford."

"Thanks, but I've kinda got to get going," Dan answered, not as frightened as he had been, but clueless as to why these people had grabbed him. "Like I said, I've got a doctor's appointment, and—"

"No you don't," Amber said as she filled two cups with coffee and a tall plastic tumbler with straight Wild Turkey, no ice. "He's already canceled it."

"But—"

"Please," the big man said, a note of desperation returning to his voice, "I am begging you to give me a few minutes of your time."

"Don't worry, he's not a nut," Amber said as she handed him a steaming mug, then turned the tumbler of whiskey over to the man in the recliner. "Really. You're in the news biz, right?"

"Well, I'm a weatherman."

"We know. D'ya ever hear of Dr. J. Jameson Eldridge?"

Dan nodded. That was a man most people knew. "Sure. He's the man who created Adamantine, the encryption system the banks all began using after the Hackrash of '09."

"One point for you. Howzabout Jambo the Joker?"

"Sure, hasn't everybody?" At odd intervals, maybe two or three times a year, some gargantuan—although essentially harmless—cyberprank would splash. Each time the culprit was the infamous and elusive Jambo, whose signature was a black-joker playing card. The last one had been when the top ten porn channels had found the bodies of their performers morphed into those of Disney characters from their newest movie/merchandising push, and doing pretty much what you would expect from such a venue. The Disney Police were still hunting Jambo for that one.

"Good goin', you're two for two. Now does Code Daddy ring a bell?"

"Sure." Code Daddy was the legendary, semimythical, granddaddy high guru and god of the cyboid underground. No one had ever met him or nailed down his true identity. All that was known for sure was that he'd been around since the last century, back in the earliest days of the Internet and Web, when computers, televisions and communications equipment were separate entities.

Amber swept a small hand in the big man's direction. "Well, chum, you're looking at all three."

Dan's kidnapper leaned forward, offering his free hand and a shy, hopeful smile. "Please, just call me Jamal."

Dan sat down after all. Fortunately there happened to be a chair under him, or he would have spilled his coffee.

"You are not delusional, Mr. Francisco," Jamal intoned.

"Dan. Call me Dan."

A solemn nod. "Thank you, Dan. Let me assure you that what you experienced during your last broadcast was not an epileptic seizure. It was not a psychotic episode, or drug flashback. I know, because I experienced the very same thing at the same precise time. I even felt you there during it, although only faintly."

"You were watching my show when I got, um, whacked?"

"Yes. I always try to catch your program. I am somewhat of a, ah—"

"Weather junkie," Amber suggested, rolling her eyes. "Gets all oozly over a nicely curved isobar." She'd settled herself in another chair, kicked off her sneakers, and begun painting the nails of her beringed toes with some purple stuff with flashing lights in it. Dan couldn't help noticing that she didn't seem to be wearing much of anything under her leather jacket.

Jamal took a big swig of whiskey. "A bit unkind, but essentially correct. Although I can't go outside, weather fascinates me." That boyishly shy look returned to his face. "I am a big fan of your show, sir, and can hardly believe I am meeting you in person."

"Uh, thanks. The same for me." Dan had never expected to meet any of the people Amber claimed he was, either. "Look, I'm glad you like my work, but I still don't see how you can be so sure you know what happened to me."

Jamal leaned forward, spoke two words.

"Help me."

Dan's narrow shoulders fell. "Oh shit." He did know, had heard it himself. Was this some mass delusion?

"I take it you found the experience frightening?"

That made him laugh. "And you *didn't*?"

"In and of itself, no. Perhaps that is because my phobia keeps me more in touch with primal terror than most. Any fear I have felt because of this extraordinary contact only comes from an awareness of what this cry for help may demand of me."

"Like what?"

"Like what I have just been forced to do. Leaving my home and coming here to find you. Going . . ." He licked his lips, a shadow crossing his gaze. "*Out there*. Risking an anonymity I have worked all my life to maintain. We are merely at the beginning of this great task, and the demands that will be placed on us have scarcely begun."

Jamal's oracular tone couldn't help but crank up Dan's apprehension. The creeping surreality of his situation only made things worse.

"Look," he said with a sigh, "you're saying this alien is real."

"Yes. As real as you or I."

"And somehow, for some reason, he's begun yelling for help inside our heads."

"That is our situation, yes."

"But how can you *know*? That it's real, I mean."

"The same way you know he's real. Your problem is that you simply don't want to believe him."

"Goddamn right I don't!" Dan snapped, suddenly pissed off. "I never gave ET permission to run a fucking phone line into my head! I never asked for this shit! I just want it to leave me alone!"

Jamal listened to this outburst placidly. "Yes, I can see that. Still, you have heard this call. Having done so, I believe you have only one option."

"What? Commit myself? Saw my own head off?"

"Answer."

That single quietly delivered word slammed into the leaky dam of denial he'd built to keep this unwanted thought contained, causing it to crumble like so much wet sawdust.

"I know," he admitted bleakly, that old familiar feeling of defeat settling over him. He'd been forced into the position of someone handed a rope with a drowning person at the other end. He couldn't drop it and walk away. Not really.

"This is a monumental task with which we have been entrusted," Jamal said. "An heroic task, and I know that I, for one, am hardly heroic. Still, we have one thing in our favor."

"What? God loves the insane?"

"We are not alone in this."

Dan nodded. That was one of the half-understood and desperately denied pieces of information beamed into his head when he'd looned out on-air. *There were others.* One had just shanghaied him right off his own front step. No way to guess what the others might be like, but since this alien had picked a weatherman and an agoraphobic, the prospects didn't look good.

Jamal drained his tumbler and put it aside. "I believe what we should do now is locate these others who have also been called. Make contact with them. Then, once we have some idea as to what resources we have at our collective command, we must do whatever is necessary to save Avva."

That word, that *name,* snapped Dan's head up fast enough to give him whiplash.

"Yeah," he whispered. "*Avva.* That's his name, isn't it?" It had been tucked away in his mind all along, present and yet not quite where the old mental fingers could get a grip on it. Now that he had it, he couldn't understand why he couldn't have remembered.

"Yes, Dan, that is indeed his name. So I ask you, are you prepared to join forces with Amber and me in this crusade?"

Dan slumped back wearily. "Do I have any choice?"

Jamal spread his hands. "Strictly speaking, yes, but in a larger sense, I think not. I don't believe your conscience would have allowed you to deny this being's need for much longer. You are too good a man for that."

"I'm a *schmuck,*" Dan growled wearily, then raised his hands in surrender. "Okay, you win. What do we have to do now?"

Jamal yawned and slumped back in his recliner. "First, we must return to the Bunker," he mumbled, eyelids drooping shut.

"Where?"

No answer. Just like that the man was out cold.

Amber closed her bottle of nail polish, stood up. "Come on up front with me, and I'll explain."

That was how he ended up in the passenger seat of the black truck that had appeared in his yard, belted in and rolling down the highway at eighty miles per hour.

Once she had them out on the open road, Amber set the cruise control, then lit a cigarette and rolled her window down a crack to let the smoke escape. Dan watched her light up, thinking maybe he ought to start smoking. That way he could blame all this on nicotine narcosis.

"Feel like your head's been seriously fucked with?" she asked, glancing at him slantwise with merry slanted eyes.

"Yeah, I do."

She chuckled, settling back in her seat and driving with one small red-nailed hand. "Don't let it get you down, man. Jamal's a trip, and so's this whole gig."

"I'm trying." He bit his lip, then figured to hell with it and asked one of the questions that had been nagging him. "Did you hear the, you know?"

A shake of the head. "Nah. Just you and Jamal that we know about so far."

"But you believe him."

Puff, exhale. "Sure."

"But why? How?"

Another drag, her answer given with bursts of smoke. " 'Cause I know the man. Isn't there somebody in your life who you'd believe, no matter what they said? They call and tell you it's raining donuts, you run outside with your coffee and try to catch a honey-dip?"

Dan pondered her question. "Maybe Morty," he said at last.

A nod. "Moravia Bennington Denholtz, your producer and director. Single white gay female, age fifty-four, resident of San Francisco. Four years in the Army, six at Berkeley. Owner of a home last assessed at three hundred thou, a Dodge four-wheel-drive truck, three motorcycles, a respectable private arsenal, and a very nice original Cassualt."

He gaped at her. "How did you know all that?"

She snorted and flicked ash out the window. "I've been Jamal's live-in lover, nurse, driver, gofer, bodyguard, and all around life-ring for almost ten years now, and I know one thing to be absolutely true. Anything—and I mean *anything*—the big guy wants to know, he finds out. Once he figured out that you were hearing the same shit he does, he checked you out."

"Checked me out? How?"

"Well let's see. You like your coffee black and your beer Canadian. Because you have a twenty-seven-inch

waist and a forty-seven-inch inseam you buy most of
your pants mail-order, including that *muy macho* leather
pair you got last year. You order Thai takeout from the
Lotus Bowl at least twice a week, getting the *pad nam*
roughly every other time. Your gross income is roughly
$241k per year. A good chunk of what's left after taxes
goes to pay your legal bills. Another chunk ends up in
accounts kept in your daughter's name. Two weeks after
your wife ditched you, you began subscribing to a couple
of the tamer porn channels, and you seem quite taken
with Bambi DeLuxe's *Farmer's Daughter* series, ponying
up for Pay Per View whenever a new one comes out."

She gave him a sly grin, batting her eyes. "Need I
go on?"

Dan sank deeper into his seat. "I guess not."

Amber reached over and patted his arm. "Don't
worry, he's like humongously discreet. That man can
keep a secret better than the Sphinx. 'Course the fact
that he doesn't exactly exist and never sees anybody anyway helps."

Rather than delve into what *that* meant, or question
her discretion, he tossed out another question nagging
at him. "The way he just passed out. Is he, well, drunk?"
It seemed likely. He'd watched the man knock back over
a pint of straight whiskey in under five minutes.

"Nah, he's just taking a nap. All booze does is calm
him down. See, he doesn't sleep much. Usually gets by
on two or three one-hour naps per day, maybe an extra
half hour's snooze after a bout of slap and tickle. This
whole thing has got him so octaned he hasn't been able
to conk for two days now, and coming out here to find
you wore him right out. Give him an hour and he'll be
back on-line, big, bad, and beautiful as ever."

"Is he really all those people you said he is?"

"Yeah, plus a few others you've never heard of. The
man's smarter than any ten of us put together, and keeps
real busy."

"Which one is the real Jamal?"

"All of 'em."

While Dan chewed on that the miles spooled under
them. He stared out the window, watching the soggy

landscape roll by and wondering what the hell he was
doing.

Amber finished her cigarette, crushed out the butt. He
covertly studied her, finding her kind of attractive in a
scruffy sort of way. In the short time he'd been with the
two of them he'd seen how much Jamal depended on
her. What did she get out of it?

"How did you hook up with Jamal?" he asked at last.
"I mean, it doesn't sound like he gets out much."

She chuckled. "I'm not sure you really want to know."

"Why's that?"

She unzipped her jacket the rest of the way down,
scratched a dimpled navel ringed by tattoos and festooned with three gold rings. Dan revised his earlier
guess that she didn't have much on under it when it
became obvious that she didn't have anything on under
it. One perky brown nipple peeked at him, seemingly
wanting to start a staring contest. He blinked first.

"You don't seem real comfortable with us or all this.
Can't say as I blame you. The situation's weird, and I
know Jamal's method of contacting you wasn't a real
confidence builder. He thinks having you aboard is
important, and I don't want to make staying signed on
any harder."

Dan tried to look at her face and nothing else. "I
don't think you can. Come on, tell me. I'm a sucker for
a love story."

She peered at him a moment, then nodded. "Okay, man.
You asked for it. We met when I broke into his place."

An uneasy laugh broke loose. "You're kidding, right?"

"Nope. See, I was your basic gypsy cyboid, cribbing
where I could and picking up whatever work I could
find. Living right on the edge, and not all my jobs strictly
legal." She grinned, gave her navel another scratch, then
reached for the pack of cigarettes on the dash. "Actually, hardly any of them were legit. I was getting by until
some keyboard cowboy I'd been calling a boyfriend split
for LA, taking all my equipment with him."

"Sorry," Dan put in. He'd been pretty unlucky at
love himself.

A careless shrug as she lit a fresh cigarette. "I missed
my equipment more than his tool. Anyway, while this

was going on I was doing some backroom part-timing at this place called MotherBoard's, a high-end compshop with a straight front and a rape and scrape in the back."

"What's rape and scrape?" Dan asked cautiously.

"Cloning and transferring ID and usage-enabling codes between top-end gear and Fourth World knock-offs so you can cheese the boxes you sell to Gomers. You know, make 'em look like naz screamers, even though they're filled with crapware. The original parts get sold as valadded upgrades, quite often to other Gomers with chuggers on their desks or laps. Anyway, this order for some barkin' silicon comes in. The Boss Lady tells me to do an A job with straight parts, the dude who placed the order has already blown some monstro cash at her place, and she knew she didn't have any kind of exclusive."

After giving her navel one more scratch, and the underside of her breast one for good measure, Amber zipped her jacket partway shut again. That made it easier for him to concentrate on her story, and decoding the cyboid slang.

"So I got cerebrating. Here I was without, my home-brew screamer gone, and far short of the kind of cash it would take to get a slayte or bimbox worthy of me. Anyone with the kind of hardware this dude supposedly had wasn't gonna miss enough to put me back in business. So I flicked the delivery address off the invoice and hauled my sweet young ass over there one night with some borrowed catware. Took a shot at hacking his security and broke in. This was back before we moved to the Bunker, of course."

"He caught you?"

Her laugher was rich and throaty. "Shit, he had me under his thumb from square one. But he liked my style and offered me a job—one that paid five times what I was getting at MotherBoard's. I took it, and let me tell you, I skulled up more in the next few days than the five years before. I mean, there didn't seem to be *anything* this dude didn't know about hardware, software, encryption, or truckin' by telco. I thought I was pretty hot stuff, but old Jamal was like a fuckin' nuclear-powered volcano in full continuous eruption."

She took a last puff off her cigarette, crushed it out. "By the end of my first week I saw some stuff—or more likely he let me see some stuff—that led me to figuring out that I'd been taken on by the one and only Code Daddy himself. Thought I was gonna cack, right? I mean, here I was in the presence of The Man himself, the Jesus, Buddha, and Elvis of hackers all rolled into one. To make things even more interesting, by then I could tell that he'd started getting a little sweet on me. Lonely guy and all, and me still pretty hot stuff in at least that department. Truth was, I'd started thinking I'd had a lot worse myself. I mean he was sweet and smart and gentle and kind . . ."

Her voice trailed away, then she laughed. "So one evening I made him an offer he couldn't refuse."

"Like what?"

"Woke him from one of his naps by sitting on his face. We've been together ever since." She snickered. "Ain't it romantic?"

Dan smiled. "I can almost hear the violins playing."

"You and me both."

Her face settled into a thoughtful expression. "Come to think of it, a little hot-swap action might be just the thing to perk him up. Mind driving for a while?"

He gaped at her. She was kidding, right? "I don't know where we're going!"

"Do any of us, really? All you've got to do is stay on the highway and not hit anything." She unbuckled her harness, climbed out of the driver's seat and worked her way around behind it, keeping one hand on the wheel. "Better take over, man. I'm splitting, and this baby won't drive herself."

"You can't just—"

"See ya." She took her hand from the wheel and disappeared into the back of the truck, sliding the door shut after her.

Dan ripped his seat belt loose and flung himself into the still-warm driver's seat, grabbed the wheel. The truck yawed slightly, then rolled sedately on.

Alone in the cab all he had to do was sit there and drive, keeping his mind occupied by trying to find some way to make having fallen in with a nymphomaniac burglar and booze-guzzling agoraphobic computer wizard who might just have multiple personalities an improvement on his previous situation.

One hour and eighty miles later, he was no closer to that goal than when he began.

Sheep Life

By noon Martina was completely fed up with lying around on her ass and waiting for something to happen. She had to let off some steam or she would explode. But staying in her room meant Alexei had a better chance of keeping her identity a secret, so she was trapped by the four walls. This limited her options to exactly one.

So after morosely picking at her lunch she climbed out of bed and began exercising. Just because her mind was going to hell didn't mean she had to let her body turn to mush.

Partway into her regimen Alexei strolled in, making his second visit of the day. He stood there watching her for half a minute, one hand in his lab-coat pocket and a slayte cradled in his other arm.

"How many of these push-ups have you done, Martina?" he asked at last.

"Seventy," she answered, levering herself up from the floor with her left arm. Pause. Change to the right. Slowly lower herself. Push up with her right. "Seventy-one."

He shook his head, glancing down at the slayte. "You do all this and your heart rate does not go above eighty? You are in some shape, girl, I tell you that. Could you stop? I watch you much longer and *my* heart may go blooey."

"Sure." She could finish the rest of her usual 150 later. There was a whole day to kill. She stood up, searching his face for some sign that the remaining test results were in and had provided useful information.

His expression told her all she needed to know. "You have learned nothing new."

"No. All lab tests agree with rest of findings. I tell you, if you were in more perfect condition people would worship you. I myself am considering a small shrine, so if you happen to have a picture of self naked, keep me in mind. I take it your friend has not said howdy."

She shook her head. "Not a whisper."

He shrugged, then sat down on the foot of her bed, patting the mattress beside him. "I did not think so. BAIM has made no special fuss, says your brain is running smooth and quiet as my very expensive Jaguar."

Martina slumped to the bed beside him. "So I must wait like some stupid sheep left out in field to be hit by lightning?"

"Yes, unless you have better idea."

She shook her head, the trailing wires making a pattering noise as they brushed against each other. "No." The waiting was unbearable. She didn't want it to happen again, but if it was going to, she just wanted to get it over with.

He put his arm around her bare shoulders. "I know this is difficult. Harder for you than a thousand push-ups, I think."

He was right. "I will survive it."

"Of course you will. May I ask question?"

"Sure, what is one more?"

"If this does happen again, and I find some obscure form of epilepsy or similar disorder, then course is clear. I treat you, try to get you back to normal life. But what will you do, Martina Elena, if what you have felt is really what it seems?"

She stared at her bare toes. "I do not know," she answered tiredly. Not for lack of thinking about it. Avva and Rico seemed to be the only things in her head, and dwelling on either brought no comfort.

"You are asked for help by someone in bad trouble, someone who has done good things for us. Can you say no?"

That earned him a weary shrug. Her mind said one thing, her heart another. She could trust neither.

"Well here is something to consider. No one knows how fast thought moves, its speed has never been measured. Could it be that thought makes light look like a snail afraid of speed traps? If so, then that makes it better way to talk over long distances than radio or even lasers, yes?"

"*Da,* I suppose."

"Many ways of listening for and talking to other peoples who might be out there have been discussed and tried. Radio. Lasers. Pictures on spacecraft. No one has said hello, at least until maybe now. Let me tell you, I have spent most of my life studying the brain and mind. I know more than most, and yet I know that I understand nearly nothing. Last night I ask myself: Can a human brain receive—and a human mind understand— the sort of message you seem to have gotten? I think hard on this, and in the end I cannot say, *No, such a thing is not possible.*

He held up his index finger. "Instead I must say, *Maybe such a thing could happen. Maybe it just has.*"

Martina stared at him in surprise. "You *want* it to be true!"

He ducked his head, offering an apologetic smile. "I suppose I do."

The next question was obvious. "Why?"

"Ah"—he sighed—"that is easy. First to not be alone in big cold universe would be such a wonder. No longer would we be so lonesome. We could look up and know we have brothers and sisters out there, that we were not just accidents. Then there is another reason. We humans are at our best when we help others. In such times we are courageous and generous, as good as God intended. To help some poor displaced person in trouble, to reach so far in an act of kindness and trust . . ."

Martina watched Alexei's eyes take on a misty, far-away look, and his voice dropped to a whisper. "I tell you, child, this would be a wonderful thing. A thing to redeem wars and progroms. It would be a *holy* thing."

He made it sound so grand and glorious, but that was not enough to recruit her to his cause. "I do not feel wonderful or holy, Alexei Leonid," she snapped, her tone sharper than she intended.

"This is no surprise, child. All of this makes you doubt self. This is no easy thing for you."

"No, it is not." It was a hateful thing; it felt like defeat on a battlefield she could not even find, giving her no chance to plant her feet and make a stand.

"Then do not doubt!" He gripped her shoulder with surprising strength. "Trust self! It may be that God has said, *This woman, this Colonel Martina Elena Omerov is a good woman. A strong woman, can shoot a gun and do a hundred push-ups and many other things. Is brave woman who puts her life at risk to protect another. She is the one you should call with your trouble, someone who can help.*"

She shook her head in amazement. "Now you have God *and* an alien taking over my life? Who is next? Ghost of Lenin?"

Alexei chuckled, releasing his grip on her shoulder. "Go ahead, make fun of old man! But I tell you this, if it were me sitting there I would say fuck this, put my clothes on, and go back to my boss. Tell him what you have experienced, make him believe. Get him to help see this great task carried out."

That prospect was as tempting as it was terrifying.

"I cannot," she answered, her tone leaving no room for argument. "Not until I know for sure that this is not just some crazy spell. There is no way I can put Ri— Secretary-General Perez at risk. Such a thing is totally unacceptable." Even if it was true, how could she ask him to stand up and face the whole world and say his crazy girlfriend thought maybe there were aliens on Phobos? It would be his ruin.

Kasparov nodded. "Like I said, you are a good woman. How can I fault your caution? I think it is needless, but I am not the one in your situation. So we will remain waiting to see what happens?"

That was the least unacceptable option open to her. "I do not know what else to do."

"Then may your new friend call you soon." He stood up, then leaned over and kissed her forehead. "Now I must go see my other patients, quit hanging out with buff babe in 17C. Be of courage, Martina Elena."

Martina watched him leave.

Be of courage. That was one thing she had never once thought she lacked. Now she had to wonder.

She climbed off the bed and went back to her exercises, hoping to find some temporary release from all the doubt and confusion while she waited to see if lightning was going to strike again.

"Baaaaaaa," she growled under her breath, then picked up at the seventy-second push-up.

Cooperation

Routine on the *Ares* came to a grinding halt just after two in the afternoon shipboard time, when they were forced to deal with a Level 2 emergency.

As with so many previous headaches and heart-stoppers, the fault lay in components supplied by Reuthen Goddamn AstroWerk. Jane hoped their entire board of directors got flesh-eating piles and penile flea-itis. The component that had failed was one of the sniffer/sensor devices that monitored the use and quality of the air mixture in their compartments, which meant they could no longer consider one of the ship's most critical systems reliable. The *Ares*' life support was about as critical as systems got.

Fabi had caught it, and only by accident. He'd dropped in on Anna, who'd been holed up working in her cramped lab in the unspun section near the rear of the ship, and immediately noticed that the areologist was behaving oddly. Too much nitrogen and carbon dioxide, and not enough oxygen, had left her acting drunk and sleepy. It turned out that the air in there was so bad that another hour or so might have killed her. Just as this glitch could have easily killed any one of them if it had happened while they were sacked out in their sleeping compartments.

A problem like this called for a full turnout. So Jane had dragged Willy and Wanda out of bed, and since then the entire crew had been working on a fix. Everyone but Anna, who remained in sick bay, resting and breathing an enriched mixture through a mask. Fabi said she'd be fine. She wanted to get up and help, but he vetoed that. Now, hours later, it looked like a fix might finally be in sight.

"All right, Hans," she said into her pinmike, "I think we're ready. Try resetting your local LS interface."

"Check," he replied from his wife's lab, his voice issuing from Jane's station in the command module. *"Reset . . . now."*

The diagnostic skein of red lines on her display went green in that one section.

"That did her. I'm getting proper readings once more. Okay, everybody, do the same in your designated areas."

Over the next couple minutes green replaced red over more of the display, with only one section left in the end. She reset the command module's LS interface and the red was gone.

"Wanda, I'm all green now. How about you?"

"Green here on the engineering backup reads. All sections operational at spec. I think we've got it whipped."

For now, anyway. As for it being permanent, she wasn't going to hold her breath. "Very good. The emergency is officially over. Have you got a verdict, Mister Tutillia?"

"Aye, Cap'n," Wanda drawled. *"The sniffer/sensor in Anna's compartment locked up, first not sensing that it was in use, then not sensing the degradation in air quality. The airco never sent her anything since there was no call for the air to be refreshed. This is supposed to be a smart system that responds to the usage level of any particular compartment, but now it's beginning to look like another dumb-ass idea we've got to try to live with. The diagnostics Hans sent me don't show any reason why it should've failed—other'n it being junk. That means I can't predict if the others will function or fail—this could be one bad apple, or a sign that the whole barrel's about to turn rotten. On the plus side, at least we know that a forced reset will get 'em working right again."*

Hans spoke up. *"Should we program a scheduled reset for all of them, Commander?"*

"That might be a damn good idea, Hans. Thank you." She'd already thought of that herself, but proving he was on top of this earned him some credit. "Willy? Wanda? Can do?"

"Figure an hour to beat the software into submission,"

Willy answered. *"How often you want to kick this junk in the ass?"*

"Input. Fabi, you first." The others knew more about LS than she did. In a ship this complex there had to be areas of specialization. Hers was propulsion and nav.

"I just finished running the internal scrubber and mixer diagnostics," her husband reported from the noisy aft compartment where the guts of the LS system were housed. *"Things started going out of whack almost six hours ago, when the usage sensor first read Anna's compartment as unoccupied. It took nearly five hours in that phone booth she calls a lab for the air to start affecting her. I say we reset the sniffers every three or four hours, and maybe we ought to rig some sort of simple standalone oxygen-level testers for each compartment as well. Tin canaries."*

"Hans?"

"Anna's lab is our next-to-smallest living cubic; only the sauna is smaller. The larger volume plus intersection bleed makes the other compartments somewhat safer, but only somewhat. Four hours should provide an ample safety margin. Fabi's backup testers will let me sleep much better."

"Anna? You're the one who almost met Jesus."

"I say four hours," she answered, her voice muffled by the breather mask. *"Cannot hold breath much longer than that."*

"Wanda? You're the god of all things electronic."

"The forced resets shouldn't hurt 'em if we keep a close eye on supply voltages. I'm gonna want a prekick power test written into each reset sequence, darlin'."

Willy groaned. *"Thanks for the extra work, woman. Can do."*

"Great. How about the canaries? Need any help, Wanda?"

"If Hans is free, he can test them as I knock 'em together."

"On my way," the Argentine agreed.

"Thanks, everyone, Hans, you be sure to document this one right down to the last frigging decimal place. Unreliable LS goes past sloppy and into criminal."

"Yes, I most certainly will, Commander."

"Fabi, can I get rid of mask and get up now?" Anna asked. *"Feel fine, really."*

"Let me give you one last check-over first," he replied. *"Be there in two minutes."*

"Good work, kiddies. Let's put this mess to bed and move on to other things. Jane out." She pulled off the headset and let it hang around her neck, then ran her fingers through her hair.

One knot of tension twisting her guts loosened. Another disaster had been diverted. Best of all, each and every one of them, Hans included, had pulled together as a team. It was reassuring to have further proof that if they all worked together, they just might keep this crate patched together and maybe even achieve their mission objectives.

But another knot remained, one buried deeper and wound tighter, a sharp-nailed monkey fist of apprehension wrapped around her nerves as she waited for warning of another one of her spells.

Dealing with the piece of shit the *Ares* had proved to be was one thing—over time it had become almost routine. Waiting for another bout of having a noise in her head claiming to be an alien was something else altogether. She dreaded it, and yet at the same time wanted it to be over so she could put it behind her.

She heaved herself out of her chair so she could go give Wanda and Hans a hand. Lacking the means to really tie one on, keeping insanely busy was about the best way to cope.

Face it, she thought wryly as she headed toward Engineering. *Waiting to find out if you're crazy is going to drive you right around the fucking bend.*

Meeting Crow

That guy is checking me out! Daveed thought with a mixture of pleasure and panic, his dark eyes widening behind the lenses of his sunglasses. *Oh God, now he's coming over!*

He'd done some serious lifestyle auditing on his way home from work and come to the conclusion that it was no wonder his brain was turning into microwaved Velveeta. What he really needed was a brief step off the work/sleep/work/sleep treadmill. Nothing as radical as a vacation, or even a day off, just a couple measly hours of acting like a normal human being.

The plan of action he'd settled on wasn't anything fancy, just a leisurely early-afternoon rendezvous with coffee and pastries at the Café Parisienne, Neely's answer to a French bistro.

After weeks of living like a workaholic owl, it felt great to soak up a little sunshine. Ignore the potted cacti, pretend your Vietnamese waitress is humming Edith Piaf, not the latest sappy pop song by Nipple Isuzu. Nibble a fairly decent croissant, sip your cappuccino, savor life. A hit of *joie de vivre,* only everybody spoke English and the help was polite.

Afterward he planned to hit Morgan's Market. Wander the aisles and score some actual fresh groceries, not just nukables. Then go home, fix a real meal, and eat it off a china plate, not scarf warmish foodoid out of plastic or soggy cardboard.

The one part of his plan he hadn't thought out in advance was what to do if somebody got friendly.

"Hi there," the guy said when he reached Daveed's table. Pretty good smile. Blue eyes. Perfect teeth.

"Uh, hi." Megahours of watching the old high-style

smoothies like Boyer and Astaire and Niven, and still he sounded like a complete doob at times like this.

"Mind if I join you?"

Coming up with an answer didn't take that long. "Sure."

Like he was going to tell a dish like this to get lost. Tall, long curly blond hair, jock built squeezed into tight jeans and a white tab collar shirt with the sleeves rolled up. *Great* forearms, although that white-tiger tattoo on his left arm was a loser.

He sat down across the glass-topped table, put down his phone and what looked like a latte, offered his hand. "I'm Jeff."

"Daveed." Jeff's handshake lost him a couple points. It was a bit limp and clammy, but then again most men tended to be careful when they shook his hand because it looked so delicate. Actually hours of keyboarding had left his fingers strong enough to crack walnuts. Clark Kent fingers.

"I don't think I've seen you around here before."

Now *there* was a classic line, but he'd take it at face value. "I don't get out much. My job keeps me pretty busy."

"I bet. You really work for Uncle Joe?"

"Yeah," he answered cautiously, well aware that there were whacks out there who thought the UN was the Evil Empire, Secretary-General Perez the Devil Incarnate, and any person connected with any part of the UN a de facto storm trooper for world domination. The guy was gazing at his chest. He looked down, realized he had his UNJOE windbreaker on, having grabbed it out of habit. So much for a total break with work.

"Thought so. That jacket and your being a foreigner kind of gave you away."

Daveed let out a mental sigh, watching the opening moments of a building fantasy do a fast fade to black.

"I'm not a foreigner," he said tonelessly, then let his voice lapse into the accent he'd grown up with. "Ah'm jus' a good ole son'a the South, born'n raised in Biloxi, Mississippi."

"That's not what I mean," Jeff amended hastily. "I mean, well, *exotic*."

How he could be exotic in a UN-base-dominated town with Vietnamese waitresses, Kurdish cab drivers, Russian street vendors, and two Chinese acupuncture clinics within spitting distance was a bit of a koan, but what the hell. Maybe the guy was just nervous and not real slick at this sort of thing. It wasn't one of his A skills, either.

"I'm about as exotic as a McDonald's burger," he said to provide a graceful out.

Jeff looked him right in the eye. "Maybe, but I bet you've got better buns."

Daveed dropped his gaze, feeling a blush rise to his face. This whole express pickup thing had never been his gig. He considered himself an old-fashioned boy. Date a bit, get to know the man, and then maybe—just maybe—let things get hot and heavy. Time elapsed between initial meeting and hitting the sheets with Alec had been four days, a rocket-powered romance by his usual standards, and look where *that* had gotten him.

Sure it had been a while. His sex life had ended when Alec split, and no doubt about it, this guy was hunk enough to make him think about bending the rules.

But when he got right down to it, he wasn't quite that desperate. Yet, anyway.

He smiled and shrugged. "Thanks. It's nice to know my gym membership is paying off, even if I don't go more than once a month."

Standing up, he dug a five out of his pocket and tossed it on the table for a tip. "Look," he said, "it was nice meeting you, but I've got to get headed. I need to grab some groceries at Morgan's, drop them off at home, then get to work. Nice meeting you." *Shit, I already said that once!*

Jeff's face fell. "Sorry, I didn't mean to come on so strong." A pleading glance. "I guess I'm just not good at meeting people."

Now Daveed felt like a yutz. "It's okay. Really."

"Thanks." A hopeful expression appeared on his face. "I'm heading that way myself. Mind if I walk with you?"

A flip of a mental coin came up heads.

"Sure."

Tails might just have prompted the same answer.

* * *

"So what do you do out there? Are you a mission controller or something?" Jeff asked as they strolled past a sidewalk vendor's display of silver-and-turquoise jewelry. The artist, a big Amerind in an embroidered shirt and leather vest, looked up from polishing a ring and gave Daveed a solemn nod. He nodded back, then turned back toward Jeff.

"No," he said with a laugh, "nothing like that."

"Satellite dishwasher?"

"Good one. No, I'm chief mediartist for MU—that's Media Uplink. We gather, edit, condense, censor, and program up media packages to be sent to the *Ares*. We're sort of like their very own personal 'net, keeping them up on most of the news, the latest music and movies, and make sure they don't miss a single episode of *Doobville*."

Jeff's face lit. "I *love* that show!" He carried his phone in his hand, and now pointed it at Daveed. *"Dun't make me use this!"* he growled, imitating Deputy Brickbat, an overweight, updated Barney Fife who was always grabbing the wrong thing while trying to arrest people.

Daveed rated the show as submoronic, but wasn't inclined to quibble over the man's taste in sitcoms. "So do a couple of the crew. They get it, and everything else, with maybe a tenth the commercials of normal feeds."

Jeff looked surprised. "You send them *commercials*?"

"Sure. See, commercials are such an integral part of popular culture that editing them all out would leave the crew missing quite a few references when they return. But we spare them the massive redundancy and repetition the rest of us have to endure."

"Lucky bastards." Jeff shoved the phone into his pocket, then cracked his knuckles. A bad habit that reminded Daveed of Alec, who used to do the same thing.

He shrugged. "Depends on how you look at it. Too many would drive them nuts anyway. It's not like they can step out to score a beer or a pizza if an ad gives them an itch."

"I guess not. Still, it's—" Jeff looked away, then stopped and pointed. "Hey, look at that!"

Daveed looked where the other man directed, went

cold inside. They were passing an alley between a shoe
store and a Korean deli. At the rear of the alley, back
in the shadows past the Dumpsters, a woman was
sprawled on the ground. Her skirt was rucked up around
her waist and one arm was flung across her eyes. On the
pavement lay her opened purse, its contents spread
across the asphalt.

"Oh jeez," Daveed gasped. "It looks like she got
mugged!" He pushed past Jeff and ran toward her, his
heart pounding in his chest.

Skidding to a halt beside her he knelt, trying to remember everything from the mandatory first-aid class
he'd taken when he signed on with Uncle Joe. He was
relieved to see that there was no blood, and that she
seemed to be breathing normally. At first glance no
bones seemed to be broken, and since it was pretty obvious that she still had her underwear on, she probably
hadn't been raped. Getting mugged was plenty bad
enough.

"Are you okay, lady?" he asked gently. Did he have
his phone with him? Yes. Hers was lying right there
beside her, but that might be evidence. He started to
reach into his pocket. "Just hold still. I'll call the police
and an ambulance."

When she lifted her arm off her face and he saw that
there was no blood or bruising, his first thought was one
of relief that she hadn't been given a street makeover.
On the heels of that came the realization that she was
grinning up at him.

"Probably gonna need that ambulance, monkey boy,"
she said with laugh. "Or maybe a hearse."

A second later something slammed into him from the
side. His phone went flying from his hand, and the next
thing he knew he was curled on the ground, arms
wrapped around the fire in his ribs. His sunglasses hung
askew, and he peered past them to stare up at Jeff.

Who wore a grin to match that of the woman.

Oh shit, he thought, as the woman stood up, dusted
herself off, and retrieved her phone and purse.

"We got us a nice slab of faggot monkey meat here,
Bets," Jeff said with a laugh so cold it made Daveed
shiver. "What you think we ought to do with it?"

"Please," he whispered, searching the blond man's face for some spark of mercy or humanity. There was none.

"Looks to me like the meat could use some tenderizing," the woman answered, eyeing him like a dark smear on a toilet seat.

"Sounds good to me. Queerboy here makes TV shows for the niggers and foreign trash on the *Ares*. Don't you, Paki?" With that Jeff lashed out, driving his booted toe into Daveed's back. "Fuckin' towelhead said he was an *American!*"

"Please don't," Daveed groaned. He looked toward the mouth of the alley, but there was no one there. He began trying to crawl in that direction, wanting only to get away.

"We're not done with you yet, queerbait!" Jeff snarled, grabbing him by the arm and hauling him back. He gagged on a scream as he felt something tear in his elbow. The couple moved in, and went to work with their fists and feet.

All he could do was curl into a tight ball and try to survive. Then one blow caught him behind the ear, and just like in the movies, everything . . . faded . . . to . . . black. . . .

"Easy, man. Don't move."
Daveed tried to open his eyes. Only one seemed to work, and not all that well. He blinked, and the blur finally resolved. Bending over him was the big Indian with the sidewalk turquoise stand.

"Wh—" he began, then lost the rest to coughing. *What happened? Why aren't I dead?*

"They're gone now. You're safe." In the distance he could hear a siren growing louder. "Hear that? The cavalry is on its way."

Daveed swallowed hard, tasting blood. "Did you . . ."

"Chase them off? Yeah, I did." The siren stopped, followed by the sound of slamming doors. "Now you just lie still and let me handle this."

His savior stood up, turned toward the mouth of the alley. He reached into his shirt, pulled out something shiny, and held it out for the approaching policemen to see.

"UNSIA," he called. "Captain Jasper Crow."

United Nations Security Intelligence Agency? Daveed thought woozily. They sell *jewelry*?

"What we got?" asked one of the cops, a rawboned, leathery-looking cowboy type. Except for the blue Neely PD uniform, he could have stepped from any one of a million Westerns.

Crow knelt back down beside Daveed. "Fists beat the living hell out of one of our people. I couldn't ID the male assailant, but recognized the woman. It was Betsy Ross Jones." His gaze flicked past the cops. "You've got an ambulance coming, right? This dude needs it pronto."

"Don't worry, one's coming," said the other cop, a short, heavyset Italian-looking man with a big mustache and sad Pacino eyes. He tapped the bud in his left ear. "ETA one minute."

"Great. Have your office pull Jones's jacket. This bitch is bad news. What we have here is one of her usual gigs, posing as a mugging victim. Has an accomplice maneuver her quarry so they'll see her. When they come to help they get one nasty surprise."

The cowboy cop shook his head in disgust. "Shit, I thought we had a handle on all the Fist-fuckers 'round here."

"She usually works the East Coast. She came in under our radar, too."

Daveed lay there listening to this exchange, feeling like he'd wandered into some gritty police drama. Then he heard the distinct and distant sound of an ambulance siren.

"I'll go out, grease the skids for the medics," the shorter cop said. "We'll have you outta here in no time, kid." He turned and ran toward the mouth of the alley, moving pretty fast for a guy his size.

"Your limo's almost here," Crow told him with a smile. "Hang in there a little longer."

"You got ID on the victim?" the cowboy cop asked.

"Yeah. His name is Daveed Shah." A glance up, his face expressionless. "American-born, third-generation. A full citizen of this great country of ours."

The cop sighed and pushed his hat back on his head. "I'm not some dumb-ass redneck, Captain Crow. Way I figure it, the UN emplacement is the best thing ever happened around here. Kept this town from dryin' up and blowin' away. Best thing ever happened to me, too."

"How's that?"

"Met my wife, Miriam. She's a translator. Comes from Senegal." A significant look. "That's in Africa."

Daveed watched this really wonderful smile spread across Crow's face. "Some say we all do, brother," he said, then looked past the cop and his smile grew even wider. "Here come the paramedics, Daveed. Gonna have you fixed up in no time."

Seconds later he was surrounded by intent faces. Gloved hands were all over him, probing and prodding. He managed to hang on until they transferred him to a stretcher.

When that happened a vast white surge of pain washed everyone and everything away.

He came to again flat on his back in a hospital room. After a few seconds of getting his head screwed on right again he remembered how he'd gotten there.

Jeff. The attack in the alley. Captain Crow. Cops.

"Welcome back to the land of the living," someone said quietly over on his left.

He turned his head. Captain Crow was sitting there in a chair beside his bed, a UN-issue slayte in his lap.

"Thanks," he whispered. He swallowed and tried again, his voice coming out a little stronger and clearer this time. "So I'm not dead?"

Crow shook his head. "Naw. You're banged up, but not totaled. Got a mild concussion. Two cracked ribs. A bruised kidney. Various abrasions and contusions. Your right elbow got separated, but don't worry, I had them fix it just the way you wanted."

Daveed looked down, saw that his left arm was in a cast. But instead of being at a right angle, the cast left it halfway between bent and straight. He looked back up, puzzled.

"You don't remember?"

"No." He didn't even know there was anything *to* remember.

"Well, you came sort of half-to in the emergency

room. I stuck with you, telling them I had to make sure you didn't blab any top-secret stuff. You seemed to understand the doc when she said she was gonna put your arm in a cast. You got real upset and started saying the same name over and over again, telling her you wanted it fixed like his."

Still no bells rung in his head. "Like whose?"

"Les Paul."

Daveed scowled, then got it. "Wow." He blinked. "Was I on drugs?"

"Oh yeah. Lucky for you I know my guitar hero history."

The famed guitarist and producer had been in an accident which destroyed his right elbow. Paul had the doctors set it in a permanent guitar playing angle. While Daveed didn't play music, the angle of the cast would allow him to use his deck's pads and keyboard.

"Thanks."

"No problem." The man's smile faded, leaving his copper-skinned face solemn and sober. "I'm really sorry about this, Daveed."

He managed a half-assed shrug. "It's not your fault, Captain."

"Jasper. No, but it's my job to be on the lookout for these skugs, and I could have been a lot faster on the uptake. You and pretty boy walked by, there one minute, gone the next. I was positive your Uncle Joe jacket wasn't just a souvenir, but it took longer than it should have to get your ID locked down. You did come up gay, but your PR was only one."

"PR?" What did public relations have to do with this?

"Promiscuity Rating—and by the way, that puts you on the hermit side of normal. You and pretty boy didn't look or sound all that hot to trot, but that didn't mean you hadn't flexed into that alley for some trashy privacy. Then I got a hit on my description of your companion, mostly thanks to that tattoo of his. No name, but a red flag saying someone who could be his twin was a White Fist, and had been spotted at some fag and wog bashings. Once I knew that, I hauled ass to check on you."

"I'm glad you did."

"Me too, brother." Crow stood up, tucked the slayte

under his arm. "I've got to book now and file my report, but if you don't mind, I'll drop in later to check on you."

"You really don't have to."

"I'll inform your section heads and get you put on medical leave for the time being. You're going to be here overnight. Got any pets need caring for?"

"No."

The big man smiled. "Me, I've got a cat. Her name's Ungrateful Bitch. Fits, too." He patted Daveed's hand. "You take it easy, man. I'll be in to see you later."

"You really don't have to come back," Daveed repeated.

Jasper Crow looked him in the eye, his bronze face utterly deadpan. "Maybe I want to. You rather I didn't?"

"No. You saved my life. If you want to come back and kick me out of bed and take it for yourself, you've earned it."

"Naw, I don't believe I'd ever kick you out of bed." With that, he turned and headed for the door.

Daveed just stared. *No, it couldn't be.*

Crow turned back for a last look, winked, then went on out the door whistling an old pop song. As the door closed behind him the name of it came up.

It was the old Beatles tune "I Want to Hold Your Hand."

Maybe . . .

He was still lying there in a daze, trying to decide if what he thought had just happened had really happened when a stout, dark-haired woman in a nurse's uniform bustled in.

"Oh, you're awake now, Mr. Shah," she said. "How are you feeling?"

Even though it made his face hurt, he still smiled. Couldn't have stopped if he wanted to.

"Better now." He settled back, checking out the screen facing the bed and wondering how many channels it pulled.

"Not in any pain?"

"Not anymore."

Bunking at the Bunker

Dan was *impressed*.

Not that he wasn't still wondering why the hell he was there, and if leaving might be advisable—or even possible. These issues had just gotten sort of relegated to the bottom of the pile, superseded by uneasy wonder.

"This is some shanty you have here, Jamal," he said, setting a new personal best for understatement.

The big agoraphobe nodded absently as he headed for one of the at least two dozen stand-alone workstations, media decks, and other high-tech who-knew-whats filling the room. "Thanks. Please allow me a minute here, then I shall be able to give you my undivided attention."

"Sure. It's not like I'm going anywhere." That comment topped his first understatement, hands down. He was definitely on a roll. The place where Amber and Jamal lived was called the Bunker, and the name sure as hell fit. There were probably maximum security prisons where it would be easier just to step outside for a minute.

Soon after Amber returned to resume driving—grinning from ear to ear and reeking of sex—they crossed into Ohio, got off the highway, and began following a series of increasingly smaller and less-traveled roads, finally ending up on something called Nil Road, out on the back side of nowhere. She turned off this country two-lane onto a long asphalt driveway leading to a blocky, windowless, aggressively nondescript two-story building. It didn't look like a house or much of anything else; it was just a giant concrete cube with two doors in front. A small sign over the larger steel overhead door read J & A ENTERPRISES.

As they rolled up the drive she retrieved a purple-plastic XoLog slayte off the dash, and began hammering in words and numbers one-handed. By the time they reached the building, the overhead door was lifting before them, a set of far thicker inner doors behind it sliding back out of the way. She drove inside, steering the truck past three other vehicles parked inside the cavernous structure; a new-looking blue Mercedes sedan, a sleek black motorcycle, and a pink 1950s vintage Cadillac complete with ragtop and tailfins. Once on the far side of the building she parked the truck on a steel platform beside what looked to Dan like Fort Knox's loading dock.

Working the slayte two-handed now, more codes and passwords caused the platform to move smoothly sideways, taking the rear side door of the truck closer to the dock. An airlock sort of thing came out from the wall and pressed up against the side of the truck, providing a sealed passageway.

"A rich survivalist named Millard Funston built this place," Amber explained as she got out of the driver's seat and led Dan into the back. "Remember the Panic of '13? That sent him here to wait out the end of the world."

The Panic had been set off by the second Chinese civil war of the new millennium, the one where they came too damn close to swapping nuclear insults. The Modern Moderatists had won that one, and things had been pretty calm since. There, anyway.

She collected Jamal, who was deeply engrossed in something on another slayte, this one a high-end CyZilla. He never even looked up from its screen as she led him by the arm through the enclosed lock and into an elevator big enough and fancy enough to carry a rajah's favorite elephants. The doors were not just beautiful, all ornately carved wood panels with brass fittings, they looked like they'd been designed to stand up to anything just short of a direct hit by a nuclear bomb. When they closed Dan couldn't help but notice that the elevator had no controls.

"Down," Amber said. The elevator chimed in response.

"Dumb fucker died down there," she continued as they began to descend. "My sweetie here was the one who hacked—remotely of course—the codes to let the cops and the crew from the meat wagon in. Picked the place up from his estate for chump change afterward."

"What did he die of?"

She shook her head, her expression turning grim. "Terminal case of RTFM got him. Lemme tell you, it was awful."

Dan swallowed hard, imagining some sort of virulent disease. "RTFM? Is it, um, contagious?"

"Prevalent, yes. Contagious, no," Jamal rumbled, finally looking up from his slayte and giving his companion an amused sideways glance. "RTFM stands for Read the Fucking Manual, an old computer term from the days before smartware. Funston turned off all the external air sources before learning how to make the scrubbers and reprocessors work. The man wasn't exactly a rocket scientist to begin with—he came from old money—and anoxia dumbed him down even further."

"Yeah, like to dirt," Amber cackled.

The elevator slowed, stopped.

"How far down are we?" Dan asked as the doors opened on a marble-tiled vestibule with yet another armored door opposite them, one that looked like it had come from a yard sale at NORAD. Beside the door was a cast-iron lawn jockey painted in grinning blackface, an antique computer mouse dangling from his hand.

"About a hundred feet."

Jamal stepped out of the elevator and crossed to the far wall. His thick fingers danced across the keypad set beside the door. Another chime sounded, and there was the muted thump of locks releasing. "Used to be a voice saying welcome, but Amber killed it," he explained as the door swung open with a soft whirr. "You should hear her argue with vending machines."

As it was opening a shrill buzzer sounded, making Dan jump.

Amber hauled out her phone, glanced at its screen. "Delivery," she groused, turning and heading back into the elevator. "You boys play nice now."

"I'll leave the door open for you," Jamal said, propping it open with the lawn jockey, then motioning Dan to follow him inside.

Dan didn't know what to expect. What he walked into was a place worthy of the featured layout in a special edition of *Better Homes and Gardens* devoted to eccentric survivalist software moguls; call it *Better Homes and Bomb Shelters*.

Right after they went inside Jamal excused himself to go commune with his waiting equipment, leaving Dan to stand there and sightsee.

The place was an odd melange of megabuck mansion and cyboid playpen. The high, barrel-vaulted ceiling was done in varnished blond wood, darker wood beams supporting brass paddle fans and crystal chandeliers. The walls were beaded wood wainscoting and gray-veined white-marble tiles. The room had to be forty feet long and just as wide, the center of the parquet floor covered with a thick Persian rug that looked like it had to be worth more than he made in a decade.

The furniture and art objects scattered around all had the look of serious money and good taste—except for the odd lava lamp, monkey-in-a-fez candle, life-size Lego-block nude, and pinball machine. As for all the high-tech equipment, he had the feeling that one wrong keystroke might just launch a nuclear strike or crash the stock market. It seemed like a good idea to wait in a spot with no buttons or breakables nearby, and keep his hands firmly in his pockets.

"There," Jamal said after a couple minutes of intense work, pushing his chair back and rising. "Pardon the interruption."

"No problem. Now what?"

"We lay our plans and prepare. Come on, follow me."

The big man led him through an arched doorway on the left side of the room and through a wide hall that looked like it belonged in the castle of some semimajor nobility. An opening off that took them through a wood-paneled dining room dominated by a carved oak table large enough to seat thirty, an elaborate HO gauge train set spread across its top. That led to a modern kitchen most chefs would kill for. Jamal went to a fancy chrome-and-glass coffeemaker that looked capable of producing your choice of regular coffee, espresso, or cold fusion, and began filling it.

"I like my coffee better than Amber's," he said over his shoulder as he worked. "Please don't tell her."

"Sure. Your secret's safe with me."

"Thank you. This should be ready in a minute. We might as well get comfortable while we wait."

There was a smaller antique oak table with matching ladder-back chairs in one corner of the kitchen. Once they were seated, Jamal leaned back and sighed. "Home again." He made it sound like a return to Nirvana.

"Relieved?" A bit of a homebody himself, he knew how good it felt to be back where you belonged. Now Jamal was, he wasn't, and he had to wonder when he'd get back again.

"Stupendously. I am just as relieved that you consented to come with me. It makes facing the task we undertake seem much more achievable."

Finally, it looked like he was going to get some sort of handle on what was happening. That would be nice for a change.

"Look," he said. "Mind if I talk a minute before we get into some sort of strategy session? Lay out where I stand?"

Jamal spread his hands. "The floor is yours."

Dan took a deep breath and tried to organize his thoughts, a process not unlike attempting to pick up peas with a knife.

"Okay. I start hearing this voice in my head. First it says it wants my help, next it says it's an *alien*, and wants my help. Then you show up, tell me you've heard it, too, that it's real, and you need my help. I don't want to believe that, but I seem to anyway. I let you drag me back here—hell, I even drive part of the way!"

He paused, realizing he was getting cranked when he wanted to stay calm and logical. He held up his hands. "Okay, I'm here. But I have to tell you, I sure hope you have some sort of plan because I happen to be entirely fucking lost!"

"I know this is difficult," Jamal said in a kindly tone. "Your life has been turned upside down."

"More like inside out."

"I understand that. Unfortunately, our situation is only likely to get more complicated."

Dan slumped morosely back in his chair. "Oh good."

"But be of good cheer. We are not without resources, both internal and external." A discreet beep sounded. "Speaking of which, our coffee is ready."

Dan waited while Jamal bustled about preparing a tray, then returning with cups, a thermal carafe, and a fairly expensive-looking bottle of brandy. He poured coffee for both of them, and after adding a liberal dollop of brandy to his own, offered the bottle to Dan. He shook his head no. Getting hammered again might be necessary later, but for the moment he was determined to get his shit more together, not less.

"Saving Avva will be difficult," Jamal said after taking a sip from his own cup, a pinky the size of Dan's thumb genteelly extended. "The more help we have, the greater our chances of success. Fortunately, we are not alone in this."

Dan found himself leaning forward and nodding. It was more a feeling than a roster of names, but his last contact with the alien had left him with that distinct impression.

"So logically our first order of business should be to identify and contact these others, just as I did with you."

"How? It was just luck you saw me spaz out on-air."

"We have more than luck working on our side. I already have a flock of flying monkeys at work on this very task."

"A flock of *what*?" Dan asked, thinking maybe he'd let himself get hijacked by a maniac after all.

A shy smile. "Aware software agents of my own design. I send them out to search for what I want and bring it back to me. Just like the flying monkeys in *The Wizard of Oz*. I have a certain peculiar fondness for that movie."

"Whew. You had me worried there for a minute."

Jamal's smile turned sad, a hint of the sort of pain his life caused him moving behind his face and eyes. "I am quite neurotic, severely phobic, and by most conventional standards extremely eccentric." He regarded Dan with a hurt and hopeful look. "But I assure you, I am not insane."

"I never thought—" Damn, he hadn't meant to hurt

the poor guy's feelings. "This whole thing has made me kind of jumpy, that's all."

"No, your reservations are quite understandable. Your life has become overtaken by forces you don't understand and cannot control. In my clumsy attempt to contact you and gain your help I have become yet another of these forces. For this I most humbly apologize. It was never my intention to frighten or intimidate."

"No, that's okay. *Really.* You and Amber are a little weird, maybe, but you're a helluva lot better prepared to deal with this than I am or could ever be. To tell you the truth, I don't know *what* use I can be to you or our friend on Phobos."

Jamal gave him a grateful smile. "Thank you, Dan. As for your ability to help, don't sell yourself short. I think it quite likely that each and every one of us who has been contacted has some unique quality and ability necessary to the completion of this task. We were not called at random, but carefully chosen by a highly acute intelligence."

"Maybe, but I hope the others have better résumés than I." He took a sip of coffee, then an appreciative gulp. It *was* better than Amber's. "Okay, enough mutual admiration and apology. How do you plan to find these others?"

"Largely through the gathering and sorting of information. For instance, you sought medical help as a result of being called. It is quite likely that some of the others may have done the same thing. So my monkeys are out sticking their clever noses into everything from medical-record databases to login help lines, searching for people who report 'symptoms' similar to those we experienced. If I am not mistaken, the delivery Amber went up to collect is devices which will let us fine-tune our search."

"What are they? Nut detectors?"

Jamal laughed and topped off his cup with brandy, then held out the bottle, one eyebrow cocked in question.

"Sure. Why not?" A *little* couldn't hurt.

"I have procured two devices called BAIMs," Jamal explained as he poured. "That stands for Brain Activity Imagining Monitors. They are a standard neurological testing device. You and I will each wear one for the next day or two. That way when we are contacted again, any unusual cerebral activity created by this event will be identified and quantified. If atypical activity is recorded, we will create a composite from our two profiles, and then search for other instances of a similar profile being taken. While all this is going on we shall also be monitoring the media for reports of people who say they have experienced episodes similar to ours."

Dan swallowed a mouthful of brandy-laced coffee. "Going to find a lot of crackbrains that way, aren't we?"

"No doubt. But we may also find allies."

He put down his cup. "Okay, say we do find others. What then? Do we start a support group?"

Jamal chuckled. "In a sense, yes. Together we must use whatever means are at our collective disposal to accomplish this mission with which we have been entrusted."

"Save . . ." It was still hard to say the name out loud; somehow that made the whole crazy business all too real. "Save Avva."

"Precisely."

"How?"

"There is only one possible way. That is to get the *Ares* mission diverted to Phobos."

Dan slumped in his chair. "*That's* the big plan? We convince the UN to divert a zillion-dollar space mission to go rescue a little green man that a handful of people say they are hearing in their heads?"

A solemn nod. "As I said before, the task ahead of us may be difficult."

With that remark, Jamal took from Dan the title for reigning Master of Understatement.

About an hour later, after Amber had returned with a box containing two BAIM units and associated hard-and software, Dan had a small unhappy revelation. It came when Jamal slotted a slim black wafer into a stand-alone bay already bristling with such devices. It was the word he used to describe it that made Dan slap his forehead in consternation.

The word? "Daughterboard."

"I've got to use a phone," he groaned, slapping his pockets and finding his own NokiTel nowhere on him.

Then he remembered getting it out during his stint as truck driver, thinking about calling Morty so at least somebody would know where he was. Amber had come back before he'd made the call. His phone was probably still up on the dash of the truck.

He looked around, trying to figure out which, if any, of the millions' worth of electronics around him might be or could at least act like a phone, and feeling a bit like a Stone Age handyman lost in the hardware department at Sears.

Jamal glanced up from his work. "Something wrong?"

"My daughter, Bobbi. I was supposed to call her last night, but didn't. Shit!" *That's because you were dead drunk,* he reminded himself, *and it slipped what was left of your mind. Great father you are.*

"A phone call, eh? We have the technology. Come on over here." He collected a chair and parked it at the console beside him, then tapped a couple buttons. "There you go."

"Thanks." Dan sat down facing the screen. It read READY. NUMBER/ADDRESS? He took a moment to compose himself, then pecked in the number for Tammy's house and the extension for Bobbi and Susannah's wing.

The display went orange, with the yellow-and-black Maximum Retaliatory Response security warning triskelion prominently displayed.

"Van Buren residence," a robot voice said in a cold, brusque tone calculated to freeze the blood of any wrong number or phleech. *"You are hereby advised that your number has already been traced and logged. Please state your name and the reason for your call in the next five seconds or this connection will be terminated and retaliatory action commenced. Have a nice day."*

"Bobbi? Susannah? It's me, Dan!"

"Oh, Mr. Francisco!" The warning screen vanished, replaced by Susannah's image. As usual she was in her working uniform of a dark shapeless sweater, starched Peter-Pan-collared blouse with a cameo pin covering the modestly buttoned top button. Her wheat-colored hair was up in a tight bun, and her round scrubbed face wore a stiff, proper smile.

"How are you doing, sir?" she asked with an air of cool formality.

Her tone and attitude, and the *sir* he'd gotten her to drop after the first couple months were a tipoff that his dear sweet ex was in residence. She'd been known to eavesdrop on his calls to his daughter before. That way she could make better offers and tell the child everything her daddy said was wrong.

"Better," he replied, the lie slipping glibly off his tongue. "I was sicker than a dog last night, and slept most of the evening. That's why I didn't call."

"I saw you become unwell during your broadcast, sir. Your daughter did not, and I withheld mention of it, believing it best not to worry her. Nor did I mention the arrangements for next weekend. I do hope you are better. I know you won't want to miss a trip to Skyles Lake. I am rather looking forward to it myself."

"I'm fine now, really."

"I am so glad to hear that."

"Thanks. Is Bobbi there?"

"Daddy!" she squealed, materializing beside her nanny. "Where have you *been*?"

Her blond hair, the same color as her mother's, was pulled back into two pigtails that had partly lost their grip. Proof of paternity—not that he needed any, he'd fallen so deeply in love the first time he'd seen her he wouldn't have cared if she'd been Avva's child—showed in her miniature copy of his build, all bony limbs, and sharp elbows and knees poking out of pink biballs and a Rockett Raccoon tee shirt. Her face was somewhere in between. Tammy's features and some—but thankfully not all—of his nose made her look like a young Cleopatra.

"Under the bed," he answered, his heart melting like a chocolate kiss in the sun from just looking at her. "Wrestling dust bunnies." He made a tragic face. "They won, Pumpkin, taking me two falls out of three. I had to say uncle to make them let me go."

"You didn't call last night!"

"I know, hon. I was sick with a bug and didn't want to give it to you."

"Daddy, you can't get bugs over the *phone*!"

He frowned, pinching his chin thoughtfully. "Are you sure about that?"

" 'Course I am." She glanced at her nanny for confirmation. "Right, Susannah?"

"Perhaps some bugs," she offered diplomatically. "We can look it up later. But for the moment, aren't you glad your father is feeling better now?"

"Oh, sure." A gimlet-eyed look that carried a faint echo of her mother appeared on her face. "Susannah says we're not coming to stay with you this weekend. Mom's taking us to Paris, France, instead."

"That's right. Your mom has to go there, and wanted to take you along. I said it was okay." Under duress, of course.

Out came the lower lip. "But I don't *want* to go to Paris! I want to stay with you! We were gonna carve punkins!"

"We will, Sugar. You see, since you're going with your mom this weekend, next weekend you, Miss Roberta Francisco, get a fabulous, all-expenses-paid, three-day trip to the cabin with me!"

Her eyes lit, and the bright spark of her joy crossed the distance between them like it wasn't even there, lighting up his insides with a father's bliss. "We're going to the *lake*?"

"That's the place."

"Do I get to go *fishing*?"

"You bet. We can go out in the boat, drown millions of worms. Pick wild apples and bake them in a pie. We can even go hunting bears in our pajamas." He shook his head and frowned. "Can't have bears running around wearing our pajamas."

"I want to go *now*!"

"I know. But you'll like Paris. I bet Susannah knows all sorts of glide places to go and naz things to see. Isn't the Taj Mahal in Paris?"

His daughter giggled, a sound that always undid him. "No, silly, that's in India. The Eiffel Tower is in Paris."

He bit his lip. "You're sure about that?"

"Uh-huh. Then there's the Loofa."

"That's the *Louvre*," Susannah corrected gently, trying to hide a smile.

"Yeah. She took me on a virt. They have pictures and statues of naked people!"

"*Naked* naked?" he asked in mock shock.

"Naked naked *naked*! Why?"

Dan bit back the impulse to say *ask your mother*. After all, she was the one who kept getting "accidentally" prazzied bare-assed, coincidentally goosing her ratings each time the tabloid sheets and shows splashed her tits and ass.

He scratched his head. "Maybe somebody stole their clothes?"

"I guess," she said, sounding unconvinced.

"Okay, Bobbster, I've got to go now. You be good, and have fun in Paris. Remember, next weekend we camp."

"Can we have beans for dinner?" She giggled. "Musical fruit! Have beans for supper and all go toot! Even Susannah. Fart-O-Rama time!"

"*Language* . . . Bobbi," Susannah chided in a choked voice. The poor woman looked like she was about to burst from the effort of keeping her laughter contained.

"We'll make beautiful bean music together," he promised. "Right, Susannah?"

He couldn't begin to decipher the look she gave him. "I will do my best to participate in any recreations you propose, sir."

"Then it's settled. 'Night now, Bobs. I love you."

"Bye, Daddy. I love you, too." The screen went blank.

Dan let out a sigh of relief that his lapse had not scarred the poor kid for life, then turned his chair toward his host to say thanks. Jamal was staring at him with a sad and pensive look on his bearded face.

"What's wrong?"

He shook his head, producing an unconvincing smile. "Nothing."

He picked up the electrode-studded BAIM headweb on the table before him. "Let's get you wired up for the night."

PART 4

Attempted Response

The Speed of Thought

Life is good, Daveed mused as he sat there watching the crimson sun sink lower and lower, its edge just touching the distant horizon.

Captain Crow had come back to the hospital not long after dinner, and with the nurse's blessing, helped him into a wheelchair. After taking him down to the ground floor he'd pushed him out onto a west-facing flagstone patio at the rear of the hospital, then appropriated a chair from a nearby table and sat down beside him. Nobody else was out there.

First they talked about his case. There was an APB out on the woman who had attacked him, the infamous Betsy Ross Jones. He didn't know how to feel about being trashed by such a famous terrorist. It was the sort of dubious honor he would have gladly gone without.

The UNSIA agent warned him that the chances of capturing Jones and Jeff weren't great. She had been a federal fugitive for over two years, managing to evade capture each time the law closed in, and twice her escape had been purchased at the cost of police officers' lives. Jeff was an unknown quantity, but there were reports of a man answering his description linked to several ugly hate crimes over the past year, three of them resulting in fatalities. A composite sketch of him was in circulation, but aside from his tattoo, he just wasn't that distinctive-looking. Jasper was pretty sure the long hair had been a wig.

Official opinion, largely based on what they knew of Jones's usual habits and methods, was that the two of them were long gone. Daveed hoped so. The only time he ever wanted to see them again was on the news, after they were behind bars.

Jasper—they were definitely on a first-name basis

now—went on to tell him that the incident had been reported to his superiors as a simple case of Daveed being tricked by Jones's pretending to be a mugging victim. No one would think he'd gotten into this jam while trolling. No one but the Goat, who was guaranteed to think the worst, no matter what happened.

Talk moved on to more pleasant matters. The good and bad points of having the UN for an employer, and of living in Neely. The *Ares* mission, and how life on what seemed like perpetual overtime had blasted both of their personal lives into space as well.

After a while the talk trailed away, and they sat there in a companionable silence, soaking up the magnificent desert sunset. Jasper slouched in his chair, legs crossed at the ankles and puffing on a small cigar, seemingly not the least bit eager to go—or be—anywhere else.

The shadows lengthened. The distant hills turned purple, and the sky became the color of a seashell's secret insides. Daveed tried to remember the last time he'd sat down to watch a sunset, that most ordinary and spectacular of events. Had it been weeks ago? Months ago? He supposed that was what happened when your life got eaten up by your work. You became a blind drone, scuttling between work and home, noticing nothing outside or in between. Missing almost everything.

"Sure is beautiful," Jasper said quietly.

Daveed opened his mouth to answer, but all that came out was a strangled sound, like he had a chicken bone caught in his throat.

But the problem wasn't there, it was in his head. *Again.*

The vista before him went out of focus, and his ears began to ring. The wheelchair beneath him, the man beside him, and the patio they were on ceased to exist as the presence he'd felt before returned, in swelling light and sound and sensation, in complex conflicting emotion lifting and buffeting him like a fragile kite in a high wind rising to hurricane force.

He heard Jasper call *Daveed?* in the moment before another voice came to him from the rising chaos, sweet and beautiful, vast and strange.

*   *   *

Alexei Kasparov's meditations on the speed of thought were being proved out, for at the very same instant Daveed felt the intruding touch of an alien mind, so did the others.

Martina was stretched out in her hospital bed at the Kasparov Institute, watching the tube. She'd accessed ICNN and asked for all available news on Secretary-General Perez. Now a half dozen Ricos in a variety of situations and poses were on her screen, sitting in meetings, making speeches, and joking with reporters.

She feasted on the sight of him and drank in the sound of his voice, aching with the urge to be at his side once more. When her head once again began filling with Avva's presence the remote slipped from her fingers and fell to the floor. She sank back into the pillows, clenching her teeth and fists as she tried to fight off the intrusion, but in the end she could only surrender and be taken by it.

In a fancy kitchen buried deep underground, Dan and Jamal, both wearing BAIM headwebs like electronic Rasta wigs, stopped dead in the middle of dinner. Dan dropped his fork, a splash of red sweet-and-sour sauce spattering like blood across his shirt. Jamal was better able to control himself. He put down his cutlery and composed himself to receive whatever it was Avva wanted to impart. Amber looked from one man to the other, shook her head and, whistling the theme song from *The Twilight Zone*, stole the eggroll off her lover's plate.

The Reverend Ray Sunshine was alone in his study, forging plans for the great crusade to come. *"Thank you, Jesus!"* he gasped as contact swept over him. THANK YOU, JESUS! the dictation program he was using dutifully echoed, writing the words across his desktop's screen. The next things it wrote were less coherent and followed by a hash of <???> marks, asking for confirmation or clarification.

Four light-minutes closer to Phobos, it was Girls' Night on the *Ares*.

Jane and Anna and Wanda had taken over the wardroom for their weekly gathering. The three of them drank watery nonalcoholic beer as they gabbed, laughed, and did each other's hair. Wanda was the mainspring behind these soirees, and thanks to her clowning and natural ability to repair damn near anything, people included, Anna's face had lost some of its haunted look. Even Jane felt herself beginning to slough off some of the tension she'd been carrying, at least until she felt a sudden chill followed by a warning twang of her over-stretched nerves.

They had been working on Wanda's hair. She dropped the braid she was plaiting and, pleading a sudden cramp, fled for the head. She was just barely able to bolt the door behind her before contact came, dropping her to her knees.

No! was the last coherent thought she had for a time.

They were not the only ones who experienced Avva's touch, but the few others felt it only glancingly, a whispering eddy off a great mental slipstream. It was those few who caught the full force of his mind-to-mind connection, and they heard the voice of the sender even more clearly and comprehensibly than the time before. There could be no misunderstanding of what he wanted.

This did not make any of their lives any easier.

Naming the Spirit

Daveed peered through the tears blurring his eyes into the concerned face of Jasper Crow. The salt made the cuts burn. He wiped his face on the sleeve of his good arm.

"You're back," the UNSIA agent said. "Are you okay, man?"

Daveed returned a shaky nod. "Yeah, I'm all right."

"Good. Want to tell me what just happened?"

He looked down at his hands. "I don't know if I can." *Or should.*

Jasper leaned closer and closed the strong bronze fingers of one hand ever so gently around his own. His one hand was the size of both of Daveed's. "I'm a good listener, Daveed. Real good."

That was true, it was one of the things he liked best about the man, but he had to shrug.

"It's . . ." He shrugged again. How did you describe the indescribable, and explain the inexplicable? Plus if he did, that pretty well guaranteed a fast end to this first date, if that was what this really was.

"Let me tell you what I saw," Jasper said quietly. "You seemed to have some sort of fit. At first I thought you were in pain, but just as I was about to holler for a nurse you went real still and began to talk. Not to me, either. Made the hair stand up on the back of my head." He lifted his long braided ponytail to illustrate. "Wish you coulda seen it."

"Why didn't you call for the men in the white coats? It's obvious I'm off my nut." Jasper still held his hands, and the big man's grip was warm and reassuring. He wanted to grab on hard and hold tight, but was afraid that would make him pull away.

Jasper chuckled and gave his fingers a squeeze. "You're forgetting that I grew up in a different culture than yours, white man. I've seen stuff like this before."

That made him look up. Jasper was watching him, a crooked smile on his face. "You have?"

"Sure. My gramma was a shaman. She talked with the spirits all the time, just sat there jawing away with nobody anyone else could see. Afterward, she'd tell someone where to drill their well, or what was wrong with their corn, or why their luck had gone bad. Folks listened to her because what she said was mostly always right. This spirit of yours have a name?"

"Avva," he whispered, for the very first time, saying out loud the name that had been haunting his thoughts.

"Avva," Jasper repeated. He shook his head. "Never heard of that one." He lifted one eyebrow. "Asian import, maybe?"

Daveed couldn't help smiling. It was a tired smile, and still muted by fear and doubt, but it felt good. "He's not a spirit."

"Ah. What is he then, a ghost?"

"No, not a ghost either." Daveed summoned all his nerve, then gazed straight into the steady brown eyes of the man who held his hands, and now maybe other things as well.

"Are you sure you want to get tangled up in all this?"

Jasper did not look away. "Yes," he said without a single trace of uncertainty. "I want to know everything about you, Daveed."

So as the sun vanished below the horizon and the first stars came into view, he began to tell the story of how a voice had come to him out of the void, and the strange, unbelievable message it spoke. .

Hard Data

Martina was still slumped against the pillows, gloomily staring at nothing when Alexei came running into her room wearing the face of a man who has just won the lottery.

"You have it *happen*!" he crowed excitedly. "Yes?"

"Yes," she agreed dolefully.

"Is *incredible*! I have computer BAIM is slaved to page me if unusual activity occurs. It goes beep, I run like bastard to monitoring station. Episode is over by the time I get there, but I have record of whole thing!" He thrust the elegant silver-and-rosewood Mont Blanc slayte he was carrying in her direction. "See?"

She ignored the device and stared at him. "You say machine has done its job. Am I insane, Alexei Leonid? Tell me truth now."

Just like the times before, the experience—and the loss of control it entailed—had shaken her to the very roots of her being. Her whole life had been dedicated to protecting herself and others, and yet against this she had once again been utterly defenseless, flattened like a cream puff under a tank tread.

His excitement fragmented, and his face fell. "Forgive me, Martina Elena. I get carried away, this is all so amazing. As for your being crazy, best answer I can give is no, I think not."

She didn't know whether to be relieved or not. If she wasn't rowing the Volga with only one oar in the water, then she had become a telephone booth for a space alien. The first could at least be treated. How did one get an unlisted brain?

"Tell me what you have learned," she said, forcing herself to sit up.

Alexei parked himself on the bed beside her, resting the slayte on his knees. He used his index finger to select from an on-screen menu. A graph appeared, a skein of convoluted green lines that looked something like an old-style voiceprint laid over a yellow gridwork.

"This is your normal brain activity. Each wavy line charts activity in certain part of brain. Yellow centerline is baseline, dotted yellow lines on either side are PAA and LAA, or Peak Activity and Low Activity Averages. Solid yellow lines above and below them are EPB and SLB, Extraordinary Peak and Subnormal Limit Baselines, standards set for this test to give scale."

He stroked one of the myriad lines with his finger, turning it pink. "This is language center. See here you go a bit above PAA, and up toward EPB here and here? Is no surprise as you are bilingual. Now I have treated writers and multilinguals and see them often hit EPB, again no surprise—language is strong, active part of brain. If lines runs too close to LAA too often, this could maybe indicate a problem with speech and language centers. But not always; visually oriented people like artists quite often run low in this line but high on others. One thing we use is what we call Composite Activity Average, a sort of middle ground where most people fall. With some people all bets are off. I have seen savants, plus Yogis and other adepts create peaks in certain centers at snap of fingers, drop lines like scythed wheat."

Martina thought she followed this so far. "So this picture of how my brain works is not so bad?"

"Is *boring*," he answered with a chuckle. "You have brain not worth second look. Never get picked up at Brain Singles Bar."

"I will try to be glad of this. What happens when . . . it happens?"

He eyes sparkled with excitement. "Ah, now we get to really interesting part!"

He called up a menu, chose. Another voiceprint appeared, nothing like the first. "You are red lines now."

She peered at the slayte's screen, trying to make sense of what she saw. "I hit, what was, EPB in several places?"

"Yes, for while there your mind was racing like car at Indy 500. Language. Cognition. Almost every area pass PAA, rise toward and some reach EPB. Is wonder smoke did not come out your ears!"

For all she knew it had. "Okay, then what are white lines?"

"Wait and see." He tapped the screen, and the display scrolled sideways. The small snarl of white lines that had overlain her own suddenly exploded, turning into jagged peaks so far above EPB their tops were clipped off. An orange line crossed this limit, bearing the legend: READING OFF SCALAR?? CHECK FOR MALFUNCTION??

"This is *other* mind," he said with quiet triumph.

She looked up. "Second mind in my head?"

"In manner of speaking. Only way to describe it."

"So I am like split personality?"

He shook his head. "No, nothing like! Split personality only show one pattern at time. This is second *concurrent* pattern. I have put this out for anonymous consult, but expect no answer. I never see this before, and am pretty damn sure no one else has either. Is unprecedented. Scale of second mind alone is unbelievable. You have mind whose activity level at least five times size of yours or mine come into your head."

"Lucky me," she said mournfully. "How can this be, Alexei? Is my brain not already full of me?"

He waggled his free hand. "Yes and no. See, much of brain not used. Colleague named Dr. Greta Glass once calculate that normal brain activity even running ENA in all centers still only using less than twenty percent of full power and capacity. I believe something came in and used these unused parts. Here, let me show you something else."

He scrolled the graph forward, stopped it. "Tell me what you see now."

She studied the lines. "White lines change, begin to match mine?"

"Correct!" He tabbed a couple menus, and the graph became narrower and longer. "Here is last thirty seconds of episode. By now white lines mirror yours almost exactly. For fifteen seconds they maintain nearly perfect overlay, then begin to disappear one by one. Afterward your pattern shows signs of confusion, emotional upset, hard thought, and other things, but is no doubt that it is your mind and your mind alone."

She could remember—there was no way to forget—that brief interval of oneness with Avva just before he left. That was in its own way the most disturbing part of the experience; such total intimacy with such an absolute stranger and strangeness. It was not sexual, yet within it was a taste of the connectedness that came with the best of sex. She had trouble enough with intimacy with the man in her life. How was she supposed to deal with ten times as much from an *alien*?

She dared not dwell on that. It was more important to get as close to the bottom of this as she could. To size up the intruder. "So how does this happen?"

Alexei shrugged. "I do not know, but here is guess. Think of it like this: Your brain is like antique computer. It sits there in your head all day, loafing along and playing solitaire and minding own business. Then suddenly a high-speed-communications line it does not know it has opens, and a bigger and smarter computer connects. This surprise visitor very advanced, much of what it can do beyond your computer. Visitor starts running communications functions unknown to you, first establishing protocol, then uploading and downloading whole bunch of stuff faster than you can absorb it. Near end it stops to play hand of solitaire with you and then disconnects, leaving your machine blinking its lights and going *What fuck just happened?*"

"Sounds about right. That last part most of all."

"Jury is out whether brain can receive signals from outside normal sensory range and equipment," he said in a musing tone. "Some believe, some sneer at idea. For me, I say we still know too little about it to make big statements about what it could not possibly do without risking egg on face. Maybe brain is like radio and *can* bring in some kind of telepathic shortwave, only no one is sending over this band before. This guy, maybe he's got thought broadcasting like you got muscles. He *lifts* you, carries you."

"So I get Radio Free Phobos playing in my head. Why *me*? Why not everybody?"

He spread his hands. "Who can say? Maybe you are more sensitive to this band than most. Maybe you are chosen special, you shine like beacon he is drawn to. This is one I believe. Only way to know for sure, I think, is to ask next time he calls."

"So you think this will happen to me again?"

"Don't you?"

"Da," she agreed with a sigh. She was certain of it. The one sure thing in all of this was that it was not over, but just beginning.

Now We Are Three

"Welcome back to Earth, boys," Amber said as she placed bottles of Labatt's Blue in front of Dan and Jamal. "Bring me any souvenirs?"

Dan blinked, drew a shuddering breath. Looked across the table and locked gazes for a long moment with Jamal. They looked down, picked up their beers, and tipped them back in unison.

It had been different this time. As before, Avva had filled his head like a symphonic Technicolor cyclone blown into a child's balloon, only this time he hadn't been exactly alone. Jamal had been there, too. Or Jamal had been there, and he'd sort of hung around the edges and tried to keep up.

The traffic between Jamal and Avva had been heavy stuff indeed, like two humungous Cray-Infinico mainframes connecting while he, a Fisher Price KidPad with flat batteries got maybe one byte in a billion. Then at the very last there had been this sort of *shift*, and for a few seconds the three of them had been linked and synched.

The experience had given a glimpse inside Jamal's head, inside his . . . soul? Not a long look, and this high-speed flash left behind more of a vivid impression than a concrete memory.

The mind of the man across the table from him was a tremendous and beautiful thing, overflowing with light and motion and sound and endless multilevel activity like some emerald-towered Oz in full celebration. Yet this scintillating spired wonder was a fortress, surrounded by a dark, Mordor-like, blasted expanse of deepest darkest terror.

He could only guess what the other man had seen

inside him. Probably something on the order of a shallow brown puddle with a half-submerged rubber duck in it.

"Thank you, Amber," Jamal said softly as he put down his empty bottle. "We needed that."

She looked from him to Dan and back again, shook her head. "You guys look like you could use another round. I *will* expect to be tipped."

"Well, Dan?" Jamal said as she headed back toward the refrigerator.

"Jesus." He tried to run his fingers through his sweaty hair, only to get them tangled in the coils of wire from the BAIM headset. He pulled it off, dropped it on the table. "No way around it. Avva's real."

"As real as you and I," Jamal agreed, pulling off his own crown of wires. He glanced up at his paramour as she returned with fresh beers for all of them. "Maybe even as real as my lovely Amber."

She made a face as she distributed the bottles, sat down. Jamal reached over and took her hand. She looked into his eyes, then lifted his hand to her lips and kissed it.

Dan chose his next words carefully. "He really does need our help. Desperately."

Jamal nodded. "Matter of life and death."

Now for the Big One. "You were right. It wants the *Ares* to come to it. Come for it. Come for him."

"That is his only hope of survival."

Dan shoved back from the table, got up and began to pace. "Okay, I accept all that. But I still don't know what the hell he's doing talking to *me*! I'm just a fucking weatherman! Not even a real weatherman, but a virtual one! I don't—"

"Dan."

He turned. "Yeah?"

Jamal's face was dead serious, his gaze unnervingly direct. "I saw you. I saw *inside* you. You are a good man. A kind man. A caring and honorable man. I don't think our friend could have chosen any better."

Dan's shoulders slumped. "Thanks for the vote of confidence." He gazed at these two new friends, tried to smile. "So what do we do now?"

A raucous jungle sound suddenly filled the kitchen, a happy *ook! ook! ook!*

"Ah, my monkeys call," Jamal said, standing up. "Shall we go find out who else is with us?"

Dan looked over Jamal's shoulder, watching his thick fingers fly across the keyboard in an ebon blur, hammering away like a ragtime pianist on speed. He explained what he was doing while he worked.

"I had our BAIM results composited and fed to my flying monkeys as soon as they came in. It looks like they already located a match. Let's see what they found us."

The display blanked, then text began to appear.

```
<<<PRIORITY POSTING
REQUEST: Consult on BAIM reading
ROUTE: @AMA; @IPA; @INDB; @USGMDB
STATUS: Confidential/secured/blind
QUERY/ACTION: Pattern match with ap-
pended [dw9467hsi356yrjs39]
BAIM profile?/Positive reply only/in-
quiry rejected
REPLY@LOC:3*********.*********.0*********4
ENDIT>>>
```

"Okay," Jamal said, "this is a machine-level query about a test result being sent to the American Medical and International Psychiatric Associations, the International Neurological Database, and the US General Medical Database. I'd say that whoever took it hasn't ever seen anything like it before."

He spun his chair toward Amber, who had settled herself in at one of the other workstations and gotten busy. "Can you get me this file?"

"Working on it. Kindly old Dr. Moriarty is asking for it right now."

"Who?" Dan asked.

"Me, of course," Jamal answered. "Moriarty is a vid-entity front we maintain to stay wired into the medical community. While she's working on that, let's see who sent this." He pounded out three bars of the "Maple Leaf Rag" in 72/4 time.

```
!PROTECTED ROUTING PROTOCOL: REQUEST
DENIED!
```

wrote itself across the display.

"Ah, going to make me twist your arm?" Jamal said, stroking a touchpad and pulling down an icon that looked like a pipe wrench from the toolbar across the top of the screen. He positioned it over the protected numbers.

The wrench latched on with a metal on metal *skreek!* The text shattered and fell to the bottom of the screen. The asterisks turned into letters and numbers and

```
REPLY@LOC=Kasparov Institute of Clini-
cal Neurology/Manhattan/New York/USA
```

appeared below them.

There was a moment's pause, then

```
Mail routing/access numbers to be
supplied?
```

appeared meekly afterward.

Jamal stroked his beard. "This is quite intriguing. Kasparov is one of the top men in the brain-function trade. Twice now he has been on the short list for a Nobel prize. Whoever we are looking for went for the biggest gun they could find."

Amber spoke up. "Klagged the file, did a comparison with the one you dudes generated. Whoever it came from is one of you, poor devil."

"Excellent. Now for some real fun." Dan watched Jamal type in the thirty-six-digit alphanumeric, apparently from memory. The display flashed orange, and up popped the yellow-and-black Maximum Retaliatory Response triskelion.

"Trouble?" he asked softly.

Jamal chuckled. "Hardly. I wrote several critical portions of the code for old Max. But let's pretend I didn't." He pulled another icon down, laid the small glyph over the center of the MRR sigil. It flashed, then expanded to become a playing card. A black joker, the signature of the infamous Jambo. Under the belled cap was a grinning stylized face that Dan now recognized as a younger cartoon version of Jamal's.

"Who's the joke on?" the Jester asked with a giggle.

"The joke is on me," Jamal replied.

The Joker threw his head back and laughed, his painted mouth stretching wider and wider, soon covering the screen's entire workspace. There was a Klaxon honk, then suddenly a glossy new menu appeared in tasteful silver and black, KASPAROV INSTITUTE OF CLINICAL NEUROLOGY emblazoned across the top.

"And I was hoping for something difficult," Jamal rumbled half under his breath.

Dan knew that Maximum Retaliatory Response was supposed to be bulletproof and hackproof. It was *the* big-ticket private compucations security, and at least 99 percent as good as Adamantine itself. Messing with it was supposed to be like shampooing your hair with fish blood and sticking your head in the mouth of a starving great white shark.

Jamal had just breezed through it like so much cobweb. It appeared that Amber's estimation of the man's skills wasn't just love talking.

"Now we see who has received our call." Jamal cursored over to a search box, typed in PATIENT RECORDS, clicked.

```
Password?
```

popped up.

"Charming." He pulled something that looked like a one-armed bandit off the toolbar and superimposed it over the password box. A tap of the touchpad pulled the lever down. A tinny version of "Luck Be a Lady Tonight" began to play.

Jamal glanced back at Dan. "I used to try to break these the hard way. I still do on occasion, just to keep my skills polished."

Just as the third bar of the show tune began the slot machine's wheels stopped spinning and the word CHESSMAN appeared in its windows. That word typed itself in at the prompt.

That went away, INPATIENT/OUTPATIENT? Appearing in its place. Jamal chose INPATIENT.

A tabbed display of nearly thirty patient names appeared.

"No need to check them all," Jamal said, pulling down the search box and entering *BAIM testing*.

Over half of the folders remained.

"Popular toy around this place," he mused, going back to the search box and this time entering *awaiting consult results*.

Now only one folder remained. MARY DOE read the tab.

"Either this lady is in hiding, or being hidden," Jamal commented. "Interesting."

Mary Doe could be anybody. "So we can't find out who is it after all?"

"Be serious," Jamal chuckled. He clicked another icon. A cartoon dog jumped down from the toolbar, sniffed the Mary Doe tab, grabbed the folder with his teeth, and pulled it off the left side of the screen. A few seconds later it dragged the folder back again, and this time there was a different name written on the tab.

"Martina Elena Omerov," Dan read over the big man's shoulder, then frowned. For some reason that name sounded familiar. Was she a Russian ballet dancer? Pop star? *Playboy* foldout from his misspent youth?

"Now we have a name. Would you please run her, Amber?"

"Already started, oh impatient one."

"See why I pay her the big bucks?" Jamal said with a grin as he opened the woman's folder. "Look here. She came in yesterday, and is a patient of Kasparov himself. See this notation? Even the clinic staff aren't being told her real name. I wonder why her identity is being kept such a strict secret."

"Holeee fucking shit," Amber drawled. "Get back!"

"What is it?" Jamal asked, swiveling his chair toward her workstation.

She faced them, a peculiar expression on her face. "Okay guys, guess what this Martina Omerov does for a living?"

Suddenly at second hearing Dan knew why her name rang a bell.

"Unless she's some other woman with the same name," he said, "she's *Colonel* Martina Omerov, the personal bodyguard of UN Secretary-General Ricardo Perez."

"Bingo," Amber agreed. "She hears your voice."

"And it made her commit herself," Dan added, knowing just how she felt.

"And now we are three," Jamal said with a satisfied smile.

Deadline

Never in her entire life had Jane felt so lost. So alone. So utterly and unbelievably *helpless*.

Commander of the farthest-reaching manned space mission ever mounted, and here she was hiding in the head. It was ridiculous. It was absurd.

But she didn't feel much like laughing.

The most recent episode had been the most intense yet, like having some sort of mental and emotional booster rockets strapped to her brain, blasting her up to where she could receive heavy message traffic like some unstable satellite, then be sent splashing down into herself again, confused and changed.

When the voice was there in her head she believed it and what it said. The experience was too intense and all-encompassing to be doubted. It was like your first time in zero gee; it seemed unreal, and your body insisted that it couldn't be happening, but you floated anyway.

Now that it was over, she was left to struggle with the Sisyphean task of marshaling the denial logic demanded. The rock kept rolling back, crushing her objections under the weight of her experience.

I must be going mad to believe this could possibly be real, she thought wearily. *I've cracked under the strain and ended up with bats roosting in my belfry. Or at least a single bat who calls himself Avva, and he flies in, tangling not my hair, but my mind.*

She knew she couldn't go on like this much longer. Creeping around on pins and needles while waiting for another episode to begin, trying to find someplace to hide when one hit, being whipsawed between belief and self-doubt until it felt like she was going to either snap or shatter.

She *couldn't*.

But she had to. She wasn't in a place where she could take a week's sick leave and go off somewhere to, as her mother used to say, get her head together. Coping was her only option.

Jane made herself stand up. Take a deep breath. She turned her head to look at herself in the mirror. Staring back at her with haunted eyes was a middle-aged woman who had grown new lines in her face seemingly overnight. The woman in the glass looked exhausted. Scared.

"What should I do?" she asked her image in a hoarse whisper.

The answer to that question was as obvious as the grooves bracketing her mouth and eyes. *She had to tell Fabi.* Let him find out if there was something wrong with her head, and if that was the case, fix it before it, before she, became a danger to the rest of the crew and the mission.

Was she dangerous? She leaned closer to the glass, searching for signs that she was turning into a Queeg or McManus.

No red **I** for insane burned on her forehead. No movie-maniac gleam shone in her eyes. No warped satisfaction twisted her mouth into a psycho's knowing smirk. She looked the way she felt: old and bewildered and worried, like a woman whose life has been built on a knowledge of her own capabilities feeling control and self-assurance slipping through her fingers like mercury, like smoke.

Worst of all, and heavy enough to bow her shoulders like a five-gee lift, was this terrible sense that time was running out. Not just in terms of hiding what was happening to her. They were drawing closer to Martian space with every passing hour, and the rules of orbital mechanics were unbreakable and unforgiving.

If Avva was not a figment of her misfiring mind, she could not in good conscience refuse him what he asked. If that was going to happen, their flight plan would have to be altered soon. Just off the top of her head she was left with a figure of no more than three days. Probably less.

That was her deadline. She had to know if she was a sick woman or had a shot at saving him before then. Mounting a rescue meant convincing the rest of the crew of something she still could not herself entirely believe.

That left her back with only one way to go, one way to begin.

"You have to tell Fabi," she told herself in the mirror. Jane watched herself return a grudging nod.

Then she plastered an unconvincing smile on her face and made herself go back out to endure the rest of a Girls' Night gone suddenly and terribly wrong.

Night Voices

"I'll swing by in the morning to help you check out of this place and get settled back in your apartment," Jasper said after helping him back into bed.

"You really don't—" Daveed began, then decided not to be a total moron. He nodded. "Thanks. That would be great."

This brought him an approving smile, one he wanted to keep seeing and seeing, like for maybe the rest of his life.

"As for that other stuff," Jasper continued, "Don't let it make you nuts. Think on what this Avva has told you. Consider how you might help him. And if I can help you help him, I will."

"Thanks," Daveed repeated. "For everything."

"My pleasure." Jasper stood there a moment, looking back at him with a question flickering in his dark eyes.

He must have given the right answer because a moment later Jasper bent down and kissed him on the left cheek, which was about the only undamaged part of his face. "Good night," he husked softly. "Get some sleep. Get better."

"I will," Daveed answered, feeling heat rise to his face.

The UN spook straightened up, flashed one last smile, then sauntered away, his long braid swinging.

Daveed gave himself a minute just to lie there and revel in the warm feeling, thinking that in spite of getting the shit beaten out of him this just might have been the luckiest day of his life.

He was still smiling when he leaned over, and using his good arm, retrieved the slayte Jasper had brought him to use. He flipped out the keyboard, and yes, his cast let him get his fingers where they could go walking.

Although he was fairly bagged, these were his usual waking hours. It wouldn't hurt to spend an hour or so looking to see if the impression Avva had left with him was true. That there were others out there who had also been called.

Maybe one was out there right now, someone who might have some idea how he could help answer this cry for help. He sure hoped so.

Bending over the slayte, he went out to see what—and who—he could find.

Dan was also in bed—or at least on it.

He was stretched out, still dressed, atop the quilt covering the antique four-poster in the room Jamal had given him. Not only was he dressed, but stressed. Although numb with fatigue, he remained so restless any attempt at sleep was bound to be a fruitless sheep chase.

For the past several minutes he'd been locked in a staring match with his phone. The NokiTel sat there on the bedside table, just daring him to use it. Amber had retrieved it from the truck for him, and rearranged its guts. Now any calls he made would, thanks to the use of the borrowed excess bandwith of a couple Defense Department satellites and clandestine land lines, be totally secure, and traceable only to a nonexistent street-corner phone booth in Nutbush, New Jersey.

The hows didn't interest him much, but the why nearly had him pinned. What he really wanted to do was call Bobbi again. Just to check on her. Hear her voice again, see her smile. His call earlier that day had been too short, just like his visits with her always ended far too soon. He never got enough of her, and right now, stuck in a strange bed in a strange place and facing an even stranger task, he needed another fix. Plus it might be a while before he could call again. God knew where this Avva business was going to lead him next.

But even taking the earlier time zone into account it was too late to call her. She'd already be in bed. That might have decided the matter then and there, except that he could still call Susannah. She would at least tell him what his favorite girl had done that evening, and in the morning she would tell Bobbi that her Daddy had called. Of course, the way his luck had been running lately he was far more likely to get Tammy. On a scale of one to ten he'd rather talk to Avva. Or Satan.

He frowned as a maybe-memory surfaced, one that might just change the odds. He reached out a skinny arm and hooked the remote from the bedside table, fired up the giant flatscreen facing the bed. Called up EdgeNet, leaving the sound off.

Yes! His brain wasn't entirely sludge after all! This *was* the night his net was running that awards show. He couldn't remember which one, and it didn't really matter. The important thing was that they were carrying it *live*. And there was his darling ex-wife doing a stand-up, fluffing it like crazy with some vapid pretty boy in a tux. Unsurprisingly she was tricked out in a sparkly paint-thin gown so filmy he could see the Victoria's Secret logo on her thong-bikini panties, and even the severely visually impaired could tell she hadn't bought the matching bra. But Dan hadn't dialed her up for fashion criticism, but for proof *She! Wasn't! Home!*

Ten seconds later the phone was in his hand and he was pushing buttons. Ten seconds after that the warning Jamal had called old Max was showing as an inset on the big screen.

"Susannah? It's Dan," he said after the beep. "Please pick up."

"Dan?" she answered after a longish wait. The inset remained black, blank, and she sounded half-asleep.

"Yeah, it's me. Sorry if I woke you," he mumbled, instantly feeling guilty and stupid for getting her up. "I probably shouldn't have called."

"No, that's quite all right. Hang on just a tick." The inset lit, and her image appeared.

Dan's eyes nearly popped out of his head. Instead of her normal working uniform, or even the severely modest flannel nightgown she customarily wore when she and Bobbi were staying over, she had on this *very* filmy, *very* revealing peach-silk nightie. Her hair was down, tousled from sleep and cascading over her half-bare shoulders. Plus she was in bed. Looking just right there, too.

"I—" Down, boy! Get a grip! "I, um, just called to make sure Bobbi is okay." He fingered the remote, splashing Susannah across the flatscreen's breadth and reducing his ex-wife to a Barbie-doll-sized pip in the lower right corner. The view got better. One hell of a lot better.

She smiled, as if aware of what he had just done and approving of it. "She's fine. I put her to bed a couple hours ago. We read three chapters of *The Wind in the Willows*. That one always makes her think of the lake."

"Great." He struggled manfully to keep his eyes above her neck, but they kept wanting to wander off and see the sights. Trying to keep them corralled was nearly giving him a cramp.

He knew Tammy sneered at the younger woman behind her back, calling her fat. He'd always thought of her as pleasingly plump. Now that estimation was being upgraded to *very pleasingly*. Maybe even *breathtakingly*.

"Do you like my new nightgown, Mr. Francisco?" she asked with a faint smile.

"Very, uh, nice," he answered, his voice cracking. "Now that you point it out, I mean. Not like I was looking before. Not that I wouldn't want to look, or it doesn't—" He shut his mouth, marshaled a sick smile, and tried again. "Yes, very nice."

"Thank you," she replied in a queenly tone. "I purchased it right after I learned that we were going on a trip to the lake. As I was preparing for bed tonight I decided to wear it as a sort of test drive." She looked him dead in the eyes. "Now I am ever so glad I did."

Oh boy. He'd always kind of sort of wondered if there might have been some maybe possible chemistry there, but hadn't pressed the matter. Aside from his lousy track record with women, starting something with his daughter's nanny—and his ex-wife's employee—could only lead to complications that Tammy would, of course, use to make his life miserable.

But right then, looking at her, he couldn't help but think that maybe just *one* more complication might not be so bad.

"Me too—I mean, well," he stammered. "I'm sure we'll have a good time. Camping I mean."

"I have long been of the opinion that you could show a lady a good time, sir," she purred, leaning back. The view got even better in spite of losing the close-up. The hem of the thing she had on just barely brushed her creamy thighs. The skimpy panties were emblazoned with the same famous logo as Tammy's, and she, too, had passed on the bra. He doubted that the gartered black silk stockings were part of the set. But they worked. They *definitely* worked.

He knew he had to tell her what he'd called about before rational thought ceased altogether. "Uh, here's the thing," he began, trying to assemble some reasonable facsimile of composure. "I'm going to be, well, kind of busy the next few days. I won't be home, and might not be able to call Bobbi."

Susannah instantly became all business, leaning forward and her face intent. "Something wrong, Dan?"

Oh, only an alien in my head wanting me to help hijack the mission to Mars, that's all. No big deal.

"No, there are just some, um, things I have to deal with right now. Nothing for you or Bobbi to worry about."

She nodded soberly. "I understand completely. Bobbi and I will be quite all right. I can distract her if necessary."

You sure as hell are distracting me!

"Thanks, Susannah. I know I can count on you. I hope to get everything cleared up by the middle of next week. Believe me, I don't want it to interfere with going to the lake." Now he had even more reason to want the trip to become a reality.

"I do hope so." Her face softened and she relaxed back against the pillows once more, looking like an old master odalisque, her image suitable for framing and hanging on a saloon wall. "I am quite looking forward to staying at your cabin again. It is such a cozy place. So private. It has always made me feel a bit more free, perhaps even a bit more wild."

Free and wild sounded good to him. Really good. "Me too."

He thumbed the remote, calling up a simple split. Now on the screen before him were both Susannah and Tammy, side by side, and each getting half the display. It was impossible not to compare them, and yet there was no possible comparison.

Tammy admittedly looked like a million bucks, her perfect, personal trainer-toned size three bod poured into a designer cashbag that looked painted on over washboard abs and firm, rivet-nippled tits. Her fashion-magazine face had been painted to perfection, and was framed by a sexy hairstyle that other women would be copying by the weekend.

On the other side was a woman who was shorter and wider, at least a size fourteen, face and form what nature gave her, not repackaged by the plastic surgeon's knife. Her face would never get her a Revlon ad, but when she smiled the intelligence and sweetness and joy that shone through made Tammy look like a turd in a greasy paper sack because Susannah's sparkle was genuine, not cold paste. Her belly was soft and her hips wide. Every part of her was curved and yielding and inviting. Her chubby breasts pointed slightly down and outward. Dan was overwhelmed with the sudden urge to put his face between them and make motorboat noises.

"I guess I better, um, let you go back to sleep," he said thickly. "You probably have a lot of packing to do for that trip to Paris."

She shrugged, that gesture setting off motions which made him swallow hard. "That shall be a minor task. Bobbi and I are each allowed only a single small carry-on bag."

Dan knew the drill on that one. "Whereas Her Majesty will take six suitcases, at least as many garment bags, and a frigging steamer trunk for all her jewelry and makeup."

Susannah laughed. "I suppose she will."

Dan knew he had better cut this short before he blew it by making a fool of himself. "Okay, I'll let you go. Sorry I woke you up."

"That is quite all right. I am quite glad you called. Feel free to do so again when you get the chance."

"Thanks." A loopy grin broke onto his face. "Next time I'll try to call when you're dressed."

Susannah gazed back at him, her face taking on that cool, reserved expression she wore while working. "You need not spoil your fun on my account, sir." Her side of the screen blanked.

"Whoa," he muttered, closing the phone and collapsing back on the bed. Life had just gotten one hell of a lot more complicated.

Up on the left side of the screen Tammy postured and posed, a reptile in the body of a beauty queen.

"Enjoy Paris, darling," he chuckled as he pushed the button that banished her from the screen. He kissed the remote and put it aside, then settled back with his hands behind his head.

"Me, it looks like I might just be spending some quality time exploring one beautiful part of the British Empire."

"I hoped you would call, my dove."

The voice-only connection made Rico sound as if he was right next door, and yet like he was a million miles away.

"Rico, I am so sorry," Martina whispered into her phone. "Is not fair of me to treat you this way. But I have no choice."

"Do not talk of what is fair, just tell me you are all right." He sounded concerned, maybe even worried. She could only imagine how he would sound if he knew where she was and why.

"I am fine. You know me, strong as ox, wear bullet-proof clothes. I just have some, ah, things I must do before I return."

"What kind of things?"

"I cannot say. Is very difficult situation." She closed her eyes, damning herself for the moment of weakness which had led to making this call. Where had her strength gone?

"So is sleeping without you by my side. I tell you I am a wreck."

You have no idea what wreck is. "Is same for me."

"I miss you, Martina."

"I am missing you, too. Very much." The thirty-some hours she had been gone from his side felt like that many years, she who had always been so solitary and self-contained.

"When will you return to me?"

Martina opened her eyes, gazing dully at the room where she had hoped to find the answer to that question.

"I cannot say for sure."

"Come back. Now! Come be by my side. Whatever this problem is, let me help, Martina."

When and if she went back, that would be the decision she faced. Involving him in the madness that had blighted her life would put him in a terrible, perhaps even dangerous position. Yet if what she was asked to do was true and necessary, then she might have no other option. Until then she had to keep him uninvolved, protect him the only way she could.

"Maybe I come back soon. I sure want to." Half a lie, half truth. Less than he deserved, but as much as she dared give him.

"I hope so. Whatever your trouble is, let me make it my trouble, too. Let me in, Martina. Do not keep me out in the cold. I am from the tropics, remember? Cold will kill me!"

"Rico, you do not know—" She shook her head, knowing that she could not keep on refusing him much longer. He could extract a yes from her where trained interrogators equipped with all the tools of pain could not make her open her mouth. "I must go. Be safe."

"I care for you, Martina," he began. She knew what he was going to say next, and cut him off before he got the chance.

"I care for you, too," she blurted, then cut the connection before either of them could say more. She closed the phone, hefted it in her hand wondering if she should break it to put temptation out of reach.

But that would be stupid. Did she plan to break her own head to damage the communication equipment implanted there?

Sighing, she rolled over to put it back on the bedside table. Before she could put it down, it began to ring.

She stared at it, frowning. It wasn't an ordinary con-

sumer phone, but SS issue. She'd been sure it was set
for location blanking and callback evasion. After flipping
it open again she rechecked the settings. Sure enough,
it was on full security mode. Which meant it was flat-
out impossible for anyone to be calling her.

Well, not *entirely* impossible. Rico could have gotten
one of her team, maybe Duffy or Swenson, to phreak
his phone. They had access to the restricted tools, and
the know-how.

It beeped again. Only one way to find out. She hit the
TALK button. "Hello?"

"Do I have the pleasure of speaking to Ms. Martina
Omerov?" said a deep resonant male voice she did not
recognize.

"Yes. Who is this?" Her tone sharpened. "How did
you reach me?"

A low chuckle. "Do not be concerned, Colonel Omerov. Making this call a reality was no simple task, even
for me. Your hiding place remains secure, as does your
phone. As for who I am, I suppose you could say that I
am a friend of Avva."

Her blood froze at the mention of that name, and she
gripped the phone with fingers which had suddenly gone
numb. "I know no one by that name," she said in a
flat voice.

Another chuckle. "Not in the flesh, no. Tell me, have
you seen the results of your BAIM testing?"

How could this man know about that? *How?* Was this
the work of some intelligence agency? The Israelis,
perhaps?

She licked her lips, forced herself to speak in a cool,
level tone of voice. "I am afraid I do not know what
you mean."

The caller sighed. "I see. Let me assure you, I fully
understand your reticence. You have found yourself in
a most difficult and uncomfortable position. Will you
permit me to speak freely for a moment? It may well
help simplify matters for the both of us."

"I am listening." She wanted to hang up, but if this
stranger really did know something about what was happening to her she had to hear him out.

"*Spacibo.* First and foremost, let me assure you that

you are not mad. I can understand why you reacted the way you did; a woman in your position cannot afford to take chances. Still, by now it must be becoming clear that there is no medical cause for what you have been experiencing. The reason for this is simple. There is nothing wrong with your mind."

"Who said there was?" she rasped.

Laughter returned to the man's voice. "I rather doubt that you checked yourself into the Kasparov Institute because all the good hotels were full, Ms. Omerov. Hearing Avva made you doubt your sanity. This was an entirely sane reaction to such an inexplicable event. Still, our friend Avva is quite difficult to disbelieve, isn't he?"

Martina pressed her lips together, refusing to answer. Either a yes or a no would be an admission.

Her mysterious caller continued on as if she had answered.

"I believe part of the reason for this is because he had no choice but to contact us, and no sound rings so true as a cry for help. Furthermore, he has much in common with us. He is not a creature such as H. G. Wells wrote about, an intellect 'vast and cool and unsympathetic.' He is in serious trouble, and I for one cannot bring myself to ignore his plea. Already I have begun the task of finding others who have also been called. One man has already joined me. Now I am asking you to join us as well, so that we may attempt to answer this cry of distress."

He made it sound so simple, like signing up for a gym membership or picking new shoes. "I—" She took a deep breath. "This is no easy thing you ask of me."

The man laughed. "You have an excellent—and I might point out, entirely lucid—grasp of the situation. From my talks with my new friend Dan I come to understand that each of us absorbs information from our contact with Avva in his or her own way. Are you aware of the service he and his late colleague have been rendering us?"

"Defense from big space debris?"

"Very good. Then you know we already owe him much. Do you know how he wants us to go about rescuing him?"

It was bad enough that she'd answered his first question. This one led onto very dangerous ground. "I am not sure," she said cautiously. "This is hard for me."

"I quite understand," he replied quietly. "It will be hard for all of us. Trying to get the *Ares* mission diverted to come to his rescue will be a demanding, difficult task. Perhaps that is why you and I and Dan are the ones being asked to do it."

"To divert *Ares*. You heard—you felt—this, too?" Could such a crazy idea come from two separate lunatics at the very same time, like two men in an asylum arguing over which one was Stalin, and so should be in charge of the crayons?

"I did. So has Dan. I admit that our understanding of this being is not perfect, but I believe it is good enough for us to take him at his word. The goodness we feel coming from him is no ruse, nor is his cry for help. We must trust him, trust ourselves, and do everything we can on his behalf."

Martina said nothing, not daring to open her mouth for fear she would agree. He spoke the arguments of her heart. Arguments that for the last few hours had been speaking louder and more persuasively than those of her head.

"This has changed our lives," the deep, mellow voice in her ear continued. "These changes have, I fear, only just begun. The great wheel of destiny turns, rolling toward a new age. We have been drafted into the position of the axis around which many events will revolve."

His voice dropped an octave, and she detected a note of weariness. "I must confess that I am not a brave man, Ms. Omerov. Already I have been forced to confront some of my deepest fears, and I know that further terrors await me. My new friend Dan may well be in for an especially rough time because of his family situation, but he has a great and powerful goodness in him, and a sense of duty and loyalty stronger than steel. I am honored that he has joined me in this great undertaking. I tell you all this so that you will know our commitment has already cost us, and will surely cost us more. Yet we are prepared to pay the price. Are you a brave woman, Colonel Omerov?"

It was finally her turn to laugh. "I always thought so. Now I am not so sure."

"A sense of caution is not a lack of courage. You are in your right mind, and you are not alone. We are here to help you, and hope you will help us. There, I have presented my case and now I will allow you your night's rest. Please give me a call when you have made your decision."

"How? I do not know who you are."

"Simply call 1–000–HELP AVVA."

She frowned. "Is no such area code."

The man chuckled in amusement. "Nor is there any way for me to have reached you over the phone in your hand. But I have. Good night, Colonel Omerov. I'll be waiting for your call." There was a click, and the man's voice was replaced by music, a husky voice singing. Martina listened, her frown deepening.

Then her eyes went wide as she recognized what she was hearing as the Cowardly Lion singing a song from the ancient film version of *The Wizard of Oz*.

A song about *courage*.

She snapped the phone shut. Put it aside. Turned off the light. Composed herself for sleep.

Only to lie there wide-eyed in the dark, wishing she could turn back time to those simpler days when defending Rico from armed maniacs had seemed like a lot to deal with.

In another dark place, this one a small compartment aboard a craft sliding through the endless night on the last leg of its journey to Mars, Jane finally broke the silence.

"Fabi? You awake?"

"Uh-hummm," he mumbled muzzily. "Am now."

"That's good."

He rolled over toward her, his face reddened by the dim lights. "Something wrong, *cara sposa*?"

"I—" That was as far as she got before the resolve she had so painstakingly constructed over the sleepless hours collapsed like a house of cards, leaving her lost and wordless in the wreckage of her intentions.

He got up on one elbow. "What is it, Janey?"

She had really meant finally to tell him. Had promised herself and planned it all out. Now she couldn't bring herself to follow through. Just couldn't.

"Nothing," she said with a sigh. "Sorry."

He reached out and cradled her face with his free hand, his soft fingers warm and reassuring. "You've had something on your mind for a couple days now. Maybe we should talk about it?"

Should. Can. *Big* difference. She shook her head. "I can't."

"Why not?"

"It's . . . complicated." Now there was one giant fucking understatement. Quarks are small. Space is big. Having an alien using your head to send an SOS is complicated.

He stroked her cheek, his touch as tender as his tone of voice. "I know you've been under a lot of strain lately. Keeping the *Ares* together. Keeping the crew together. Keeping Mission Control and the media largely unaware about our situation here. Then there's the worst thing of all, putting up with me."

She cupped her hand over his. "That last part is easy, old man."

He smiled. "I sure hope so. Then you didn't wake me up to tell me you wanted a divorce?"

She shook her head. "No way you're ever getting off that easy."

"Good. Is there something else wrong with the mission? Something the rest of us don't know about?"

That was her Fabi, perceptive as ever, even when wakened from a sound sleep. "I guess you could say that."

"Secret information or orders from Earth?"

Try Phobos, love. "Something like that, I guess."

"Do we need to know?"

"That's what I'm trying to get straight in my head." Among other things. Her brain, for instance.

"Are we in danger?"

A harsh, humorless laugh twisted out of her chest. "Not so far." *Ask me again if I start hoarding sharp objects or channeling Jack the Ripper.*

He was quiet for a time, absently stroking her cheek. Waiting for what he had to say made it hard to fully enjoy the sensation.

CALL FROM A DISTANT SHORE   191

"You are in command of this mission," he said at last, gazing steadily into her eyes. "You were given this commission because of your skill. Because of your experience. But most of all, I think you got it because of your judgment." He turned his hand, closing his fingers around hers. "I trust that judgment. Fully and completely."

"Thanks," she said hoarsely, a wave of love for him surging through her. But how well would his confidence in her judgment stand up to the truth? Could he hear it without becoming *Dr.* Costanza, whose training would give him no choice but to think his blushing bride had gone bugshit?

"Just remember, you can trust me, too. You can trust all of us. Even Hans in his own way."

"Thanks," she whispered again, drawing his hand to her lips and kissing it.

"You're welcome, Commander. Are you going to be able to sleep?"

"Sure," she lied.

"I can give you something if you want."

"I'm okay."

He leaned closer, kissed her. "You're better than okay, Old Lady," he said, settling back down beside her. "Try to sleep."

"I will."

She did try.

The attempt was largely a failure.

Fame and Misfortune

Dan was having a fairly decent day up until the moment he happened to pass by a Christian bookstore. After that, everything rapidly turned into an avalanche of sliding shit.

He'd slept soundly in spite of the strange bed and stranger accommodations. Somewhere near dawn he'd drifted into dreaming about a certain nanny in such a way that he'd ended up creating a rather embarrassing stain on the sheets. That shot in the dark woke him up. He nodded off again with a smile on his face, feeling a certain foolish optimism about his romantic prospects. Who knew, maybe having an alien in your head was a surefire way to improve your love life.

Breakfast with Jamal and Amber had been pleasant. The big guy had been up all night prowling cyberspace and doing who knew what else—maybe taking the Pentagon for a spin. His plan was to take a nap after eating, resting up for a busy day. After that they would get serious, but until then matters of coping and conspiracy were put on hold as an aid to digestion.

Jamal's nap might have left Dan at loose ends, but Amber was going to run into town to do a bit of shopping, and asked if he wanted to ride along.

Dan leapt at the offer. Apart from still being a little spooked by being locked away ten stories underground and feeling a mildly claustrophobic yen for a little sun and sky, there were a few things he could use. After all, he'd left his house the day before on his way to a doctor's appointment, not geared up for a protracted bivouac in a private bunker.

So he and Amber had headed for town in the antique pink Cadillac with the top down, the wind in their hair, and Chuck Berry blaring. She'd dressed for the trip in her usual ragged jeans and ratty black-leather motorcycle jacket, a Plutonium Enema Quintet tee shirt on under it as a nod toward modesty.

She drove fast with the seat buzzed all the way back, one small hand on the wheel and long black hair blown out behind her, cherry red ends snapping in the slipstream. Her eyes were hidden by immense purple plastic-framed mirrored shaydes. He hoped she was watching the road and not veering the drive into some vehicular mayhem vidyo game.

She told him the name of the town where they were headed was Drakeville. They bypassed the obligatory Walmart and strip mall on the outskirts, and headed straight downtown. Amber parked the Caddy near Sven's Outfitters, a Big & Tall men's store where she thought he should be able to find clothes to fit him, then went off on foot to do her own errands.

Sven's had a reasonably good selection, and it didn't take him long to pick out two spare pairs of pants, three shirts, extra socks, and underwear. Then he scored some toiletries from the drugstore next door, along with a box of Belgian chocolates to share with his new friends. Before checking out he lingered over the offerings in the birth-control section, musing on when and if he might need such accoutrements. But buying anything right then seemed a bit presumptuous and premature. A gentleman bought a lady posies first, then prophylactics.

Shopped out, he headed north along Drakeville's main drag, looking for the gourmet market where Amber said she'd meet him. Maple trees lined the street, and autumn had turned their leaves to fire. A farmer's market had been set up in the town square, filling the air with the smell of coffee and apples and fresh-cut flowers.

Dan hadn't really been thinking about much of anything in particular, a K-Tel Zen state that had come naturally to him up until the last couple days. The most troublesome thing on his mind was a mild regret over that fifth pancake and sixth sausage he'd scarfed down. Amber was one hell of a cook for a retired burglar.

He'd just ambled along the shady streets, enjoying the sunshine and fresh air. Then came the fatal step, the one where the cartoon character puts his foot down on the nothingness past the cliff edge. He didn't fall or plummet, but he did begin a long hard drop, suddenly the helpless and hapless subject of forces far beyond his control.

It began when he heard something that made him stop midstride, turn his head, and look around in owlish puzzlement.

Oh shit, not more voices, flitted through his mind.

Then he heard it again, the last name he ever expected to hear in public. He whirled around, homed in on the sound. It was coming from the open doorway of a nearby storefront. He got his feet moving, and then his long legs, winding up to a headlong run by the time he crossed the threshold.

Even in his distracted state he could tell what kind of store it was because smiling, frowning, praying, and variously crucified Jesuses were everywhere—watching from the shelves, kneeling on the floor, and nailed to crosses on the walls in sizes ranging from Junior to Jumbo. Angels covering the seraphic spectrum from the sappy to the downright sinister perched on high shelves and hovered above him, hanging by lengths of dusty, earthly monofilament. Tables, counters, and shelves were crammed full of books, tapes, ROMs, framed pictures, and uncountable religious geegaws.

He gave none of these pious—and largely tacky—commercial offerings a second look. What had drawn him into the store, and now yanked him across the floor, was the big Zenith widescreen blaring and blazing away in the far corner. On its screen a tall, broad-shouldered, silver-haired man in a black suit, silver lamé shirt, and string tie leaned on an ornate wooden pulpit and preached away in a passionate evangelical singsong pitched to raise the dead and reach the deaf.

Dan recognized him as Reverend Ray Sunshine, yet another of the endless supply of Billy Graham wanna-bes. If he hadn't, the *Call Reverend Ray Sunshine with your offerings NOW!* stripped along the bottom of the screen with a flashing orange toll-free number would've been an obvious giveaway.

"*GAWD* has said we should come to the aid of this

poor creature crying in the wilderness!" Sunshine bellowed in ringing augmented stereo, eyes blazing and gold fillings flashing. "*Gawd* has told me that he must be saved, so that he may be *saved*! And *Gawd* has told me that I am not the only one who has heard Avva's *plea*! Have *you* heard it, brothers and sisters? If not, can you hear *me*? Will you stand up and *join* me in this Holy Crusade? We need the help of every man woman and child for *Gawd's* will to be *done*!"

Dan watched Sunshine gaze out across the parishioners in his studio audience as if searching for those who might just decide to pass on his invitation. He gripped the pulpit even more tightly, and in a shaking voice intoned, "I said *Gawd* has told me I am not the only one to hear this call! I know of one other sinner upon whom he has laid this great *task*! I know this sinner's *name*!"

The preacher flung his arms wide, raising hands winking with rings toward heaven. He took a deep breath, his chest expanding.

"*Where are YOU Dan Francisco?*" he roared. "Why have *YOU* not come *forward*? Why have *YOU* not raised up your *voice*? Do *YOU* try to hide from this Holy Task *Gawd* has—"

"That Reverend Sunshine sure can preach, can't he?" The store's clerk had appeared at his elbow, a gangly black-haired young woman in a modest tartan skirt and pilly pink sweater, her face glowing with holy spirit and acne.

"I guess," Dan croaked, feeling his breakfast rising up in the back of his throat and tasting of maple syrup and bile.

"Are you bathed in the blood of the Lamb?" she inquired, plucking at his sleeve.

"More like up to my neck in deep shit," he muttered, whirling around and stumbling toward the door.

Amber put the top up and the hammer down for their trip back to the Bunker. Dan found the final minutes of the *Sunshine Hour* on the Caddy's small nonperiod deck. At the moment a white-robed choir was on, belting out "When Jesus Is on My Screen God Is in My Heart," each singer reduced to the size of a tiny ecstatic moth.

The sound was turned down to a Wurlitzer-driven gospel buzz.

"This is bad," Dan fretted for maybe the fiftieth time since he'd found Amber haggling over the freshness of the salmon fillets at the gourmet market. "Real bad."

"I know," she repeated, her round face intent as she sent the Caddy screeching around a hairpin turn, gangster whitewalls squealing in protest. "Pacify yourself, man. Jamal will be able to fix it. He can fix anything."

He really wanted to believe that, and what he'd seen so far of the recluse's abilities made it seem almost possible. But only almost. There as no way for him to banish the Alberta-Clipper-sized forboding of utter doom that had swept down on him.

He worked media, even if only in one of its low-flash backwaters, and knew how the system worked. Sunshine had just painted a big fucking flashing neon bull's-eye on his back. If the majors picked up on it, they would come after him like steroid hounds on the tail of a palsied fox, hunting him down and fighting over his carcass.

The knot his insides had turned into tightened when his phone let out a chirrup. He stared straight ahead through the windshield, trying to pretend he hadn't heard it.

It chirruped again.

"Maybe you better answer that," Amber suggested, peering at him over the top of her shaydes.

"Why?" *Chirrup.*

"Could be important."

"Could be more frigging trouble." *Chirrup.*

"Just answer it, willya?"

Chirrup. His shoulders slumped in defeat. "I guess I can at least see who it is." He pulled the phone out of his pocket, flipped it open, checked the caller ID. A big sigh of relief escaped him when he saw the number.

"It's my producer." He thumbed ACCEPT. "Hi, Morty."

"Hi yourself," the big woman rumbled, eyeing him from the phone's small screen. She didn't look happy. "You got any possible idea why I'm calling, Dan my lad?"

"Maybe a little," he admitted cautiously.

His answer didn't make her look any happier. "So you *know* this Sunshine asshole?"

"No, nothing like that. I just happened to, um, over-hear part of his broadcast and heard my name, well, mentioned."

"Mentioned." Her eyes narrowed, and her cigar shifted from one side of her mouth to the other. "So are you *really* hearing Jesus and aliens in your head, Danny? Tell me the truth now."

"No, Jesus hasn't said word one."

"That's good news. What about this alien?"

He tried to smile. "No comment."

"Shit oh goodness," she groaned, squinting back at him. "*That* was what your little spastic act was about?"

There was no point in lying. "Yeah, it was."

"So you *do* hear this Avva spaceman talking into that big space between your ears?"

"Just three times."

"Oy. How's this Sunshine clown know?"

"I don't *know*!" Dan wailed. Then something clicked, and he stared at his old friend uncertainly. "You *believe* me?"

Morty unplugged her cigar and regarded it thought-fully, thick ring-bedizened eyebrows drawing down. "I know *something* happened to you the other day, and you aren't the sort of guy to make shit like this up."

Her gaze shifted back to him, and her heavy face was utterly serious. "More importantly, something is happen-ing to you *now*. The machine's got your name, sweet-buns. EdgeNet brass have already called me up asking if you are the who, and before long the other nets are gonna be on this like flies on shit. One of 'em will figure out that the Dan Francisco Holy Joe is yammering about is the one and only Dan Francisco, virtual weatherman. When that happens you're gonna be famous. *Big-time.*"

"Nobody knows who I am," Dan protested.

"Not now, but I bet you a thousand bucks and my Steely Dan Deluxe that your smiling face is gonna be plastered on every screen from here to Sri Lanka by suppertime."

He knew she was right. The media machine was like some vast relentless swarm of robot termites. They'd burrow and dig and gnaw, and in no time flat they'd bring the rickety house of anonymity he'd constructed and maintained down around him.

"Oh man," he moaned, sinking deeper into the Caddy's leather seat and wishing it would swallow him altogether. "I'm fucked."

"Soon as the foreplay's over. But look on the bright side."

"There is one?"

"Only if you get a woodie over the thought of your NRQ blowing Tammy's clean off the charts."

Why did she have to keep being right? He knew the drill. They would seize on a name, a situation, and go into a feeding frenzy that made a school of starved piranhas look like picky eaters, running the poor slob's Name Recognition Quotient from zero to infinity so fast it was a wonder the letters didn't melt. Truth, reason, and restraint would get trampled in the rush for the holy grails of Exclusivity, Preemptivity, Splash Factor, and Ratings.

Odds were that by this time tomorrow they would be interviewing his first-grade teacher, and making pronouncements on his aberrant behavior based on her hazy recollection that he had once wet his pants during finger-painting class.

"So what should I *do*, Morty?" He prayed an old hand like her would have some sort of tidy solution in mind—one short of suicide, or massive plastic surgery and a hasty relocation to Tibet.

"For now, hide. Where are you, anyway?"

Dan glanced at Amber, who shook her head. *No.*

"Maybe it's better if I don't say." That earned him a thumbs-up.

Morty nodded. "Maybe you're right. You got a good place to hide?"

"*That* we got," Amber muttered.

"Yeah, I do."

"Get there. *Stay* there. Set your phone to ignore all calls other than from me. I'll get back to you as soon as I can."

"You think you can get them off my back?" he asked hopefully.

She made a face. "We'd have better luck getting me crowned Miss America, and that's even if I shave my legs. You know what you're going to have to do, don't you?"

"What?" He was afraid he did know, but this one time it would be so nice to be wrong.

"Go public. Tell your side. The longer you wait to confirm or deny, the more bullshit you're gonna have to face when you do come out." This terrible pronouncement made, she cut the connection.

"Almost home," Amber said, slowing the Caddy below Warp Factor One and going into her secret-code routine as they neared the aboveground entrance to Jamal's hideaway.

Before, all Dan had wanted to do was get out for a while. Now he could hardly wait until he was safely a hundred feet underground and locked behind all those nice thick steel doors. He hoped that was deep enough and barricade enough.

"Does Jamal's place have a *cellar*?" he asked as the overhead door and armored inner doors opened before them.

Dan entered Jamal's inner sanctum like a seeker entering a shrine in search of a curative miracle. He was mightily glad to see that the source of possible salvation was up, around, and at work.

"I take it you are aware of your new celebrity," the big man said. His short nap seemed to have done him a world of good. He looked rested and ready to take on the world. Dan sure hoped so.

"Yeah, I saw the crusade in town," he answered as he headed for where Jamal was working at one of his elaborate desktop machines. "You can fix this, right?"

Jamal shook his hairless head. "I am good, but I am not God. The best I can manage is the creation of confusion and delay." He indicated the screen in front of him, which was filled with text and numbers.

"Toward that end I have caused your credit-card usage this morning to vanish, and doctored the records with several bogus transactions. Within the last four hours you checked into a Holiday Inn in Tampa, Florida, and bought a bus ticket to Boise, Idaho, at a Greyhound terminal in Atlantic City, New Jersey. You also rented a Lexus in Winnipeg, Manitoba, and took a two-hundred-dollar cash advance at an ATM in Fairbanks, Alaska. These diversions will make it impossible to track you that way."

"That's great!"

Jamal didn't look all that pleased with his work. "Dan, sooner or later they will just change tactics. I believe we can safely assume that they will try to smoke you out."

He knew Jamal was right. "Still, they can't find me here, can they?"

"No." He stood up, laid his hand on Dan's shoulder. "Come on, let's go to the kitchen. I believe it is time we held a council of war."

Once they were all settled in at the kitchen table, each with a medicinal jolt of brandy added to their java, Jamal assumed his rightful role as generalissamo of their motley group.

"Let us begin with what we know," he said. "I have already done some checking on this Reverend Sunshine. He launched his so-called Avvatine Crusade just this morning, claiming that God put him in contact with Avva so that he can be rescued, and presumably converted."

"I caught that much," Dan said after taking a big slug of spiked coffee. This was definitely a morning for drinking before lunch. A little, anyway, to settle his nerves. "He must be hearing Avva, too, right?"

"So it would seem. We knew there were others."

"Yeah. But we also thought they'd be keeping a low profile."

"An assumption in error in this case, but which I believe holds true for the others."

Amber took Dan's next question right out of his mouth. "What are the chances that this will just get written off as another religious nut trying to grab headlines?"

Jamal shook his head. "No doubt it will by a good number of people—at least at first. But the Sunshine ministry is quite large, and not so fringe as to be considered laughable. There is a daily one-hour syndicated show seen on CrossNet and other Christian outlets, plus radio shows, vidyo, and the usual cybic links to the net. His viewers worldwide number in the millions, a following which has earned him several invitations to the White House. His ministry brings in something over two hundred million dollars a year, and while some goes to the obligatory mansions, limousines, and yachts, a surprisingly high percentage of his take is plowed back into good works. Soup kitchens, shelters, that sort of thing. Whether this is cleverness or conscience I cannot say."

He took a sip of coffee, put down his cup. "In other words he is too well known, and has too much clout to be ignored. Nor does he lack an understanding of the media. He gave a somewhat spottily attended press conference first thing this morning, promising that his service would reveal what he called 'the best good news since the word that Jesus has risen.' His after-service press conference ended just before you arrived, and it was *much* larger. He has the media's attention, and he's using it to proclaim that everyone who believes in a merciful God should, and I quote—"

Jamal's voice rose into the high, singsong cadence Dan had heard before, " 'Rise up and in one mighty voice cry out that this lost child of *Gawd* should be *saved* and brought into the *fold*!' "

"*Hell*afuckinglooya," Amber muttered. "Of course he also wants 'em to send money. Lots and lots of money."

Jamal smiled. "Of course."

The humor drained from his face. "There were two avenues of attack I had envisioned us taking. Call them plans A and B. Plan A was to locate any others who were called, and then see if between us we had the means to accomplish our objective behind the scenes. When we learned that Secretary-General Perez's bodyguard had heard Avva, I began to hope that this sub rosa approach might just be possible. It took some doing, but I managed to call Martina Omerov last night after the two of you went to bed."

This was news to Dan, thanks to a mutual decision to keep this whole mess away from the breakfast table, and not get back into it until Jamal had finished his nap and he and Amber returned from town.

"What did she say?"

"She did not refuse to join us outright, but I must admit that our conversation tarnished my initial optimism. When I got up from my nap, my flying monkeys presented me with several bits and pieces which led me to someone else who has heard Avva. His name is Daveed Shah, and he is a mediartist working at Uncle Joe's Neely New Mexico Uplink center."

Dan felt a spark of hope. "You mean he could contact the *Ares* directly?"

Jamal nodded. "Quite possibly. This still leaves us with the question of how we are going to convince Commander Dawkins-Costanza and her crew to believe us, but a step closer to our objective may be in sight."

"That's great!"

Jamal sighed. "Yes, but unfortunately this morning's events may force us also to attempt plan B."

Dan had to ask. "Which is?"

"That is for one of us to go public."

He almost choked on his coffee. "Are you crazy?" he sputtered.

Jamal held up his hands. "Believe me, I am no happier with this idea than you are, but it had to be considered as an option. Now it may have become a necessity."

"Nobody would believe us!" Dan argued. "Sometimes *I* don't believe us!"

"They might if someone with sufficient credibility and name recognition were to speak up. Besides, this is America. One in five people still believes Elvis to be alive."

Amber stared at her lover aghast. "You mean he's *not*?"

He patted her hand. "Sorry, love."

"Well shit," she groused. "All these years of saving myself for the King wasted." Then she shrugged and settled back in her chair. "Hell, the kids woulda had a weight problem anyway. So you're saying someone's gonna have to come out of the Avva closet."

"Yes, and soon. This Reverend Sunshine may well be sincere in his drive to save Avva, but if his is the only

voice to be heard, then Avva's existence—to say nothing
about the possibility of rescuing him—will never be
taken seriously. A less hysterical, more secular voice
must speak up."

"Right," Dan said with a derisive snort. "Sign me up."

Jamal just stared at him, and he didn't like the look
in the man's eyes one bit.

"Hey," he wailed, his voice cracking. "I was just *kidding*! There's no way in hell you'll ever get me to do
this!"

"You have to make some sort of statement anyway,"
Jamal pointed out in a reasonable tone. "Reverend Sunshine has seen to that."

"But the media will eat me alive!"

Jamal's expression was rueful and sympathetic. "We
both know they are going to do that anyway."

Dan reached for the bottle of brandy.

Just as tying a certain kind of knot in a rope and
tossing it over a handy beam is no great challenge, putting together the means to dangle himself in the public
eye had been frighteningly easy. All it had taken was a
single call to Morty.

That was how Dan ended up perched on an uncomfortable straight chair, facing her image on the screen.
Sweat dribbled down his sides, soaking his nice new
shirt. An anxiety attack hovered somewhere nearby,
teasing him with tics and minor palpitations until it
swooped down and claimed him full blast.

For all the thousands of times he'd been on-air, it had
been more years than he could remember since he'd
shown his actual face. When the camera went active he
wasn't going to be good old Dan the Virtual Weatherman, safely hidden behind a cybernetic mask and cracking canned jokes. This was full frontal, and he felt
horribly underequipped for the task. His palms were
sweaty, his balls shriveled tight, and his brandy-soaked
breakfast squirmed uneasily in his gut.

"Are you ready, lover?" Morty asked.

He blotted his face yet again with a sodden handker-
chief. "No." He'd refused a monitor, afraid seeing how
bad he looked would distract him.

"We can still knock together a script if you want."

He shook his head, glancing over at Jamal. The big man was crouched over a keyboard, a worried look on his face. Christ only knew what was going wrong now.

"No, I know what I have to say," he said, facing his producer once more. "Now all I need is a shot for lock-jaw so I can get it out."

"Relax, Dan," she said in a surprisingly gentle tone. "We can retake and edit as much as we want. But you're a stone pro, remember? You'll do just fine."

He nodded, then took a deep breath and faced the unforgiving lens pointed at him. "Let's do it."

The red light above it winked on, telling him it was hot.

Showtime.

"Hi," he began in the sanest, calmest, most modulated tone he could muster. "My name is Dan Francisco . . ."

Homecoming Bash

Daveed had only two things on his mind as he rode the elevator up to his floor of the condo. Getting off his feet was the top issue. He couldn't believe how tired just checking out of the hospital and riding back here had made him. Of course being up half the night might have also been a contributing factor. Taken together they left him feeling, like they used to say where he grew up, like he'd been writ in grease and half wiped off.

Once he got off his feet he intended to recontact this Jamal guy and find out what he knew about Avva. Hearing someone else use that name had made him feel much better.

Then, to be perfectly honest, there was a third thing on his mind. That was the man standing beside him, the one and only Jasper Crow.

The UN spook had shown up at seven sharp with a Thermos jug of good coffee and fresh warm bagels, and stuck around when the doctor came in to poke, prod, and pronounce Daveed capable of going home. Jasper has driven them back to the condo in a funky old Volvo electric, and been ever so solicitous helping Daveed out of the car into the building. Probably would have carried him if he'd asked. His neighbors, largely senior citizens, would've cracked their dentures gossiping about that.

"You okay, man?" Jasper asked.

"Doing fine."

"You're not feeling faint or anything?"

"No." Actually there was yet one more matter weighing heavily on something other than his mind. "My only problem is hanging on until I can hit the bathroom."

"That's because of the stuff they gave you to keep flushing out that bruised kidney."

He shuffled his feet, trying to ease the pressure in a safely dry manner. "Well, it's working."

Jasper laughed as the elevator stopped and the doors slid open. "Which way, *kemo sabe*?"

"Right. I'm in 5F." Which, he realized, was probably a complete disaster area. This guy was going to take one look and run screaming. "I better warn you, it could be dangerous, the dust bunnies gone saber-toothed and rabid."

"I'm not armed, but I'll still take my chances."

They started out along the corridor, Jasper staying right by his side and letting him lean on his arm. That was something he could really get used to. "It's just up ahead, right after the hallway turns."

"Gotcha. Great old building."

"Thanks. My unit used to belong to my aunt Marina. When she died my family decided to keep it as a sort of desert hideaway—that plus real estate being a lot more serious religion with them than Islam. My sister Miriam is an artist, and she stayed here a couple years, going out into the desert to paint almost every day. When I got a job at the Center, we swapped. I moved here, and she took over my apartment in New Orleans. Now she's doing this really packed series of portraits of drag queens."

"Big family?"

Daveed rolled his eyes as he pulled out his keys. "Big enough to be scary. Three brothers and two sisters. Enough cousins to form an army." He unlocked the door and pushed it open. "Come on in, make yourself comfortable. I'll be back out of the john in a jiff."

"Thanks. Seems a bit stuffy in here. Want me to open the door onto the balcony?"

"That would be great." It did smell a bit funny. He peeled off his jacket and hung it on the back of a chair on his way to the bathroom. Went in, closed the door, got in position and unzipped before he embarrassed himself.

"Ahhhh," he sighed with pleasure, the ache in his innards settling back down to a low throb. Just as he was about to zip back up again he thought he heard a sort of heavy thump.

Damn, he hoped the poor guy hadn't tripped over his junk. Before he could call out and ask Jasper if he was all right, there came from his living room the muffled sound of a female voice. One he would never forget for the rest of his life.

"Well, if it isn't the blanket nigger."

He froze. Oh God, Betsy Ross Jones! What the hell was *she* doing here—and what had she done to *Jasper*?

Next he heard the other voice he had never wanted to hear again say, *"Wake up, Chief! Where's the Paki?"*

If Jasper gave any answer he couldn't hear it. He slapped his pockets looking for his phone, then remembered it was still in his coat, out in the other room. Looking around in rising panic his gaze fell on the bright yellow Sony SportPad he'd used in the tub a few nights ago. And had to stop using because its batteries were nearly dead.

He snatched it up, parked it on the vanity, and turned it on. It activated sluggishly, the red low-power warning flashing. He ignored it, calling up its message function. The slayte's screen blanked, then relit with a message window.

Yes! He typed in the odd destination code Jamal had given him, grateful his cast let him work, then began a message.

HELP! B R JONES AND OTHER WHITE FIST IN- TRUDER HERE AT—

Something slammed into the bathroom door. The knob rattled.

"You in there, fag-meat?" *Jeff.*

Daveed stood stock-still, fingers poised over the slayte's keys, afraid the sound of typing would be heard. The knob rattled again. "Answer or I just start shoot- ing!"

"Wh-who's there?" he called in a quavering voice.

"It's your old buddy Jeff! Open the door, or we fuck up Cochise big-time. I'm gonna count to three. *One!*"

Daveed thumbed the SEND button, praying there was enough juice for it to generate a signal, whirled around, and stuffed the slayte in the dirty laundry hamper. He buried it under a couple of funky towels and a dirty shirt.

"Two!"

"I'm coming! Don't hurt him!" He faced the door, reached for the knob. Going out there was going to be bad. Real bad. And if they'd hurt Jasper—

"Now, raghead!"

His heart slamming against his bruised ribs, he turned the knob and opened the door. Waiting on the other side was Jeff, a rifle in his hands. The butt of the weapon's hardwood stock was bloody.

"Welcome home, queerboy," Jeff drawled with a grin, grabbing him by his good arm and hauling him toward the living room. "Come on, join the party."

He laughed, his handsome face warping with cruel hilarity.

"It's gonna be a real bash."

Sabo Express Righteous

Martina had turned on the news, thinking it might help distract her from thoughts of Avva and Rico. Instead it did the direct opposite.

She watched the nervous, uncomfortable-looking man with the long bushy brown hair make his statement one more time, then turned the sound down when he was replaced by some toothy announcer who seemed to find the whole thing hilarious. *Aliens from space!*

The image on the screen switched to that crazy American preacher shouting about Avva at the top of his lungs and naming this poor man, forcing him to go public and say that he had heard Avva, that he was real, and he really needed whatever help Earth could give him. His plea had been desperate and heartfelt. It was obvious that he believed.

The name of the tall, skinny, long-haired man was *Dan*. That had a very familiar ring to it. She doubted it was a coincidence.

Sighing, she picked up her phone and punched in 1–000–HELP AVVA, wondering if anyone would really answer.

"Hello, Nowhere here," a female voice answered before the second ring.

"My name is Martina," she began cautiously. "I believe someone there has been expecting me to call?"

"Have we! Hang on, lemme get the big guy."

Moments later she heard the voice of the man who had called her the night before. "Colonel Omerov," he said, "I am extremely glad you called." He sounded rushed and harried, which partially confirmed her suspicions. He also sounded more than a little relieved.

"I just saw a man named Dan Francisco speak of

Avva on a news bulletin. This is the friend of yours you mentioned?"

"He is indeed."

"For a media person he did not seem very happy being in the spotlight."

"He isn't. We had hoped to keep this a private matter, accomplishing our goals quietly and behind the scenes. Unfortunately, something came up that forced him to go public."

"This Ray Sunshine person, yes?"

"Good, I'm glad you know about him. It will save some time. Reverend Sunshine has indeed put us in a difficult situation. Now we have yet another problem laid on our doorstep. One which a woman of your unique talents might be able to help us solve."

"What problem is this?"

"It is rather complicated. To begin with, earlier this morning I located yet another person who has heard from Avva."

"You are very busy man. Very resourceful." In fact, he sounded like a one-man intelligence agency. If there was not a dossier on him, there damn well should be. Later, a job offer might even be in order.

"I try, Ms. Omerov. My initial contact with this man was brief, and he promised to get back to me as soon as he could. I just received a fragmentary and quite disturbing message from him. His name is Daveed Shah, and he works as chief mediartist and editor at the *Ares* mission North American Command and Uplink Center outside Neely, New Mexico."

"I know this place." She had accompanied Rico on a tour through the Center right after the *Ares* had begun its long journey outward.

"Here is the situation: Yesterday Shah was attacked and severely beaten by two members of the extremist group the White Fists of Uncle Sam. One of his attackers was an extremely dangerous woman named Betsy Ross Jones. A UNSIA undercover agent named Captain Jasper Crow intervened, probably saving Shah's life. Shah spent the night in the hospital and was released just this morning, leaving in the company of Captain Crow. Just a few minutes ago I received a partial mes-

sage from Shah, sent to an access node I provided. He
has been attacked once more by Jones and her accomplice. It appears that he was interrupted before he could
disclose his location or other information."

"But you think you know where he is."

"Yes. Jones and her confederate are still at large, and
it occurs to me that the home of a hospitalized victim
might be a good hiding place. That is reportedly where
Shah was being taken by Crow. Furthermore, all in-
access to Shah's condo was terminated just a short while
ago, and I found signs that two calls were made from
there before Shah left the hospital. These calls went to
a ghost exchange, and I am still trying to trace their
destinations with no particular success. The logical conclusion is that she was waiting in the apartment and has
taken Shah and Crow prisoner for purposes of either
revenge or leverage."

"I know of this Betsy Ross Jones," Martina put in.
"You are probably correct. We must assume that she
has taken these two men hostage." Jones's face was
graven into her mind. A fanatic of the first water, she
was on the FBI's Ten Most Wanted list, and UNSIA
had a Contain and Capture order out on her.

"I certainly hope that is the case," the mystery man
said softly.

Martina frowned. "Why do you say this?"

"Because it is better than her killing them outright.
Which my information leads me to believe she is quite
capable of doing."

She closed her eyes a moment. "*Da,* you are correct."

Eleven slayings, and a bombing which killed twelve
and wounded nearly fifty were attributed to Jones. She
would not hesitate to kill them, not unless she thought
they were more valuable alive.

"There is one further factor to consider. The woman
is obviously a xenophobe—one who hates and fears others than her own kind. I shudder to think what would
happen if she learned that Daveed was communicating
with a real alien—which is bound to happen if Avva
contacts Shah while he is a prisoner."

"That could be very bad." Worse than she could
imagine.

"Now for the hard question. Can you help rescue Daveed?"

Martina considered his question. She was gaining nothing by hiding in this room like some old turtle in her shell. All the evidence pointed to Avva's being real. Which meant she had to help save him—or at least come to the aid of those who might. If this Shah could be freed, and then contact the *Ares*, this end might be accomplished without getting Rico involved.

"Yes," she said, swinging her legs over the side of the bed. "I will go there and see what I can do."

"I suppose we should, too," the mystery man said in the voice of a man discussing his own funeral arrangements.

She stood up. "This is a problem?"

An unhappy bark of laughter. "Like many fine wines, I do not travel well."

Martina glanced at her watch. "I should be able to get there in maybe four or five hours. Can I reach you at any time?"

"Yes."

"I assume you can contact me if you need to."

"That is a safe assumption, Ms. Omerov."

"Then we do this. But before we go further, would you please tell me your name?"

"Ah, please pardon my lack of manners, Colonel. My friends call me Jamal."

"Call me Martina. I will see you in New Mexico, Jamal. How will I recognize you?"

A soft, sad laugh. "I'll be the distinguished-looking black catatonic."

The connection ended on that peculiar note, making her wonder just what sort of people she was getting herself involved with. But it did not matter. More lying around and she surely would go mad, if for no other reason than from the continued struggle to suppress the urge to come to this Avva's aid. The fight was over, and while in one way she had lost, she did not feel defeated.

She closed the phone and dropped it on the bed. Went to the locker where her clothes were stored, peeling off the hospital gown on the way. She pulled on shirt and slacks, strapped on her shoulder holster, then shrugged into her jacket. The one-shot CerTek went on one calf, the Ripski combat knife on the other. Thus dressed, she straightened up and began distributing the other tools of her trade in various obvious and hidden pockets.

Clothed, rearmed, and with the sort of task she'd been trained to do before her, she was beginning to feel like her old self again. One more thing to do, one which gave her pause. A look of wry amusement broke onto her face.

You are some strange woman, she thought. *At drop of hat you agree to go take on a pair of armed terrorists, and are even looking forward to it. Yet the thought you might have to talk to the man you sleep with gives you the nerves of old woman hearing prowler in the night.*

It was a risk she had to take. She allowed herself a brief moment to prepare, then plunged in.

"System, active." The implant behind her ear tingled, signaling that it was on. "Tac Three. Mister Chan, please." Since Chan's team acted as outrider, there was less chance of his being near Rico.

There was a momentary pause, then inside her ear she heard a surprised and uncertain *"Ma'am?"*

"Good day, Mister Chan. I trust you are keeping Secretary-General Perez safe in my absence."

"Ah, of course, ma'am."

"Good. I count on you and Mr. Fayed to continue this work. I cannot return to take command of unit just yet. In fact, I must leave for New Mexico within the hour, so you will be on your own for some while yet."

"Did you say New Mexico?"

"Yes, I—"

"Listen, Colonel," Chan broke in. *"I think you better talk to Secretary Perez."*

"Chan! Wait! I—" He was already gone off-circuit. There were a couple clicks, then a long period of faintly humming silence. *"Dermo,"* she growled, wanting to just sign off, but not daring to. If Rico needed her, she had no choice but to answer.

Another click, then his voice came to her over her implant. *"Martina?"* he said uncertainly. *"Are you there?"*

She closed her eyes. "Yes, Mister Secretary."

He chuckled. *"No one is listening, my dove. Mr. Chan and Mr. Fayed have cleared the circuit and stepped back a discreet distance. Mr. Fayed even whistles to prove he is not listening."*

"That is good of them," she said tonelessly.

"Sí, you have very good people. I am glad you called. We have problem, need your help. A message was just brought to me by courier. It is from the White Fists of Uncle Sam. One of their members, a woman named Betsy Ross Jones, claims to be holding two UN personnel hostage. Their names are—"

"Daveed Shah and Captain Jasper Crow," she finished for him. Why take hostages without making demands? But they *were* hostages, which meant they might still be alive when she got to them. If she got to them fast enough.

"How do you know this?" In her mind she could picture him blinking in surprise.

A thin smile broke onto her face. "Outside source. I am aware of the situation, and am on my way to deal with it."

"Demands were made of me, as Secretary-General. No police, Jones warns that any interference will see these two men dead."

"What does she want?"

An unhappy sigh. *"Not much! Twenty million dollars, and full amnesty for her and companion. These make sense, but other demand does not. She wants Mars mission turned back immediately and prevented from, and I quote, 'infesting our world with filthy alien trash.' For once I do not thinks she speaks of colored peoples like me. It makes no sense, Martina!"*

Great, these maniacs had seen the news. Just as Jamal had predicted, Avva seemed like the Antichrist to them. "They do not. Daveed Shah is very important to Mars mission. He must be rescued. So I am going there to get him and Crow out."

"All our peoples are important, Martina! But, according to my information, Shah is a mediartist and editor, not some systems specialist or scientist critical to success of mission."

"There are, ah, special circumstances. Very special."

She racked her brain, trying to come up with some white lie that would justify what she had to do. If she could keep him unaware of the real reason Shah had to be saved, she could keep him from getting tangled up in the rising Avva craziness in the media. A craziness certain to get worse before it got better.

"Is security thing," she finished lamely. "Very hush-hush."

"Martina, you are my bodyguard—my lover! You belong with me, not running off to be a one-woman SWAT team! You know I have no choice but to reject these demands, turn the matter over to the proper authorities, and let them deal with this."

She could feel the walls closing in around her. He would not abandon mandated procedure unless she could give him a very good reason, convince him it was in service of some higher law or purpose.

There was only one way out of the impasse.

"Rico, you have seen the news lately?"

"Yes, some," he said sounding puzzled.

"You have heard about this preacher saying God wants us to divert the *Ares* mission to save alien named Avva stranded on moon of Mars? Or that another man named Dan Francisco is saying Avva is real and needs our help, but God has got nothing to do with it?"

"I have, sure. Is loco stuff." A pause. *"This is why Jones wants the mission turned back? She thinks the Mars mission is part of some alien invasion?"*

She swallowed hard, reaching for the courage she'd told Jamal she possessed.

"Yes. I tell you Avva is real, and is in bad situation this Dan Francisco says. Daveed Shah is, ah, also in contact with alien, and might be able to convince *Ares* crew to change flight plan and at least swing closer to moon and look for him."

"I . . . find this had to believe. Very hard."

"Trust me, you are not only one. But is all true."

"How can you know this, Martina?"

Now the abyss lay before her. She had no choice but to jump. Leaping out of a plane over a war zone would have been easier.

"Because," she began, summoning the will to force

the words out. It made bench-pressing an automobile look easy. "Because I, too, have heard this Avva's cry for help."

The ensuing silence seemed endless. She waited it out, bracing for the pain of his disbelief and rejection.

"This is no joke?" he said at last. *"You are not pulling on my leg?"*

"No joke," she returned heavily. "This is why I go away. I hear Avva in my mind and think maybe I am crazy. My friend Dr. Alexei Kasparov can find nothing wrong with me, and tests seem to prove Avva is real. Other people who have also heard him contact me. Either we are all crazy, or we are being begged to save life of person from other star. Even if there is only small chance of this being true, we must act. *I* must act."

Those last three words made her feel good, and more right with herself than she'd felt in days.

"Why did you not tell me about this before?"

A bitter laugh escaped her. "So you think I am crazy, too, but maybe want to help even though I might be dangerous lunatic? Or have you believe me, then risk career trying to convince others big Russian broad you sleep with hears distress call from space between her ears? Risk was too great either way. I could not allow it."

"So you have been protecting me. First from yourself, then from the political troubles this might cause."

"*Da*, that is my job."

Alexei came into her room, his eyebrows rising when he saw her dressed. She held up one finger to let him know she would be done in a minute.

"No, I think it is more than that. Much more." A sigh. *"This is some damn mess, Martina. What would you have me do?"*

Alexei gave her a wink and settled onto the foot of her bed, crossing his legs and smiling.

"Stall. Give me time to see if I can fix this by rescuing Daveed Shah. Then maybe we can contact *Ares* on sly, keep Uncle Joe and rest of world from fighting over whether to look for Avva or not." And keep you out of it completely.

"I could maybe announce press conference about Ares

*for tomorrow morning. These Fist banditos might take
this as sign I am knuckling under."*

Martina nodded. That was an acceptable level of
involvement, and might buy her more time. "Yes, very
good. As for business with Avva, pretend you know
nothing. Better for you and everyone else if we can find
way to have *Ares* crew find Avva on Phobos without
any official orders to be looking for such a thing."

"This I will do. Is there anything you need?"

There was. It was the reason she had called Chan in
the first place. "Yes. Please have my team arrange very
fast transport to Neely for me. Will contact you from
there later, with good news if all goes well."

*"I will do this. You be careful, Martina. I want you
back in one piece."*

"I . . . I want to come back. Have from the moment
I left."

*"Then do so as fast as you can. Go to the airport now.
I will have Mr. Fayed make the arrangements."*

"Thank you, Rico. Omerov out. System off."

"Must be handy to have phone built into head,"
Alexei said when she turned toward him. "Maybe I
should get one."

She smiled. "Can be handy sometimes, but getting it
disconnected can be bit of mess."

"Good point. I see you are all dressed up. Checking
out?"

"Da, I must leave now, must get to airport, catch
plane to New Mexico."

He picked her phone up off the bed. "You will be
helping Avva by doing this?"

"Da, I will."

He beamed at her and tossed her the phone. "Then I
will drive you there myself in my very expensive Jaguar."

"Comfortable back there, ma'am?" asked the chubby
black woman in the cockpit of the plane Fayed had arranged for her. The pilot's name was Winnie Sabo, and
she was a captain in the South African Air Force on
detached duty to the UN.

Crammed into the backseat of the fighter plane, all
Martina could see of Sabo was the back of her helmeted

head. The woman's voice had that musical quality she associated with African English, and it came to her over the headphones built into her own helmet. That helmet, and the special flight suit they had stuffed her into, hinted that she might be in for a bumpier ride than you got on *UN One*.

She was not particularly fond of flying, and doubted that she was going to be offered a nice calming in-flight vodka. Still, if this got her to Neely in time to save Daveed Shah, it would be worth some discomfort.

"Yes, I am ready." Not comfortable, but ready.

"Righteous. Powering up. Don't you mind the racket."

The sleek black warplane came to howling, shivering life around her. Calling the sound it made a racket was like calling Moscow slightly chilly in winter.

"Ever ridden in a Gryphon before, ma'am?" Sabo asked.

"No." The whine of the engines, even muted by her helmet and headphones, was unbelievable, and it continued to cycle higher and higher. It would seem that Fayed had taken her request for something fast to heart.

"It's a hoot! Be easy with you, we'll have a righteous ride."

There was a harsh gabble of sound Martina couldn't make heads or tails of over her headphones.

"Okay," Sabo said, "we just got a clearance to take off. Hang on, ma'am, lift in five seconds."

Unbelievably enough, the engines seemed to redouble their noise. The craft began to shudder and shake like it might just detonate and fly not away, but into a million flaming pieces. She heard a cheerful *"Two,"* over her headset before the noise made hearing anything else impossible.

She set her jaw and braced herself. While suiting up, Captain Sabo had told her that the Gryphon was a VTOL, so she was prepared for a lurch as it heaved itself off the tarmac. She'd ridden in VTOLs a half dozen times before. They wobbled their way up to forty or fifty feet, then sort of lurched off into level flight. This Gryphon was certainly louder than the ones she'd ridden before. *Much* louder.

A warning tone sounded in her ear, then suddenly it

was as if some great hand had come up under the plane, flinging it straight up with such violence that she was mashed down in her seat. The pressure increased, doubling her weight, tripling it, more. Then just when she thought her tits might end up on her kneecaps, all her weight fell away, plunging momentarily below one gee. That sent her stomach heading for the clear canopy above her.

Roughly five seconds after that initial jolt they stopped moving and seemed to hang quiveringly in the air. The noise abated slightly, down to about the sound of a Mig fighter trying to rape a Concorde in a cyclone.

"We're at five hundred meters now," Sabo reported in an offhand tone. Martina leaned cautiously to the left and peered through the plexi canopy. Somehow in that very short time the ground had ended up way the hell down there. "Got your breath back?"

"Ah, yes, I think so." And kept her lunch as well.

"Righteous pleasing. Now we zoop around to our heading." The plane began to wheel clockwise, turning almost 180 degrees. "Normally in a scramble situation we go straight from vertical lift to directional flight, cranking around to our vector on the way up. I did it this way 'cause the other can be a little stressful the first couple times."

Martina managed a thin smile. "I can see where it might be." Any more stressful, and she would have needed a privy hole cut in the seat.

"Righteous fun once you get used to it." The plane stopped turning, hung there poised and tremulous, straining at the leash of gravity. "We have our heading. Ready to start putting some klicks behind us, ma'am?"

"Ready as I will ever be."

"Trust me, this is better than sex. If my boyfriend could do this, I'd *never* get me out of bed. Standby for throttle-up."

The engines began to howl like enraged demons again. There was a short fall, and then an abrupt lurch as they snapped into level flight configuration, followed by a pause just long enough for her to think, *What next?*

Then what felt like either the plane exploding or God kicking them in the ass slammed her into her seat. Her flight suit inflated around her as acceleration tried to flatten her like a pancake.

"System . . . active . . ." she grated through clenched teeth. "Mr. Fayed, please."

"Ma'am?" Mohammed Fayed said inside her ear a moment later.

"We really must have a talk . . . about your choice in travel arrangements," she said tightly, forcing the words past the elephant sitting on her chest.

"Secretary-General Perez said you wished to get to Neely fast, ma'am," he answered apologetically.

A gauge on the firewall before her showed that they had just passed through Mach 1 and were well on their way to Mach 2. The display was a simple dial, and was marked in increments up to Mach 4. Someone had stuck a piece of tape above the right side of the dial, the unnumbered part which was a bright warning orange. There was a big **5!** scrawled on it, along with the legend **SABO EXPRESS RIGHTEOUS FAST!**

"I believe I am getting my wish, Mr. Fayed. Omerov out."

The needle went past 2 and moved steadily toward 3.

"Starting to blow the dust off now," Winnie Sabo reported cheerfully. "Once I get this bitch out of first gear we'll start doing some righteous traveling."

The needle went past 3. That was, if she recalled correctly, somewhere over 3500 kilometers per hour.

"Very good, Captain," she said, closing her eyes. "Thank you."

Next time she would know enough to say "reasonably fast" instead.

Dishing Dirt

They had been on the road for less than two hours when Jamal called Dan back into the truck's rear compartment.

Amber was at the wheel, coffee at her elbow and cigarette dangling from her purple-lipsticked mouth, taking them along the southbound interstate at a bit over eighty miles per hour. Traffic kept them from going any faster, not fear of getting stopped. Thanks to the man in the back, the truck's VID 'sponder was read by any police officers they blew past as an FBI undercover vehicle.

"Need anything?" he asked as he unbuckled his seat harness and stood up in a semicrouch to keep from banging his head.

She squinted at him through her shaydes. "Maybe a sugar jolt. There's a box of Twinkies back in the upper right cabinet of the kitchenette. Grab me a couple."

"Sure. No problem." He ducked through the low opening, then straightened up to his full height. "What's up, Jamal?"

The big man was ensconced in his leather recliner, surrounded by flickering displays, a whiskey bottle within easy reach. Packing up and leaving his underground redoubt had been hard on him. Knowing that he was going farther away from home than ever before was scaring the hell out of him. Burying himself in his beloved cybic universe was helping him cope—that plus a nearly steady stream of Wild Turkey straight from the jug.

Jamal regarded him for several seconds, then sighed. "There is a problem," he began in a low unhappy voice.

This didn't sound good. "What kind?"

Jamal beckoned him over. "That is for you to decide.

I considered not informing you about this, but you deserve to know what is going on."

"Informing me about what?" he asked as he crossed the carpeted floor.

Jamal indicated the bucket seat beside his recliner. "Sit down, and I'll show you." Dan obeyed, uneasily wondering what new disaster had befallen them.

"This is a playback of something EdgeNet ran just a few minutes ago." His thick finger stabbed a key on the keyboard in his lap.

Dan leaned closer, watched the big display in front of Jamal fill with the trailing credits for his home net's hit afternoon gossipalooza *Dishing Dirt with Donny and Dot* stripped along with an ad for al-McMecca, the Islamic fast-food chain. That cut to the usual hourtop *NewsEdge,* hosted by Fox Huntley, a cleft-chinned, distinguished-looking man with great hair and, Dan knew, the IQ of lukewarm soup.

Huntley was what they called a *cracker,* not because he was white and from the South—which he was. He was a cracker because he didn't read the news off a prompter, but only parroted what some producer—dubbed a Polly—was capable of reading at over the single syllable level whispered in his ear. The twenty-five-to-fifty female demographic loved Huntley, each month sending him a bale of used women's underwear that the mail room sent on to the Salvation Army—all except for a few carefully selected items it was rumored he kept for his own extensive wardrobe.

"Today *NewsEdge* brings you an EdgeNet *exclusive*!" Huntley breathed as if about to reveal concrete proof of God's existence. "Earlier today EdgeNet's own Dan Francisco, better known to our viewers as Dan the Virtual Weatherman, made an exclusive and quite controversial statement right here for *you*!" Dan watched his face appear behind Huntley. The shot they'd chosen was not flattering. It made him look like someone caught with his hand in the till, or maybe shoved down the front of somebody else's pants.

"This statement concerned the alleged existence of a creature named Avva, the space alien supposedly living on the Martian moon Phobos." A sly smirk quirked

Huntley's lips. "This creature is the basis for the so-called Avvatine Crusade launched earlier today by Reverend Ray Sunshine, who also says this Avva speaks to him. So far NASA, Uncle Joe, and other space agencies have denied any knowledge of such a creature."

The fact that they didn't switch to a shot of Sunshine, or stock footage from Uncle Joe, but left his picture hanging up there like a target worried Dan. It meant they weren't quite through with him.

Now Huntley tried to look serious. "Not generally known by the public is that Dan Francisco is the estranged husband of our own EdgeNet Lifestyles reporter Tamara Van Buren. We take you now to LA's Spielberg Airport, where EdgeNet reporter Lacy Bustier is standing by with Tamara. Lacy?"

Huntley was replaced by Bustier, a sultry, hard-eyed, ruthlessly wrinkle-free redhead who had a decade earlier made her mark on journalism with a series of locker-room interviews which caused at least six divorces, and the short-lived marriage of two fullbacks who had met on top of her. She was dressed for her stand-up in the airport's VIP lounge in tight black-leather pants, stiletto heels, and a scoopneck blouse that showed off some of the best work of LA's teeming legions of knockerdocs.

Beside her was Tammy. Who, Dan had to admit, made Lacy look like day-old dog meat. Hovering in the background were a stern-faced Susannah and his daughter. Bobbi appeared to be concentrating on the proceedings with her full attention, eyes and nose squinched up in a frown. Susannah had her hand on the child's shoulder, and clearly did not appreciate the two of them being used as background.

"Thank you, Fox," Bustier purred into the prop microphone. "I'm here today with EdgeNet Lifestyles reporter Tamara Van Buren." She turned toward Tammy, a concerned moue on her painted face. "Today's statement by your ex-husband Dan Francisco must have come as quite a shock, didn't it, Tamara?"

Tammy took charge of the mike and the camera the way a seasoned hooker takes charge of a client's whanger, putting on a brave but troubled face.

"It did, Lacy, it really did. I'm shocked and saddened

by all this, and must admit I'm quite worried about the poor man. While I have long been aware of Dan's many, ah, eccentricities and unusual beliefs, I never suspected that he was so terribly out of touch with reality."

Her forehead furrowed prettily, and she stared directly into the camera. "If you can hear me, Dan, *please* get help! Until you have done so, and are over this sick Avva mania, I have no choice but to protect our daughter from you. I can't risk having you infect her with this insanity, or possibly even causing her physical harm."

"Have you taken legal action?" Lacy asked, right on cue. She was trying to look concerned, but was obviously creaming her fancy Edvardo leather jeans over being at ground zero for such juicy stuff. This was something the other nets would pick up, getting her megafacetime.

A brave, reluctant nod by Tammy. "I have. His recent actions scared me, and made me fear for my daughter's safety. The court agrees with my concerns. In light of his unstable behavior, which I understand began with some sort of seizure during one of his little broadcasts, I have been awarded sole custody of my darling Roberta. Dan has been restrained by the court from any and all contact."

That last sentence left Tammy's lips with a gloating edge. Dan sank into the chair, weighed down by defeat and feeling part after part of himself wither and die.

"Are you leaving the country out of fear for you and your daughter's safety?" Lacy breathed worriedly, shooting Tammy her next cue.

"No, she's accompanying me to Paris where I'll be covering the kickoff concert at Nipple Isuzu's new world tour." A come-hither look appeared as she slid onto her pitch. "I do hope my faithful viewers won't hold this unpleasantness against me, and tune in Saturday night at seven Eastern, when I—"

"I've seen enough," Dan croaked, turning his face away and feeling like he was going to puke.

This was it. He was absolutely and entirely fucked. He should have *expected* Tammy to use this to grab facetime and get some licks in. His career and reputation were in ruins. Worst of all, he would never see his daughter again.

"Keep watching, Dan," Jamal rumbled quietly. "It does get better."

"How?" Short of Tammy spontaneously combusting right then and there, leaving him the sole-surviving parent, he was screwed.

"Just watch."

He forced himself to look at the display. Tammy nattered away for a few more seconds of bald-faced pitch, then Lacy asked her if she felt sorry for her demented ex.

Tammy adopted a mournful tone and pensive stance as she went back to the knifework. "Of course I do, Lacy. He's not really a bad man. While Dan was of some small help to me at the beginning of my career, I had to leave him to be free of a number of quite unreasonable expectations he had of me."

"Yeah, like monogamy and motherhood," he growled at the screen.

"—did not take our divorce well, nor my being awarded primary custody of Bobbi. His career has not been anywhere near as successful as mine. To be honest, I have to wonder if seething resentments over these failures contributed to his now running around claiming aliens live in his head. Still, I can't let my pity allow me to—"

"Watch now," Jamal warned.

Suddenly Bobbi pulled away from Susannah and bolted toward her mother and Lacy. She slipped past Tammy, who made a futile grab for her, then put herself right in front of Bustier.

"I would like to say something if I might, please," she said in a cultured, no-nonsense tone that was pure Susannah.

"You're Roberta, Tamara's daughter, aren't you?" Lacy said, producing this obscure fact in a tone that threatened to give the poor kid diabetes. "How are you, sweetheart?"

Bobbi smiled back, her face bright as a new penny. "Quite well, thank you." She went up on her toes, staring curiously at the reporter's mouth. "Are your teeth really real?" she asked in the piping little-girl voice she only used when being sarcastic.

Uh-oh, Dan thought nervously. *The kid's about to go for the jugular.* Tammy got a real nervous look on her face, but dared not interfere.

Bustier only partially managed to hide a frown. "Sure they are, honey. Why do you ask?"

Bobbi's face was all picture-book innocence. " 'Cause I heard my mom tell the cameraman that you'd blown so many brass to keep your job that you had them all pulled to save the trouble of brushing afterward." A big-eyed look. "What's *blown* mean?"

The newswoman nearly swallowed her teeth, real or not.

"Bobbi!" Tammy gasped, her face going the color of her lipstick as she made another grab for her.

"My daddy's not CRAZY!" she shouted, eluding her mother's hooked fingers and heading for the camera. "He's *NOT*!"

Finally, Tammy managed to grab her by the arm. She jerked her back, her face twisted with fury. "Turn that fucking camera *off*!" she snarled. *"Now!"*

All at once a very confused-looking Fox Huntley was back, blinking uncertainly. "I guess," he began, letting out an uneasy laugh, "I guess the kid is upset by these rapidly developing, uh, developments."

He produced a glassy smile that turned to one of relief when a voice in his ear put words in his mouth once more. "That's *NewsEdge* for now. Stick around for—"

"That's it," Jamal said, freezing the image. He smiled at Dan. "Your daughter is a real spitfire."

"She sure is," he agreed glumly. "Takes after her mother, I guess." If a spitfire was like the fetal stage of a dragon.

"She really loves you."

"I know." Tammy hated that, and had from the moment Bobbi was born. What she'd wanted in a daughter was slavish devotion to herself alone, like the kid was some dim-witted lapdog. How long before she was finally able to poison Bobbi's mind against him now that she had sole custody?

"I know this is a terrible setback. I am sorry."

Dan shrugged. "I'll live." This wasn't the first time

Tammy had fought dirty, but it was the absolute worst. He couldn't even begin to imagine any way to fight back.

"Can I ask you a question?"

"Sure."

"Are you still going to stick with this? With us?"

Dan slumped in a weary heap, considering his options. He could call Morty back and get her to help him try to retract his earlier statement. Say it had been faked, or made at gunpoint, or something.

Nobody would buy it. He'd had a hard enough time staring into the camera and telling the truth. Trying to lie would make him look like some scam artist caught by an ambush news show, and any additional public statement would only further seal his fate as media fodder.

Besides, somewhere along the way he'd made a commitment to Jamal to help Avva, for whatever his help was worth. It was too late to back out. He would see this mess through, and then try to retrieve the broken fragments of his life from the landfill afterward.

"I'm staying." Plus, he just realized, he didn't have anywhere else to go anyway. His house would be staked out by a swarm of reporters, and unless he shaved his head and shrank a foot, he'd be recognized no matter where he went.

"Thank you," Jamal said, letting out a relieved sigh. "I was afraid we were going to lose you."

"No, you're stuck with me for a while longer."

"I'm glad." In spite of his words, the big man looked almost ready to cry.

"Hey, it's no big deal."

Jamal shook his head. "It is a very big deal, Dan. I will freely admit that I don't know many people. Not in person, anyway. So my telling you that you're one of the best people I've ever met doesn't count for much. But it is true, and your assistance is more appreciated than I can adequately express."

Dan nodded, touched by the man's shy sincerity. "Thanks. I'm glad you came after me."

He was better off now than when he'd felt crack-skulled and alone, even if now he still mostly felt like some ineffectual comedy sidekick. Jamal made things happen. Martina was headed to Neely to rescue Daveed. He rode shotgun and kept Amber amused by pointing out some of the more interesting vanity license plates.

"So am I." Jamal cleared his throat, a grim expression appearing. "As for this custody business, rest assured that what your ex-wife has done cannot stand."

"Why? Can you go in and change court records?"

"Actually, yes," he answered, a rascally gleam that reminded Dan this man was the infamous Jambo in his spare time coming back into his brown eyes. "But I don't think that will be necessary. When we prove Avva exists, her assertion that you are crazy and therefore an unfit father will fall apart."

"I guess." He looked the other man in the eye. "You really think we can pull this off?"

Jamal nodded, his face settled into a determined expression. "Yes, and now we have more reason than ever. I promise you, if I have to turn cyberspace inside out to save Avva and get your daughter back, then that is precisely what I shall do."

Dan believed him. In fact, this new disaster seemed to have made the agoraphobe more able to cope with the fears he was facing by going out into the world. A little of the haunted look had left him, replaced by resolve.

Dan stood up. "I better let you get back to work. Thanks for telling me about this."

"I almost didn't. But you deserve the truth."

"You did good."

"Thank you. We're all in this together, Dan. One for all and all for one."

"I think you count as all three Musketeers all by yourself. But that's okay. Amber and I will keep your swords sharpened and your muskets loaded."

In an heroic attempt to be an asset to their enterprise, he got Jamal a fresh flagon of Wild Turkey before taking Amber her Twinkies.

Yeah, he thought as he went back up to the front of the truck. *How can we lose with a guy like me on our side?*

The John Gambit

While Martina was crossing the continent at a significant multiple of the speed of sound, and Amber was wheeling the Jamalmobile along a westbound interstate at as far above the posted speed limit as she dared, Daveed was getting nowhere fast.

He and Jasper had been tied up back-to-back, sitting on the hardwood floor of his condo's living room just a couple feet away from their captors. Jasper hadn't said a single word or moved a muscle since he had been overcome by the White Fist zealots. He hoped the man was just playing possum, but the one good look he'd gotten before they had been bound together had made him sick with fear for the man.

Jasper's face was a mess, bloodied and bruised by Betsy's and Jeff's fists and feet. It was probably a blow to the skull with Jeff's gun butt that had brought him down. Blood matted the dark hair on one side of his head. His face was so lax and expressionless it made Daveed wonder if his brain had been permanently damaged.

He'd gotten off a bit easier, probably because he hadn't put up a struggle. They had just slapped him around a little before trussing him up. AIDS was pretty well beaten, but the 'phobe fringe refused to believe it, and they might have been worried about catching something. Either they didn't know Jasper was gay, or they figured he was government-inspected or something. It was hard to tell just what they might be thinking. All he knew for sure was that both had heads full of seriously bad wiring.

The hours since their capture had been at once terrifying and tedious, filled with a horrible combination of monotony and menace. His face hurt. The arm these same assholes had wrecked the previous day ached. His butt had gone numb from sitting on the hard floor.

And now he had to use the bathroom again, his bladder feeling like it was the size of a basketball.

"Uh, excuse me," he said meekly.

"Shut the fuck up, wog," Jeff spat, his attention riveted to colorized goosesteppy bits of Nazi propaganda marching across his living room's SceniView Ultra widescreen. Jasper's guess about the wig had been on the money. Jeff's hair was so short and so blond he could have posed for a Gestapo recruiting poster.

The two fanatics had settled into a sort of peculiar domesticity, raiding his kitchen, then settling back on the couch with weapons across their laps while they snacked and tubed out. Two-thirds of the SceniView's two-meter screen was set to display some encrypted pirate net styling itself "The Victory Channel." This vidyo abomination spewed out a sickening stream of propaganda films, *Greatest Hits of the Third Reich*, "educational" programming, and slobbering lunacy calling itself news and editorial. It was as bad as anything he'd ever seen before.

The other third of the screen was a split between CNNI and EdgeNet. Compared to the Victory Channel, EdgeNet looked like a model of sanity and probity.

While he had been getting checked over and checked out of the hospital, the shit had hit the fan back on the East Coast. Finding out about Ray Sunshine's Avvatine Crusade had been a shock, as had been his naming of Dan the Virtual Weatherman as someone else tuned in to Avva. This quickly shot to the top of the news curve, first boosted by Francisco's statement, then getting another push when Tamara Van Buren's public whipping of her ex on her home net had gone badly off script. Avva was running saturation everywhere.

He almost felt insulted that his two noxious houseguests had known about all this before he had. On the other hand, if he survived this and ever got the chance to meet Dan Francisco, he owed the man a beer. Jones and her mad-dog boyfriend had seen Dan's statement about Avva not long before he and Jasper had arrived, and that was what made the two decide to keep them as hostages rather than kill them outright. They'd believed in Avva instantly—or at least a version of him suited to a late-night Creature Feature. He and Jasper were supposed to be the garlic and crucifix which kept it away.

EdgeNet continued to play the whole Avva thing for laughs, banging hard on the exclusivity angle. CNNI had unsurprisingly taken a far more serious—and ominous—approach. They'd dredged up archived material from an incident in the mid-nineties, when members of a cult called Heaven's Gate committed mass suicide so they could board the alien spaceship they believed to be hiding behind the comet Hale-Bopp.

This was very creepy stuff, these people stretched out dead in new sneakers and jackets with some sort of interstellar busfare in their pockets. Their leader, this void-eyed spook who called himself Doe, was being compared to Francisco and Sunshine.

The pundits were unanimous: Avva did not exist, Dan was delusional, Sunshine was running some sort of scam, and Uncle Joe should not even think about considering changing the *Ares*' mission profile.

Daveed found all that discouraging but unremarkable; the news machine running off in the wrong direction as usual and chewing up everything in its path, like a threshing machine with a drunken chimp driving.

The Victory Channel's reaction was considerably more extreme. One lead commentator, a smug, sneering, triple-chinned blob, kept waving a thick manila folder, informing his viewers that he had right there in his hand Super Top Secret documents which proved that this had been the *Ares*' covert mission all along: that the UN intended to contact this alien race and bring them back to Earth so they could take over the world, impregnate the cream of white womanhood with little green babies, and treat the rest of the White Race as the other White Meat.

Daveed would have laughed at such bubbleheaded bullshit, except that he had two heavily armed extremist wingnuts parked on his couch, sucking it up, and nodding in agreement, murmuring *Right on!* and *The truth be told!* at the most moronic kibs of babble.

He hoped the Victory Channel's viewership was as low as its fairness quotient because the running theme behind all this gibberish was an ongoing call for action. For all the good, right-thinking people of America to rise up, load all their weapons, and take aim at the enemies of White Humanity. The best way to do this? Surround the center at Neely and declare war on the UN, putting an end to their perfidious machinations.

Several hundred heavily armed paranoiacs was just the thing to make the drive to work even trickier than the random deer or armadillo. Not that getting to work was his current problem.

Just a few minutes ago one Victory Channel talking headcase made a veiled allusion to "two heroes of the White American struggle" who were taking independent and decisive action to stop this interplanetary abomination. Betsy and Jeff had grinned and elbowed each other, getting off on this backhanded acknowledgment.

Daveed knew that his and Jasper's use-by dates were coming up fast, because he also knew the UN rule about exchanging hostages for concessions. That rule was *no way, Jose.*

Their only hope was this Jamal. The man seemed totally wired in, and maybe even up to miracles. He figured if he could get back in contact, they might just get out of this alive. Which meant getting back to the bathroom and the slayte hidden in the dirty-clothes hamper.

"Uh, excuse me," he tried again.

"I said shut *up,* fag-meat!" Jeff hissed. "One more word and I knock your fuckin' head off!" He started to get up, probably to make good on his threat.

Jones laid a restraining hand on his arm. "What?" she said coldly.

"I, well, I need to go to the bathroom."

"Hold it."

"Normally I could, but the doctor gave me this stuff to make me pee a lot. See, one of my kidneys got bruised yesterday when, well, you know."

"Fag bastard got off easy," Jeff growled, his upper lip curling as he eyed Daveed and Jasper. "I still think we shoulda killed the blanket nigger, paid the bastard back for sticking his nose in our business."

"Two bargaining chips are better than one," Jones replied. She was clearly the brains of the outfit, toting the nastiest-looking assault rifle and in charge of the remote. "Besides, the way Geronimo's acting, I don't think there's anybody left at home in his teepee. When you hit him on the head you scrambled his brains."

"I hope so. Fuckin' UN puke. Oughta kill 'em all!"

"We will." Jones stared Daveed in the eye. If Jeff was like some mad dog, maybe a pit bull on whack, she was a poisonous reptile, like a Komodo dragon with tits and a perm. "You really have to go?"

"Yes ma'am," Daveed whispered meekly. "Sorry."

She sighed. "Jeff, take him."

He shook his head. "Fuck no! I don't want to watch some raghead queer play with himself!"

Jones sighed again, stood up, and slung her rifle over her shoulder. She stepped past Jeff, then squatted down and began untying Daveed. He tried to keep from flinching every time her fingers touched him.

"Okay, get up," she said curtly once he was untied. Her voice was hard, and as empty of kindness as the weapon slung over her shoulder. He stood unsteadily. His legs had fallen asleep, and he could barely feel them.

Jones glanced at Jeff. "You keep a close eye on Sitting Bull while I'm gone."

"No problem." He lifted his rifle and jammed the muzzle against Jasper's temple. The UNSIA agent's face never changed, still retaining the blank expression it had worn when Daveed saw it last. "Either he's a good Injun 'cause he behaves, or he's a good Injun 'cause he's dead."

Seeing the shape Jasper was in, and how hot Jeff was to kill him, trashed any vague hope he'd had that getting one of their captors off to one side would give the UNSIA agent a chance to do something James Bond-y. That left it up to him. While not exactly a rugged action hero, if he could just get a minute alone he might be able to help them out of this. Thirty seconds, even.

He shuffled unsteadily toward the bathroom. Stepped through the doorway and reached for the doorknob.

"No." Jones said sharply behind him.

"Can't I just pee in private?" he asked, trying to

sound harmless and pathetic. No real stretch at this point.

She shook her head. "No."

"But you're a *woman*," he wailed, fluttering his hands and mincing for all he was worth. If it took playing a flamer to get a few seconds alone he'd do it. Jasper was depending on him. "I can't, you know, do that in front of *you*."

Jones reached into the waistband of her skirt, pulled out an extremely deadly-looking revolver. It swung up toward Daveed, pointing at his face and suddenly looking as large as a cannon.

"Your filthy Paki dick is of no interest to me. If it is any value to you, get it out and use it." Her eyes narrowed, pure mean craziness bubbling behind them. "Right now."

Daveed swallowed hard and turned slowly around. Walked stiff-legged to the toilet, Jones two steps behind him. Unzipped with the hand of his good arm, which was a trick because it was shaking so badly. Went hunting for a penis which seemed to have gone into hiding—and who could blame it. Finally, grappled the little fella out and began trying to convince muscles which had clamped his plumbing tighter than cooked macaroni in a bench vise to loosen. When and if he looked up, he could see her reflection in the mirror over the toilet. Seeing the gun pointed at the back of his head didn't much help him relax.

"Betsy!" Jeff yelled from the living room.

"What?" She called without turning her head.

"You gotta come look at this!"

She stepped back toward the open doorway, her head half-turning, but her eyes still fixed on Daveed. "What *is* it?"

"I think it's *working*, Bets! That greaser Perez just announced he'll be holding a press conference tomorrow! About the *Ares*!"

Jones took another backward step, trying to see the screen from the doorway. Her head and face were now half-hidden by the doorframe, and her gun was no longer centered on the back of his head. He risked a longing glance back and to the side at the hamper. Gingerly changed hands, leaving his good left arm free.

"Did he say anything else?" Jones demanded.

"No, just that it's important! You think this means he's gonna meet our demands? Should we risk checking that message drop we gave him?"

"Maybe. Let me think."

Think hard, Daveed pled silently. *Think in the other room. You and your brain-damaged buddy put your worm-filled heads together and noodle this thing out.*

She did move farther away, and now all he could see of her was a narrow slice of her back. This might be the best chance he was going to get. He leaned backward and reached toward the hamper with his free hand.

It was too far away. He wasn't going to be able to get his hands on it as long as he was using the toilet.

And there was the rub. Now that he'd finally gotten started, he couldn't stop. What seemed like a gallon of urine had started to flow, and seemed inclined to keep going until every wretched yellow drop had expressed itself.

Jeff had cranked the sound way up. Now some plummy-toned CNNI pundit was speculating on whether Perez's press conference had been prompted by this Avva business, and concluding that if Perez did alter the mission to investigate, his career as Secretary-General would be over.

Daveed struggled on with the Leak from Hell. *Enough, already!* he begged his recalcitrant bladder, trying to clamp down while arching his upper body backward for another try. His hand pawed the air near the hamper as if coaxing it to come closer. The stream became a dribble. He leaned back a little farther. His fingers just grazed the plastic cover.

Almost! Just a little far—

He started to lose his balance and made a desperate grab to catch himself with his other hand. His arm moved too slowly and would not extend to its full length because of the cast. All his hand grabbed was thin air.

He toppled over backward, crashing into the hamper. Bounced off and landed on the floor. The hamper flipped over and spilled its contents around him.

"What the fuck are you *doing*?" Jones began, reappearing in the doorway. For just a second it looked like she was going to laugh, but only for a second.

Daveed lay there on the floor. Flat on his back, dick peeking out of his fly, dirty clothes and towels scattered around him. And there on the tiles between them, bright yellow and too big to miss, was the Sony SportPad.

He watched her gaze go to it, her eyes narrow, and her face go stiff and hard.

"You filthy sneaking third world *turd*," she hissed, stamping on the pad and kicking it away. Then she aimed another kick at his head. He tried to squirm out of the way, but having only one arm to work with slowed him down. Her toe caught him in the forehead. Pain strobed, making him gasp.

"You rotten little Paki cocksucker." Another kick, this one catching him behind the right ear. The bathroom wavered, too bright and too dim in a sudden fog. He only semisaw the third kick coming, her shoe exploding from the haze, and could do nothing to avoid it.

Nor did he feel it connect.

Diversion

Neely's Kofi Anan Airport—so renamed after Uncle Joe had quadrupled its size—was far busier than the last time Martina had been there. But apparently Rico had reached out to grease the skids, because in spite of the heavy air traffic Captain Sabo was given immediate clearance to land.

Nor did his influence end there. When they got inside the terminal, and she flashed her ID and asked for a quiet place with a fully netted computer, the liaison aide ushered her and Captain Sabo straight to a small but quite luxurious VIP lounge. He left telling her to call if there was anything—*anything*—else they needed.

According to her phone there were several messages waiting for her, the bulk of them large downloadables. So she had gone straight to the computer, logged into the indicated space.

The mysterious and ever-resourceful Jamal had provided her with all sorts of useful items. A set of blueprints for the condo where Daveed Shah and Jasper Crow were presumably being held. Info to help bolster that presumption, such as that his apartment remained blocked to in-access, and for the past few hours it had been receiving the Victory Channel, a militiacentric pirate feed with obvious White Fist leanings.

He had also provided a précis of the last few hours' events in the media. She reviewed it with a sinking feeling in her gut. She saw the statement made by Dan Francisco's ex-wife and the pronouncements of those comparing him to a dead cult leader. The poor man's reputation was in ruins, with his own home net gleefully bulldozing the smoldering remains every hour on the hour.

To her it looked like America was doing what it always did, which was focusing on one thing or event and going completely insane. EdgeNet had begun running an hourly fifteen-minute Avva update complete with fancy graphics and theme music, rehashing the stuff they already had, and filling in with the ever-popular political and celebrity reaction and shots of the dozen or so pro- and anti-Avva protests that had been staged so far.

Then there was the special lunacy the good old US of A produced with the same efficiency as pizza and software. In Kentucky a naked man who was being described as "quite large and clearly aroused" had accosted a female cop, demanding that they have sex so Avva could watch human mating rituals. The man had run away when the cop had hauled out her own woody, and the search for him still continued. A second-string psychic in Tampa claimed she was in contact with Avva, and could pose personal inquiries about life and love for a quite modest fee, considering. The latest in a series of has-been actors shilling for a lobby better stocked with ammunition than logic was making statements about how all these events proved there should be no gun control.

On the tactical side, the Command and Uplink Center was in the process of becoming a war zone. A full-security alert had been declared. Already it was partly under siege, a locust swarm of media camped outside its gates. The Fists and other extremist groups with similar delusions and goals were converging on the area, and Reverend Sunshine's Avvatine Crusade had likewise gone into high gear. The televangelist had bought large blocs of time all across the media, and was using them to exhort his followers and good Christians everywhere to join him at Neely where mass prayer meetings would attempt to bend the *Ares'* course toward Phobos. Cars, vans, buses, and pickups filled with the sorts of nuts and hustlers this sort of thing draws were causing traffic jams on the highways leading into Neely. Roadblocks were being set up.

New Mexico governor Julian Blackhorse had already called out the National Guard to help the UN troops being brought in to deal with the rapidly developing situation.

She pushed back her chair, running a hand through her short white hair. This was turning into what the Americans called a clusterfuck at an alarming rate. Any chance of her slipping into the Center and quietly requisitioning help was gone. Just getting past the media encampment without causing a stir would be impossible. It looked like she was on her own.

Martina rubbed her burning eyes, then her gaze settled on the broad back of Captain Sabo, who stood by the window gazing out onto the runways.

"Do I need to release you so you may leave?" she called. The woman's warplane had already been refueled, a crew beginning that job while they were still heading for the terminal.

Sabo turned, shrugged.

"Be easy with you, ma'am," she answered. "My orders were to get you here ASAP and render aid as necessary. So I figured I'd stick me around. Maybe you'll want to get somewhere righteous quick, or strafe someone."

"I wish it were that simple," Martina said heavily, getting up to go stand beside the other woman and stare out the window. A steady stream of transport planes flew out of the setting sun, landed to disgorge loads of troops and equipment, then lifted off empty. Helicopters darted in, unloaded, and darted out like cyborg dragonflies. Everywhere there were soldiers, trucks, forklifts, and fuel trucks. This level of activity had to be felt in Neely itself. Sooner or later it might just make Jones panic and cut her losses. The situation was explosive, and the fuse had already been lit.

The South African woman leaned against the wall. "Could I ask what the problem is, ma'am? I can keep a secret. I even have the papers to prove it."

Martina parked a hip on the windowsill. The pilot did have a good security clearance—she'd checked on that back in New York. A sounding board might help her come up with a viable plan.

"Okay, here is situation: There are two men, both UN personnel, being held hostage in a fifth-floor unit of an old condo near here. Hostage takers are extremists, members of White Fists of Uncle Sam. They are certain to be armed, very dangerous. I need to get these two men out. The two sole entry points to the apartment where they are held are front door and fifth-floor balcony."

"You can't ask for help from the police or our troops?"

"I would rather not. On practical side, balcony faces street, making it too easy for unusual activity to be spotted. Plus locals already have hands full. Then are other, ah, considerations."

The woman nodded thoughtfully, then headed toward the gleaming glass-and-steel Braun InCafe set up on one side of the room. She glanced back questioningly. Martina nodded. Maybe caffeine would crank her brain into high gear.

"So what you're saying is you have to do this sort of sideways of official channels," Sabo said as she returned with two steaming cups.

"Yes," Martina agreed, gratefully accepting one. "Very sideways."

"I figured, what with the way my orders came down. Hush-hush, full scramble, top secret and all of that droff. Can I ask why these hostages are so special?"

Martina smiled over her cup. "No, not really."

The pilot shrugged, unconcerned. "Be easy with you. You got a map of the area where this building is?"

"Probably." She pushed off from the windowsill and went back to the computer, calling up a listing of the myriad files Jamal had sent. Snorted and shook her head. "You can take your pick, Captain. I have satellite overview current within the last hour, virtual model, utilities routing—you name it and I have it."

"Virtual model would be righteous handy." Sabo started to reach past her, hesitated. "May I, Colonel?"

Martina stepped back. "Help yourself. Is all yours."

The woman called up the virtual map, studied it for a moment. Then she pulled a set of banana yellow, decidedly nonmilitary shaydes with pink flamingos on the earpieces out of her flight suit's breast pocket, and slipped them on. Martina stepped back out of the way and stood there sipping her coffee as she watched the pilot move around and sweep her head from side to side, the flat-screen representation changing dizzily.

"I think I see how I can help do this," she said at last, pulling off the shaydes and dropping them back into her pocket. "You go in the front door. I'll provide a diversion at the balcony."

"What kind of diversion?"

Sabo grinned. "We rode here in her."

"Your Gryphon? You can fly to that balcony?"

"Righteous easy. It's against the law to pilot a fighter inside civilian space, but I figure you've maybe got enough pull to keep me cool on that."

Martina felt something like optimism beginning to return. "*Da*, I probably do." If not, she knew who did.

"Barkin'." Sabo's grin grew wider, her teeth very white against her coal black skin. "I bet I can scare me the living shit out of these bleachy assholes."

"Yes," Martina chuckled. "I just bet you can."

The pilot tossed off the rest of her coffee. "I'm ready to go anytime you are, ma'am."

She clapped the younger woman on the shoulder. "Save the ma'ams, Winnie. You might as well call me Martina since it is looking like we are going to be working together."

Subsection Nine

Jane's watch had started badly and gone downhill from there. Then just when she thought it couldn't get much worse, it did.

Yet another sleepless night had taken its toll. She dragged herself out of bed feeling old and tired and stupid, a hollow shell of her normal self. Plus she felt like a total shit for having wimped out and not told Fabi what was going on. A quiet, easy day was what she needed, but that wasn't what she got.

She was beginning to think the *Ares* was jinxed. Maybe even cursed. While the previous day's patchup of their life-support systems was holding, a new problem had sprung up to take its place. This most recent headache was not life-threatening, but it did put their primary mission objective in jeopardy.

The Mars lander and associated equipment were to be tested biweekly, inspection duty rotated among herself, Wanda, and Hans, whose turn it was this time. The probes and minisats they were to deploy had tested fine, but Gluck had encountered a problem while running a check in the propulsion systems of the Mars Eagle, the craft that was supposed to take him and his wife down to the Red Planet's surface to plant the first human footprints and take samples.

So the three of them had taken on the task of trying to track down the problem, leaving Willy, Anna, and Fabi to manage the daily shipboard routine. First they pissed away several hours working by telemetry with the Eagle's own onboard diagnostics, getting zilch for their efforts.

That left them with only one option. She and Hans had to suit up, go out into the unpressurized bay where the Eagle was berthed, and go over it in person. That bay was a clamshell-doored nacelle in the aft section of the *Ares,* just ahead of its engines. The lander filled most of the compartment, and although its short stubby wings were retracted to vestigial fins, that still left them very little space in which to work.

They labored side by side under its bulk, the harsh glare of the bay's halogen lamps casting knife-edged shadows against the Eagle's curved blue flank. It was basically a VTOL rocketplane, bastard cousin to the new Gryphon and Shrike classes of combat aircraft. Like them, it was powered by a custom version of the small, ultraefficient "Dragon's Breath" neoceramic engines. Custom in this case meaning lacking the endless hours of use and perfecting the standard engines had going for them. Finicky, untrustworthy kladge, in other words.

The belly hatches covering the systems that fed the engines were open. Color-coded cables snaked from the Eagle's guts to the diagnostic board that hung from a strap over Jane's shoulders like the tray carried by a cigarette and condom girl at some retro club.

"Okay, pressure test section Gamma 40," she said tiredly. The problem seemed to lie in the overbleed system. Oxytonic Fuscol fuel was pressurized and preheated, fed to the engines through insulated high-pressure lines at a point just a hair shy of spontaneous combustion, the amount used metered by the throttle. Excess was shunted back into the feed loop to help preheat fresh fuel from the tanks being prepared for burning. Foolproof in the Gryphons. Not here, of course.

"Testing," Gluck replied, his voice coming in over her helmet's speakers. He sounded tired and depressed. If they couldn't find the problem and fix it, he wasn't going to get any closer to Mars than the *Ares'* orbit.

"What does the telemetry read?" she queried Wanda back in engineering, repeating the question for what had to be the three hundredth time.

"I've got nominal and green," the engineer replied, then yawned. "Sorry."

Jane frowned. They were all wiped out, Wanda most of all. Her watch had ended hours ago. "I know it's past your bedtime. If we don't get this pinned down in the next few minutes, we'll pull the plug and try again tomorrow."

"I'll make it, Cap'n. At least I get coffee, not suit-water."

"Rub it in, you bitch. Hans, we both have green. Do you see anything to contradict?"

"Nothing."

"Okay, then on to Gamma 41."

"Check." He began moving the sensors and test leads to the next section of the fuel system. Jane turned her head to take a sip of warm, flat water, wishing it was coffee, which she also wished Wanda hadn't mentioned. The test board's display read WAITING. She was glad it was built by Seiko-Shamrock, and not more Krautgentine trashware.

"Ready," he said once the last lead was in place.

"Pressurize." An itch started on her left thigh, right on the edge of her panty line. *Just* what she needed. She closed her eyes a second and squirmed inside her suit, trying to relieve it. Just as she managed to hit the magic spot a new, and equally recognizable sensation replaced it.

A chill ran down her spine, instantly setting off a spike of adrenaline.

Another visit from Avva was coming. Fast.

Not now! she wailed inwardly, her eyes flying open and her gaze sweeping across the test board, then snapping back to the red dots lighting its surface. *Shit!*

"I . . . have red," she said in a hoarse voice. *It was coming. Now. Nowhere to run. Fuck! FUCK! Not NOW!*

"Read confirmed," Wanda said. "You okay, Jane?"

"Looks like the problem is in safety sensor of section Gamma 41-C," Hans said sourly. "I suppose it could be worse. I can pull it in about half an hour, but I, for one, am beat and think the repair, test, replace, and retest should wait for tomorrow. What do you say, Commander?"

His question went by half-heard as the first tentative touch of Avva crashed over her. All she could do was check her tether and mentally hunker down.

"Commander? *Jane?*" His tone sharpened as he realized that something was wrong.

She was no longer exactly there to answer.

* * *

When Avva departed, awareness of her surroundings rolled back into focus like bounceback from a high-G blackout.

Hans had her in the airlock, the outer door just closing. A detached part of her noted this, and approved of how quickly and decisively he'd acted. According to the clock in her suit just under two minutes had elapsed since she lost it. Much better than drill-spec. If nothing else, the arrogant son of a bitch was efficient.

Voices swirled around her, filling her helmet. Crisp emergency voices.

"I'm okay," she rasped, her mind still reeling from what she had just been through. The contact had been shorter than any of the others before, but had packed an emotional wallop that had threatened to trip her breakers. Her brain felt nuked.

"Suit telemetry confirms she is stable," Fabi agreed in a flat, passionless voice. His *Doctor in Charge* voice. "Biostats returning to normal. I want her brought straight to sick bay immediately. Willy and Anna are standing by the lock. They will bring her here and help me get her unsuited."

"I said I'm *okay!*" she repeated, anger at their treating her as if she wasn't there sharpening her tone. "I just had a—" A *what,* old girl? Well, she knew what it had been, knew for absolute damnsure now; all doubts had been blown clear away by this contact. The question— the problem—was what to do about it. *Big* question. *Big* problem.

"—a small dizzy spell, that's all," she finished lamely.

"I hear you, Janey," Fabi said, emotion creeping back into his voice. "It was more than that, I'm afraid. I believe you suffered some sort of seizure."

"It wasn't a fucking *seizure!*" she snapped, instantly regretting her loss of cool. She could see Hans staring at her through his faceplate. Could see the calculation in his eyes as he examined her for defects. She had an absurd, nearly overwhelming urge to stick her tongue out at him.

"It was just a dizzy spell," she repeated, trying to sound calm and reasonable. "Blood sugar, maybe."

What was it her aunt Tess had that caused blackouts? Oh yeah. "Or maybe potassium." She tried for a light-hearted tone. "Just peel me a banana, and I'll be good as new."

"You were talking out of your head . . . Commander," Hans said in a flat voice. He glanced away as the lockstack changed to yellow, then regarded her again. Stonefaced. Watching and waiting for her to go bananas again? "You kept yelling the name Daveed."

Daveed! Her knees went weak at the mention of his name, and dizziness eddied through her.

The visitation from Avva had begun as usual, disjointed and largely incomprehensible imagery and sensations filling her head, riding a rising emotional carrier wave. But then he had sort of hesitated, and an instant later she'd *felt* him suddenly fix on one of the other people he was contacting, sending what he found and how that felt rushing into her and the others' heads in a massive ungoverned blast of empathic juice that had threatened to stop her heart. It was as if he'd gathered them all in close and *screamed*.

Up until now all she'd had was this vague, indefinable sense that there were others. Now she knew for sure. She could even *name* most of them. A preacher named Ray Sunshine. Jamal, who answered to several other names as well. Dan. Martina. Another woman whose identity was hazy, but seemed somehow connected to Jamal.

And most of all Daveed Shah, the mediartist from MU in charge of stitching together bits and pieces of the world the *Ares* had left behind. Before he had been no more than a name she had traded backchannel quips with, and thanked for knowing her taste so well. Now she knew him from the inside, with an immediacy no normal contact could have created.

Daveed. Hostage to two terrorists. Beaten. Semiconscious. Terrified for himself and his friend, and in terrible terrible pain.

Avva had not once repeated his plea for help this time. No, when he had made contact with Daveed and understood his plight, he had abandoned all thought of his own situation in an instant, terror and concern for

Shah overwriting everything in letters a thousand feet high. Avva's frightened/horrified/desperate cry of ***SAVE DAVEED*** still boomed through Jane's nerves like a storm distilled into feelings, tremendous, frantic, and irrefusable.

There was no longer any way for her to try to rationalize Avva away. Nor was there any way for her not to trust or believe him. The being's concern had not been for what Daveed might have done for him, but for the man and his dreadful situation. That had rung so pure and so true and so potent that the memory of it threatened to bring tears to her eyes.

Yes, she had surely cried out Daveed's name. Probably screamed it, echoing the cry in her head. She shrugged in answer to Gluck's question-slash-accusation, an entirely pointless gesture in a pressure suit.

The stack turned green, and the lock's inner doors began to open.

"Can you walk?" Gluck asked tersely. "Or should I carry you?"

He said this as if he had been carrying her all along. "I can walk."

His helmet dipped in a nod. "Then let us get you looked at by Dr. Costanza." A last hard-eyed stare. "Then we will see what must be done about this situation."

Jane set her jaw and submitted to having Willy and Anna and her husband help her out of her suit like she was some helpless cripple. Once that was done, Fabi banished everyone from the sick bay. Anna and Willy left together, giving her cautiously hopeful looks over their shoulders as they went out. He very nearly had to remove Hans by force. Gluck must have shed his own suit in record time, because he made it to the sick bay while they were still getting her undressed.

It was unlikely this had been so he could see her in her unmentionables. He seemed to have decided his job was to keep an eye on her, probably to physically subdue her if she started acting strange again. His face and posture suggested that he was just itching to try out his chokehold.

The door finally closed behind him, leaving Jane and her husband alone. She sat there on the examining table in her sweaty underwear, shoulders slumped and dreading what was to come. Now she had no choice but to tell him what had been happening to her, and thanks to her earlier cowardice, it was going to come out when she already had a couple strikes against her.

Fabi came back, knelt so he was looking up at her. His dark eyes searched her face for some clue as to what had happened.

"What gives, Janey?" he asked gently.

She gazed down at him, once again skating on the edge of tears. Where to start? How could she make him understand?

"I'm not sick," she said at last. "Or crazy."

Dismay flickered across his face for just an instant, then vanished. He nodded. "All right."

"At first I thought I might be. Thought I had to be."

"Can you tell me why you had thoughts like these?" The pitch of his voice warned her that this question was as much headshrinkerly as husbandly. Maybe even more.

"I want to. I've wanted to all along. But it's hard." Her hands fretted each other nervously.

"I know." He closed his hands around hers, stilling them. "You can tell me, love. You can tell me anything."

She hoped that was true. "I—I've been hearing something. In my head." She got those words out, but it would have been easier to confess that she had been spreading her legs for some other man. That at least was explicable and normal. He hadn't been trained to treat infidelity as a disease.

"What kind of something?" he said with a frown. "A ringing in your ears?"

"No, something else."

His brow furrowed slightly. "You mean like a voice?"

She nodded, hung her head. "A voice. Plus pictures. Sounds. Emotions and feelings. It's almost like sex in a way." That sounded wrong. "I mean not physically, but this feeling of near total connection with someone else."

"Do you know who this voice belongs to?" His tone detached, as if reading from a workbook.

Now for the really sticky part, and she could already feel herself losing him. "Yeah, I do."

"Can you tell me?"

"His name is Avva. I'm not really sure he is male, but I think of him that way."

"Who is this Avva?"

She took a deep breath. "Avva is an alien."

"An . . . alien," he repeated, his face losing all expression and a note of despair finally entering his voice.

"I *know* it sounds nuts," she admitted, looking him straight in the eyes. "Believe me! But I know he's real. As real as you or I."

Fabi didn't look very convinced, but at least he continued on as if taking her assertion at face value. "Where is this Avva, honey? What does he want?"

"He's on Phobos. It's not so much what he wants, as what he needs."

"What would that be?"

"Our help. He and another of his kind were, um, stationed there. The other one died. He's young and all alone, and can't maintain his place or emplacement or whatever you want to call it all by himself. He wants us to come to his rescue. *Needs* us to."

By then Fabi, her Fabi, was staring at her like she was a stranger.

"Us meaning the *Ares* mission," he said at last.

"Yeah." She tried to smile. "It's not like there's anybody else nearby."

"So this is what happened out in the bay? He, ah, came to you and told you this?"

"He never got the chance because something came up. Besides, he'd already told me all this before. Today was different."

"How?"

"Well, Hans said I was calling Daveed Shah's name, right?"

A solemn nod. "Yes, I heard it, too."

"You know who he is?"

"Chief editor at MU, right?"

"Yeah. He's been hearing Avva, too, and now he's in bad trouble. Avva learned this and put Shah's welfare ahead of his own, begging the rest of us who are hearing him to help the man. Things are getting crazy back home." She tried for another smile, coming closer than before. "Even worse than here."

"What do you mean by crazy?"

Her smile died and she bit her lip, realizing that she had better not throw that word around too freely.

"It's hard to explain. See, when Avva contacted me this time I got these, I guess you could call them *impressions* from the others who are hearing him. Bits and pieces. There is a preacher named Sunshine who's started a public crusade to save Avva. Remember Dan the Virtual Weatherman from EdgeNet? He went public after Sunshine named him, and his daughter has been taken away from him because of it. The White Fists want our mission stopped. They believe Avva exists, only they think he's like the granddaddy of all nonwhites. Two of them took Daveed and a friend hostage. A woman named Martina, she's UN Secretary-General Perez's bodyguard, is on her way to rescue them if she can. Working with Dan and Martina is this guy named Jamal . . . who I think might also be Jambo the Joker. Then there's another woman I'm not sure about, but I think her name might be Amber."

"I—" She watched him shake his head and look away. "This is a lot to absorb, Janey."

She snorted. "Try doing it in thirty seconds flat while linked to an alien brain."

"That would be . . . difficult," he agreed in a cautious, clipped tone. "There has been nothing about any of this in the news, Jane. Not a word."

"Our news is censored. Remember?"

He straightened up, rested his hands on her shoulders. "I don't know what to say. This is all quite difficult to believe." He shook his head. "Extremely difficult."

"I know, believe me *I know*. It's taken me a lot of time and pain to come to terms with it myself. But I know what I know, and I think if we look hard enough, we'll find proof."

He regarded her soberly. She could see how badly he wanted to believe her, but he possessed far too much knowledge about the myriad ways the human mind could malfunction to entirely accept her story. She was his wife but also their commander, and so held their lives in her hands. He dared not wink at a possible breakdown.

Before either of them could say anything else the intercom came to life, Hans Gluck's voice blaring out of the overhead speakers.

"General meeting in the wardroom immediately, all hands to attend. Dr. Costanza, please bring your patient with you. Gluck out."

They exchanged a glance, both well aware what this meant. Gluck was going to want to know if she was fit to continue commanding their mission. She searched her husband's face for some sign of what answer he would give.

Fifteen years of reading that mug and she didn't have a clue. This was not a good sign.

"Fabi," she said, unable to keep the desperation from her voice any longer, "I'm not crazy. There really is someone from another planet trapped on Phobos, and he needs us. He needs us bad. He's going to die if we don't come."

He turned away, going to a locker and removing a coverall. "Here," he said, bringing it to her. "You better get dressed."

She hopped down from the table and began pulling it on. It was one of the spare one-size-fits-nobody jobs, and far too big for her, making her look like she'd shrunk. Maybe she had, the past couple days gnawing her down to a fragment of the strong, self-confident woman she'd been before this all began.

"I know you have a responsibility here," she said tiredly as she zipped the coverall shut. "I understand that you have to be absolutely certain I'm not a danger to this mission or anyone on it." She took hold of his arm, relieved that he didn't flinch. "I'm not. You believe me, don't you?"

"Partly, anyway," he said with a sigh. "But I'm not sure belief is going to be good enough for Hans."

She had no answer to that.

He took her by the hand, another hopeful sign. At least he wasn't afraid of her.

"Let's go get this over with," he said.

She had no other choice.

The moment they entered the wardroom she knew she was in for a battle.

Hans was sitting in her chair. The command chair.

He'd changed into his dress uniform, every button buttoned and brass gleaming. His face was hard, cold, his mouth set in a tight line. He looked prepared to court-martial her on the spot, and act as one-man firing squad afterward.

Easy now, she warned herself. Remain calm. The way you act may be the deciding factor in how this turns out.

The rest of the crew were already there. They looked up when she entered. She smiled. They smiled back, but not with the easy camaraderie of old.

Anna looked the most apprehensive, almost as if it were she who faced punishment. She tried to smile, only partly succeeding. Wanda toyed with her decorated braids, rearranging the bits of electronics as if trying to build some new device. Her smile was stronger, and reassuring. As usual Willy had a slayte in his lap, his blunt fingers dancing ceaselessly across the foldout keyboard.

"Please sit down, Commander," Gluck said in a formal tone.

"Thank you, Mr. Gluck," she answered, trying to sound calm and confident. She sat, crossed her legs, folded her hands in her lap to keep them still. Fabi slid into the seat beside her and gave Hans the eye, his face tense and wary.

Gluck stood, his back rigid and his chin thrust out. "I have called this assembly under Article Twelve," he announced in a flat, emotionless voice. There was a stir. Each and every one of them knew what that meant.

Willy looked up from his slayte. "Don't you think maybe you're overreacting, Hans?" he asked mildly. "Jane just had a dizzy spell, that's all."

"There is more to it than that," Gluck replied. "Perhaps you have noticed that for the last few days Commander Dawkins-Costanza has seemed preoccupied. Jumpy. Even furtive. Now less than an hour ago she suffered some sort of seizure right in the middle of a critical procedure. I am glad she has recovered from this episode, but in light of recent information which has come into my possession, I am forced to come to the conclusion that she is no longer fit to command this mission."

There, he's said it, Jane thought numbly.

"What information might that be?" Fabi asked. His tone sharpened. "I don't recall having given any sort of diagnosis yet, Mr. Gluck."

Hans stared back at him. "You have not offered one, Doctor. I cannot hold this against you. As her husband it is entirely natural and understandable for you to be biased in her favor."

Jane watched Fabi's eyes narrow, felt his anger rise. "I ask you again, what information are you talking about? If it is what I suspect, *you* may be the one in need of treatment. I'll be able to diagnose your condition easily enough. I'll have caused it."

Gluck's mouth tightened. "Please, Dr. Costanza. This is not the time or place for threats. We have a serious matter which must be decided. One best approached in a cool, clearheaded manner."

The ghost of a smile appeared on Fabi's face, and he bowed. "You are right, of course." His smile widened. "If necessary I will wait until afterward to ask you to step outside, you snot-nosed, goosestepping, impotent little anal-retentive prick."

Gluck's face paled, and the muscles in his jaw knotted, but he made no direct response to Fabi's insult. Instead he stiffly turned toward the other members of the crew and held out his hands.

"As you can see, Dr. Costanza's impartiality is in question on this matter. But that is not the issue we must deal with at this time. This is." He leaned down, tapped a command into the board before the chair he had taken as his own. The big wall display behind him lit.

Jane's stomach sank down to her bowels when she saw herself sitting on the examination table in her underwear, Fabi kneeling before her. Their hushed voices filled the wardroom.

"I'm not sick. Or crazy."

"All right."

"At first I thought I might be. Thought I had to be."

"Can you tell me why you had thoughts like these?"

"I want to. I've wanted to all along. But it's hard."

"I know." A pause as he closed his hands around hers. *"You can tell me, love. You can tell me anything."*

"I—I've been hearing something. In my head."

"What kind of something? A ringing in your ears?"

"No, something else."

"You mean like a voice?"

"A voice. Plus pictures. Sounds. Emotions and feelings. It's almost like sex in a way." She watched herself make a face and shake her head. *"I mean not physically, but this feeling of near total connection with someone else."*

"Do you know who this voice belongs to?"

"Yeah, I do."

"Can you tell me?"

"His name is Avva. I'm not really sure he is male, but I think of him that way."

"Who is this Avva?"

On the screen before her the bedraggled woman who was herself took a deep breath and delivered her own indictment, her own damnation. *"Avva is an alien."*

"An . . . alien." His disbelief was obvious.

"I know it sounds nuts."

Gluck froze the playback. "I believe this evidence speaks for itself."

"You sneaky fascist cocksucker," Fabi growled, pushing up from his chair. "You filthy peeping—"

Jane laid a restraining hand on his arm, shaking her head when he broke off his verbal assault and looked down at her. He stared at her a moment, then sat back down in tight-lipped fury.

She faced her accuser. "Spying, Hans?"

"Trying to maintain the safety and security of this mission and its crew," he answered stiffly.

"Ah. Most commendable." She leaned toward him, resting her forearms on the table. "So you believe I pose a danger to this mission and the rest of you?"

A curt nod. "I do, yes."

"Based on what evidence?"

"You say—you *confess*—that you are hearing an alien

talking in your head." He tried to smile, looking like a man who has just had an accident with his zipper. "This is hardly normal behavior, Commander."

"No, I don't suppose it is." She straightened the crease in the leg of her coverall, arranging her thoughts at the very same time. "There is one thing you haven't considered, Hans," she said at last, looking up at him once more.

"What is that?"

"What if I'm right?"

He eyed her with a baffled scowl, then turned toward his wife. She paled at the look on his face, flinching back in her chair.

"Have you seen any evidence of an alien living on Phobos?"

"Phobos?" she echoed uncertainly.

"The Martian moon," he said, as if talking to a stupid child. "Surely you must have heard of it. Later she says that this is where her spaceman lives."

Anna looked toward Jane, her face stricken. The poor woman didn't want to anger her husband further, or get Jane in trouble.

"Go ahead, Anna," Jane said quietly. "You can answer."

"*Ny*—no," she said at last. "But have not been look-ing—"

"That will be all," Hans broke in. "Thank you."

"But maybe I—"

"That will be *enough*!" His command silenced her like a slap. She huddled deeper into her chair, shoulders hunched and eyes downcast. Although she made no sound, tears ran down her round cheeks.

Wanda gave the areologist's hands a sisterly pat, then spoke up. "Jane is one of the sanest people I know," she drawled with just the slightest edge of challenge in her voice. "She says there's an alien campin' out on Phobos, I say get out the marshmallows." The engineer gave her a broad smile. "I s'pose he wants us to drop by and say howdy."

God she was glad this woman was her friend! "Actually, he wants us to rescue him."

"Makes sense," Wanda agreed with a nod. "Who else

is he gonna call? It's not like Triple A's gonna send Bubba's Wrecker out."

"This is *absurd*!" Hans snapped, slamming his hand down on the table. "There is no alien. The woman is deluded. Delusional. Under Article Twelve I am relieving her of command."

Those words hung in the air like poisoned smoke. No one breathed or moved until they'd been given a few seconds to dissipate.

"Hans," Anna whispered meekly, cringing back and covering her mouth at the black look he gave her.

Willy looked up from his slayte, his stubby brown fingers finally ceasing their endless motion. His round face was thoughtful, but Jane couldn't help noticing how his dark eyes gleamed with suppressed merriment. He was up to something, she was sure of it.

"It seems to me what we've got here is a problem in logic," he said in a musing tone. "We have before us two propositions. Proposition *A* is that our Jane's brain has started dealin' her jokers, and she should be relieved of command. Proposition *B* is that she really has been contacted by this Avva fella, and we should be haulin' ass to Phobos to help."

"This is not a debate or a democracy," Hans snapped. "I have followed the rules and relieved her of command. I am in charge now, and there will be no vote."

"Very well, sir," the chubby Samoan replied imperturbably. "Then by those same rules, I am hereby appointin' myself her advocate."

Gluck frowned. "Her *what*?"

Willy beamed at him, his hand briefly flickering across his slayte's keyboard. "I direct you to look at the copy of our mission rules I have put on the screen in front of you. I quote from subsection nine: *'In the case of an Article Twelve action, the accused has the right to an advocate who may in his or her behalf investigate mitigating, explanatory, or exculpatory factors.'* Since you are insistin' this is a psychological problem, the job would normally go to Fabi. But since you seem to doubt him almost as much as Jane, I'll volunteer."

Hans was scowling when he looked up from the display. "I have never seen this part of the rules before."

"It's in the appendices. If you don't believe me, call Earth up and ask—but remember, you're gonna have to explain why you want to know. A change in command like this for a reason like this would probably cause them to scrub our mission. Anyway, the way I figure it, proof of this Avva's existence would make one damn good mitigating, explanatory, *and* exculpatory factor."

"You cannot prove this."

"I sure as hell can try, brah. I'm allowed to solicit any help I deem necessary to defend and help exonerate the person for whom I stand as advocate. The pickin's are a bit thin, but I'll make do."

Willy turned toward Gluck's wife. "Anna my love, I want you to give Phobos the hardest eyeballin' you can. Use every sensor and trick you can think of to find some proof of Jane's friend. Can you do that?"

Jane watched the chunky woman sit up straighter, set her jaw. "I damn sure will." A defiant glance in her husband's direction. "Even if I must sleep in my lab to do so."

"Thanks. Now Fabi, I want you to test our girl six ways to Sunday, proving there's nothin' wrong with her."

Fabi smiled. "I plan to. By the way, Jane told me that they know about Avva back on Earth—a bit of information Lord Admiral Gluck saw fit to withhold when he played back his spying."

Tutillia nodded. "Excellent. That would certainly help prove her assertions. Wanda, would you mind lookin' into that? May have to sneak past the censorin'."

She bared her teeth. "It would be my pleasure, sugar."

Hans had listened to all this, seeing his control of the situation slipping away. Jane did have to give him some points for what he did next. Of course the rules Willy had come up with, real or not, gave him little choice. Still, buried under all that knee-jerk bullshit there just might be a tiny rice-grain-sized seed of leadership.

"Very well, then we are agreed," he said, trying to sound like Willy's advocacy had been his idea. "This situation is difficult, and the circumstances extraordinary. I will retain command while you try to prove that her assertions are not a delusion." An unconvincing smile.

"If there is indeed a little green man living on Phobos, I will of course relinquish command."

He faced Jane. She could see the steel shutters coming down inside him as he braced himself for what he felt he had to do next.

"Yes, Mr. Gluck?" she asked, as if giving him permission to speak.

He took a deep breath. "For the present time, Commander, you should consider yourself relieved of all command duties and confined to the sick bay. Will you accept these constraints, and abide by them?"

Jane locked eyeballs with him, reading fear, determination, and a not entirely suppressed glint of appeal. She knew she could tell him to go fuck himself and there wasn't one damn thing he could do about it. Odds were that one word from her and *he'd* be the one confined. On the other hand, even though she had been ousted, this had come closer to a draw than she had first thought possible.

In lieu of rules there is only anarchy. It was for the best if they both played by them.

"This will be acceptable," she replied in a queenly tone.

His face gave nothing away, but a trace of the rigidity left his shoulders. "Very good. You are all dismissed. Thank you."

Willy, Wanda, and Anna stood up. They faced her, came to the strictest attention she'd ever seen them manage, then in unison snapped up their hands and sharply saluted her.

"Thank you," she said, feeling a lump in her throat. They dropped their salutes and left the wardroom together, pointedly ignoring their new commander.

Fabi stood, tugged on her arm. "Come on, let's get away from this fascist bastard."

Jane rose to her feet and faced her usurper. In a way she felt sorry for him. He had no imagination, no empathy, no flexibility, no charisma, and scarcely a trace of the other indefinables that made a good leader. His taking command was a hollow gesture. If it hadn't been clear to him before that one word from her and the rest of the crew would follow, this last demonstration of their loyalty had surely gotten through.

"Hans, I know you are doing what you think is right. But you are wrong. Avva exists, and we're the only ones who can save him."

He sat down in her chair, eyes on the keyboard rather than her. "I cannot believe that," he said, sounding more like the odd man out than the man on top.

"I know. I had a damn hard time with it myself."

He finally looked at her, naked appeal twisting its way onto his face. "There is no *proof,* Commander! I cannot swallow this madness or allow our mission to be diverted without proof! You know I cannot!"

Jane smiled wearily.

"Well, with a little luck maybe we can find you some."

Virtual [Im]possibility

Dan was at the wheel of the Jamalmobile when things spun completely out of control.

They'd gotten off the interstate, and were heading for a strip mall where they could not only tank up with fuel, but score extra liquor and groceries for the long drive through the night. Amber had gone into the back a few miles before the exit, supposedly to work on a list with Jamal.

The amount of time she'd been gone made him think maybe Jamal had needed some distraction to help him cope. That was fine with him. If it took regular heaping helpings of sex and booze to keep Jamal from freaking, then let him slurp and screw all the way to Neely. Without Jamal they were *nothing*.

The only problem with Amber being gone to administer some sexual TLC—and it turned out to be a big one—was that left him all alone in the cab when Avva called. What ensued was like one of those stupid bumper stickers come to ugly life: *When the Rapture comes, somebody grab my steering wheel!*

When Avva left him alone in his head once more the truck was no longer moving, and he was surrounded by deflating crashbags. The big vehicle was sitting at an odd angle, and the inside of the windshield—and everything else, himself included—was covered with the fine gray-white powder the bags were packed in.

He wiped a clear spot in the glass with his hand, then peered uncomprehendingly at the bucolic vista on the other side. The truck's headlights fanned out over an expanse of green grass and red dirt, spotlighting a herd of cows who didn't look like they'd expected visitors to their yard. They stared back, equally puzzled.

There was a multisecond lag as his still-reeling mind absorbed and tried to process this, then what it all meant finally added up.

He'd crashed the truck.

"Oh Jesus," he wailed. *"Amber and Jamal!"*

He pawed desperately at the buckle of his seat harness, finally getting it open, then lurched from the seat and banged his head on the padded roof. The door into the back was half-open. He shoved the panel out of the way and ducked into the rear of the truck, his heart in his throat.

Fortunately most of the big stuff was securely fastened down, and had stayed were it belonged. But smaller items were scattered everywhere, and the place reeked of the whiskey leaking from a bottle of Wild Turkey lying on the floor. There were no bodies, which was good, but where the hell were Jamal and Amber?

He heard a groan from way in the rear. Picking his way across the tilted truck bed he headed for the curtained area back there. Swept the drapery aside, trying to brace himself for the sight of blood and broken bodies, and froze when confronted by something else altogether.

"Oh *man*," a buck-naked Amber groaned, shaking her head groggily. "I think I felt the earth move!"

Jamal was sprawled on his back under her and in a similar state of undress. He looked up at Dan, a lopsided grin splitting his bearded face. "That was, ah"—he blinked—"intense."

Then a pained look drove the smile off his face. "Oh Lord," he whispered, *"Daveed."*

"Yeah." Dan collapsed shakily to the bed beside them, relieved that they were all right.

"I think I may have killed the truck," he confessed. The need to do something about Daveed jangled in his nerves, and he knew he'd just ruined their means to do so.

Amber crawled off her lover and crouched there, staring at Dan with dazed eyes. "I *felt* it," she said in an awed voice. "Him. *Avva.* Through Jamal. I felt you, too."

He nodded, trying to keep himself from staring at the

quite remarkable tattoos that began just below her pierced navel and went all the way down to her ankles. "I know." He'd felt her there on the edges, along with everyone else.

Jamal sat up and rubbed his bald pate. "I was feeling extremely tense. We slipped back here for a little relaxation." He gestured toward the upholstered padding surrounding the bed. "It would seem a good thing that we did."

"I'm just glad you're okay." He stood up. "I guess I better go out and see how badly I've screwed up the truck."

"I'll go with you," Amber said, climbing across Jamal's bare legs. She went to a cabinet and took out a big flashlight. Dan couldn't help noticing that the tattoos covered her naked buttocks and the back of her legs as well.

He swallowed hard. "Don't—don't you want to get dressed first?"

She looked down at herself, shrugged, then grabbed her leather jacket and headed for the side door.

They walked around the truck, feet squishing in the muddy field. When they got up by the hood Amber squatted and directed the flashlight's beam across what remained of the truck's front suspension.

There wasn't much. The stone fence they had crashed through on their way into the pasture had seen to that. Both front wheels were twisted inward, the bumper wrapped around one of them. One big rock was still lodged in the grille.

Unlike Dan, Amber seemed to know what she was looking at. So he sort of stood guard, keeping a wary eye on the cows.

"We're screwed," she said as she straightened up. "The front axle is busted, along with all the steering linkages and suspension mounts. The frame may be bent, too."

Dan hung his head. This was all his fault. What a fuckup. He couldn't even be trusted to *drive.*

"I'm sorry," he sighed, sounding as pathetic as he felt. She patted his shoulder. "Are you kidding, man? I only caught a little of what you guys got. *Nobody* could've driven through a mind fuck like that."

Obviously he couldn't, but hearing her say that did make him feel a bit better. "Thanks for the vote of confidence. So what do we do now?"

She rubbed her round chin, peering at him through the gloom. "We have to get out of here and get our asses to where Daveed is. To Neely. As soon as fucking possible."

He nodded in agreement. "If anybody can rescue him, it's Martina, but we're going to be needed afterward. Jamal most of all. He's the brains of this outfit."

Amber kicked a clod of mud with her bare foot, then pulled a phone out of her jacket pocket. "I guess our first order of business is to scare up a wrecker."

Dan looked back along the deep ruts leading across the pasture, through the bulldozed fence and to the road beyond.

"Better make it a *big* one."

"No," Dan said in the steeliest tone he could muster. "We are *not* going to leave you here with the truck."

"You must," Jamal insisted. "The two of you can catch a plane and be there in just a few hours." He sank deeper into his recliner, taking a long pull from the fresh bottle of Jim Beam Amber had brought him, the only part of the bar to survive the crash. "I should have known better than to attempt this trip. I'm simply not cut out for this sort of thing."

"We need you, love," Amber insisted. "Daveed needs you. Avva needs you. Dan and I need you."

The big man hung his head in defeat. "I know," he rumbled morosely. "But I am barely maintaining by hiding in here. I can't go out there. I . . . just . . . *can't* . . ." He began to tremble and withdraw, overcome by the mere thought of leaving the truck.

Part of Dan wanted to argue with him, to tell him that he could surmount his phobia. The only problem with that was he'd had an inside glimpse of Jamal's fears, and knew the bitter truth: Jamal and the truck were inseparable, at least for now.

There was a warning blast of an air horn, then the

truck lurched as the wrecker began dragging it back toward the road. They had lucked out on that count, finding an oversize wrecker at a service station just a few miles away, and the driver had come right out. He'd even agreed to pass on a couple hundred bucks compensation for the flattened fence to the field's owner. They had problems enough without being pursued by some guy on a tractor armed with a pitchfork.

Dan wondered if he could convince the guy driving the wrecker to haul them all the way to New Mexico. That would be slower than driving there under their own steam, but at least it would get Jamal there without going catatonic.

Not much of a plan, but better than nothing. Still, there had to be some better way to get something this large halfway across the country . . .

His eyes went wide as another idea wobbled uncertainly into his head. It was seriously nutty, but so was this whole misbegotten enterprise.

"Amber," he said, jerking his chin toward the cab of the truck. She nodded and followed.

"Just how well off is Jamal, anyway?" he asked once they were out of earshot.

She snorted. "As rich as he wants to be."

He frowned. "What's that mean?"

She lit a cigarette and leaned against the frame of the door leading into the cab. "He keeps some of his money visible under a couple of his identities, but most of it is hidden. Earns big bucks for his legit work, and some of his sidelines bring in a barkin' chunk of cash. Then again, some cost us a bundle. But the thing you've got to remember is that not only is he seriously rich on his own, he basically wrote the security system for the international banking industry."

"You mean he can tap into that?"

She blew a stream of smoke, giving him an odd smile. "Let's just say money is not a problem. Why?"

Dan took a deep breath, let it out. "Okay, here's what I was thinking . . ."

The tall, prune-faced older woman in the starched gray uniform did not look at all happy. She stood ramrod straight behind Dolgeburg Airport's single counter like the commandant at some military kindergarten, eyeing Dan and Amber like two toddlers who had been caught playing doctor.

Dan, still a bit ghostly from crash bag powder, and whose pant legs still let loose of the occasional clod of drying mud and whose bushy hair looked like it had been styled by Oingoboingo of Borneo, clearly worried her—although not half so much as Amber.

Jamal's gal Friday was still barefoot, rings winking from several of her muddy toes. She had put on a pair of skintight pink Capri pants to go with her battered leather jacket, but as seemed to be her habit, had eschewed a shirt to go under it.

To Dan it looked like the clerk, whose name tag read CLOVIS GARELICK, was clearly thinking about calling security. Assuming this small-town airport had such a thing. If not, she seemed inclined to haul out a hogleg of her own and put it to use. He kept a close eye on her, planning to hit the deck if she made any sudden moves.

"Yew can't just walk in and rent a plane," she repeated once more in the tone of voice one might use on the insane.

"A *cargo* plane," Dan repeated patiently. "Why not?"

The woman's lipsticked mouth puckered tighter, and her narrow nostrils flared. "Well, first yew have to make such arrangements far in advance. Deposits must be made at the very beginning." A raking, dismissive glance in Amber's direction. "*Large* deposits."

Amber squinted up at the woman, reaching into her open jacket to scratch a breast. "How large is large, honey?"

The woman looked smug. "Oh, I should imagine at least ten thousand would be necessary for the sort of craft you're talking about."

A grin skidded dangerously across Amber's face. "Shit, is *that* all?" She dug around in her jacket pocket, pulled something out and nonchalantly flipped it on the counter. It made an odd chiming sound when it hit. "This oughta cover any petty bullshit like that."

Dan found himself looking at an object he'd only ever seen in the movies, a clear, credit-card-sized wafer of solid cultured diamond with a filigree of gold circuitry embedded in one edge. The only marking it bore was a tasteful satin black infinity sign.

James Bond and Martin Braintree and other such high-style fictions invariably carried Diamond Cards, but not real people. At least none he knew.

Up to now. That card meant Jamal had a literally unlimited line of credit. They could use it to buy the whole airport. Probably the entire county, and make a downpayment on those surrounding it. Like Amber had said, money was not a problem.

The woman behind the counter stared at the card with bulging eyes, her hand poised uncertainly over it.

"Is this *real*?" she asked in a voice cracked with awe.

"Fuckin' A it is." Amber went up onto her toes, putting her hands on the counter and her face inches away from that of the older woman.

"Now *Clo*-vis, I suggest you get the board outta your ass and get us a plane, pronto. *Buy* the fucker if you have to. *Capisce*?"

"Yes ma'am," Clovis Garelick answered meekly, bending to her terminal. "Right away, ma'am."

"*FUCK!*" Amber bellowed, kicking the soda machine with a bare, beringed foot and leaving muddy toeprints. "I can't fucking *believe* it!"

"Attempts to damage, deface, or defraud me will result in criminal prosecution," the machine warned in a sweet bubbly voice. "Thank you for drinking Pepsi!"

"*Eat carbonated shit!*" she hissed, kicking it again.

"Calm down," Dan said soothingly. "We'll figure something else out."

They were going to have to. No cargo plane large enough to carry the crippled truck was available, not for the next fourteen hours, no matter how much money they threw around.

So much for getting Jamal, truck and all, to Neely. The only thing immediately available was a twelve-seat charter jet that had happened to be making a short layover in Dolgeburg to deliver some presents to the mother of the man who owned the service before deadheading back to the West Coast.

"Look, if we can get Jamal in that jet we *can* get, will he be all right? He'll be inside, right?"

She scowled and stared at the floor, hands stuffed in her jacket pockets. "I don't know, man. He's never flown before, and the damn thing's got all those windows. Maybe if he hides in the bathroom or something . . ."

"I say we try. We really don't have any other choice."

She gave a curt nod. "Okay, let's do it."

They marched back over to the counter. Clovis watched their approach nervously, a faint tic starting in her right eye.

"Okay," Amber growled. "This one stinking little toy plane you *can* get. Has it got a bathroom?"

The woman blinked. "Excuse me?"

Amber rolled her eyes in exasperation. "I said has it got a *bathroom*? You know, small room, china bowl, paper by the roll? A tight-ass like you must use one at *least* once a week."

"Uh, yes ma'am," Clovis stammered. "I'm sure it has a bathroom. Positive."

"Then we'll take the goddamned thing," Amber said in the voice of a woman settling for something less than even second-best. She held up a warning finger. *"If."*

"If?" Clovis echoed breathily, the tic increasing in tempo and intensity.

"If we can make a few special arrangements."

Half an hour later the wrecker halted with a *squonk* of air brakes, parking so that the damaged truck stood just off the jet's port wing.

Amber gave Dan the nod. He opened the truck's side door, letting in a wave of hot air smelling of jet fuel. The pilot was already on board, and the clamshell door into the plane's passenger compartment stood open, a puzzled-looking stew standing just inside.

"Okay, honeybunch," she said gently. "All we have to do is get from here to there. Piece of cake, right?"

Jamal nodded, but his eyes bulged with fear from just facing the open doorway. Sweat beaded his face, and his skin had gone ashen. He made himself stand up. Took a tentative step forward. As he tried for a second he faltered, his massive body beginning to shake like an oak in an earthquake.

"You're doing just fine." Dan tried to sound encouraging, but was already fairly sure this wasn't going to work.

"I—" Jamal croaked in a strangled voice. He tried to make his legs move, his entire frame quaking from the effort, staring out the door like it was the gateway to Hell. He began to hyperventilate. His legs folded under him, and he went down, still a yard from the door.

"Aw, sweetie." Amber sighed, bending beside him. He curled up in a tight ball and began to weep, wrapping his arms around his head and gasping for breath between braying sobs. She stroked her lover's broad back, looking on the verge of tears herself. She glanced up at Dan, shook her head.

He closed the door, then scrubbed his face with his sweaty palms. There had to be something else they could do. He looked around the back of the truck, desperately searching for some idea or item which would help.

Half-baked plans came and were discarded. Could they throw together some sort of tunnel? What about a handcart, blindfold, and heavy sedation? Maybe if they moved everything from the back of the truck out there and he focused on that he could convince himself he was still inside . . .

Unless they came up with some brilliant plan, getting him across those thirty feet of open space would be virtually impossible.

He blinked, then giggled. Amber shot him a puzzled look.

Maybe, just maybe, it would be virtually possible instead.

"The door's closed now, old buddy," he called to Jamal, going to ransack the place for what he needed. There was a top of the line CyZilla slayte. Good. Now if there were only some—

There were.

Five minutes later they were ready to try again.

"All set?" Dan asked, speaking into the pinmike curving around in front of his mouth.

· Jamal took a deep breath. "I think so."

Then it was time to give this a shot. He gave Amber the sign. She palmed the control that opened the truck's side door.

"Where are we now, big fella?"

Jamal turned his face toward Dan. "Home," he said, sounding half-convinced. Wraparound Gargoyle eyephone shaydes covered his eyes, silvered to total opacity. Headphones covered his ears. Sweat sheened his broad forehead, and he clutched the CyZilla like a life-ring, stylus ceaselessly moving across the screen.

Dan wore Amber's purple shaydes himself, what Jamal was seeing a translucent heads-up over the real. "That's right, we're home. Back in the Bunker, safe and sound a hundred feet underground. What're you doing here in the Bunker?"

"Walking around. Working on this slayte."

"Good. Let's step down into the living room."

"O-okay." Jamal took two steps forward, paused, then a third that carried him through the truck door. First one red-sneakered size 14 foot landed on the tarmac, then the other.

Dan let out a sigh of relief. *One small step for man, one giant leap for Mister J.*

He and Amber stepped down beside the big man, each keeping a loose hold on an arm. "What are you doing on the slayte?"

An uneasy chuckle. "Trying to crack the UN Uplink Center."

Plus managing the VR re-creation surrounding him, building it on the fly from wakened computers back at the Bunker. Well, the busier his mind was the better. Let him take over NORAD and declare war on every used-car dealer in America if that's what it took.

"That's great, Jamal. Let's keep walking. Makes the blood flow to the old brain. How's the hack going?"

"Their main system for the Center itself is easy. I've already gotten in there. The problem is that there is no way to contact the *Ares* other than through Uplink. That section is completely isolated from the rest of the system."

They walked past an insubstantial Chippendale chair.

A book titled *The Psychology of Phobia* rested on the seat, opened to the chapter on agoraphobia. A picture of Jamal illustrated the chapter head. Nice touch. "Completely? Not just some firewall or icewall?"

Jamal shook his head, glancing Dan's way with blind robot insect eyes. "Gelb's Law: The only total security is total disconnect. Uplink is separate and standalone."

That wasn't good news. "So we have to physically get inside Uplink. Eventually."

Behind them the wrecker began hauling the crippled truck away. Well-tipped airport personnel rushed to reopen the gate so it could drive off the landing field. Dan was pretty sure the driver of the wrecker had recognized him, and was willing to bet he was probably already on the phone trying to sell his story.

This just increased the immediate need to get on that plane and the hell out of there.

"Yes, we do." They were over halfway there. Amber stayed at her lover's side, her face hopeful. Dan lowered his shaydes and threw her a wink. She smiled and held up her free hand. Her fingers were crossed.

"Which means we need Daveed."

"I believe so." Jamal traced endless mazes and filigrees across the face of the slayte as he continued to create the vreality he and Dan moved through. They passed a ghostly workstation. *The Wizard of Oz* was playing on its screen. A Wicked Witch of the West who looked like Jamal was sending a horde of Flying Monkeys into the sky. She turned and smiled uneasily, holding up a green-black hand clutching a rabbit's foot.

"No word from Martina yet," Jamal continued in a strained voice. "I wish I dared contact her again, but believe it is best if we wait. We don't want to joggle her elbow in the midst of the task she has taken on."

"I guess not. But I bet she'll pull it off. She's good." Contact with the woman through Avva had been like encountering an iron tower. One which, surprisingly enough, had been full of birds and butterflies. Her strength and competence and force of will were massive, and yet inside was this amazing supply of humor and warmth.

"Indeed she is. Her qualifications are formidable."

They were getting closer all the time. The stew, a baffled, bulimic blonde in a powder blue miniskirt uniform and pillbox hat, hovered uncertainly in the open doorway of the plane. Amber let go of Jamal's arm, took three quick steps toward the rear of the craft, dropped her pants, and squatted. The stew watched this, painted eyes widening and rouged mouth turning into a shocked O.

Amber rejoined them at the foot of the ramp. "Bathroom's gonna be tied up," she said by way of explanation.

"Stairs now," Dan warned. "Six steps."

"No stairs in my place," Jamal mumbled. Dan blinked as the virtual representation of Jamal's retreat suddenly sprouted an ornate iron staircase leading up into the dining room. "Got some now." He licked his lips. "Hope we get to the kitchen soon. I'm getting kind of, ah, thirsty."

"We'll get you set up once you're in the plane's bathroom—I mean your kitchen."

"I think I can hold out that long."

They went up the metal stairs, Dan leading, Jamal in the middle, Amber behind. The big man's legs were starting to get a bit wobbly, but he was beginning to think they might just make it.

The stew stepped back as they entered. "Uh, welcome aboard," she said uncertainly.

"Turn here," Dan prompted, ignoring her. He guided Jamal toward the rear of the plane.

Amber planted herself in front of the stew. "You serve booze on this thing?" she demanded.

"Yes ma'am. I can start serving as soon as we're in the air."

Amber shook her head. "New rules, Blondie. Happy hour starts *now*," she explained in a voice that brooked no argument. "Beer for me and the hairy stringbean, a martini for our friend." She glanced back, watching the two men's slow and painful progress aft. "Better make that *five* martinis. Triples. Very dry, and no goddamned vegetables."

"Almost to the kitchen now," Dan said as he reached

out and opened the door to the head. "By the way, how are your monkeys doing?"

"Still out there," Jamal returned in a shaky voice. "Still flying."

Amber turned back, saw the stew gaping at Jamal.

"You got something against monkeys, sister?" she growled.

"No ma'am!"

"Good. Now shag your skinny ass and get us those drinks."

Dan let out a sigh of relief as he settled back into one of the plane's butter-soft leather seats. He and Amber had taken seats facing aft so they could keep an eye on their charge.

"This was damn good thinking, Dan," Amber said as she settled in beside him. "I think we're gonna make it."

"I sure hope so." He touched his pinmike to activate it, and toggled the sound to ambient so she could hear. "How're you doing back there, big fella?"

"My situation is improving. See?" The head door opened a crack and a large black hand pushed an empty martini glass out. The door slammed shut again. *"The seat is rather hard, though."*

"Want me to bring you a pillow, sweetie?" Amber asked.

They heard a slurping sound as he downed another martini. *"No, but I may need another round before too long."*

Dan shook his head in bemused admiration. "Just yell when you're ready. Do you think you can make arrangements for the other end?"

"I have already begun that task."

"Great. We're about to take off. Will you be all right by yourself back there?"

A mordant chuckle. *"Well, if it turns out that flying scares the piss out of me, I am at least in the right place."*

The plane shuddered, began to move.

"I guess you are."

The plane began moving faster.

They were on their way to Neely once more.

Glory

Martina's period of rapport with Avva caused far less trouble than it did for some of the others. It hit while she was in the back of the cab carrying her to Daveed's condo.

Stealth was the key to the operation's success, and she hoped arriving by cab would help keep the terrorists unaware that trouble had arrived. To aid the process she'd traded her tailored jacket for a blue nylon souvenir **NEELY TALKS TO MARS!** windbreaker, and a fairly preposterous broad-brimmed straw cowboy hat to hide her face from above. As the personal bodyguard to one of their most hated foes, she was sure her face was as well-known to the Fists as Jones's was to her.

After Avva delivered his frantic message and departed, she found the cab's driver, a tiny Cambodian woman with a blue-black Moe Howard haircut, gawking at her in the rearview mirror.

"We are almost there?" she asked in a voice graveled by tension. The sense of urgency she'd had before was now amped a hundred times over thanks to Avva. Gone were any residual doubts about the alien's existence and intentions. This new certainty felt good, but she wished he could have given her some useful tactical information while he was at it. A nice person for an alien, but a civilian nonetheless.

"Almost, yes, sure," the cabbie answered, nodding rapidly. "Very soon, you see."

Martina checked the tripmeter readout set in the back of the seat, frowned at the number displayed. Then she sighed and reached into her shiny new jacket, pulling out her badge and a fistful of matte black Dumbrov automatic pistol. She held both up for the driver to see.

"I am in big hurry," she said tonelessly. "If I were to begin thinking maybe you were maybe taking long way to get there, I would be most upset."

The cabbie's eyes widened. "I no take slow way! For sure!" An unctuous grin. "But maybe I can find faster way! Yes! I think so!" She wrenched on the wheel, sending the cab slewing across two lanes of heavy traffic and took an abrupt left, moving much faster than before. "We get there soon! You see!"

"Good." Martina settled back, reholstering her pistol but leaving her jacket open so it was obviously within easy reach. "You do not want to blow tip."

"I no want to blow *nothing*," the woman piped. "We get there fast! You see!"

All was quiet at Shah's condo, proof that Rico had managed to keep a lid on things. Security at the place was a joke, but Martina was not laughing.

The building's front entrance was unlocked and unwatched, anyone who wanted to could just stroll right in. While there was a desk with someone at it just inside, the old babushka in a baggy rent-a-cop uniform who was supposed to be on security duty was snoozing blissfully away, her head resting on the counter and her hearing aid lying nearby. Both surveillance monitors were tuned to soap operas.

Shaking her head at such incompetence, Martina stalked past and went to the elevator, a heavy *Viva New Mexico!* duffel bag hanging from one hand. There was no lock or access control on the elevator either. Such pathetic security measures offended her professional sensibilities. Jones and her confederate would have had a harder time getting into a Walmart. At least there they checked to make sure visitors were unarmed.

She thumbed the UP button. The door opened almost immediately. She stepped inside, pushed the button for the fifth floor. Right after it started moving she hit the emergency stop button, halting it between floors.

"System active. Sabo, please," she said as she pulled off her cowboy hat and began shrugging out of the windbreaker.

"Sabo here," the pilot answered after a moment.

"I am in the elevator and getting ready now." She removed her shoulder holster and other pieces of concealed weaponry.

"I am ready to take off at any time."

"What about clearance to take off?"

A laugh. *"I will be gone off their radar so fast they will think they dreamed me."*

"How long to get here?" She opened the bag, pulled out the hard black ballistiplaz leggings from the body armor she'd convinced the head of airport security to loan her. It was his own personal gear. Unfortunately, the man was half a head shorter, and thirty kilos lighter. Her own custom-tailored body armor was back in New York, so this would have to do.

"Oh, about two minutes. Less if you don't mind me breaking a few thousand windows."

"Two minutes will be fast enough."

"You're the boss. Let me know if you change your mind."

"Thank you, Winnie." She buckled on the hardshell vest, finding it a tight fit. Thank God she was flat-chested, or it would have been worse. Still, badly fitting armor was better than nothing. The elevator call bell chimed as she was trying to make the short man's equipment fit her long legs, someone on the third floor wanting the car. She ignored it, continuing her preparations. Once the body armor was on, she began strapping her holsters in place. After that her other weapons and odds and ends went into convenient holdits and pockets.

She twisted her body and swung her arms and legs to make sure the armor wasn't going to limit her movement too much. The fit was terrible, but it would work.

"Okay, I am heading up to the fifth floor now. Wait for my word to take off."

"No worries."

Easy for you to say. She punched the button to let the elevator resume its trip upward. It stopped at the third floor, and the door slid open.

She found herself facing two older women in fringed cowboy shirts, fancy ruffled skirts, and ornate cowboy boots, all duded up for an evening of Country and Western dancing. They found themselves confronted with a very large, very intense white-haired woman armed to the teeth and dressed in matte black body armor.

"Going up?" Martina asked politely, holding the door open.

"Down," one woman said in a very small voice.

"We'll wait," said the other with a nervous smile.

"Good choice." Martina let the door close, and the elevator started up once more.

Martina stepped silently back from the door to Daveed's apartment, stuffing a listening device back into a hardshell pocket. So much for high tech. A water glass would have worked just as well, or as badly.

"All I can hear is damn tube babbling," she reported to Winnie Sabo. She'd hoped to hear something that would help her pin down the location of the people inside.

Tactically, the situation sucked. She'd be going in alone and blind. The only thing on her side was the element of surprise.

Nothing she could do about it. Just like the night so many years ago when several vodkas had convinced her it was time to learn how to drive a tank, all she could do was pull hard on a lever and hope for the best. "Well, Winnie, ready to raise some hell?"

"Righteous ramped and ready!"

"Good. Let me do one more thing, and we begin." She reached down, removed her phone from an armored pocket. Punched in three numbers.

"Nine-one-one Emergency," a professionally calm female voice answered.

"Need ambulances and emergency medical personnel at fifth floor of Ortega Condominiums Building, 2364 Sandstone Road. Cops, too. Lots of them."

"What is the nature of the problem?" the dispatcher asked, her tone sharpening.

"Shots fired."

"How many?"

Martina chuckled darkly. "We will soon find out." She slapped the phone shut, stored it away. "Winnie? Go."

"On my way!" Over her implant she could hear/feel the Gryphon explode into life before the noise suppres-

sors compensated. She placed her back against the wall facing Daveed's door. Tightened her grip on the Dumbrov.

The need to get in there and save Daveed roared inside her like a bonfire, one that threatened to burn away all caution. But she knew his life hung on her being in control. Avva's life hung on Daveed's. Rico would never forgive her if she got herself killed. Never. She would not be very pleased with that herself.

She began forcing such thoughts aside; they were only impediments, distractions that could dull her edge.

"ETA thirty seconds," Sabo warned. Already she could hear the distant shrieking roar of the warplane coming at them like some furious demon from Hell.

She focused on the door, all expression leaving her face.

"Twenty seconds."

Her breathing slowed, her mind stilled. *Combat Zen,* her Manchurian Special Training instructor had called it. Barely fifty kilos and pushing sixty, he could break concrete blocks with his fingers and remain smiling while taking down four attackers three times his size. One learned his lessons, or became hospitalized.

Twenty years later she still remembered and knew how to use what he had taught. As she centered herself anxiety faded. Urgency drained away. She was, waited to do.

"Five seconds." The howling of the approaching Gryphon was unbelievably loud, filling the corridor.

"Three. Gonna be a bump." The floor and walls began to vibrate.

"Two." She took a deep breath, her muscles tensing like steel springs. The door filled her field of vision, an obstacle that would not be allowed to slow her down.

"One." Her entire world narrowed down to the noise and the shaking and the door. The entire building could have come down around her and she wouldn't have blinked.

The building shuddered when the Gryphon hit it, the banshee scream of its engines beyond deafening.

Martina launched herself at the door to Shah's unit like a human battering ram.

*   *   *

Combat Zen.

Everything happened with the slow dreamy deliberation of a sleepwalking opium smoker dancing the waltz.

She hit the door like a hundred-plus solidly packed kilos of meat and muscle fired from a cannon, body armor stiffening on impact. The lock parted with a crack, and the door split lengthways, bursting apart before her. Momentum carried her through, ducking low and primed for action. Her eyes swept the room, taking in the situation and feeding it to the training and practice-created tactical computer between her ears.

Chaos reigned inside the apartment. The sharp black nose of the Gryphon was wedged through the wall where the sliding glass door onto the balcony had been. Deep scratches ran across the UN logo, and the twisted remains of the ornate wrought-iron balcony were draped across the fuselage like a mustache. The machine shuddered and shrieked as if frustrated that it could not get more of itself inside, the whole building thrumming and trembling in sympathy.

Two battered, brown-skinned men on the floor, tied back-to-back, both looking semiconscious at best. A tall blond-haired man stood between them and the plane, firing at it with an assault rifle and screaming at the top of his lungs. Ricochets thudded into the walls around them. The widescreen exploded in a shower of sparks, pixolaminate glass flying everywhere.

Him first. She leveled the Dumbrov and began settling into a two-handed stance.

Before she could fire she was staggered off balance by impact like a blow in the side from a sledgehammer. She dropped, rolled to her left, seeking—

She caught a fleeting glimpse of Betsy Ross Jones ducking back down behind the counter in the kitchenette. Returned two shots, bullets punching through the wood paneling in a spray of splinters. The noise from the Gryphon was so great it swallowed the shots almost entirely, like farts in a hurricane.

"WINNIE! BACK OUT!" she screamed at Sabo, afraid a stray bullet from the idiot with the assault rifle would kill the men she was trying to rescue.

The pilot didn't answer, but the nose of the VTOL began wrenching its way back out of the apartment. The man with the assault rifle fired one last round at it, convinced he was driving it off. Martina extended the Dumbrov in his direction once more.

Just as she was squeezing the trigger another blow slammed into her shoulder. A crater appeared in the wall just past her target, not in the spot just behind his ear where she'd been aiming. Not daring to play target while trying for another shot, she swung her weapon back toward Jones, who was already ducking out of sight. She put a round into the counter anyway, trying to make the bitch stay down. Then scrabbled back, just in time to avoid a spray of bullets fired blind through the counter in her direction. One snapped by her ear, missing by centimeters.

Two against one. Split field of fire. No cover. This wasn't going well at all.

Peripheral vision let her see the male Fist finally figure out that there was also a human intruder, and bring his assault rifle around. He started to crouch, clearly planning to use the two hostages as cover. But before he could get in position and start unreturnable fire the odds changed slightly in her favor.

The Amerind UNSIA agent, Jasper Crow, suddenly opened his eyes.

In a convulsive move he heaved, rolling himself and Daveed out of the way and flat onto the floor, covering the other man's body with his own.

The terrorist froze in surprise as his cover deserted him.

Martina fired once. Red erupted from the center of his forehead and exploded from the back of his skull, painting the wall and floor behind him with gore.

She didn't wait to see him fall, instead twisting around to face the place where Jones hid. She got oriented just in time to see something fly up from behind the counter and sail in her direction. It arced through the air, a cigarette-lighter-sized slab of dull white plastic tumbling end over end as it came toward her.

Minigrenade went through her head in a flash. She instinctively flung her arm out and slapped it in the general direction of the front door, then hunkered down with her arms over her head.

The device detonated, thirteen razor-thin layers of steel and plastic fragmenting into a thousand deadly whirling flinders that chewed deep holes in the corridor's walls, ceiling, and floor. A wave of debris rolled up behind and over her.

Dust was still falling as she shoved herself up from the floor, the Dumbrov pointed at the counter.

"Come out!" she bellowed to make herself heard over the residual roar of the Gryphon's engines. *"NOW!"*

Betsy Ross Jones rose up from behind the counter, her hair wild and her eyes gleaming with fanatic malice. In her left hand was another grenade, this time a full-size model. Martina recognized it as Chinese military issue from the shape of its base. In Jones's right hand was a good old-fashioned Colt snubnose revolver.

"BACK OFF!" Jones screamed, whipping the grenade around between them.

With a chill, Martina saw that the pin had already been removed.

"There is no way out," she said in a level voice, ignoring the grenade and focusing on the woman who held it. "You must give up. Police already have the building surrounded."

This was no bluff. The wail of sirens could be heard over the Gryphon, which seemed still to be hovering somewhere nearby. Red light strobed through the hole in the apartment wall, painting everything inside the color of blood.

Jones worked her way out from behind the counter, her fair cheerleader's face twisted with hate and pain. The front of her blouse and skirt were soaked with blood. A shoulder wound bled freely, and she hunched over another in her side.

"You won't take me," Jones hissed through clenched teeth. "I won't let the UN get its filthy hands on me." She began to edge toward the living room, taking hitching sideways steps. "I'll die first!"

"No one needs to die," Martina said, watching, calculating. Once the handle of that grenade was released she had three seconds to close it again or they were all dead.

Could she shoot the woman and grab it in time? No, she was too far away, and putting more distance between them with every step. Dumbrov centered on Jones's chest, she started to follow.

"Stay back!" Jones shrieked, spittle flying. She worked her way around the two hostages, lowering her pistol to point it at Crow. He stared up at her, his battered face expressionless. The grenade still held between them, she skirted her dead comrade's sprawled body and continued to edge toward the gaping hole in the side of the building Sabo had made with her plane. Her dragging feet drew stripes of gore on the carpet.

"You cannot win," Martina insisted, claiming a third of a meter before the Colt lifted in her direction once more. "But you can live."

Jones shook her head. "Not in some UN prison filled with filthy subhumans. Better I go out in a blaze of glory."

"There is no glory in death." She took another sliding half step forward. "Just put down your weapon and give me that grenade."

Jones glanced behind her, trying to see past where the cracked concrete balcony floor turned to nothingness, then faced Martina again. "Do you think there are cameras out there?"

"Maybe," she answered cautiously. "Give up and you can make a statement."

Few things frightened Martina, but the smile that appeared on Jones's face chilled her to the marrow. "I intend to. I want the world to see how a true American hero acts."

Jones extended the Colt, pointing it at Martina's head. When Martina saw the hammer lifting she reacted instinctively, flinging herself down and to the side.

It was the wrong move.

While she was trying to protect herself from a shot that never came, Jones dropped the grenade, turned, took two steps, and launched herself off the edge of the balcony with her arms spread wide.

The grenade hit the carpeted floor, bounced. Martina scrambled desperately, a count automatically starting in her head as she tried to get up off the floor.

One.

She got her feet under her, pushed off.

Two.

Lunged forward, eyes fixed on her deadly goal, already knowing she wasn't going to get there in—

The big UNSIA agent's hand shot out, snatched up the explosive, and squeezed the spoon back in.

Three.

Already in headlong motion, she swept past him with a nod. Slid to a halt on the bloody floor. Braced herself to look out and down.

The street below was ablaze with flashing lights. Police cruisers, UN Security cars, and emergency vehicles were everywhere, with more coming all the time. Uniformed figures were scrambling madly, trying to make room for the howling black warplane settling down to land in their midst.

Martina blinked, stared. Spread across one stubby wing was the body of Betsy Ross Jones.

"Winnie?" she shouted to make herself heard.

"Here, boss. Thought I'd stick around just in case. See what I caught?"

"I see. Is she still alive?"

"I think so. I caught the bleachy bitch before she fell too far." The Gryphon settled down on its wheels and its engines spiraled into silence.

Martina sagged against the wall. "Thank you."

"Excuse me, ma'am?" someone said beside her in an odd, distracted voice.

Martina turned. Crow had crawled off Daveed and crouched there on his knees, the grenade held out at arm's length. His battered face wore a pained, lopsided grin.

"Would you mind finding the pin for this?" he asked hopefully. "Please?"

Martina felt a relieved smile break onto her face. "Since you ask so nice and polite, I will go do that right now."

It was well past midnight before Martina could wrangle the time and privacy to use her phone. She leaned wearily against the sink counter in the women's rest

room just down the hall from the hospital room where
Daveed and Jasper were being kept. She punched in the
000 area-coded number, wondering what it would bring
her this time.

"Jamal here," said the deep voice she'd been hoping
to hear. The man with all the answers and information.

"This is Martina. In case you have not seen news,
Daveed is safe. Is banged up pretty good and must stay
in hospital for the night, but basically okay. The same
for Captain Crow."

"We have been watching. The news said you were
hurt, too."

She smiled grimly. "Not so bad. Got a couple big
bruises from being shot in body armor. No big deal,
could have been much worse. The maps and things you
send were big help. Thank you."

"No problem. You did the hard part. Is there anything
else you need?"

A good night's sleep would be most excellent. Maybe
a hot bath and a tall glass of schnapps first. "I am okay.
How soon before we meet? You still get in tomorrow
like you said?"

A chuckle. "Actually we ran into a few problems with
our original mode of transport, but we managed to surmount them quite handily. We are in Neely now."

"How did you manage that?"

"That is a rather long story. If you want to hear it in
person, we're at 317 Rasbeck, right off Quinn near
downtown."

"This is hotel?" Maybe she could get that hot bath
and schnapps after all—after first locating an all-night
drugstore so she could find some liniment. Then all she
would need was Rico to rub it in. . . .

"Actually it is a basement-level compucations store
named Chips Are Down. Rather fitting, don't you
think?"

"Why are—" she began, then shook her head. Better
she asked him this and her other questions in person. "I
will be there as soon as I can."

"I'll be up." The connection ended.

She shoved herself back onto her feet, wincing as a
dozen aches and pains made themselves known.

I am getting too old for this dermo, she thought glumly. She definitely needed liniment, and a big bottle of Megasp.

But first one last check on the security detail watching over Shah and Crow. Then she could find some painkillers and go meet this Jamal face-to-face.

Maybe she'd better grab a coffee somewhere while she was at it.

It looked like this might be another long night.

Zippo

Jane looked up when she heard the knock, saw Willy standing beside the open hatch of the sick bay.

"Come on in," she said, putting her slayte aside. Forms and reports. As good a way to kill time as any, and her removal as Commander hadn't really ended its eternal flow. She should have handed it all to Hans and let him deal with it, but the mind-numbing monotony was oddly comforting now.

"How are you holdin' up?" he asked as he came over to where she sat on the deck with her back up against the wall. Besides his own ever-present slayte tucked under his arm, he carried two steaming cups.

"I'm managing. How about you?" The big man looked tired, his eyes smudged with fatigue and his top-knot partially unraveled. Even the palm trees on his shirt looked wilted.

"Can't complain. Want some hot tea? It's your favorite, McKay's Earl Grey."

"Sounds wonderful." She reached up and relieved him of one cup, then patted the deck beside her. "Come on, take a load off."

"I thought you'd never ask." He lowered his chunky body down beside her, got settled, slayte in his lap and his own tea within easy reach.

"I assume from the look on your face you haven't got good news."

"No, not really," he answered, looking around. "Where's Fabi?"

"In our compartment taking a nap while some tests are running."

"Has he found anythin' wrong with you?"

"No loose screws as yet."

"Maybe I should send Wanda in to check you over."

"It may come to that. So we're not doing so good, Mister Advocate?"

"Not really. The missus and I queried Media Uplink for an infosearch on the name Avva. Said it was to settle an argument at Scrabble. There was a long wait, a lot longer than signal lag and the usual bureaucratic sludge could account for. Finally, we got back a reply that no information was available signed by Daveed Shah's boss, some clown named Armand Gautier."

"Which tells us nothing. You think he's stone-walling?"

"Probably, they're so friggin' careful not to pass on anything that might upset us delicate astronauts. Herr Gluck came marchin' in just as we were getting the reply. Of course he took it to mean that your software's buggier than a flea circus."

Of course he would. She took a sip of her tea, trying to find some pleasure in that, then looked Willy in the eye. "I'm not crazy. I hope you believe that."

He smiled, his dark eyes nearly disappearing behind his round cheeks. "Jane, listen. After two years of trainin' with you, and then this bitch trip, I'd doubt my own sanity before yours." His smile faded. "But I have to tell you, at the moment the chances of our findin' proof to back you up don't look so hot."

"Anna hasn't seen anything either." It wasn't a question.

"Zippo—though not for lack of tryin'." His grin returned. "Fact is, our man Hans went to tell her she was spendin' too much time on clearin' you and lettin' her mission objectives fall behind sked. Guess what happened?"

She shook her head, too tired for guessing games.

"She told him to go fuck himself!" Willy laughed and slapped a meaty thigh. "Man, that's somethin' she should've done a *long* time ago."

Jane's spirits lifted slightly at this news. It was about time Anna made a stand for herself. "Good for her."

"Damn straight. Anyway, Anna's livin' in her lab, going over Phobos with a fine-tooth comb."

"I hope she finds something."

"Me too. I sure don't want to lose my first case."

They sat sipping their tea in silence until Willy put his cup down. He hit a couple keys of his slayte, then leaned in close, his broad brown face solemn.

"No one can listen in now," he said quietly. "I want to tell you we don't have to go on like this. Wanda and I are behind you one hundred percent. I talked to Fabi earlier. He doesn't understand what's happened to you, but he doesn't think you're crazy. At this point I think Anna would be on our side even if she thought you were stone bananas, just 'cause it would piss off her husband. As far as we're concerned, you're still Commander of this mission. You say go to Phobos, we go. No questions asked.

Jane shook her head. "Willy, don't."

"I'm just sayin'—"

"I know what you're saying." She sighed. "Don't think I haven't thought about it. Don't think it isn't tempting."

"Then why? I don't get it."

How to explain it to him? "Because Hans is following the rules, Willy. Doing his duty as he sees fit. Sure he's using it to get what he wants, but that doesn't change the fact he's doing the right thing. In his place, I might even have to do the same thing."

Tutillia made a disgusted sound. "Stiff-necked fucker would have made a *great* Nazi."

"Then so would I, because I'm going to follow the rules, too. At least for now."

The big Samoan didn't look particularly happy with her answer, but let the matter drop. "Okay, next item of business. Anna and I ran some plots. We figure we have to change course within the next eighteen hours if we want to be able to rendezvous with Phobos."

"I know. I ran some myself." She could feel every second ticking away, urgency a living thing under her skin.

"What if we still haven't found proof by then?"

"I don't know." She stared at the opposite bulkhead, focusing on something that lay beyond it, something beckoning and as yet unreachable. Avva was as real to her as anyone she'd ever met, his situation of more consequence than her career. He *had* to be rescued. No other options were acceptable.

"I know I'll have to do something. It's like . . . like standing on the shore and hearing someone far out on the water calling for help. I want to respond. I *have* to respond. I couldn't live with myself if . . ."

She shook her head to clear it, sat up straighter. "I don't want a fight with Hans, Willy. I don't want to do this the hard way unless I absolutely have to."

After a moment he nodded. "Okay, I can take a hint. It's time to get up off my fat ass and get back to work." He stood with a theatrical groan.

She smiled up at him. "Sorry to be such a slave driver."

"Aw, I can use the exercise." He regarded her a moment, then saluted. "I promise you, Commander. If there is proof, we'll find it."

"If?" she said, one eyebrow rising in inquiry.

"Just a figure of speech, Jane."

She let her head fall back against the bulkhead and closed her eyes. Vibration came to her through the bones of her skull, reassuring her that they were still moving closer to Mars, and to its moon.

"I hope to God you're right, Willy."

Face-to-Face

Dan listened to the pale-eyed Amazon with the white butch haircut who had come knocking at the door a few minutes before 1 A.M., glad for the distraction.

Martina had one helluva tale to tell. Supersonic warplanes. Body armor. A gun battle with armed fanatics. Juggling hand grenades. What she'd been through made their little adventure look like an exercise in slapstick comedy.

The flight to Neely had been uneventful. He and Amber had ridden in the private jet's luxurious cabin like mutant CEOs, sipping beers and munching macadamia nuts, resting up for what lay ahead. Jamal remained closeted in the head, mostly in cyberspace while slurping down martinis like a thirsty camel at an overdue oasis.

Things had gone far more smoothly when they touched down. The reason for that was simple: the big man was back in charge. While unable to do something as mundane as walk around the corner to buy a quart of milk, he could bend the outside world to his will with uncanny skill by manipulating the data damn near everything on the planet looked to for its marching orders. Of course the fact that he also threw money around like confetti didn't hurt either.

A liveried chauffeur driving a Mercedes truck with an Italian leather living-room suite in the back had met them at a landing field about forty miles from Neely's Anan Airport since traffic was stacked up so badly around Anan, and there were likely to be fewer media types lurking in the bushes. The driver had backed the truck almost up to the plane's door, which made it easier for him and Amber to escort an eyephoned and surprisingly sober Jamal inside.

They had headed straight to Neely, Jamal's magic touch with VID records breezing them through the roadblocks, going directly to the potential hideout he had located while in the air. That turned out to be a cellar-level compucations store in downtown Neely. They arrived an hour before its ten o'clock closing.

Once inside the store Jamal had cautiously removed his wraparound shaydes and headphones. Finding himself in a cavernous, windowless space filled with computer equipment had put some shine back in his eyes. He went right over to a fancy BlitzTek workstation on display and already running. The store's owner had smelled a hot customer and descended on him, bubbling over with salesmanly bonhomie.

"How much?" Jamal had asked before the guy could even open his mouth. The store owner quoted the displayed price, then slid into his sales rap about how maybe—just maybe—he could come down a little.

Jamal cut him off with his next question, one which had nothing to do with onboard memory or service contracts. "No," he'd said, "you misunderstand me. How much for your store and entire inventory?"

That had set the guy back, making him blink like he'd been slugged with a sockful of twenty-dollar cartwheels. "The whole *store*?" he'd stammered. "You mean for like all the equipment? And the *building*?"

"Well of course," Jamal had answered as if that was the way most folks shopped. He wanted to buy the stock outright, and rent the store itself for the next, say, week. So what would the hardware—which by the way he knew was largely vanilla sloware and off-brand knock-offs—store rental, security deposit, and a reasonable sum to cover lost sales run to? Would half a million cover it?

The guy got pretty wonky at that point. Jamal had just sighed, and said, "Amber, darling, please deal with this man," 'faced his CyZilla with the BlitzTek, and pretty much dropped off the mercantile plane.

Amber had hooked the man by the arm, towed him back to the sales counter, and begun dickering like a Turkish rug merchant. Five minutes after she'd hauled out that Diamond Card, Dan helped her escort the dazed store owner off the premises. They closed the

door after him and locked it, then turned the CLOSED
sign so it faced out.

The next couple hours were spent in service to Jamal's
King-Kong-grade nesting instinct.

By midnight they'd turned it into a home away from
home. Every deck, workstation, and slayte was on, filling
the place with light and noise. Dan had covered the sole
window, the one in the door, with a piece of plywood
he found in the back. Amber had gone out, returning in
a cab filled with food, beer, and liquor. In the interim,
orders Jamal had placed while still on the plane began
arriving.

Soon they had a half dozen sleeping bags and self-
inflating mattresses to crash on, and two coffeemakers
to make getting up again survivable. An apartment-sized
fridge held beer, soda, drink mixes, and the remains of
the Thai takeout that had arrived shortly after Amber
returned. The portable Jacuzzi, set up near the employee
bathroom, had just finished filling when Martina arrived.

It was that period before the big Russian woman came
calling that had put Dan in severe need of distraction.
He'd made the mistake of sitting down at one of the
decks and checking to see if maybe his fifteen minutes
of fame had expired.

No such luck.

The entire media had grappled on to the whole Avva
business and gone into bombard mode, EdgeNet leading
the attack as his own personal *Enola Gay.* In the hours
since the first mention of his name during the *Sunshine
Hour,* the splash had rippled outward, building higher
and gathering strength as it was fed by a zeal for ratings
and other Avva-related occurrences.

His face was everywhere, hanging behind countless anchors and ax-grinders. His statement and Tammy's fiasco
were getting heavy rotation, and now they were describ-
ing him as *Unavailable for comment and presumed to be
in hiding.* While this was essentially accurate, it didn't
do much to make him sound sane, stable, or ideal parent material.

Of course Tammy hadn't passed up the chance to
wring more facetime from the situation. She'd grabbed
air again, this time with an "interview" from Paris, the

whole thing canned and as carefully orchestrated as a pro wrestling match; there would be no unexpected fall this time.

The interviewer, Talmadge Beale, was a legendary tail-hound. He clearly had getting the old horizontal hold on Tammy in mind, fawning and drooling over her from word one. Since he was head of EdgeNet's EuroBureau, he'd probably gotten his wish.

The clear spin Tammy was humping—and Beale was slopping on the KY for—was that his mind had completely snapped thanks to smoldering resentments over his career being in the doldrums while the woman he'd helped—only a little, of course—get her start had gone on to be a star. That and certain hinted-at, but never clearly defined "instabilities" had led to this Avva mania.

Going underground and hiding from the media, the authorities, and the mental-health-care professionals he obviously so desperately needed were further proof he'd become a major-league headcase. Then she'd capped off with an Emmy-grade tearful plea for him to turn himself in and get help. If not for her, or for himself, then for the sake of their dear, dear daughter.

Bracketing this carefully crafted exercise in self-promotion and character assassination had been updates on the Avvatine Crusade and the anti-Avva gun-nut fringe. The followers of Ray sunshine were maintaining around-the-clock prayer vigils in a field on the outskirts of Neely. This was given big play. Beatific-looking believers holding flickering candles while being watched over by National Guardsmen holding guns made great vidyo. There were fewer shots of the Guard and UN forces trying to locate and contain the increasing numbers of White Fists and their sympathizers.

The only other thing competing for top play was Martina's rescue of Daveed and Jasper Crow. News crews had caught the kind of footage producers would kill for: Betsy Ross Jones's swan dive from the gaping hole in the side of the building; the South African pilot swooping in and executing a seemingly impossible maneuver which let her catch the woman's falling body like a flapjack on a skillet; Daveed and Jasper being taken out on stretchers under the watchful eye of Martina, whose fearsome appearance and evil eye was enough to make the cameras maintain a respectful distance. According to official sources, Jones was hospitalized in stable condition under armed guard at an undisclosed location.

The Fists and other screaming xenophobes were going ballistic, demanding that she be released and treated as a hero who had been brought down by the forces of evil while trying to prevent an alien invasion.

Everything came back to the alleged alien on Phobos. He somehow had become "Mr. Avva," a shadowy, Fu Manchu–like presence behind all the madness. Martina's arrival was a relief, giving Dan reason to quit watching.

By then, the arrival of a gang of unemployed Roto Rooter technicians moonlighting as attack proctologists would have been a welcome diversion.

"So," Martina said after she had told her tale, and Jamal had told theirs. "What do we do next?"

It was weird. They were strangers, and yet Dan felt he knew this woman better than he'd ever known Tammy through the first couple years of their marriage.

Jamal spread his hands. "For now all we can do is wait. You are certain Daveed and Captain Crow will be released tomorrow morning?"

Martina nodded. "That is what doctors tell me." She shrugged. "I made them understand anything less than best care possible would be unacceptable. Since doctor in charge had to make fast visit to men's room after our talk, I think is safe to say they will honor my request."

Dan was willing to bet she could convince them to donate their own lungs or kidneys if needed. On the spot, and without any troublesome paperwork or anesthetics.

"Then I am sure their care is assured," Jamal said with a smile. "I believe we should all get together as soon as possible after Daveed's release. Then we can plan our next move."

"To get inside Uplink and contact Jane Dawkins-Costanza."

Once again it was a case of their knowing someone they didn't really know. The last visit from Avva had left them aware that the commander of the *Ares* mission was one of them.

As they had come physically closer together, the interconnect between them when Avva called had increased. Jane, being the farthest away, had been the least drawn into this loop. To Dan she had been no more than a fuzzy, unidentifiable smear in his mind. But this last time Avva's desperation had made him lose some of the reserve he'd exercised dealing with their smaller minds. Jamal had not only been able to weather this blast, but to work inside it to some degree and pull her into slightly better focus during the final seconds of their contact.

Knowing that she was hearing Avva meant they had a potential ally up there. That was cause for a fragile optimism.

"All I could read from her was worry and concern," Jamal confessed. "I have searched for information about her situation, but so far my efforts have been to no avail. There is nothing in the news, and nothing in any of the Uncle Joe command-and-control sectors I have crashed."

Martina yawned. She looked whipped. That was no surprise, considering what she'd been through. "You think she lies low?"

"That is quite probable."

"She's got to be scared," Dan put in. "Think about it. She's running the show up there, then suddenly she starts hearing Avva. Every one of us except the Wizard here figured we were going looney tunes. Even if she didn't, even if she believed it right from the start, then what? She doesn't dare tell the rest of the crew. They'd think she was going off the deep end."

"Good point," Jamal said, stroking his beard and looking pensive. "We should also consider the possibility that she was not able to hide her episodes. If so, she could be in trouble. The lack of news may be due to her situation being hushed up, perhaps at the very source."

Martina rolled her broad shoulders and yawned again. "In either case hearing from us should be a relief. This will be most true if we can make contact look official."

"Yeah," Dan said, "but even then, what are the

chances that the other five crew members will believe her and us?"

None of them had an answer to that question.

"Can't sleep?" Jamal asked, as Dan slouched in and parked himself in a chair next to the BlitzTek where the big man was working.

"No. Thought maybe a drink might help. You got one to spare?"

Shortly before two, Martina had left for the hotel room Amber had gotten for her. Amber crashed for the night right after she left. He'd gone to bed at the same time, mostly to keep himself from spending the rest of the night watching his life go down the china bowl of the media like some flaming turd. An hour of tossing and turning passed before he gave up and got back up.

"The bar is always open," Jamal assured him, reaching down to grab a fresh bottle of Wild Turkey from the case under the table. "Worried about tomorrow?"

Dan jerked his chin toward the clock on the wall. In a few minutes it would be three o'clock. "It *is* tomorrow."

That made the man smile. "Figure of speech. For me it's always today." He cracked the cap, took a swig, and held it out.

"I guess it would be." He accepted the bottle and took a slug, shuddered as the liquor clawed its way down. When his eyes quit watering he handed the bottle back, looking closely at Jamal's face and seeing the fatigue etched into it. "How are you holding up, big fella?"

Jamal took another snort, then put the jug down where both of them could reach it. "I am managing. This isn't home, but it's enough like it to keep me from turning into a babbling turnip."

"Are you going to be okay tomorrow—I mean later today?"

He shrugged. "I know I have to go to the Center with the rest of you. Using the shaydes and my virtual Bunker should let me avoid any embarrassing lapses into catatonia."

Dan helped himself to another snort. This time the whiskey went down easier. "You'll be fine. Another couple days of this and we'll have to tie you down to keep you indoors."

"That seems a trifle optimistic. Thank you for thinking of a way for me to come along, Dan. I didn't want to stay behind, but I simply couldn't . . . make myself go out there."

"I know." He did, too. He'd tasted the man's terror, and knew he couldn't have overcome it if it were his own. "Me, I was scared of trying to pull this off without you. Amber's like the heart of this outfit, and Martina's the hands. You're the head. Me, I guess I'm kind of like the appendix."

Jamal shook his head. "Nonsense. I wouldn't be here now if it weren't for your cleverness and determination. I owe you an enormous debt of gratitude."

He waved it off. "Forget it."

"Never. So what about you?"

"What about me what?" The whiskey was really kicking in now. On the plus side, it was soothing his nerves. On the minus side, it wasn't helping his tired brain run at anywhere near top speed. He hoped Jamal didn't decide to talk about anything complicated.

Jamal met his gaze squarely. "I am well aware that media attention has only grown greater and more cruel, and your difficulties with your ex-wife and daughter have not lessened."

Not what Dan wanted to talk about—not if he was going to get any sleep at all that night. He stalled by taking another swig, this one going down like water. But it didn't quite wash away the need to let a little of it out.

"The noise will blow over eventually." He sighed. "It always does. As for Bobbi, I'm trying not to think about it. About her. I guess if we pull this off and get the *Ares* to Phobos, and they find Avva, Tammy will have to back down." He scowled, realizing how unlikely that sounded. Tammy never backed down or gave away anything she'd glommed on to. She made a black hole look fair and generous.

Jamal smiled and took the bottle from his hand. "She most certainly will."

He raked his hair back, then let his hands fall to his lap. "God, I hope so."

"You really miss your daughter, don't you?"

The question made him slump in on himself like it had turned his spine to Jell-O. "Oh Jesus, yes." The ache was huge and endless, and it filled this vast hollow space where the knowledge that he could at least be with her now and then used to live.

"I was supposed to have her this weekend. Tammy called midweek, wanting to take her to Paris instead. I agreed, striking a deal to let me have her next weekend for four days. I was going to take her camping at this cabin that's been in my family since I was a kid. Just her, me, and Susannah."

"Susannah is her nanny, correct?"

"Yeah." He had to laugh in sour amusement. "Tammy managed to wreck *that,* too."

"That?" Jamal echoed. His eyebrows went up, his eyes bugged out, and his mouth hung open. "No!" he gasped, clutching his chest. "You weren't messing around with the *nanny*? Putting the old bumbershoot to *Mary Poppins*?"

He had to laugh at Jamal's clowning, and this time there was some pleasure in it. "No," he said, still chuckling. "Hell, we haven't even kissed! But it was beginning to look like maybe something was going to start."

His pleasure faded, leaving him feeling doomed and more than a little tipsy, like a town drunk who somehow strayed onto the *Titanic.* "That's all shot to hell now. I doubt I'll be seeing either of them anytime soon."

"This isn't over yet. You may get that camping trip with your daughter and your lady friend after all."

Bitterness rose up in a black wave. "It would take a fuckin' miracle."

"And being contacted by Avva isn't one?" his new friend asked quietly.

Dan shrugged. "I guess. Like the loaves and fishes, only I keep getting slapped in th' chops with a dead mackerel." He grabbed the bottle, took a long pull. If it knocked him flat on his ass, fine. He just wanted all this to stop, or at least go away for a little while.

Jamal took the bottle from him, then rested a gentle hand on his back. "I think you've had enough, Dan. Go back to bed now. Sleep. Dream of nanny-nookie, and better days to come. All right?"

"Sure." He got up, and after giving the room a few seconds to steady, shambled back to his pallet. Dropped onto it and pulled the sleeping bag back around himself. Unless he bent his legs, it only came up to his chest.

Amber lifted her head and peered at him blearily. "You okay, man?" she mumbled.

He forced a smile. "Sure."

"Remember, you've got friends here, and we don't take shit from *nobody*."

"I know."

"Don't forget it." This message delivered, her head sank back to the pillow and her eyes closed. In seconds she was snoring.

When he closed his eyes the room began to spin, but that was all right. On one of the turns it flung him off into the sweetly forgetful depths of sleep.

The Media Junkie

Daveed was glad to be leaving the hospital. Again. Hopefully for the last time.

They'd promised him a morning release, and while five minutes to noon was still technically morning, he'd been hoping to be gone long before this. Thanks to the wonders of medication he was feeling pretty good, considering he looked like he'd gone three rounds with a homophobic kick boxer in combat boots.

As the nurse wheeled him into the hospital elevator he turned his head to look at Jasper. The UNSIA agent looked just as bad as he did, but damn fine in spite of that. The bandage around his head looked almost like a headband. Jasper smiled and held out his hand, his fingers bandaged from where he'd cut himself using a fragment of broken glass to sever the ropes holding him. Daveed took it carefully in his own.

The nurse pushing his chair let out a sniff of disapproval from behind him.

"You have problem, nurse?" Martina demanded in a voice calculated to pucker the woman's butt so tight her uniform gave her a crippling, maybe even fatal wedgie.

"No ma'am," she said meekly. The orderly pushing Jasper's chair grinned and stifled a snicker.

"Is good." She glanced down and gave him an exaggerated wink. "Doctors are supposed to need nurses, but I can arrange it so this is working other way."

Daveed had found that he really liked this very large, seriously tough woman who had saved his and Jasper's lives. She had a gift for deadpan that would have made old Buster Keaton crack up.

"So, Jasper," she continued, "your file tells me you are dancer. This is not good Russian ballet, I bet."

"No, it's traditional dance." He patted his bandaged leg. "I'd do a rain dance for you, but the best I'd probably get with this is light drizzle."

"We are inside. Maybe instead you set off sprinklers. Is probably best if you sit still. I have already had shower this morning."

Daveed listened to the two of them bantering, glad they liked each other. Both were so brave. Everything after being caught with the SportPad was kind of fuzzy, but between the two of them he'd gotten most of the details of just how brave.

Jasper had given him the rundown on her one-woman assault, saying that she was the toughest hombre he'd ever seen. She'd been equally complimentary, explaining that even though he'd been hit in the thigh by a ricochet from Jeff's firing at the warplane stuck in the side of his building, he'd kept up his zombie act. He'd palmed a shard of broken glass and gone to work on his ropes, waiting for the right moment to act.

It hadn't been until midmorning, just after they'd taken Jasper away for a final set of scans, that he and Martina had managed a few minutes of privacy. She'd used it to bring him up-to-date on other matters.

Learning that she, too, was hearing Avva had messed his personal reality around a bit, as had finding out that she was in close contact with the guy he'd tried to contact with the SportPad. Enough of his first message had gotten through for Jamal to have located him, and then sent her to the rescue. How he could be giving orders to a Colonel in the Special Security division of the UNSIA remained a bit cloudy, but she promised to fill him in on the details later. Even more amazing was the news that this Jamal, his girlfriend Amber, and Dan the Virtual Weatherman were in Neely, waiting for him and Martina to join them so they could begin planning how to enter the Uplink Center and ring up the *Ares*.

When he heard that, he wanted to get right out of his bed and get moving. It was about time he helped bail someone *else* out for a change.

Martina insisted that they wait until the doctors gave their final okay. It would not do for her to have to give him first aid, she warned. The last person she'd given

CPR to was an Olympic wrestler from Turkey, and while she had saved the man's life, she'd also broken five ribs in the process. Him she would probably break in half. She was a lousy nurse, she continued in a glum voice. No delicate touch. Might try to give him an enema with a fire hose, or worse.

Once he'd stopped laughing, she'd broached the question of Jasper. What did he know, and how involved was he?

Daveed related the story of how they met. Told her how Jasper had been present during one of his Avva visitations, and taken it in stride better than he had. Then he recapped the ugly tale of their being taken hostage. That was harder going.

Martina had listened quietly, only interrupting near the end to point out that his message was what had started the wheels of rescue rolling, and that Jasper had saved all three of their lives by grabbing that grenade. This part of the whole horrible experience remained a blank. All he could remember was noise and terror and pain.

Then she asked him point-blank if Jasper should be included in the trip to meet Jamal and his crew.

A sudden shyness and uncertainty made him answer that she was better off asking Captain Crow that herself. He knew what he wanted, but had no right to speak for the other man. The past two days might just have been enough to make him swear off men in general—and a certain 'sippipak mediartist in particular—for life.

When the orderly brought Jasper back she'd done just that.

He'd stared at Martina several seconds, then asked if she was armed. She'd said yes. He'd said then *maybe* she could keep him away, but not to count on it. Indians could be damn sneaky when they wanted to.

Martina had left her weapons holstered, and now here they were, two beat-up gay men with a female Terminator Fairy Godmother watching over them. Riding the elevator down to the basement level so they could be sneaked out past the media in a milk truck, on their way to join one of the oddest conspiracies ever mounted.

Daveed watched the floor numbers diminish, trying to

come up with his own script for the task ahead. Getting several uncleared strangers past the Center's front gates wasn't going to be easy, but maybe between them Martini and Jasper had enough UNSIA mojo to pull it off.

If they did get past the gate and into the Center, that still left the ultrasecure Uplink Ops to crash. That was going to be voluminously harder.

If by some miracle they did get in there, having a bunch of nonpersonnel wanting to use the Big Dish to tell the *Ares* they ought to cruise Phobos-ward to look for Avva was going to make his old buddy the Goat blow several major fuses, plus a gasket or three. He might even spontaneously combust.

Daveed began to grin as the elevator doors opened.

First Jasper, and now this. His luck had definitely changed.

Admit it, he thought wryly sometime later. *You're just a media junkie.* Here he was, part of the tatterdemalion cabal planning how they were going to fake out the UN and pretty much the rest of the world by forcing contact with an extraterrestrial life-form. This was *history.* Win or lose, this meeting was going to be the stuff of endless miniseries to come.

So what was *he* doing? Sitting off to one side while they plotted and planned, sucking up a badly needed news fix.

Maybe because he too could only truly exist in a wired state, and understood how the pixelated-infomonkey bit, the big bearded black man Jamal had turned a couple decks in his basement hideout over for him to use. They were just cheapo consumer sets, but he wasn't inclined to complain.

So there he sat on the periphery like a shy wallflower at the big dance, maybe 5 percent of his attention given to listening to Jamal and Jasper and Martina discuss the sort of security concerns they would be facing, the other 95 percent dialed into putting him back on top of the happening curve.

That curve was a spike shooting straight up into the stratosphere. It was getting crazy out there, the good old USA wobbulating into one of its periodic bouts of being the place where *anything* can happen, and probably will, in full public balls-out, megamultichannel howling Chinese fire-drill lunacy.

He now understood why Dan Francisco—who was even taller and thinner than he appeared on the tube—looked so tired and preoccupied. The poor bastard was the guest of honor at a cybervidyc crucifixion, nailed up on screens worldwide and being jabbed continuously to keep him bleeding. Media-driven sympathy was solidly behind his ex-wife, Tamara Van Buren. No surprise there; she was out there providing a steady stream of lap-stroking public statements timed to ride the wave. Anybody half-bright enough to know which end of the remote to point should have been able to see that her act was phony, a two-fisted facetime grab and opportunity to whup her ex while he was down. But this was Amurrica, where the soap opera would get sucked up first, and get thought over later, maybe.

Dan's silence and unavailability proved whatever the media said it did. Stills from his single statement that showed him in a sweating Nixonian light hung bug-eyed behind a cavalcade of smirking anchors. The infovacuum left behind was being filled with the usual incendiary media Molotov cocktail of rumor, innuendo, and half-assed speculation.

FlashNet was even running a dingo of some goateed "psychological expert" with a Stalag 13 accent who was of "der konsidered hopinion" that Dan fit the profile of a bomber, and warned that his next act might be a "pathetic, desperate, and hexplosive attempt to reclaim his manhoodt, forcing der worldt to take him serious."

It would have been funny if it weren't so fucking horrible.

Nor was that the end of the horror show. An estimated three hundred White Fists and other heavily armed xenophobic extremist whackos had set up several encampments in the desert between Neely and the Center. Most were remaining hidden, but there were enough running loose for every news spot to feature clips of crazed, gun-toting white folks in camouflage carrying signs with such Hallmark sentiments as NO OFF-WORLD SCUM! THE UN WON'T FEED *OUR* KIDS

TO ALIEN MONSTERS! and BETSY ROSS JONES IS A HERO!!

Playing dippy doves to the mad dogs were some fifteen hundred Avvatine crusaders who were maintaining around-the-clock prayer vigils. Reverend Ray Sunshine himself had helicoptered in late the previous night, and was presently on stage before them. Daveed had Cross-Net's coverage running on one corner of one display, Sunshine's voice one of the mere four the unit could carry.

He bumped that feed's sound a notch. This guy had heard Avva, too, although he seemed to be operating entirely on his own agenda.

The sound level came up, Sunshine's voice rising over the muted babble of the other feeds. *"— believe you, Child of GAWD from another WORLD! We hear your cry for SUCCOR! We have invoked the HOLY power of PRAYER to turn help your way! But this is a world of CYNICS! A world of UNBELIEVERS! So we beg you, Brother Avva, give us a SIGN! Show us—"*

"Daveed!" Martina's shout broke through, and he realized that it wasn't the first time she'd called his name. He'd tuned the real people out in favor of the ones on the screen. Occupational hazard and bad personal habit.

Whoops. He guiltily muted both decks. "Sorry," he mumbled, turning his back on the displays to face the others.

They were all looking at him, seemingly amused by what they were seeing. Martina appeared to be working hard to hide a smile, her face stern but her lips twitching.

"This Armand Gautier, your supervisor," she said. "What is this man like?"

"He's an asshole," he blurted.

More smile leaked through. "Will this asshole listen if you try to tell him that we must inform the *Ares* about Avva?"

"Not a chance. He'd probably try to have security shoot me."

A nod. "I see. So you think he must be neutralized?"

"Hey, you can neuter him for all I care."

"I will consider this proposal," she said, finally letting her amusement show. "What we must know is this: If we can get you inside Uplink and keep Gautier and security contained, can you contact the *Ares*?"

"Sure. I can probably finesse a sideline from my cubicle, but our best bet is to use the board in the Goat's office."

"Thank you." The big Russian woman looked around at each of them in turn, her smile fading. "Is not much of a plan, but you heard Jamal. Time left before *Ares* must change course is nearly gone. Jasper and I will try to get us inside Center, then Uplink. I have more rank, but he is better known there. Once inside, we contain this Goat person, contact the *Ares*, and help Commander Jane convince rest of crew they must go to Phobos."

Amber spoke up. " 'Scuse me, but how are you gonna get us there? All the reports I've seen say the roads are closed to all but you UN types, and there's a shitload of armed jackoffs running around between here and there. If they spot you, Dan, Jasper, or Daveed they'll be all over us."

"That is something Jamal, Jasper, and I have covered with a bit of creative requisitioning."

Daveed looked toward Jasper, getting a *just you wait* grin and a wink in return.

They broke for some food and to get better acquainted, afterward going back to the search for some better plan.

By four o'clock they hadn't made any progress. It was an hour before his regular shift would have normally begun, the time they were to begin their half-assed assault. Just as the stroke of the hour arrived he heard an approaching rumble, like a bulldozer or something was coming down their quiet side street.

"Our ride is here," Martina announced, standing up. "Let us get moving."

They all got up and headed for the door.

Martina led the way. Dan and Amber followed, shepherding an eyephoned Jamal. He and Jasper brought up the rear of their unlikely strike force.

All he could think as they climbed the concrete stairs was *Wait until the Goat gets a load of us!*

Spam Can

Dan had come to the conclusion that he liked the back of Jamal's wrecked truck one helluva lot better than the passenger compartment of the vehicle that had waited for them on the street above Chips Are Down. It was far roomier. Quieter. And considerably more comfortable.

Still, he had to admit, it did feel safe.

The back of the armored personnel carrier that Martina, Jasper, and Jamal had wrangled was cramped, claustrophobic, and smelled like some industrial robot's armpit—a heavy, oppressive mixture of sweat and machinery. There were narrow benches running down each side, and at the back an armored tailgate sort of thing just now closing and shutting out the afternoon light. Headroom was at a minimum. He'd clonked his skull twice just getting in and seated.

He hunched beside Jamal in a sort of question-mark-shaped crouch, Amber on the other side of her lover. Jasper and Daveed had taken the seat facing them. Martina had gone up front to ride shotgun with the driver, a short heavyset guy with a British accent who was dressed in sand-colored desert fatigues and a sky-blue UN beret.

"The door is closed now," he told Jamal, raising his voice to be heard over the throaty rumble of the APC's idling engine. He took off his shaydes and pocketed them.

"Thanks." Jamal removed his own shaydes as the vehicle lurched into motion, looking around and expressionlessly taking in the cramped, windowless space.

"You okay with this?"

The agoraphobe smiled. "Actually, I kind of like it."

"Really?"

"Sure. I may just have to get one of my own. It seems just the thing for those Sunday drives in the country."

"Yeah, Occupied Serbia, for instance," Daveed suggested.

Amber snorted and elbowed her man in the ribs. "Next you're gonna tell me you want a convertible."

He turned toward her. "I believe I already own one, don't I? An antique Cadillac, if I recall correctly."

"Yeah, but you haven't ridden in the damn thing in over twenty years."

"True, but that could change." He put an arm around her. "I never thought I would ever stray this far away from home, either. Or fly in an airplane. The wonders have still not ceased."

She stared back at him, her tough-chick facade melting.

"You've done just fine, baby," she purred. "Been ever so brave and strong."

They kissed, then snuggled together and began exchanging whispers like two teens in the backseat of Dad's car. Dan watched for a few seconds, then looked away.

Across from him, Jasper and Daveed sat side by side and holding hands, off in the midst of their own intimate whisperfest.

Ain't love grand, he thought glumly, leaning back and trying to get comfortable. The vehicle bounced and swayed like a tractor as it drove through Neely's streets. The seat beneath his skinny butt was padded, but not much. The squashed caterpillar green militaristic decor was depressing, and the fact that Martina had thought they needed this thing did not bode well. The road was supposed to be clear, but obviously she wasn't counting on it. Who knew what they might be heading into.

The APC lurched around a corner and accelerated. The others remained oblivious, happily drifting down the Tunnel of Love.

He stared at his feet, wondering what Susannah was doing now. What she thought about all this crazy shit that had fallen from the sky to land on his poor head. Probably not much. Chances were whatever approval of—and attraction to—him she'd felt before were history, wiped away by his new status as Dan "Hale-Bopp, here we come" Francisco, world-class whacko.

Nice woman like that, there was no way she could help being turned off. Even if she wasn't, she was an ocean away and under Tammy's thumb. His darling ex wouldn't be letting him near his daughter or her nanny for at least the half-life of plutonium.

Susannah, I'm still me, he thought, trying to send a message to her the same way Avva beamed them at him. *Don't believe everything they're saying. I'm not dangerous. I'm just a bit of a loser who's gotten into trouble trying to do something really important. Something I have to do, no matter how bad things get.*

No answer. He tried to summon her up in his mind, to see her the way she'd been the other night. Her hair down, her ripe milk white form barely hidden by that flimsy nightgown. Sweet and sexy and thinking of him.

The image that manifested in his mind's eye was far less titillating and a lot more foreboding. It was Susannah as he'd first met her, fresh off the boat and her head still filled with Tammy's propaganda. Stiff and cool, watchful and professional. The kind of woman who'd give a guy like he'd become the same kind of wide berth she'd give week-old flyblown roadkill. *Skunk* roadkill.

He knew he loved Bobbi. At least a hundred times more than her own mother, maybe even as much as he did. She would protect his baby from the shitstorm raging through their lives, and to do that properly she would probably have to protect Bobbi from him. Which was all the more reason to make him wish he could at least explain all this to her. Say he was sorry, and thank her for doing the right thing.

No chance for that now; he was down to the level of opportunities and options of a meat scrap caught in a garbage disposal. Somehow in the space of just a couple days he'd managed to lose everything. His daughter. The woman who might have saved him from being alone. His career and his reputation. All of it gone, and probably past reclamation.

This somber train of thought wasn't taking him anywhere he wanted to go. Much more and he'd figure out how to open that back door, jump out, then run around in front of the APC and try to throw himself under its six big rubber wheels.

"Going up front," he mumbled to no one in particular, unlatching his seat belt.

Access to the vehicle's cockpit from the troop compartment was through this narrow crawl space and hatch sort of arrangement. He worked his way forward on his hands and knees, putting a couple more dings in his skull as he tried to thread his long limbs through the narrow channel and the hatch at the end. Fortunately, there were handholds.

Martina sat crammed in the vehicle's tiny passenger seat. She turned back toward him as he managed to stand, the opening at the level of his hips. He had to crouch because there wasn't any more headroom than in back.

"Dan, you come up to backseat-drive?"

He shook his head, pushing stray hair out of his eyes and peering out the windshield to see where they were. "I just felt a little out of place back there in Lover's Lane."

They were outside Neely, following a winding two-lane road that curled around crags of red rock. There wasn't any other traffic in sight. Maybe this leg of their trip was going to be hassle-free. That would be a nice change.

"Jamal told me you have some troubles in that department."

He rolled his eyes. "Lady, I've got nothing *but* troubles in that department."

"This is too bad. I know how you feel."

Now there was an Oldie but Goodie from the Meaningless Platitude Top Ten. Normally he would have let it slide, but hearing it now seemed like the final insult.

"Do you?" he snapped.

"Maybe some." She twisted her body around and leaned closer, putting her mouth next to his ear. "You know I am personal bodyguard to Secretary-General Perez," she said in a voice pitched for his ear alone. "Well, for couple years now he and I have been lovers."

He blinked as that sank in, then stared at her uncertainly. "Really?" He spoke in a loud whisper, not wanting the driver to overhear. That was pretty unlikely. The guy wore bulky headphones, and the APC was noisy as hell. He had no idea who built the thing, but it sure wasn't Rolls-Royce.

"Really. Is pretty damn complicated, you know? If it ever came out, my job would be gone like snap of fingers."

"Couldn't you still stay together? Like as a couple?"

"Maybe so, but it would no longer be me in charge of keeping him safe. This is something I think I can do better than any other."

Dan didn't doubt that; she'd already proved that she was a one-woman army. But he didn't think that was what she meant. "You're the best one to protect him because you love him."

A slow cautious nod, but no direct answer. He could see that those were words she couldn't bring herself to say out loud. Funny how that one little word "love" could shake a woman capable of facing armed terrorists. But it did have a strange power, and had gotten him into plenty of trouble.

He sighed and shook his head. "Don't love suck?"

"That is whole other subject," she said, her face breaking into a bawdy grin. "Not sure I know you well enough for loose-lipped talk about such things."

He grinned back at her. "What, you're saying your lips are sealed?"

She regarded him askance, her expression haughty. "I can only say that the Secretary-General speaks perfect Spanish and has pretty good command of English tongue. In my book this make him cunning linguist. Other than that I have no comment."

This woman was *good*! "I suppose you'd know, being head agent of his security detail and all."

Whatever comeback she might have made was interrupted by the APC's driver. *"Colonel Omerov,"* he called in a tight voice.

Instantly Martina turned back to face the windshield. "Yes, I see," she said. "It would seem we have trouble."

"Bloody hell," the driver growled. "I have to stop,

ma'am." He began bringing the APC to a halt, pulling back on the yoke and working the pedals with his feet.

Dan peered past Martina's shoulder, the bottom dropping out of his stomach at what he saw before them. They had just rounded a curve which swept around a tall rock outcropping, and come onto a short stretch of straight raised road. The path ahead was blocked by three large four-wheel-drive pickups parked side by side, grim-faced men in camouflage at their wheels. Standing in front of the trucks were more militia types, all carrying weapons. Not just the men, but the women and children as well. He didn't take time to count, but there had to be at least twenty of them in all.

"Where's the National Guard?" he asked, his voice cracking. "Aren't they supposed to be keeping the road clear?"

"They have own problems," Martina answered tonelessly, pointing off to her right. He leaned forward to squint through the grated side window. His stomach did another half gainer when he saw a green troop truck overturned on its side maybe twenty yards from the raised roadbed. More armed, camouflaged figures stood watch over a dozen or so uniformed Guardsmen huddled on the ground with their hands on their heads. The five nonwhites he saw in this group of captured soldiers, three men and two women, had blood on their faces.

"Colonel," the driver said in a hushed voice, "I've just been advised that a group of armed Fists broke through the cordon and may be heading for this road."

"Tell them we have found these Fists." Dan couldn't believe how calm she sounded.

"I have, and am relaying the situation from my fore and aft cameras." He looked Martina in the eye, his face solemn. "ETA for assistance is fifteen minutes from now."

"Can't we just turn around and go home?" Dan suggested hopefully. The mob in front of them had begun advancing on the APC. They didn't look friendly. Not at all. The children ran at them and slapped their hands on the APC as if it had become home in a game of tag.

"Do not use Charge Defense System," Martina said to the driver. He stared at her a moment, nodded.

"We cannot leave. See?" She reached up and tilted a display over her head so he could see it. More trucks and guns had come out from behind the rocks and closed the gap behind them. They were boxed in.

"Can't we—can't we just run over them?" He couldn't believe he was suggesting such a thing, but staring into those angry faces made it perfectly clear that sticking around was suicide.

"No, because we are not in zone of declared war. I guess I must call on my new friend for help once more." She plucked a microphone from the console between her and the driver, then tapped in several commands on a keypad she folded out from the dash in front of her.

"Captain Sabo?" she said when READY appeared on the small screen above the keypad. "Come in please."

"Here ma'am," answered a woman's voice crackling through the overhead speakers, blaring loud enough to be heard over the vehicle's engine.

"Could use some help here, Winnie." She leaned forward, tapped a couple more keys. "You have my location and situation?"

"Got it clear. Preparing to lift. ETA three minutes."

"Be careful, Winnie. These people are armed."

"So am I, but I bet I won't need to fire a shot. Hang tight. Sabo out."

The extremists had pretty much surrounded the APC by then, a tightening noose of people who looked like the very thing responsible for everything that ever went wrong in their lives had just landed in their laps. One man, his fat stubbly face stretching into a rictus of hate and outrage when he saw Martina, the woman who had brought down Betsy Ross Jones, swung his rifle up, preparing to smash the gun butt against the windshield. Dan cringed back, bracing for broken glass. She only stared back at him, her face expressionless.

There was a sharp *crack!* as the wooden stock connected. But instead of the glass breaking, the rifle stock splintered in his hands, slivers sliding down the glass. He went ballistic with rage, hammering at the APC's armored flanks with the remains of his weapon.

"Better prepare for a ride," Martina said quietly.

The driver reached up for a switch on a panel above

the windshield. "Will all passengers please make sure their crash harnesses are secure. The screen in the forward bulkhead will show our situation. Sit tight, help is on the way."

He said this in a firm, no-nonsense voice, then turned toward Dan. "You better strap in too, sir. There's a harness right behind you."

"Why?" He twisted around. There was a padded area behind him, thick nylon straps dangling around it. He had to bend his knees to get lined up with it, then began shrugging the straps over his shoulders. The buckles were simple enough, but apprehension had him fumbling with them like a four-year-old.

The reason for the safety harnesses soon became self-evident. The entire group mobbed the vehicle, and after several seconds of fruitlessly thumping and banging on its steel sides, changed tactics. They slung and holstered their weapons, then began rocking the APC from side to side. The sound of their screams and shouts sounded like the buzzing of angry hornets.

"Can they really flip this thing over?" It seemed unlikely, but not impossible.

"*Da*, they can."

Not the answer he wanted to hear. "Can't we do anything to stop them?"

"No. Vehicle is equipped to send electric charge through outer armor to drive them off, but UN rules say we cannot use it in this situation. So we must let them rock and roll us."

The APC lurched from one side to another, bouncing on its shocks. Dan found handholds on either side of him, grabbed on.

"What they do is called 'catching a turtle' in some places," she continued as if giving a lecture on some very dull subject.

The vehicle rocked again, harder this time. The furious buzzing outside had taken on a definite rhythm.

"Others call it *opening the Spam can.*"

This he took to mean an attempt to get at the soft pink meat inside. Which was him and his friends.

"Can't we do *something*?" he repeated, knowing he

sounded freaked, but too freaked to sound any other way. "This is fucking *insane*!"

"You see the children in front of us, ones who grabbed us first?"

"Sure." Three of the six or seven he'd seen were at the windshield, two making faces and obscene gestures, the other scrawling WHITE AMERICA FOREVER on the glass with a bar of soap. They clung like monkeys as the vehicle tilted, farther this time, then bounced back to level.

"You want to kill them?"

"No, of course not, but—"

"Adults know UN mandate is to avoid harm of children at any cost. So they are here to prevent us from electrifying vehicle, charge can kill a child. Most groups do this now, use children as human shields."

The APC rocked again, and this time it was horribly obvious that they'd managed to get the wheels on one side off the ground.

"Is very effective tactic. Rule is sometimes bent in poor countries where chaos is high and no one watches close, but here in America we must play by book. Do not want to hurt nice patriotic citizens exercising civil rights."

They came down hard enough to rebound. Laughing shrieking faces filled the front and side windows, mouths stretched with shouted obscenities and epithets.

"Children are cheap renewable resource," she continued blandly. "In North Korea, Sungite rebels strap explosives to their girl-children and those of villages they occupy. In Africa there are still armies of kidnapped children. Their lives are considered to have no value."

Dan had no idea what had prompted this horrible stuff, not until she turned toward the vehicle's driver. "Do you have children, Sergeant?"

"Yes ma'am," he said in a thick voice as the vehicle lurched and tilted sickeningly. His fingers gripped the yoke white-knuckled. The APC seemed to hang there forever, then dropped back onto its wheels. "Two. A boy and a girl."

"You are a lucky man. Children are very precious."

"I think so, ma'am."

The rhythmic shouting seemed to reach a crescendo. The armored vehicle began tilting up to the right, higher than ever before.

Oh fuck, this is it! He held tight to the handholds, trying to brace himself for what was coming next.

Then he saw something through the canted windshield and over the heads of the women and children in front of them. "What—" he began, not daring to let go and point.

The thing went from a black dot on the horizon to a howling immensity seemingly inches over their heads in half a heartbeat. The mob surrounding the APC scattered like windblown leaves, blown away by a tremendous backwash.

They hung there, the heavy vehicle balancing on its right wheels and wavering as if deciding which way to roll. The driver wrenched on the yoke, cursing under his breath, and the APC wobbled drunkenly, then slammed back down on its wheels with an impact that would have driven Dan to his knees if he hadn't been strapped in.

Through the driver's side window he saw an angular black warplane stand on one stubby wing, circling back and rising. In an instant it was out of sight.

"Where—?" The plane suddenly plummeted out of the sky and fell into the space between them and the trucks blocking their way. He gasped and flinched back, sure it was going to crash and blow them all to hell.

With a deafening banshee scream and a wall of displaced air that made the heavy vehicle shudder and slide backward, it halted its precipitous fall mere feet off the asphalt, facing in their direction and filling the windshield. He blinked in bewilderment as a black woman in mirrored sunglasses and a sky-blue helmet waved gaily from the cockpit. Martina nodded in acknowledgment, a smile working its way onto her face.

The plane did a ponderous and yet graceful pirouette, wheeling around so that it faced in the other direction. Then it began moving forward.

"Do follow her, Sergeant," Martina yelled to make herself heard over the noise of the plane's engines.

"Yes ma'am!" He worked the yoke, and they began creeping along after their rescuer, a process not unlike

trying to stay on the coattails of a small fierce tornado. The APC bucked and shuddered, but kept moving.

When they passed the point where the blockade had been, there were two trucks overturned in the ditch. There was no way to see what had happened to the other one; the blown dirt and sand raised by the Gryphon reduced visibility to less than twenty feet. A glance in the screen showing the rear view was more helpful. The other pickups were racing away at high speed, their backs filled with militia. The Guardsmen by the overturned truck remained hunkered down, but now it was just to protect themselves from flying sand and debris. Their captors had fled.

The pilot's voice crackled from the overhead speakers. *"The road seems to be clear now. I think you'll make better time if I escort you from above."*

Martina retrieved the mike. "Thank you, Winnie."

"No, thank you! Hanging with you is a righteous blast!"

One moment the plane blotted out the road ahead, then there was what seemed like an explosion and it was gone. The APC bucked and nearly stalled. The driver kept it going, muttering encouragement under his breath.

They emerged from a cloud of swirling dust. The road to the Center stretched out in front of them, free of obstruction.

"We made it." Dan sighed shakily. "I can't believe it."

Martina glanced back at him. *"Da,* now all we must do is get past your comrades in the media."

He wiped his sweaty face with the side of his arm.

"At least they won't have guns."

The airspace over the Center was restricted, which prevented the media from deploying their beloved aerostats and helicopters. Still they had managed a tremendous turnout before the sole road leading there was closed the evening before. At least a hundred communications-dish-encrusted trucks, vans, and motor homes were clustered just outside the front gates like some encampment of high-tech gypsies who read satellites instead of palms.

The bored wandering of techs, reporters, makeup people, and producers turned into frantic swarm behavior when they saw the APC heading their way. They descended on the vehicle en masse, aiming cameras, waving microphones, and shouting questions.

This raucous horde retreated just as quickly when it became apparent that the APC's occupants didn't plan to stop to toss off a quick sound bite or pose for a photoop. One cameraman in a *Le Monde Interactif* windbreaker stood his ground in front of them until the last possible second, flinging himself aside just before he became an asphalt crepe. Dan heard the driver mutter, "Run, you frog bastard," half under his breath.

The *LMI* camera operator and his news-gathering brethren swept onto the road behind them and tried to follow, a pack of baying newshounds hot on the trail of the only quarry within sight. A phalanx of troops in skyblue helmets turned them back before they could get within thirty yards of the gate.

We made it, Dan thought with amazed relief when their chariot rumbled to a stop at the guardhouse before the gate. *This far, anyway.*

Beyond the fence lay the Center, a low, sprawling concrete building the size of a shopping center, its silvered windows gleaming in the lowering sun. Antennas and various-sized dishes covered the roof, and beyond it stood another dish at least two hundred feet across, mounted on a frame rendered spidery by distance. Daveed had told them that this was what they had to commandeer, one of the six circling the globe and creating a communication line to the *Ares.*

Martina did something with the controls in front of her. A hatch over her head unlocked and flipped back with a hiss of hydraulics. She grabbed some handholds over her head and pulled herself up so she was standing on the seat, her upper body thrust out the opening. This gave him a fairly up-close and personal view of her backside. He tried not to stare, but it was hard not to. The woman had more muscles in her ass than he had in his entire body.

"Colonel Martina Elena Omerov, UNSIA, SS Division," she called to make herself heard over the APC's engine, leaning forward to show her ID to one of the

blue-helmeted guards. The woman, who had a red maple-leaf patch on her arm and looked like she might be at least part Native, passed a handheld scanner over it. She blinked in surprise and her mouth moved, but he couldn't hear what she was saying.

The other soldier at the gate, a beefy blond guy who also had a red maple leaf on his shoulder, moved so he could get a better look inside the APC's front compartment. He peered at Dan, a puzzled look appearing as he tried to figure out why the skinny hairy guy looked so familiar. Dan crouched there trying to ignore him and Martina's butt, striving to look like someone else.

"Da," Martina said above him as she straightened back up again. "Is very crazy, this alien stuff and these White Fist maniacs. I am glad I came in this, believe me. You are doing good job, soldier. Thank you."

The female guard saluted smartly, stepped back, and made a hand signal. The armored gate began rolling back. She yelled at her partner, who blinked and stepped out of the way, still staring and frowning. The driver started the APC rolling forward.

"That guy almost recognized me," Dan told Martina as she lowered herself back into her seat. "I looked familiar to him, but so far he can't figure out why."

"Let us hope it stays that way." She glanced at a blinking light above the keypad in the dash, stabbed a button, and picked up the microphone. "Winnie? Martina here."

"I've been recalled for more escort duty. You and your passengers should be safe now."

They rolled through the gate, coming that much closer to their objective. The relief Dan felt was tempered by worry about what would come next.

"Yes," she answered. "I thank you for your help. Could not have done any of this without you."

"Has been righteous hoot working with you. Call if you ever need a flyer again."

"I will, believe me."

"Sabo out."

"Now what?" Dan asked as above them the Gryphon swept around and blasted back toward Neely as if fired from a cannon.

She stared straight ahead at the Center.
"Now comes hard part."

Martina's prediction soon proved to be something of
an understatement.

They had gotten into the Center proper without much
fuss, but right after that things got sticky. *Real* sticky.
Dan had a feeling he now knew how visitors to a Roach
Motel felt.

Security had taken one look at the motley crew accompanying Martina and freaked, albeit in a tightly con-
trolled, military sort of way. In spite of her protests that
they were there at the express bidding of Secretary-
General Perez himself, the entire group was immediately
hustled into a rather spare, and he nervously noted,
somewhat cell-like room, where they were watched over
by armed guard. It seemed unlikely that this was VIP treatment, not unless they were visiting cannibal dictators.

He supposed he couldn't really blame them. Avva's
tribe didn't make the best of first impressions.

He knew he looked like shit, all hollow-eyed and
twitching with anxiety like some skinny dope fiend,
skulking around and trying to keep his face averted from
everyone. Amber was in her usual state of half dress,
and she bristled like an angry pug anytime anyone with
a gun came anywhere near her beloved Jamal. Because
the room had windows—barred windows—the big man
held her hand and clutched his slate to his chest, his
color off and his movements stiff and robotic. The three
of them taken together had to look more like refugees in
search of asylum—not necessarily political—than anyone
with even marginal UN status.

Then there were Daveed and Jasper. While they did
have proper credentials, the two men clearly belonged
in the hospital, not running around with bad company in
the midst of a security alert. Even Martina was looking a
little rough around the edges, her hair standing in spikes
and her suit smudged and wrinkled. She did not appear
at all amused by their treatment, and her blue eyes were
lit with a gleam the soldiers seemed to find quite worrying. Once one came too near her. She eyed his rifle
and muttered, *"Ne khochesh li proprobovat eto?"* half

under her breath. Dan knew that bit of well-known Russian from the popular cop show *Moscow Knights*. The kid must have watched the tube enough to know she was asking if he wanted to eat his rifle, because he backed off and maintained a respectful distance.

They were at an impasse. Back at Chips Are Down, Martina and Jamal had cooked up a communiqué from Secretary-General Perez saying that he was sending a delegation, and wanted them to be let into Uplink. That had been accepted as genuine; the problem was with a certain Colonel Franz Czarne, the Belgian UNSIA man in charge of the Center's internal security. He didn't feel that their group fit his definition of delegation, even though she, Daveed, and Jasper possessed sufficient bona fides.

The three of them might have been able to get in, but their insistence that the others must come too was keeping that from happening. They couldn't bring themselves to separate, not after all they had been through. Just as Jamal had said back in the beginning, it was one for all and all for one, just like manic mutant Musketeers.

Martina had gone nose to nose with Czarne, using her Special Service status to invoke Top Secret, straight from the Secretary-General, super hush-hush, no-need-to-know orders as the reason she needed to get her shabby comrades inside Uplink.

Czarne wasn't buying it, wouldn't even take it as a free download. Worse yet, he refused to contact Secretary-General Perez for confirmation until they provided some reasonable explanation for wanting into Uplink.

It may be that nature abhors not only a vacuum, but also an impasse, because just as Martina was running out of verbal moves—and clearly considering resorting to more physical ones—the situation began to unravel fast.

One of the soldiers guarding the door had been staring at Dan the same way the one at the gate had been. All he'd been able to do was keep his head down and pray the woman didn't recognize him, that his infamy was one hell of a lot smaller than it had seemed the last time he checked.

God must not have been listening. Suddenly the sol-

dier's eyes widened in recognition. She sidled over to
her superior and whispered in his ear.

Dan watched Czarne turn to stare at him, making a
face like he was sucking on a pickle. The Belgian
marched over, looked him up and down, then said, "You
are Dan Francisco? The man who says he hears an alien
in his head?"

Oh shit. "Well, ah," he stammered. Stopped and
squeezed out a queasy smile. "You can't, you know, believe everything you see on the news."

Colonel Czarne turned back toward Martina, his thin
mustache twitching with fury. "What are you trying to
pull here, Colonel Omerov?"

Martina never got a chance to try to come up with a
good answer to that one. Before she could open her
mouth, the old Avva hot line rang.

Each visitation from Avva had been somewhat different than the one before. This time was no exception.

Dan's ears began to ring and his vision to double as
that now-familiar feeling of presence and pressure filled
his head once again. But this time instead of being
plunged into a mental maelstrom it came on slowly, feeling tired and tentative. A great alien weariness washed
over him, threatening to buckle his knees. His heart
clenched at the knowledge that the poor being was wearing down and losing ground.

"Oh Jesus." He sighed.

"Hey, yeah, JESUS!" Daveed yelled. *"Sure!"* Dan
turned toward the mediartist in confusion, his thoughts
beginning to roll loosely around like marbles on a plate,
saw Daveed seize Jasper's hand and begin pulling him
forward. Then he switched Jasper's hand to the one in
a cast and grabbed Martina's hand. *"Show—show us a
sign!"* he called, that cry a faint whispering mental voice
in Dan's wobbling mind.

Jamal moved then, taking Amber's hand, and Jasper's.
"Show us a sign!" he echoed, his voice booming through
the room and sounding like some great bass horn in
Dan's head.

He was already stumbling forward to join the others,
uncertain why, but knowing it was important. Took Mar-

tina's free hand, and then Amber's, closing the circle. It was like grabbing a live wire. Or maybe a life wire, because that was the juice that suddenly surged at the connection.

A sense of kinship, of shared strength and determination, swept through him and the others when the circle was completed, transforming into a warm rising cyclic wind that lifted him/them up as the weaknesses of one were buttressed by the strengths of the others. Their bond took on a shape, a fragile house of cards suddenly solidifying into a kind of great graceful tower, a construct solid and perfect and beautiful rising up into the sky and beyond at a speed light could not match, and with a strength only love could ever hope to equal.

Show us a sign, Avva! he shouted with his mind with the others, that cry multiplying in power as their grouped contact with Avva deepened like a waking interior symphony, their entreaty becoming a steel hymn of hope and encouragement as the room around him faded away.

Please, you must show us a sign!

Madwoman

Jane came back to herself from otherwhere, found that she was on her knees and weeping as what felt like an ocean of emotion receded. She wiped her face with her arm and let out a shaky sigh, then looked around, her vision blurred by tears.

Fabi and Hans were in the sick bay's open doorway. Watching.

The expressions on their faces told her the whole story. They'd seen it all. Her husband looked concerned, she could see and feel his need to come to her. To hold her. To see if she was all right.

Gluck held him back, eyeing her with the scowling caution you would use when faced with some dangerous and unpredictable creature.

"It's all right," she said hoarsely, straightening up. "I won't bite."

"You are through being a madwoman?" Gluck asked in a voice sharpened by doubt as to that possibility.

She sighed and levered herself up off the deck. Faced him squarely. "I am in full command of my faculties, Mr. Gluck."

Fabi shoved his way past the younger man, came to her, and wrapped his arms around her. She held him tightly, sparing just a moment to close her eyes and feel his warm strength and his love. In the aftermath of Avva's contact she felt oddly lost and alone in her head, and this was just what she needed to make the feeling go away.

She could have stayed that way forever, but dared not. She made herself open her eyes and stare unflinchingly back at Hans over her husband's shoulder.

They stood that way for nearly a minute in a silent

battle of wills. At last he turned away and stalked off, white-faced and tight-lipped.

Fabi gave her one final squeeze, then held her out at arm's length. "You are really okay?" he asked in a shaking voice.

She nodded. "I'm fine, considering."

He tilted his head and studied her face, as if searching for something to give him proof of that.

"You kept calling 'Show us a sign!'" he said quietly. "You were asking this of, ah, Avva?"

"Yeah, me and the others. Most of them are at the Center in Neely now. They were trying to get into Uplink and contact us here." Frustration welled up, some her own, some secondhand. "I don't think they're going to make it now."

"Did . . ." He licked his lips. "Did Avva hear you? Did, ah, he understand what you were saying?"

She could see how hard it was for him to believe in the alien. But it was enough that he believed in her. Agreeing to go out with him even though he wasn't a macho cockpit cowboy like the other men she'd been helling with at the time had been the smartest move of her life.

"Maybe. I think so."

"What kind of sign can he give us?"

"I have no idea." Her gaze went distant as she remembered his confusion, and then that spark of what seemed to be understanding at the end. "I just hope it's something everyone can see. He's so tired, Fabi. So goddamned tired. I'm not sure he has the energy left to do much of anything."

"If it doesn't?"

All she had been through on her long journey from denial to commitment filled her mind, along with glimpses of what the others back on Earth had faced in their attempt to reach her, to answer the call. The thought of failure was more than she could bear.

"*Fabi,*" she said in a choked voice, falling back into his arms. There was nothing more any of them could do for now. Unless Avva came through in the next few hours, she was going to have to seize control of the *Ares* back, and Hans would fight her tooth and nail. She wasn't sure she had enough strength left in her for such a battle; everything except bitter determination seemed to have been wrung out of her.

"It's all right, *cara mia,*" he whispered in her ear. He stroked her forehead, fingers tender and loving. "Everything will turn out all right."

Jane held on to him as if her life depended on it, hoping with all her heart that he was right.

The Gambler

When the contact ended, it took Martina considerable effort to recover. She took a deep breath and let it out, then opened her eyes and gazed into the faces of those with whom she held hands. Her friends and comrades. Her brothers and sisters. She'd come out of their contact with a deeper knowledge of each of them, and to look on any one was to feel a great pride in knowing them.

She saw Dan first. He tried to smile, only partially succeeding. Inside him was a battlefield equal to any she had ever visited, an internal army of fear and loss and doubt held at bay by his simple dogged determination to see this thing through. There was an odd gentle heroism in him, and it flowed from deep wells of love and loyalty and kindness. His was not a soldier's courage, but that of a father, and in his mind Avva had taken on something of the aspect of a lost child. One for whom he had put his chances to be with his own child in serious jeopardy.

Her attention was drawn to Daveed and Jasper as they turned toward each other. Before, in her mind, they had been almost one single presence. Now it was easy to see why. Their time and troubles together had forged them into a unit, and no two other things in the whole world could have fit together as well as they did. The innocent, unreserved elegance of their bond made her feel a pang of envy. In a day they had reached a place she had not been able to come near in two years.

"Oh mamma! That was one *serious* motherfucking rush!" Amber cackled, giggling and shaking her head as if to resettle her brains. Martina had to smile, still able to taste the woman's fierce eccentric love for Jamal, one so great there wasn't any force on Earth she wouldn't challenge or privation she wouldn't endure in her determination to keep him safe and happy. Tough and tender. She showed that you could be both.

Beside her Jamal took a deep breath. A smile stolen from the Buddha unfolded on his bearded face.

"He heard," he said softly.

"What can he do?" She knew he was the one most likely to have an answer.

They had all been linked together when they tried to contact Avva back and send their message, and most of them had touched the radiant and exquisite power of his mind only lightly, forced to keep a safe distance from Avva's too-vivid intellect; the sheer size and strength and complexity of it was too bright and potent for any of them to bear.

Any of them but Jamal. Although terrified of the everyday world most of them took for granted, he plunged into this outré alien presence with a sort of childlike exuberance, like a man dancing in a vast, cascading waterfall of sense and cogitation, gleefully turning his face up to touch and taste what he could from a rush that would have crushed the rest of them flat.

It was through him that they saw Avva more clearly, and it came to her then that Avva and Jamal were strangely alike. Which made both of them very beautiful indeed.

The big man shook his hairless head, still smiling. "I am not quite sure. But he is going to do something."

"Colonel Omerov!" A sharp voice from outside their circle. The wider world intruding with a harsh reminder that they had been stopped short of accomplishing the task before them. A task that demanded completion. Word still had to be gotten to the *Ares,* if for no other reason than to help Jane Dawkins-Costanza convince her crewmates to look for the sign Avva was hopefully going to give.

Martina turned her head. Colonel Czarne wore a forbidding expression now, and he had his sidearm out of its holster.

"Yes, Colonel?" she replied, trying to sound as if nothing out of the ordinary had just happened. They

released each other's hands, but stayed close, a belea-
guered family facing the wrath of a commissar.

"I am afraid I must place all of you under more formal
detention." The soldiers at his command had arrayed
themselves around them, weapons at the ready, and
stared at them like they might just be aliens themselves.

"For what reason?" she asked, as if she didn't know.
Had she seen a performance like they had just given,
they would all be in cuffs and on the floor. Which might
just be what came next.

"Just a precaution," he answered, eyeing her warily.
"I am going to ask you and Captain Crow to hand over
any weapons you might be carrying. Please."

Could she brazen this out? It seemed unlikely, but she
had to try. "I do not think—" she began.

"*Now,* Colonel!" He backed up this command by raising his pistol so it was pointed at her forehead. "I know
your reputation, and the level of combat skills you pos-
sess. So be advised I will shoot you if you make the
slightest threatening move."

Her shoulders sagged in defeat. So this was how it
ended. She had failed Avva, failed Jane, failed the others, and what were the chances she'd ever be let near
Rico again after this?

"Very well, I surrender," she said heavily. Jane was
on her own. She might be able to take this stiff-necked
bastard, but the cost would be too high. "I will unbutton
my jacket so you can remove the weapon from my shoulder holster."

Just as she was slowly beginning to put her fingers on
the buttons, the door to the room where they were being
held banged open. Two soldiers whirled in that direction,
rifles leveled.

"Is there some especial reason why my personal bodyguard is being held at gunpoint?" a familiar voice called.
"And now me, too?"

Her heart nearly burst when she saw Rico standing
there in the open doorway, his familiar figure resplendent in a blindingly white suit. Chan and Fayed flanked
him, and the stern warning looks on their faces had the
soldiers facing in that direction lowering their weapons.

"Secretary-General Perez?" Czarne said uncertainly, snapping to attention a moment later and saluting. *"Sir!"*

"Ah, so you recognize me," Rico said with an easy smile, striding in like he owned the place. The rest of Tacs One and Three followed, fanning out around him in a protective cluster. Their presence was sufficient to make all the other soldiers lower their weapons as well.

"Of course, sir!" Czarne barked.

"Bueno. I mean good. Please be at ease, Colonel."

The Belgian dropped his hand, but his spine remained ramrod straight and his face frozen. Now his pistol pointed at the floor.

"So, how is my fact-finding mission going, Colonel Omerov?" Rico asked as he came toward her. A merry mischievous twinkle lit his dark eyes.

"It could be better, Mister Secretary," she answered blandly, adopting a professional mien when what she really wanted to do was pick him up and kiss his face off. "We have encountered some difficulties."

"Ah, these are difficult times," he said with a nod. He indicated the others with an airy wave of his hand. "I take it these are the advisors who have been helping you on your mission?"

"Yes, Mister Secretary. They are."

"Excellent." He rubbed his hands together. "Then I suppose we should head straight for the Uplink Center and begin, no?"

"Sir," Czarne began, forcing the words out between clenched teeth. "These people are not—"

Rico turned toward him, his smile warm and bright enough to turn Siberia into a sunbather's paradise. "These people are my guests, Colonel. They have aided me in a most delicate matter, and have gone to considerable trouble to meet me here. They deserve our praise, not suspicion."

Czarne looked ready to die. "Sorry, sir."

"For what? Doing your job? For this you, too, deserve commendation." Rico slapped his forehead. "Ay, this talk of jobs reminds me!"

Martina watched him turn back toward her. "So, Colonel Omerov, are you ready to take command of my security detachment once more?" One shaggy eyebrow went up, and the curl of his mustache told her he was having the time of his life.

She swallowed the lump in her throat. "Yes, Mister Secretary. I am." She wasn't going to cry, dammit. She *wasn't*!

"This I am glad to hear. Anything else you need to tell me?"

There were three little words she wanted to say more than anything else in the whole world, but they would have to wait for a little while longer, for a better time and place. Still, they would be said, consequences bedamned. She shook her head, and the words she did speak felt almost as good and right.

"System active. Tac One and Tac Three, please."

A tingle from behind her ear told her that at last she was back where she belonged.

"Welcome back, ma'am," Chan whispered under his breath, trying to hide a smile. Fayed salaamed, grinning from ear to ear, then pumped his fist in the air and went *"Yes!"* The others, Wilkins and Carelli and Duffy and the rest saluted.

Martina turned toward Colonel Czarne. "If you would be so kind as to holster that weapon and lead the way, please?"

After a moment he clicked his heels together and gave a stiff bow. "Of course, Colonel. Follow me."

"Why do you do this?" she asked Rico as they made their way down the long sun-washed corridor leading to Uplink.

He looked surprised at her question. "So you can do what you say you must, of course."

"You believe Avva is real?"

He shrugged. "That does not matter. I believe *you*, Martina Elena Omerov. Now I know you are *muy loco*, why else would you mess around with old guy like me? But otherwise you are pretty okay for a large Russian broad with a gun fetish. You say this is all true and must be done, then I believe you. So I come to help you. Just in time, too, I guess."

"So . . . you are doing this for me?" Such trust and devotion seemed impossible, such risk unacceptable.

And yet was it any less than what she'd always given him? No, it was more. What kind of lover will catch a bullet for you, but won't say how much she cares? The kind she had been.

"Of course." Then he laughed. "Plus, just think! If I am first Secretary-General to bring another planet into the UN, I will gain a whole lot of clout. Some of my favorite initiatives may finally get adopted. Who knows, maybe even those *maricons* in accounting will stop giving me so much shit over my expenses!"

It eased her mind to hear him make so light of what he was doing, but still she wanted to be certain he knew what he might be getting into.

"You . . . you are risking much here."

There in front of everyone he leaned over and kissed her on the cheek. "Only because I do not want to gamble what is really important to me."

Blushing, she looked away. Dan caught her eye, winked, then mouthed the words *I love you.*

"Me neither," she answered, saving those words for a time when she would also be able to have show-and-tell.

But just to make a start, she took his hand in hers.

Klatu Barada Nikto

Daveed's homecoming was everything he could have hoped for and more.

The moment he stepped through the door into MU the Goat came bursting from his office like an evil jack-in-the-box, almost like he'd been watching and waiting to pounce.

"What are you doing here?" he bellowed as he stormed over, his face puckered with pique at seeing his least favorite mediartist standing there in the doorway holding hands with another man. The entire crew prairie-dogged, heads appearing above their cubicle tops.

The Goat's pucker got worse when Dan, Jamal, and Amber came in behind Jasper and Daveed. Whispers started among his coworkers, Francisco's name making the rounds in seconds. No lag in recognizing him here, no sir.

"Who are these people—" Gautier howled, then stopped with his mouth hanging open when Secretary-General Perez and his entourage entered behind Dan.

"Aren't you glad to have me back, Mr. Gautier?" Daveed asked with a grin. "I brought some friends along for my coming-back party. Hope you don't mind. The pizza and champagne should be here any minute now."

"This is not—" He sputtered. "You cannot—!"

Jamal had pulled off his shaydes and found the windowless space acceptable. "Has the *Ares* mission requested information on Avva?" he asked, his deep voice booming throughout the room.

Gautier stared at him. "Who are you to ask this?"

"Answer the man," Secretary-General Perez suggested, managing to convey about twenty tons of authority with those three softly spoken words.

"I—" He stared at Perez, blinking furiously. "*Oui,* they did," he said at last.

"What did you tell them?" the Secretary-General asked in a silky tone.

Gautier drew himself up. "I tell them nossing about this foolishness, of course."

"*Boing!* Wrong answer," Daveed said. "Sorry, contestant number one. I guess we better go use your office to straighten out the mess you've made."

The Goat's eyes nearly bugged out of his head. "How dare you speak to me this way! *I* am in charge here! No snotty, smart-ass queer can—"

"*Captain Crow,*" Martina rapped in a voice hard enough to drive nails into concrete, "please take this awful man into custody."

Jasper let go of Daveed's hand and saluted. "With pleasure, Colonel." He dropped the salute and started limping toward Gautier. "If you will please come with me, sir."

"*Stay away!*" the Goat screeched, backpedaling with a look of horror straight from a Hitchcock film.

The beginnings of a smile leaked out onto Jasper's battered bronze face when he saw a thick leg sheathed in lime green fishnet stocking stick out of a cubicle behind the Goat. "I think you had better stop right there, sir," he called. Daveed knew it was Dawn's cubicle. Dawn's leg.

"Don't you come near m—" the Goat began, then his heels came up against Dawn's leg, and he went down on his ass with a screech.

"Hand him over to Center Security and return here as quickly as you can, please," Martina instructed.

"Yes ma'am." Jasper bent down, hauled a squirming Gautier to his feet by his arm, then frog-marched him away. The cubicles erupted in cheering and applause.

"Now, Mr. Shah, if you would kindly lead the way?" Secretary-General Perez said once it quieted down a little.

"Sure. Follow me."

A couple minutes later the others were all crowded around him as he settled in before the workstation in Gautier's office. Hot damn! The big board was *his*!

"Okay," he said. "See this display here? That's our present communications lag. We're at a bit over four minutes, which is pretty close to the minimum. Anything we send to the *Ares* is first digitally recorded, then compressed and encrypted. Once that's done it's queued in with the other burst transmissions. We're into the *Ares'* second watch now, where we at MU are given a little more time for our uploads, third watch is where we get the most dish time. At the moment average queue time is . . ."

He hammered in a command, watched a number come up on the display. "We can get in with only a couple minute wait if our packet is small enough. Which it probably will be. So figure a couple minutes wait in queue, then four for the signal to reach them. Not exactly like calling your family when the rates are cheapest, but it works."

He swiveled his chair around to ask the million-dollar question. "So who's going to talk, and what are they going to say?"

Every one of them looked at Jamal, Mr. Answer Man in the flesh.

"Very well," he said. "I picked up some sense of Jane's situation this last time. She believes, and part of her crew half believe, but her second-in-command does not. If I am not mistaken, he has relieved her of command because of her insistence that Avva exists and must be helped."

"She needs some clout to back her up, then," Dan said.

"Precisely. As much clout as we can muster. You, Mr. Secretary-General, have more than any of us. Give me a minute or two with that board and I am certain I can convince it that our message comes from a command sector, not media. That plus your presence should be sufficient to make it stick."

Perez nodded. "I will talk to the *Ares,* sure. Just tell me what I should say."

"Howzabout *Klatu barada nikto,*" Amber muttered.

Daveed stared at her with delight, recognizing a kindred spirit.

The Face of Elvis

Jane looked up when Gluck stuck his head in the sick-bay hatchway.

"In the wardroom. *Now.*" A parting scowl and he was gone.

She exchanged a glance with her husband. "What do you figure? Firing squad?"

Fabi shook his head. "He didn't look happy enough for it to be that."

"I guess there's only one way to find out." They hopped down off the examination table where they'd been sitting, just two old married folks taking comfort in each other's company. Hand in hand, they headed for the wardroom.

"I have a Priority One communication from Uplink," Hans said when they came in, indicating the display in front of the command chair where he had planted himself. "It is supposed to be viewed with both of us present."

Her heart skipped a beat. *Could Daveed and the others have made it after all?*

"Well, let's see what it says," she suggested in the most offhand tone she could muster as she went to stand beside him. "Mind if Fabi sits in?"

Gluck just stared at her.

"Does it say that it's for our eyes only?" she asked patiently.

"No."

"Well then?"

He scowled. "He can stay."

"Thanks." She motioned Fabi over. "I'm ready when you are."

Gluck touched a key to start the message. The Uncle

Joe logo vanished. She blinked in surprise at seeing Secretary-General Perez appear on the screen.

"Greetings to the *Ares* mission," he said with a broad smile. "I bring you most extraordinary news. Over the past few days several unimpeachable sources here on Earth have come forward to report that they have been contacted by an alien being. This being, whose name is Avva, has told them that he is marooned on Phobos, and in dire need of our aid. Avva has been very much in the news down here, although I understand that certain overzealous persons have seen to it that you have remained unaware of what has been happening."

His smile faded, his expression turning grave. "While we have not yet seen any overt signs that this Avva exists, it is my considered opinion that we must assume these persons' assertions to be correct; that Avva is real; and we must render the aid and comfort they insist he so desperately needs."

Yes! Jane had to lock her knees as relief swept through her.

Perez spread his hands. "I know that this may be hard for you to believe, and I suppose there remains some small chance that these people are mistaken. Still, I believe we must respond, and act on this plea for rescue as if it had come to us through more normal channels. To do otherwise would, I think, be utterly unconscionable."

He squared his shoulders, seeming to stare right at them. "So in my official capacity as UN Secretary-General I ask you, Commander Jane Dawkins-Costanza, and you, Lt. Commander Hans Gluck, to immediately begin the following tasks. First, I want you to concentrate all sensory equipment at your disposal on Phobos, and search for hard evidence of this being. Second, I want you to begin calculating a new flight plan, one that will take you to Phobos as soon as humanly possible."

A faraway look entered Perez's eyes. "Just think what this means, my friends! We sent you to Mars hoping to find some small sign of simple life. It may be that we are instead on the threshold of meeting someone from another star."

He regarded them steadily once more. "Even if the

odds are only one in a hundred, we dare not pass up this chance. I am certain you understand the urgency and importance of this matter. I stand by waiting for your reply."

His image froze, then blipped down to one corner of the display.

They did it! How they had gotten the fucking Secretary-General himself in on it, unless Martina had somehow managed it—the "how" didn't matter. They had just gotten orders straight from the top man. Hans had to back down now, didn't he?

"This could be a hoax," he said in a voice stripped of all inflection.

Of course it couldn't be that easy. Nothing had so far.

She looked him in the eye. "You know it's not, Hans. That was Secretary-General Perez himself. You heard what he wants us to do."

He stared up at her. "I heard him say we should look for proof! Anna has been doing that! She does that and nothing else, and still she has found *nothing*!"

She made herself speak softly because he seemed to be on the verge of losing it. "That may change. We asked Avva to give us a sign. I know you heard me talking to him."

"Give you a *sign*?" He shook his head in scowling bafflement. "I heard you yelling at *nothing*, that is what I heard! There can be no sign! There is no alien on Phobos or anywhere else! This is madness! Next you will be telling me you see the face of Jesus on the surface of Deimos!"

"Well, maybe the face of Elvis," she joked, trying to calm him down.

"This is not *funny*!" he shouted, slamming his hand flat on the table. "How do I know that this message isn't some trick Willy has made for you? I know you are all against me!"

Jane let out a weary sigh. It looked like no matter what happened he was not going to accept Avva or Perez's orders. Which meant she would have to regain command by force after all. Time was running out.

"Hans," she said gently, taking one last despairing

shot at reason. If he would not bend then she was going to have to break him. "Listen, we're not—"

Before she could say any more Anna burst into the wardroom. *"Is there! I find it!"* she yelled as she ran toward them, her round face glowing with joy and excitement.

"Find what?" Hans snapped impatiently.

"Proof of Avva!" she crowed, pushing in next to Jane behind the table, then leaning over and punching a command into the board in front of her husband. "Look! *See?*"

Jane stared down at the display, her eyes widening. *Oh my God . . .*

"This is real-time view!" Anna gushed, nearly levitating with excitement. "Is happening now! *Right now!*"

"What—what *is* it?" Hans asked uncertainly, staring at the display and frowning.

"Is column of material from surface of Phobos, dust and particles up to size of small gravel. A column like whirlwind, rising up where we can see. Was not there before, but is now." She turned toward Jane, grinning and hugging herself. *"Is now!"*

Movement caught Jane's eye. She watched Willy and Wanda enter, drawn by Anna's shouts and wanting to know what was going on. As Fabi headed toward them she leaned over and put the view up on the big screen, where they could all see. Fabi filled them in on what was happening, laughing and pointing toward her and the screen.

She stared down at the desktop display again. Phobos peered enigmatically back at her, a rusty crescent of Mars filling the left-hand side of the screen behind it. A reddish gray column continued to rise up from the small moon's surface, growing taller all the time.

"How big is it, Anna?" she asked in a hushed voice.

"Less than kilometer across, but look at scalar! Is almost two hundred kilometers high! Still getting bigger!"

"There cannot be a whirlwind on Phobos," Hans said in a flat, mechanical voice. "There is no air."

His wife rounded on him, triumph blazing in her eyes. "Is so. You know what this means."

He shook his head.

"*Durak!* Stupidhead! Means it cannot be natural phenomenon! Can only be happening because someone *make* it happen, *and that sure-shit is not us*!"

On the screen the whirling dust cloud rose higher yet, thrust up like a wobbling length of corrugated plastic pipe. Over the next minute it reached a height of just over 250 kilometers, then began to withdraw back toward the Martian moon's surface once more. Jane had a sudden image of the waving arm of a drowning man sinking below the surface.

Going down for the last time.

She laid her hands on Hans's shoulder, feeling him flinch and go rigid at her touch. Fear and denial rolled off him in waves, and she began to wonder if he was constitutionally incapable of accepting this as real. She hoped not, and took one last shot at reaching him.

"This is real, Hans," she said in a soothing voice. "This is wonderful. This is so—"

Before her mind could supply another word that might cast some faint shadow of description on the situation, it filled with the touch of Avva. No warning this time. Suddenly he was just there in her head, coming in five-by-five.

did . . . this suffice?

He sounded weary, all energy expended on the effort of raising the dusty signal flag they had just seen.

will you . . . come now?

"*Yes,*" she whispered/thought in reply. "We will come as fast as we can."

***thank you* * * *

That returning thought was like a sigh, and in an instant he was gone, leaving behind an impression of utter exhaustion tempered by relief and hope, feelings that fit like a key in a lock with the way she felt herself.

Gluck took a deep shuddering breath, then lifted his head and gaped at her wide-eyed. His mouth moved, but nothing came out.

She gave his shoulder a motherly pat. "I know, Hans. You just heard him, too." She'd felt the contact reach him, carried by her touch. If only she had known this earlier, so much trouble and pain could have been avoided.

He swallowed hard, looking ready to cry. "What—what should we do . . . Commander?" he whispered hoarsely.

She smiled and gripped his shoulder tightly. "We play it by the book, of course. Contact Mission Control. Relay our observations, and inform them that we are altering course to investigate."

He nodded uncertainly. "Can we really save him?"

"We are going to do our absolute damnedest. Right, Mr. Gluck?"

He tried to smile. "Yes ma'am. Of course."

He got out of her chair and offered it to her, then gestured toward the display where a playing-card-sized image of Secretary-General Perez remained frozen. "We must reply to him as well."

Jane reclaimed her proper place, feeling her old strength and certainty returning as she sat down.

"Oh, we will, just to keep the historians happy."

There had been only a microsecond's linkage with her allies back on Earth, but that had been enough.

"But take my word for it. They already know."

Friends in High Places

At first Dan had been up, cruising in the stratosphere and sharing the sense of relief and flat-out crazy joy that they'd pulled this whole thing off in spite of the odds and obstacles.

Things were just starting to calm down to a dull roar when Jane's official reply to Perez's message had come in. Then Dawn, the woman who had tripped Daveed's former boss, brought Daveed a sheaf of news bulletins. Several Earth- and space-based telescopes reported seeing a 250-kilometer-tall column of dust appear and then disappear on the surface of Phobos, confirming Anna's observations on the *Ares*.

The initial reports referred to it as an anomaly, but it wasn't going to take long for Uncle Joe and the world at large to put two and two together and come up with four for a change. One net had already broken in with a bulletin, a two-word graphic hung behind the excited announcer: **AVVA LIVES!**

The hugging and hooting and laughing had begun all over again. One of the hardiest partiers was Secretary-General Perez. He'd had his hand on Martina's arm when Avva had asked if his signal would suffice, and just as Amber had made contact through Jamal, heard him, too. The man was so happy he looked about to burst like a piñata.

In spite of the celebratory atmosphere, Dan soon found himself coming down from his initial high. Not slowly, but in an abrupt plummet, like an angel crash-landing in a swamp. His pleasure curdling, he drifted off and flopped down on a chair over in one corner of Gautier's office. He had some hard thinking to do, and didn't want to spoil the others' fun.

He'd barely got his butt parked when Jamal extricated himself from the melee and came over.

"Not in a party mood?" he said, settling into the next chair.

Dan shrugged. That had to be pretty obvious.

"Thinking about your daughter?"

"Some," he admitted. "Yeah."

"And Susannah?"

"Her too."

"Feeling screwed?"

"Yeah, I guess I am." He spread is hands. "Now don't get me wrong, I mean this is great. Jane and her crew can go save Avva. That's what we want, isn't it?"

"It most certainly is."

"And we got it. We did it. Game's over, and our side won. Now you and Amber can go back to the Bunker and lock the door behind you. Martina and Secretary-General Perez are together again. Daveed and Jasper found each other. Everybody gets to live happily ever after."

"All except you," Jamal said gently. "Your life got utterly destroyed in the process."

"Yeah, it did. I know I should feel like a winner, but I don't. I've got the kind of fame nobody needs, and a reputation I'll probably never live down. Tammy's got my Bobbi, and she *never* gives back anything once she gets her hooks in it. If I don't get to see Bobbi, then I don't get to see Susannah. Even if I do get the chance, I've got the media so tight on my ass I won't dare go near them for fear of seeing it on the evening fucking news."

He made a helpless gesture. "I feel like a real asshole thinking about this now, I really do. It's just—just—"

Tears flooded his eyes, and he hung his head in shame. *"Fuck,"* he mumbled. "All I want is my life back. I mean, even Dorothy got to go home after her trip to Oz so she could grow up, get laid by some big strapping farm boy, have some kids, and look up and remember every time she saw a rainbow."

"Dan," Jamal said quietly, "listen to me. You paid a heavier price than any of us on this. I know that. So do the others. Just remember, what goes around, comes around."

Platitudes from Jamal? He looked up, shook his head. "What is that supposed to mean?"

"Look around you and you'll see."

He did. The others stood there watching him, their faces filled with concern. Over him, the death of the party.

"You have made yourself some pretty impressive friends, Dan Francisco," Jamal continued. "Some of them in quite high places."

He grinned. "If you count Avva and Jane, then you've got friends in the highest places we've found. When Avva called, and we understood what was at stake, not a single one of us walked away. Well, we're still here, and none of us are going to walk away from *you*."

The big man put his hand on Dan's shoulder, his face solemn. "I haven't had a friend like you since I was a kid, or even been close to anyone besides Amber since I buried myself under a hundred feet of dirt. You changed that, and changed me in the process. As I've said before, I owe you, and I honor my debts. We all owe you. If I can't kick your wife's ass myself, then they will help. If we can't do it, then we'll find someone who can. You have my solemn promise on this. Can you believe me? Can you believe us?"

Dan looked into the faces of those around him, his friends and coconspirators, knowing them better than people he'd been around all his life, seeing and feeling how much they cared.

Daveed and Jasper both wore the same compassionate-yet-determined expressions on their battered faces, and they nodded in unison.

Amber winked and blew him a kiss, then struck a pose and stuck out her chin in a way that said, *Just let me at 'em!*

Secretary-General Perez crossed his arms and nodded gravely, while beside him Martina unbuttoned her jacket to expose the gun in her shoulder holster. She grinned and said, "If her arm cannot be twisted, then I just shoot the bitch."

He turned back to face Jamal, the man who had

started him out on this bizarre odyssey. What he had said before cut two ways. The big agoraphobic had become the best friend he'd had in a very long time, as loved and trusted as Morty.

"Okay?" Jamal said.

He nodded, smiling through the tears running down his face. "Okay. Thanks."

After all, if he could believe in a lost and lonesome alien stranded in some foreign, inhospitable place, then how could he not believe in them?

He might be a bit of a fool, but he wasn't stupid.

He stood up, wiped his face on his sleeve, and tried for a smile. "I think we ought to move this party back to Jamal's place and order in that champagne and pizza Daveed mentioned."

Jamal stood up beside him, hand still on his shoulder. "Excellent idea. I'm buying."

Secretary-General Perez shook his head. "No, this will go on *my* expense account!" He laughed. "Come, my friends! We shall go drink enough to make those *cabrons* in accounting think maybe I have bought a winery!"

Jamal put his shaydes back on. Amber took one arm, Dan the other. The Three Musketeers ready for their next adventure.

"So, you want to make a forecast, Mr. Weatherman?" Amber asked, as together they headed for the door.

Dan smiled. "Better days ahead, I think."

PART 5

The Answer

On the Wires

It used to be said that the world stopped and held its breath back in July of 1969, at the moment when the still-adolescent medium of television brought to it the image of a human being stepping off a ladder onto the surface of the Moon, a man named Armstrong's booted foot creating the most famous footprint in history.

The world was a far different place in that bygone time. Things were more simple then. Back then "the world" meant the developed nations, and just those where governments did not hold the flow of information in an iron grip, choking it off, and twisting and warping it to fit their political ends.

That world was not a place where every African village got three thousand channels, and existed in cyberspace as much as on the dusty plain where their huts were raised. Where Amazon shamans could not only upload their knowledge onto the nets from their hiding places deep in the remaining rain forest—information that helped preserve that forest—but also watch baseball games and commercials for Budweiser and McDonald's on slaytes that were as important a tool as the knife and the spear. Where the signal and the screen were so ubiquitous that there was no place they did not reach.

Back then a single image, that fabled distillation of a thousand words, could not be so instantly omnipresent in the way it could now, with a reach and saturation that would have seemed inconceivable to the men and women who disseminated those jerky black-and-white flickerings brought home from a place where no man had gone before.

A philosopher from that bygone time gained fame

from his statement that "the medium was the message."
He had been right in his way, and most of the time.

But there are times, most often in moments of triumph
or tragedy, when the message seizes the medium, overwhelming its shallow, self-referential reliance on noise
and flash, on form over content. In those moments the
shabby Frankenstein's monster of media is trans-
formed—perhaps even transfigured—into something undivided and immaculate. The endlessly thumping engine
of consumption becomes a great beating heart of unifi-
cation, connecting billions of people and uniting them in
a single shared experience.

It was night in North America when a new day
dawned in the light cast by countless screens and displays, when all across the entire planet eyes soaked up
the sight of Commander Jane Dawkins-Costanza's historic meeting with a being from another world, another
star. Her words, excitedly translated into a thousand
tongues, rang around the planet in one voice, girdling it
and covering it pole to pole.

What they saw and heard was of course warmed-over
and secondhand. It had already happened minutes before in a place so far away that light and its sister radio
had a four-minute hike home. Still that did not blunt
its impact.

Only a few experienced it firsthand, two as part of it,
the handful of others as a fleeting real-time touch. This
moment was something they had helped make possible,
and it was only fitting they had front-row seats.

The rest of the world laughed and cried and reeled
with wonder, popping champagne corks and drinking
toasts to the *Ares* and her crew. Some drank tea, some
said prayers, each celebrating in his or her own way.
Mankind being what it is, there were also those who
reacted with horror and fear and fury, and in the wake
of this event began laying black, apocalyptic plans.

Still, for the most part the people of Earth watched
together, and hoped together, and prayed together, and
celebrated together, and knew that they were in some
small way part of something grand and glorious and
amazing—not only the event unfolding before them, but
perhaps even themselves as a race.

Hush

Daveed leaned forward and fed another handful of twigs into the small campfire Jasper had started out there under the endless desert sky using the ancient native technique he called the Bic Fire Spell. The fire felt good, warding off the chill that had descended after the sun went down.

Jasper had picked the spot, saying it was a holy place. Daveed could believe it. There was something in the air, or maybe in the earth itself. A sort of peace, and a feeling of connection with larger things. Looking up was like tuning into the Forever Channel.

"Almost time," Jasper said beside him, his eyes glued to the CyZilla slayte on the hard ground between them and the fire.

"Yeah. History here we come." Strictly speaking he should be back at Media Uplink, but as the Goat's replacement, he could take the night off if he wanted to. Rank had its privileges.

The old Daveed would have been there. After all, the world was throwing up the biggest wave of infoload ever, and at MU he could have surfed that tsunami with ten thousand channels under his feet, riding the greatest swell of happening in the history of mankind.

The new Daveed had decided that they could do without him, and this one small slayte set to a single feed was enough. The wave could pass, and work wait until tomorrow. There would be plenty to do then, and in the weeks to come as the *Ares* made its long journey home.

Jasper reached over, squeezed his hand. "You all right, man? You seem kind of quiet."

"I'm fine." He glanced at the slayte. "Looks like less than a hundred feet to touchdown."

"Yeah, hard to believe this is finally happening."

The former Mars Eagle, now rechristened *Rescue One,* closed with the surface of Phobos, a breathless voice-over relaying all the details. Before it could touch down, a knot popping in the flickering campfire drew his gaze away. He watched a firefly-cascade of sparks rise, then turned to study the face the fire illuminated.

He drank in the sight, drunk with the pleasure it brought. This one was going to stick around. He was sure of it, and thankful beyond words. Beginning tonight work would always take a backseat to this man. To life.

Jasper leaned forward, grinning from ear to ear. "Look, man, they're touching down! Way to go!"

He spared only a quick glance at the screen, then returned to contemplating the man watching it, his heart swelling until it felt twice as big as the star-flecked sky above them.

"Isn't it great?" Jasper breathed in an awestruck voice.

"It sure is," Daveed agreed, ignoring the media event of the new millennium for something far smaller and more personal—and in its own way, infinitely more wonderful.

"You *sure* you want to do this?" Amber asked fretfully. "We can go back."

"I'm . . . fine," Jamal replied hoarsely as the elevator stopped moving.

"You don't sound fine. Or sure."

Well, he wasn't. But the urge to attempt this thing was overwhelming. He had to try. *Had* to.

He closed his eyes, steeling himself as best he could. "Open the door," he rasped. There was a muted chime.

"Okay, lover, brace yourself," Amber said, as he heard the elevator door slide open. Cool evening air swept in, chilling the sweat on his face. Beyond lay the small rooftop deck atop the building guarding the Bunker. It was a place she came to sunbathe sometimes, but he had never been there before.

He felt her take his hand. As always, he was amazed by just how small it was, her fingers swallowed up by his. How fragile. And yet it was strong enough to have helped hold him up all the years they had been together.

"I love you, you know," he whispered, his heart lurching in his chest, bouncing crazily between fear and fondness.

"I know, babe."

"Lead me . . . out there."

"Here we go." She led him by the hand like a blind man, guiding him out onto the deck. The wash of cool air became a breeze, and with this rare sensation came sound.

Over the heavy wheeze of his breath he could hear the song of frogs from the pond he owned and had never seen. Crickets. There was little traffic to be heard, though. No surprise there, everyone on the planet had stopped what they were doing to witness the momentous events unfolding on Phobos. Down below his trusty machinery gathered the sights and sounds for him to access later.

But right now he had to experience it this way. Or at least he had to *try*. He thought about how brave Dan had been, and asked himself if he could do any less.

"This is a good spot," Amber said. No wisecracking now, just the voice of love and concern that was always there when he needed it the most. The day she had tried to break into his old place had been the luckiest day of his life. That might just be Jambo's next prank, getting it declared a national holiday.

"If you say so." He stood there, eyes squeezed shut. Now all he had to do was summon the nerve to open them.

She moved around so that she was standing with her back against him, her shoulders warm against his chest. "Lean on me if you need to."

"I always have, my jewel," he said with an uneasy chuckle, wrapping his arms tightly around her. "Here goes nothing."

Jamal ever so slowly and cautiously opened his eyes. The great rough beast of terror rose up to its full height inside him, a hydra-headed thing that snapped and screeched and tore at his insides with cruel and savage teeth. He fought to keep it at bay. His heart slammed against his ribs, and panic swirled blackly around him as he faced the place he so feared.

"Where's . . . Mars?" He had to force the words out through a throat that had closed like a fist.

She raised her arm and pointed. "Up there. That reddish spot."

He stared, trying to blot out the endlessness on which it was brooched like a tiny dim ruby. "It's . . . beautiful."

"Sure is, baby. It sure is."

He'd remembered the night sky as being huge and filled with countless motes of light, but nothing like this. It made the world he felt as being so huge and scary seem like a cozy little place in comparison, a tiny box down in the corner of a stuffy closet in one small room of an immense mansion. This was large enough to dwarf all conception, and yet now that they knew they were not alone, not quite so empty.

Ever so cautiously he let his gaze drop from star to star until the place he feared most hove into view.

The horizon was ablaze with light. The light of streets and towns and cities, of homes and stores and churches and shopping malls and offices and factories and the countless other places where people moved and gathered.

Would he ever be able to visit those places? Walk freely among his own kind once more?

The feeling of faintness and fear he'd been fighting continued to bear down, his heart and head being crushed by the relentless enemy that had bested him in his youth. At the moment he'd entered the elevator the hydra had begun eating away at the pitiful gleam of courage he'd mustered, and now that small flickering flame was consumed.

"I—I've got to go back now," he gasped, eyes slamming shut and his body beginning to shake.

Amber silently took him by the hand, led him back to the elevator kiosk and on inside.

"Down," she said. He heard the chime as the machine acknowledged her command. On the heels of that came another sound. A distant many-voiced cheering, soon joined by the cry of sirens and the honk of car horns.

"I think Jane just landed," Amber chuckled. "Let's you and me go have us some champagne to celebrate."

As the doors were closing Jamal opened his eyes and risked one last backward glance at the outside world.

And smiled, knowing that he might just go out there again. Someday.

"Sounds good," he said, as the doors closed him in and the elevator began to descend.

Jane and Hans stood shoulder to shoulder in their heavy pressure suits, the surface of Phobos under their booted feet. This created footprints that would have been historic as Armstrong's—but for what was to come.

Behind them stood the former Mars Eagle, its cabin emptied of its original payload to make room for a passenger. When she looked up she could see Mars. Someone else would be the first to reach the Red Planet. As soon as they got Avva aboard the *Ares* they were heading home. That was all right with her. She wouldn't trade their present mission for a hundred others.

"Nervous?" she asked quietly.

Hans nodded, his face a pale shape behind the silvered faceplate of his helmet. "Yah. You are not?"

"Naw, not a bit."

"Jane, you are such a liar," he said with a chuckle.

She grinned. "What, did the yellow stains on my suit leg give me away?"

A stray thought flickered through her mind like a neon ribbon.

I am coming

"Here we go. Did you catch that?"

"I felt *something*. Since we are not touching, I did not get it all."

"Can't be helped." Her grin widened. "Fabi would've pitched a fit if I'd stuffed a younger man in this suit with me."

"Anna would not have much liked it either."

"You two are getting along pretty good now, aren't you?"

"Yes. All of this—" A wave of his gloved hand. "Has made me a little less sure I am always right. She tells me this is a very big improvement."

"Hey, we all had to grow up a bit. I have a feeling we're just starting."

As if to illustrate her point, a shaft of golden light suddenly shot up through the solid stone ten meters in front of them.

This is it. "Show's starting, kids. Willy, switch us to the monitored band." A muted click signaled the change.

"A light has just appeared," she said for those on the *Ares* and for retransmit back to Earth, a voice-over to match the images they were transmitting. She tried to keep herself from thinking about the projections that the entire population of the planet minus about nine people would be watching and listening.

The narrow beam widened, becoming a radiant pool over a meter across. The light seemed somehow alive, coiling and pulsing, golden opalescence edged with colors that shifted continuously like oil on water.

"It's getting, um, bigger." *So much for a postretirement career as a play-by-play announcer.*

A glowing dome appeared and began to rise up before them, extruding out of the solid ground without disturbing even a single grain of sand. Watching, the lines she had written and rehearsed flew right out of her head.

"Avva told us he would be inside a protective, um, thing. Like a suit made of light. That's what we're seeing now."

The dome continued to rise, slowly revealing itself as a two-meter, egg-shaped construct of glowing radiance. There was a shape inside, rendered indistinct by the glowing caul surrounding it. Avva, finally there before her. Within reach at last.

She'd wondered how she'd feel at this moment, and now she knew. She felt a heady mixture of eagerness and joy and awe, but deeper and greater was a feeling of relief.

They had done it. Her race was good for something besides watching the tube and squabbling after all.

She moved carefully closer, small units on her suit releasing micropuffs of compressed gas to keep her feet on the ground. Wanda and Willy's work, the extra tanks on her and Hans's backs giving them each one hour of being able to move as if they were under more than the negligible gravity of Phobos.

When she was just under a meter away she stopped,

dimly aware of Hans coming up beside her. "He's . . . beautiful," he whispered.

"Sure is." She raised her gloved hand, reaching toward the glowing spheroid, and some of her lines coming back at the last moment.

"In the name of all the peoples of Earth, I greet you, and bid you welcome," she said, adding in her mind, *And I'm pleased as hell to finally meet you, fella!*

A glowing pseudopod curled out of the blazing shape, reaching toward her outstretched hand.

believe me, it is the same for me

The two extremities touched, ending the extremity of one.

They became one.

Reverend Ray Sunshine stood before the billboard-sized Toshiba Megatron, bathed in the golden light flooding from the image of that first contact.

He bowed his head, hands gripping the pulpit.

"Thank you, Lord," he whispered too softly for the microphones to pick up or be heard over the jubilant cries of the faithful, speaking with the deep and abiding humility recent events had brought him.

He hoped that someday he would get to meet Avva, to see this living testament to His handiwork, and thank him for bringing him back to belief that God had a plan, and it was divine.

"Thy will be done."

A dozen cameras were trained on Secretary-General Perez as he perched on an antique couch and watched this wonderful moment he had helped bring about. Martina watched over the watchers watching him, her face professionally blank.

She checked her watch. It was about time to send this lot packing. The big moment had come and gone. Rico had made a statement. They would get another chance at him in a few hours anyway.

Before she could begin the roundup, Vlad Chemnirdin of RussNet turned her way, a microphone in his hands. His camera operator stepped back to frame them both.

"Colonel Omerov, a word please," he said in Russian.

"You had much to do with making this great event possible. You must be very proud."

"Yes, I am," she answered in English, hoping that deterred him.

He smiled and switched easily to that tongue. "Were you ever worried about the risks involved in your heroic rescue of Daveed Shah, or your attempt to reach the Uplink Center?"

Her gaze slipped past Chemnirdin's handsome face, lingered half a heartbeat on Rico, returned.

"No. I was not risking the things I felt most valuable."

Chemnirdin frowned. "But you could have died in Shah's apartment, or when your vehicle was attacked by armed fanatics."

She shrugged. "Even so."

Before he could pose another question she raised her voice. "Please, I must ask you all to leave now. It is late, and Secretary-General Perez has a most important address of the General Assembly tomorrow."

Her people moved in and began shepherding the media people back out. There was a bit of grumbling, but only a bit. They all knew that pictures of a man—even one as important as Perez—watching a picture would get only a few seconds airtime at best.

One by one they gathered up their gear and straggled out. Fayed brought up the rear, bowing deeply toward her with a poorly hidden smile before closing the doors behind him.

When she turned around she found Rico holding a stiff vodka out for her. "Here, my *paloma*."

"Thank you." She knew he was calling her his dove, a rather odd pet name for a heavily armed woman half again his size. His little bird knocked back half the vodka in a single gulp, finally allowing herself to relax a little. In the wake of Avva, public opinion was more behind him than ever before, but those who were against him and what he stood for hated him with a new virulence. Greater vigilance than ever was required.

"This has been some long day," she said as the soothing milk of her motherland hit bottom. "You must be tired."

He lifted one shoulder. "This was also a very good

day. I was thinking about a snack before bed. How does that sound?"

"Is probably good idea," she agreed, heading for the small kitchen. "What you want?"

"I am in mood for taco, I think. Yes, that taste very good right now."

Martina turned back. Rico was grinning like a maniac as he peeled off his white suit jacket, dropped it on the floor, then began working on his tie and shirt.

"So you are hungry?" she said, regarding him askance.

"Starving!" He came to her and began unbuttoning her jacket. "I bet I can find something tasty in here."

"Could be."

He opened her jacket, buried his face between her breasts, and inhaled deeply. "Yes, I smell something hot!"

"You are sex maniac," she chided with a laugh, running her fingers through his thinning hair.

He peered up at her, a comically hopeful look on his face. "You won't tell nobody, will you?"

"Your secret is safe with me, *moy lyubimiy*" she answered, wrapping her arms around him and holding him close.

"I love you, Ricardo Aldomar Perez," she whispered in his ear. "Love you with all my heart."

It felt so good to say those words out loud that she couldn't help herself. She looped one arm around his shoulders, reached behind his knees with the other, and scooped him up off the ground.

"Hey!" he cried, laughing and kicking his feet. "This is no way to treat an important, macho man like me! I should be one sweeping you off your feet!"

"You already have," she said, carrying him off toward the bedroom. "Is my turn now."

"Still—"

"Hush. Or I will put you to bed without your supper."

Ripples

A loon called in the distance, the sound echoing off the cliffs at the far end of Skyles Lake.

"This is so beautiful, Dan," Susannah murmured. She spoke softly so she would not wake Bobbi. The child had nodded off and slept snuggled against her, a slayte with the Phobos landing playing on its screen still loosely gripped in one small hand.

"Sure is," he agreed, talking about more than the moonlight on the water and the scenery. The sight of Susannah, her hair down and dressed in jeans and a sweatshirt, sitting in the stern of the boat with a similarly dressed Bobbi in her arms was something he wanted to drink in until it oozed out his pores.

She smiled, dimples appearing in her round cheeks. He'd grown very fond of those dimples over the last few days, and making them appear was like a magic trick he never grew tired of.

"So where are you now?" she asked.

He leaned over to retrieve his own slayte, accessed the node Jamal had given him. "Let's see. It looks like Marrakesh, Maui, and Minneapolis." A dedicated workstation in Jamal's underground retreat ceaselessly manipulated the cyberic universe 24/7, keeping all real traces of him hidden and sending doppelgängers out all over the world to keep the media confused as to his whereabouts for a little while longer. The Flitting Franciscos, cousins to the Flying Monkeys.

"How is the view?"

He gazed at her. "Just breathtaking." He put the slayte down again. "I can't thank you enough for—"

She shook her head. "Hush."

That was hard, it seemed like thanking her twice an hour for the rest of his life wouldn't do half the job.

Late Sunday evening Morty had called him, all atwitter and insisting that he tune in some news pronto. He'd said he hadn't really been enjoying the news all that much lately. The media were treating him better now, having promoted him from slippery fugitive maniac to elusive hero, but he still wanted to stay out of their clutches. She'd said he'd like this. Now acting as his spokesperson and publicity flack, she'd taught several prospective interviewers to be damn careful what they asked, and was having the time of her life extracting retractions of some of the more damaging statements made about him. She'd even gotten a minor makeover and begun wearing lipstick. Black lipstick, but a major change for a woman who kept a special chain saw for cutting down cosmetics billboards.

So he'd called up EdgeNet on one of the decks in Jamal's now-deserted Neely hideout. Within minutes, he learned that the public soap opera his life had become had taken a strange new turn.

That afternoon the California judge who awarded Tammy sole custody of Bobbi was given some ten hours of compressed—and expertly edited—vidyo.

Five hours were a cavalcade of sequences showing Tammy ignoring Bobbi, peeling the child off herself so she could go to parties or entertain men in her own wing of her mansion, taking away toys her father had given her, and trying to fill her head with hateful lies. They painted a picture of a cold, indifferent, selfish, and manipulative woman who at best viewed her child as an annoying possession, contested ground in the battle with her ex-husband.

The other five hours were clips of Dan and Bobbi laughing and playing together. His teaching her how to swim and how to cook eggs. Reading with her, playing games with her, clowning and telling stories, and just gazing at her with unalloyed adoration.

All this imagery had been gathered by the cameo brooch that was part of Susannah's nanny drag, a small high-resolution camera linked to a miniature digital recorder.

These materials had been delivered by a battalion of lawyers bearing Haliburton attachés full of corroborating documents and testimony, suits, writs, and other legal weaponry. Within a matter of hours the judge reversed himself, awarding sole custody to Dan.

Since Tammy and Bobbi were still in France when this went down, a phalanx of gendarmes aided by a detachment of UNSIA Special Security agents had taken Bobbi into custody, escorted her and Susannah to Orly, and put them on a UN SST headed for America. Somehow in all the confusion Tammy's visa came up missing. She was still in France, unable to leave.

For the past few decades professional nannies had routinely kept a vidyo record of their interaction with their charges, an insurance policy against charges of neglect or abuse. Tammy might have been dimly aware that Susannah was capable of recording the things she witnessed, but he knew that she *never* thought that any camera anywhere could ever be used against her, or to make her look bad.

Dan saw the sly hand of Jamal—along with help from Rico Perez, Daveed Shah, and the others—in this turn of events. Help from his friends. As promised and delivered.

More help arrived while he was still watching the news, this time in the form of a limousine and driver to take him to Anan Airport. From there a chartered jet flew him to an airfield forty miles north of Skyles Lake, where he found Susannah, Bobbi, and a brand-new Lincoln SUV filled with food and camping supplies waiting for him.

What goes around comes around, Jamal had said.

Things seemed to be coming around his way now.

Susannah glanced down at the pad in Bobbi's lap. "Avva is going back to the ship with Commander Jane and Lieutenant Commander Gluck now," she said. "Now they can begin bringing him home."

He nodded, having caught flickers of communication between Jane and the alien. Avva was getting better at talking to just one of them at a time. What he was getting was like hearing a whispered conversation in another room. One almost half an AU away.

She looked up, and the way she gazed at him was like all the sunshine he'd ever predicted in thirteen years as a weatherman shining into his soul. "You should be proud of what you did to make this possible, Dan. I most certainly am."

"I guess so, though it still seems kind of unreal." He smiled shyly. "So does this. Having you here, I mean. Wanting to be with someone like me."

"I wanted that almost the moment I met you."

"Really?"

"Really, and the first time I saw you with Bobbi I knew I wanted you to be the father of any child I might ever have."

Dan grinned at this revelation, thinking he might just bust if things got any better.

Bobbi wriggled around and opened her eyes. "Daddy, can we go back home now?" she asked in a voice slurred by sleep.

"Do you want to go to bed, sweet one?" Susannah asked, stroking the hair off the child's forehead.

She nodded. "Uh-huh."

"Me too," Susannah said, lifting her head and looking him in the eye. "I think that is where we all belong."

On the slayte in his daughter's lap the events on Phobos continued. A camera that had been left behind showed Jane, Gluck, and their passenger lifting from the surface of the desolate, now-unoccupied moon, heading back to the *Ares* so the six humans and the source of the voice that had disturbed Dan's sleep and changed his life could begin their own long voyage home.

Thank you for rescuing me, Avva.

No answer came, but that was all right. Someday he'd get the chance to tell him in person.

"Then I guess it's unanimous. Back to the cabin we go."

He unshipped the oars and began rowing their own small craft toward the warm, welcoming light on shore.

Off in the distance the loon gave another lonesome cry, the sound echoing across a lake silvered by moonlight and gleaming with stars dancing on the ripples made by their passage.

This time its call was answered.

Coming Next Month From Roc

Arthur C. Clarke

2001: A SPACE ODYSSEY
Featuring a Special New Introduction by the Author

Oliver Johnson

THE NATIONS OF THE NIGHT
Book Two of the Lightbringer Trilogy